The Running Club

About the author

Ali Lowe has been a journalist for twenty years. She has written for bridal magazines, parenting titles, websites and newspapers in London and then Australia, after she moved to Sydney sixteen years ago on a trip that was meant to last a year. She was Features Editor at *OK!* in London, where she memorably stalked celebrities in Elton John's garden at his annual White Tie and Tiara ball.

Ali lives on the northern beaches of Sydney with her husband and three young children. *The Running Club* is her second novel.

Also by Ali Lowe

The Trivia Night

ALI LOWE

The Running Club

HODDER &
STOUGHTON

First published in Great Britain in 2023 by Hodder & Stoughton
An Hachette UK company

1

Copyright © Ali Lowe 2023

A CIP catalogue record for this title is available from the British Library

Hardback ISBN 978 1 529 34885 9
Trade Paperback ISBN 978 1 529 34887 3
eBook ISBN 978 1 529 34886 6

Typeset in Plantin by Manipal Technologies Limited

Printed and bound in Great Britain by Clays Ltd, Elcograf S.p.A.

Hodder & Stoughton policy is to use papers that are natural, renewable and recyclable products and made from wood grown in sustainable forests. The logging and manufacturing processes are expected to conform to the environmental regulations of the country of origin.

Hodder & Stoughton Ltd
Carmelite House
50 Victoria Embankment
London EC4Y 0DZ

For Joey. 'There's nothing like a sister to understand the *real* you.'

WELCOME TO THE

ESPERANCE
RUNNING CLUB

Please fill in the following details so we can set up a running profile for each member, compare lap times and make sure that everyone's keeping on top of their training!

 Name: Carole Latimer

 Best lap time: 119.0 seconds

Emergency contact 1: Max Latimer (husband)

Emergency Contact 2: Lottie Denton (best friend)

Notes: Severe peanut allergy

 Name: Lottie Denton

 Best lap time: 154.3 seconds

 Emergency contact 1: Dr Piers Denton (husband)

Emergency Contact 2: Shelby Massini (twin sister)

 Name: Freya Harrington

 Best lap time: 139.1 seconds

Emergency contact 1: Bernard Harrington (husband)

Emergency Contact 2: Lottie Denton (childhood friend)

 Name: Shelby Massini

 Best lap time: 119.7 seconds

Emergency contact 1: Tino Massini (husband)

Emergency contact 2: Max "Latto" Latimer (friend)

Prologue

I turn left onto the pavement, always left. Glance down the hill towards Esperance Reserve, stop at the lights to tighten the laces of my brand-new running shoes. The rules of the running club are the same as they have always been: keep your breath steady, keep your mind sharp, record your laps! Only now there's a new one: don't get killed.

I slow down as I reach the seafront, turn to admire my slender silhouette in the French window of Esperance's most extravagant beachside home. A polished red sports car in the driveway just adds to the grandeur, sitting pretty on the verge of the expansive front lawn with a gaudy designer water feature as its centrepiece. Next, a large, white-fronted home with bottle-green Italian-style shutters and out-of-control jasmine creeping up the façade, wily in its efforts. Worth six million dollars, I heard. Every house comes with a hefty price tag in Esperance. You pay for paradise – for neat front lawns and infinity pools; for snaking, flower-lined pathways and white picket fences; for polished bus-stop windows and fancy lattes: soya milk, rice milk, oat milk, goat milk!

You pay a premium.

Perhaps even with your life.

The air is pure today, with a faint waft of sea spray. It is only if you close your eyes you might sense it: the cloying scent of death. It hung heavy in the air after they found the body in the tree-lined clearing that runs parallel to the running track. Eyes open and face set in a smirk. A fingernail neatly lacquered with her favourite shade, Cajun Sunset, standing erect, like a tiny tombstone in the mulch, long hair spread about her like Medusa. And she *was* like Medusa! She could turn you to stone with just one gaze.

That scream when her body was found was shrill enough to pierce the pendulous, grey clouds and force out the last torrents of warm spring rain. The residents of Esperance heard it as keenly as they heard the secrets that came spurting out like champagne through the neck of a shaken-up bottle in the days that followed.

So many secrets.

So many lies.

So much vengeance.

But could anyone honestly say she didn't have it coming?

Now, six weeks on, the sun has cleared the charcoal clouds that bathed our beachside town in grey in the days after her death. Esperance has a new aroma: summer. A season where things prosper and grow, where nothing dies.

In this tiny, pristine patch of the world, everyone knows you need to be perfect to survive.

I bend down, touch my toes, my legs ready to pound the pavement alongside the mulch that cushioned the decaying body of a woman who was once just like me. Who was one of us.

I really must stop thinking about it now. Lay it to rest. You can't dwell on the past, you must move on, just as I have done. I am the butterfly emerged from a cocoon, a chick fleeing the confines of the nest, a phoenix from the ashes!

I've been given a second chance at life.
I am alive. She is not.
So traumatic.
So unfair.
So wasteful.
So pleased I got away with it.

Part One: Jealousy
Six Weeks Earlier

MONDAY

Chapter One
Carole

The house is a hive of activity.

I find it easier to dedicate a particular day of the week to tradesmen, since it lessens the general household upheaval. Today the cleaners are here, and the gardener, too. I am very particular about Summerfield's lawn. I must have the stripes, in alternating shades of green, and Ryan is the only tradesman who knows this. Lottie would flinch at the word 'tradesman' – apparently they are 'trades*people*' these days – but I don't have time for any of that.

Ryan has been doing our lawn for a long time. He travels all the way down the peninsula from Shivers Beach (there are no trades*people* living in Esperance, they're rarer than hens' teeth here), but the money is worth it. We pay him a lot, because good staff are always worth the extra dollars.

'I'd like it to look like Wimbledon,' I told him when he first started gardening for us, five years ago. That's the way the lawn has always been, even before my parents handed this house over to Max and me. Alternating stripes in olive and fern.

'Wimble-*who*?' Ryan had asked.

'Don,' Max told him with a smile. 'My wife likes her lawn nice and tidy.' He winked at Ryan as if he was making some kind of lewd innuendo. 'With stripes.'

Ryan hadn't even tried to hide a look of consternation, but nodded and set about with the mower. The result?

Flawless! Alternating hues of green along the length of the front yard, only broken up by the large marble water fountain in the middle of the grass. It's very tasteful, the fountain, no kissing dolphins or anything like that, just a simple cherub with a spout, but Freya still likes to have a dig when she can.

'Oh Carole,' she lamented just last week. 'The *least* you could have done was get a chiselled Michelangelo with his cock out.'

So uncouth. But that's Freya for you. You can take the girl out of Shivers Beach, but can you really take Shivers Beach out of the girl? Although Shivers Beach is only thirty-five kilometres north of Esperance, it may as well be in another state. Esperance sits pretty at the very southern tip of a peninsula that rolls languidly along the coastline, a few kilometres north of the bright lights of Sydney. Shivers Beach sits poverty clad and unkempt at the northern point with its bulbous, ragged headland, separated from its affluent bedpartner by a buffer of coastal enclaves that get progressively rougher as the coastline unfolds: Esperance, Mooney Waters, Nash Lake, Boorie Point and then finally, Shivers Beach. It's where Freya and Lottie grew up, and my husband, too, although you wouldn't know it.

My phone pings with a text message. Speak of the devil. **What do you mean, it is "mandatory to run in our fluoro vests"?** Freya has written. **Is this a new government measure I'm unaware of?** I didn't say she wasn't smart. Sarcastic may be a better description. The kind of person who has an answer to everything. You would have thought a request to 'stay safe, stay seen' would be self-explanatory for any responsible member of a running club. But I don't have the time to get into this with Freya right now – not with tradesmen to organise. She will have to wait.

Today Ryan is topless, pushing the mower down the slight slope of our vast front lawn that leads to the fence that's almost touching the sand of the north end of Esperance beach. From the front garden, I can see the dunes on the other side of the beach. They mostly block the view of the running track, save for the far corner where the water fountain sits on a square of mosaic pavers, a haven for thirsty runners and dogs. From upstairs, you can see the twinkling lights of the city after dark, and even enjoy the New Year's Eve fireworks over Sydney Harbour. It's a much more sophisticated spot to observe the festivities than on the ground with the masses. This is prime real estate, and as such, the house needs to be well-kept. I like it to be the most attractive property on the seafront, to ensure it keeps the highest price tag in the row, should we ever decide to sell. Not that I can see that happening, because I grew up in this house and it is as much a part of me as my right arm.

I watch Ryan out of the window, his torso glistening in the stifling heat that's unexpected in September, the very start of spring. A single drop of sweat trickles between his glorious thirty-something pecs and down towards the elastic waistband of his pants. I chew on my cheek; I'm a sucker for a bit of rough. I *married* a bit of rough!

Max walks into the kitchen. I turn from the window and throw my arms round his neck. He's only been in the next room, but I like to be as affectionate as possible as often as possible. I truly believe that if you don't give your man what he needs, emotionally *and* sexually, he will stray. And I'm not giving Max up to anyone.

He puts his hands lightly on my waist, kisses me on the forehead and gently extracts me from his torso. I resist the urge to try and snuggle back in, because there has to be a sort of 'treat them mean' element to wifely behaviour, wouldn't you agree?

Max fills a glass of water from the fridge. The chiller churns and gurgles as it spits out cubes of ice. He gulps down half of the glass and exhales loudly.

'This heat's unbearable. It's meant to break on Friday.' He gestures at the laptop screen on the benchtop, where a document emblazoned with the title *Your Running Club Needs You!* strobes out of the screen. 'What's this?'

'A flyer,' I tell him. 'I'm trying to recruit a few more members to the running club. I mean it's lovely having so many husbands and wives' – all of them except Shelby – 'but it would be nice if it gathered some momentum. If we got a few more members, we could raise a little more money for charity.'

'Are people paying to join now?' asks Max.

'No, but the mark-up from the merchandise goes to Meals on Wheels.'

Max smiles. 'Well done, darling,' he says. 'Very worthy.'

I nod. It *is* worthy! I mean, we all have to do our bit, don't we?

The running club consists of myself, Lottie and her husband Piers, Freya and Bernard, although I hardly classify what he does as 'running' – it's more of a senior power-walk. Then there's Shelby and Tino. The three husbands are a late addition to the club. It started as women-only: myself, Freya, Lottie, and, by default Shelby, because she's Lottie's sister, but somewhere along the line Tino joined in and then Piers and Bernard jumped on board (I use the term 'jumped' somewhat loosely as Bernard is far too old to mount anything). By all accounts, all three of them love it, and as well they should – it's the perfect antidote to the stress of their demanding jobs. Tino creates apps for Android, and he's very kindly made one for the group which enables us to keep track of our kilometres and measures our speed against one another. I don't care where I come in, as long as it's before Shelby. A little competition is the best thing for upping anyone's fitness, in my opinion. Competing pushes you to be better, to test your limits.

The running club officially runs five nights a week at seven o'clock, although annoyingly some members seem to regard the start time as a free-for-all. Of course I run every day, rain or shine, but not everyone is quite as dedicated. Lottie runs three nights – Monday, Wednesday and Thursday – because those are the nights Piers, who is an obstetrician or gynaecologist or whatever you want to call it, is generally home on time and Lottie likes to be there when he arrives with dinner on the table. Fifteen laps of the purpose-built 400-metre running track, Olympic size, that backs onto the same scrubland that nestles the sand dunes at the southern end of Esperance beach. We meet at the water fountain and then we begin, in formation. I am the fastest of the females with a lap record of 119 seconds, so I'm always ahead of the pack. I have to be if I want to feel the burn. The only person who doesn't seem to have any routine is Shelby. She shows up when, and if she wants to, there's no rhyme or reason to it. She marches to the beat of her own drum in that arrogant way she has, like the world owes her a giant favour. She will stride out in front, or wait until we're all half a lap ahead before she starts, so she doesn't have to talk to anyone. It's incredibly rude.

'So is all this talk of recruiting runners a roundabout way of you asking me to join the running club again?' Max slices through a green apple and offers me an indulgent smile.

'Well, all the other husbands are involved, as you know,' I say, coyly. I don't want to *pressure* him. 'But it might be a little low-energy compared to what you normally do.'

'I might stick to surfing,' he says and pats my behind. 'It's more my scene.'

What's more Max's scene is keeping to himself. He finds the husband and wife cliques of Esperance a little too much to bear. 'We see them for drinks, I don't want to work out with them too,' he says.

I'd be lying if I said it doesn't hurt a little that I'm the only wife who can't persuade her husband to accompany her on the running track. Still, no matter. If I'm honest, I don't particularly want Max to see me all beetroot and flushed with sweat patches left, right and centre. It's not exactly sexy, is it?

'What have you got on today?' Max asks as he drops his apple core in the bin, and it feels a little like a change of subject.

'School drop-off, a bit of admin.' I look up at him and smile. I need to book more piano lessons for Otto – now he's in year 3 we feel he may benefit from an extra session a week, and pay Olivia's extortionate school fees. 'Keeping an eye on the tradesmen . . .'

Max glances out of the window. 'He's a good bloke, Ryan. You really don't have to worry about him.'

'Oh, I wasn't . . .' I lie.

Max is very touchy about me making generalisations about people from the town he grew up in. 'We're not all rough,' he says.

'Oh darling,' I pout. 'I know *that.*'

I do, however, have my doubts about the cleaners who also hail from the other end of the peninsula. I still can't find the diamond bracelet Max bought me for my birthday and I know for a *fact* that it was on the dresser when Leah was at the house last. Otto said, 'It's your fault Mum, you shouldn't have left it *Leah*-ing around.' That's a private school education for you.

'Are you still out tomorrow night?' Max asks.

'Yes, I'll be at Lottie's. Is that okay?'

'Of course. It's just I thought I might pop out to look at the car. Perhaps Hannah could stay on for an hour or so?'

My husband throws back the remains of his icy water. His skin is lightly tanned and his stubble fashionably short, with distinguished flecks of white. He is as handsome as he was the day I met him. More so. He still turns heads. I mean, he is so much more than a pretty face – he's a wonderful father, for starters. *Present,* I believe that's the word. Always there for the children.

'Of course,' I tell him. 'I'll speak to her. Can't have you missing out on seeing the car!'

Max is almost the proud owner of a Maserati MC20. It's a nifty little thing. It's my fifteenth wedding anniversary present to him – a few months early, but when your name rolls around on the waiting list, you have to jump on it. The car was meant to be a surprise, but the morons at the garage ruined it when they called him directly about the window tint (as in, did he want one or not?). I was livid about it at the time, but now I don't mind a jot because Max is so happy about his impending gift. It's like watching a child wait for Christmas Day to come around when they know they've got exactly what they want.

'I take it you like your present?' I say with a girlish pout.

'Are you kidding?' my husband asks, but not in the over-excited way he did the first couple of times I asked the same question. 'It's incredible. Now I have to think what the hell I can get you for our anniversary. What do you get the woman who has everything?'

Jewellery? Designer bag? Bespoke art? I really don't mind. But whatever it is, I'll be paying for it. That's the unspoken thing between us. The money. I have it in abundance thanks to my father, who has more of the stuff than he knows what to *do* with, and Max has none. I say 'none', but I mean very little, comparatively. He works, of course – the fact it's for my father's hedge fund is, for want of a better word, immaterial – but even that generous salary can't compete with the Parkes family fortune. But surprisingly, Max isn't insecure. I made it very clear from the very start, even when my parents insisted we sign a pre-nuptial agreement saying he'd get nothing if the marriage didn't last fifteen years, that what is mine is ours. Every last cent. Unless of course Max runs off and has some sordid affair or something, and then he'll walk away with nothing apart from the pants he stands in. But Max simply wouldn't do that to me. He loves me too much. He loves our *kids* too much.

Olivia skips down the stairs and leans up to kiss her father.

'How you doing, kiddo?' Max asks, and for a moment his accent sounds terribly Shivers Beach. I'm grateful for the Botox, otherwise my eyebrows might have knitted together.

'Fabulous, Papa,' she says, and turns, en pointe, towards the fridge. My statuesque ballerina. Thirteen and so poised – an Arlingford Ladies College girl, through and through, just like me. So *accomplished*, unlike Isobel Denton in her class. Poor Lottie has her hands full with that girl. Sometimes I can barely believe she and Olivia grew up together, they're so vastly different. Different toddlers, different pre-schoolers and now vastly different teenagers. But then you could say the same about myself and Lottie. Or myself and Max, I suppose, if you were being brutally honest. Both of them dragged up at the furthest end of the peninsula, a world away from Esperance.

I cover Olivia's chicken sandwich in a beeswax wrap. Otto doesn't like sandwiches, so it's a case of finding an alternative every single day. Today I have whipped up some miniature veggie quiches, or rather Hannah has. Hannah makes them, and I go through the rigmarole of packing them as if I rolled the pastry myself.

Hannah isn't a housekeeper, or a chef. She's just a regular mother from down the road in Mooney Waters, who helps out a few times a week with household chores. Whatever I need doing, she does. Last week I got her to label the medicine boxes in the pantry with a labelling machine. On the box with the antacids and Imodium, instead of writing 'Digestion' or 'Stomach', she typed out a label that read, 'Diarrhoea etc'. It was most uncouth, and Max and Otto almost died laughing.

I sniff a mini frittata. It smells heavenly. Perhaps I'll take a couple to Lottie's tomorrow and pass them off as my own. We gather once a month at one of our houses, after the running club has completed its twilight laps. Max always vacates on the occasions I'm hosting here because he says he finds the noise levels deafening. He calls it 'Cheese and *Whine*'.

We haven't got around to inviting the husbands to this particular extension of the running club yet, and it will stay that way because, after all, they do tend to feature in much of the conversation. Freya will moan about Bernard being an ancient old fart; Lottie will enthuse about how wonderful Piers is and then, when she's had a couple of drinks, she'll start crying about how she thinks she's a terrible housewife; and Shelby will occasionally make some snide comment about Tino, who could not be nicer as it happens, and who, quite frankly, deserves someone way better than her.

Max looks up as Otto walks into the room. He grins as Otto attempts to rugby tackle him and forces our son's head under his elbow, ruffling his hair frenziedly. Otto laughs and pulls away.

'Hello darling,' I say, smoothing Otto's hair back down into school-worthy smartness. 'How about I have

Hannah whip up some dinner for all of you tomorrow when I'm out?'

Max looks excited by the prospect of Hannah's culinary efforts as opposed to mine. 'Great!' he says and taps his stomach. 'Wonder if she'll do that delicious chicken risotto?' He and Otto look thrilled, which frankly makes me feel rather insignificant.

Max pulls me into his side and kisses my head. 'But Hannah doesn't cook as well as Mum, *does she,* kids?' He opens up his arms and nods at Olivia, who puts down her phone and comes to slip her arms around my waist.

'No way,' Olivia says, more earnest than Cate Blanchett doing Richard III at the Sydney Opera House.

'No! She sucks!' Otto says, as though he's disgusted by Hannah's edible offerings. Then he turns to Max, eyes sparkling, and says, 'Maybe she'll do her bolognese!'

'Ugh no,' says Olivia and I feel a glow of warmth in my chest. 'It's way too hot for bolognese!'

After I've deposited both kids at school, I get my regular weak almond chai from Only Organic and head home to attempt a surface tidy of the benchtop before Leah arrives. I shuffle papers and wipe jam off Otto's homework book. Underneath is Max's phone. He's forgotten it, which is rare for him. I pick it up and walk it over to my bag. If I drop it in to his office, I can have a quick coffee with my father while I'm there.

I'm just clipping shut my handbag when I hear the phone beep. When I pull it out again, I see a message from a number I don't recognise. It starts, **Latto, we need to . . .**

I can't read the rest, however much I jab at it with my fore-finger, because I don't have Max's fingerprints, obviously, and I don't know his passcode. He changes it frequently because he's worried about cyber security.

I feel a wave of hot anger shroud me. As far as I know, there's only one person who calls my husband by his old childhood nickname, and I want to know why the hell she is messaging him. What does it mean 'we need to . . .'? Need to what? Talk? What could *she* possibly want to talk to Max about?

I throw the phone back in my bag and march out to the car, knowing full well that I will hand Max his phone with a winning smile and not mention the text. He gets touchy about these things. You see, he's not to blame. It's *her*. She's the one who won't leave him alone. Poor Max, he feels so sorry for her. She never got over their break-up, even though they were just high school kids at the time. She just can't let it rest.

I stride down the pathway to the garage that houses our four cars and pip a key fob. It's pot luck which car I'll take today. I look up to see Leah standing in front of me with her gormless sister whose name I don't know, holding a bucket and a mop and wearing a rucksack that's actually a vacuum cleaner. She looks like she's about to collapse from heat exhaustion.

'Hello, Mrs Latimer,' Leah smiles, sweat collecting on her brow. 'Where would you like me to start today?'

'Bedroom,' I snap. 'And don't touch anything you shouldn't.'

Chapter Two
Lottie

Breathe in. Breathe out. Breathe in. Breathe out.

'You'd like to know about *me*?' I wriggle on the sweaty plastic chair, collect a snap of static. The office, tucked in the far right-hand corner of the charity shop, smells of wet animal – thanks to the overweight cattle dog asleep in a basket in the corner. The only window to the outside world is closed and the minute hand on the wall clock struts across the face with a sinister click. The room is stifling, despite the blast of cold air from the yellowing air conditioning unit positioned high up on the far side wall. I look up at the exit sign above the large, antique desk in the middle of the room. It's something I do wherever I am, a habit I can't break. Just in case I need to get out in a hurry.

Marella, the shop's manager, wears a smile and a faux-silk blouse which has attracted sweat marks under the armpits on account of the crazy humidity. My dress sticks to the side of my right calf. It's a long, floral Zimmermann maxi with layers of chiffon – extortionately expensive. Carole persuaded me to buy it, and Carole knows her fashion. 'Oh for Pete's sake, Lottie,' she'd sighed, 'just buy it. It isn't like you can't *afford* it!' She was right, of course. Six hundred bucks is a drop in the ocean here in Esperance.

Marella nods in answer to my question, offers a bright smile.

'Yes,' she says. 'Tell me about yourself.'

Sandwich residue lines the gap between her top canine and her lateral incisor, and I try not to stare, but Marella must notice where my pupils keep darting, because she sweeps her top row of teeth with her tongue a couple of times. She isn't embarrassed, though. She is obviously confident, proud of herself – if her clothes are anything to go by – and of her body, too, even though she's not slim or toned like the other women I know. She could be though, if she joined the running club and did three sessions a week for a month, under the watchful eye of Carole. Then she'd be right on track. She'd be quite attractive, actually.

I wonder what she thinks of me. I know I look well-put-together and she'll be able to tell that I'm slim with caramel tones running through my mousy brown, blow-dried hair. She'll probably think I'm high maintenance but I'm not – really, I'm not. Not on the scale of say, Carole. I don't slather myself in fake tan twice a week ('You should,' says Carole. 'People must think you've got a Vitamin D deficiency!'), but I do try to keep myself nice. I do it for Piers really.

Marella continues to smile and I realise that maybe she's not judging me at all. Her eyes are kind and she has a familiar face, a generic one. It's a face that belongs to several other people, the kind you need to see a few times before you remember it and associate it with a name and a personality.

'What I'd like to know,' she says, offering me a prompt, 'is why you would be the right person to do voluntary work here at St Paul's.'

I don't tell her that I have to get some kind of charity gig because it's what you do in this town in lieu of doing actual *paid* work. You start up some kind of club or society that raises funds in some way, like Carole has, or you get your hands physically dirty in the name of giving. You pull on rubber gloves over your Cartier stacking rings, emerald-cut solitaires and twice-weekly manicured cuticles, because it's expected of you. Or, if you really want to be seen to be giving back to the community, you do both. Carole does a day of Meals on Wheels in Nash Lake each week ('Ugh, the hat! It's like I'm in a fucking operating theatre!') and Freya works at the Mooney Children's Trust, which raises funds for the paediatric ward at Mooney Waters Hospital. She isn't a mother herself because Bernard already has grown-up children of his own and didn't want to have more when they got married. It's a shame. I've always thought Freya would be a good mum.

Anyway, we all do our bit, and places are hard to come by in the neighbourhood we live in. In fact this very position at St Paul's was just vacated by Marjorie Howard, who ran the Esperance Women's Book Club, and she only left because she opted to die instead.

My sister Shelby doesn't do charity work because she's Shelby and for her, others do not come first. Instead she works part time at Esperance Prestige Motors as an accountant; the guy who runs it hails from Shivers Beach like us and trusts her. He knows how good she is with money, with numbers. He pays her a fortune to work three days a week and keep his books in check, because, I suspect, there's something dodgy about them. Shelby does it because she likes her independence, and to make the point that she won't ever be kept by a man, even though Tino has made a fortune from creating apps. It gives her an air of superiority, I suppose, about women who don't work, whereas Carole, and to some extent Freya, have an air of superiority about women who *do*. Personally, I think it's up to the individual. Live and let live. But here in Esperance, Shelby *is* different, an enigma. She rages wildly against the machine, and that is why I always worry about her.

But then again, I worry about everything.

Marella clears her throat as she waits for an answer.

'I think the role would suit me because I like helping people . . .' I venture.

'Go on.' She smiles.

'Who are less fortunate . . .'

The smile fades and Marella sighs, adds her hot breath to the already sickly room. She changes tack. 'Do you know much about St Paul's?' she asks.

'I know it's . . . a charity that benefits the homeless.' I look up at the ceiling, awkwardly. There is mould on the top left cornice, which somehow reminds me I am enclosed in a small room which is only slightly bigger than the lifts at Mooney Mall. I take a deep breath, glance at the exit sign again.

'Correct – St Paul's is a charity that benefits the homeless. There are currently one hundred and sixteen thousand homeless folks in Australia, seven hundred on our peninsula alone. As many as forty in Esperance.'

I'm not sure she's right about that. I've never seen a single homeless person in Esperance. Our little nook of the world, at the southern-most tip of the peninsula is too – how can I put it? – too *clean* for stained sleeping bags piled in the corners of Perspex-walled bus stops. There's not so much as a patch of browning grass as far as the eye can see. Manicured, opal-green lawns abound and row upon row of residential streets are paved with spotless white weatherboard homes with ornate fretwork and pretty sandstone pavers leading up to white picket fences.

'Gosh,' I say blandly. 'I didn't realise there were that many.'

Our home is only a street back from the beach, and was architect-designed and built to our exact specifications: four bedrooms (a master, Isobel's room and two spares), a kitchen-dining area, rumpus room, three bathrooms. We don't just get sea glimpses, but generous sea views, because the bedroom window looks out to the ocean on the left, with views overlooking the southern tip of the running track on the right. I can sometimes make out Piers at the window when I turn round the corner on my daily laps. It is heaven really, utopia. Perhaps that's why it is so anxiety-inducing. It's hard to live up to perfection.

'The money we raise here at St Paul's goes towards provisions for the Shivers Beach soup kitchen, as well as providing temporary housing for women and children at the Mooney Waters Women's Shelter,' Marella tells me.

I sit up, enthused. 'I know the women's shelter. My husband is on the board, actually,' I offer, pleased to have finally made a connection, to have contributed something useful.

'Really?' Marella straightens up.

'Yes. His paid job is Head of Obstetrics at Mooney Waters Maternity Hospital, and the women's shelter is his sort of pro-bono work. Dr Piers Denton?'

'Ahh, yes,' says Marella. 'I know the name. How wonderful! In that case, you must be well aware of the number of women and children who remove themselves from dangerous situations and need to be rehomed in the local area . . .'

I nod. 'Yes,' I say, although the truth is, Piers hasn't really discussed it with me. He doesn't talk about his work at the shelter that much. But hearing Marella say this fills me with a genuine desire to get cracking, to get my hands dirty, as it were. The simple fact is, I haven't always been as lucky as I am today. Life wasn't always this easy, or privileged. And despite the stressful financial issue Piers and I are currently facing head-on, we're still better off than many. We have a roof over our heads, and a stunning one at that. Piers might argue differently – he is demented with worry about our situation. The fact is, we have an awful lot of debt from a rather sizeable bank loan he took out to invest in some aviation shares, which didn't hold their own. Then on top of this, there's the matter of school fees and mortgage repayments. The twist in the tale is that we are owed a life-changing sum of money that's currently being withheld from us by a third party. So the stress is rather intense. But Piers would be incredibly angry if I told anyone about it. He does not like us voicing our problems in public. Not that it's a problem, as such. Piers is incredibly capable and I'm sure he will find a way to make things right.

'Domestic violence happens everywhere,' Marella continues and I wonder if she's suggesting something about Piers. I mean, he may shout, but he'd never *hurt* me. 'Even here, in this perfect little suburb – although you wouldn't believe it, would you? We recently helped an Esperance woman escape a violent situation and I was approached by another local woman, just yesterday, in my capacity as a counsellor.'

'Gosh,' I say. 'How devastating!'

In the corner of the room, the dog whimpers in his sleep.

'Don't mind Rocky,' Marella says. 'He's a noisy sleeper.'

I smile and cast a glance at the mangy animal wedged into the basket.

'Lottie,' Marella says. 'I need to know that the person I hire for this important role *genuinely* cares, and isn't doing it just to get charity work on their social résumé.'

I nod earnestly.

'Well, I'm not oblivious to struggle . . .' I've started, but I don't want to finish. I don't want Marella to know my history, where I'm *from*.

But Marella does it for me.

'Right,' she says to herself. And then she fixes her gaze on me. 'You're Shelby Brennan's twin sister, aren't you?'

I flinch. 'Yes.' I twist my wedding ring on my finger. Marella looks at me expectantly. 'She's not Shelby Brennan any more,' I offer. 'She's married . . . to Tino Massini.'

Marella nods.

'How do you know Shelby?' I ask in an attempt to steer away from the subject of my sister's marriage.

'I remember her from school.' Marella's soft features harden. 'I was in your year at Shivers Beach High School. I recognised you as soon as you walked in.'

I flinch at the name, let the memories flood my brain. Shivers Beach: the town I grew up in, with flat, arid terrain; streets in a grid, yellowing and dilapidated fibro cottages with rubbish-strewn decks, rusty hand-me-down BMXs abandoned post-ride on unkempt, browning lawns. Nothing cared for, nothing loved. Not like Esperance, where the polished silver logos of sports cars shimmer in the sunshine, like the water in the travertine-framed, azure-blue swimming pools out back, tended monthly by pool boys who come recommended on the 'Esperance Mums' Facebook page where the chatter goes something like this: *Can anyone recommend a pool boy who comes in at less than $400 a month? We used to use Frankie at WaterWerx, but he insisted on traipsing mud through the granny flat with his filthy workman's boots on, so he had to go.*

I search Marella's face. Is Shivers Beach where I know her from? I try to imagine her younger, without the greying roots and the fine lines under her eyes. But I still draw a blank.

'I'm so sorry, I have the worst memory,' I tell her, but I can't meet her eye.

'It's OK, we only met a couple of times, but I remember Shelby.'

Marella's smile is forced, and I wonder what psychological torture my sister inflicted on her back at high school to make her face transform like this. Or maybe she just remembers Shelby for the way she looked. There weren't many girls as striking at Shivers High – and when I say there weren't many, I mean, there were none. Beautiful, complicated, manipulative. The one the boys wanted and the girls wanted to be. I pull my necklace out from the neckline of my dress and finger the stone: rose quartz for clarity and calmness.

'What a coincidence,' I mumble. 'Do you live here in Esperance, now?' But I suspect she doesn't. You don't live in Esperance and dress like that, faux silk with a polyester skirt. You don't carry a hessian bag with a supermarket logo emblazoned on the front, however environmentally conscious you may be. Not here in Esperance. I suspect Marella still lives in Shivers Beach, a good forty-minute journey south. Forty minutes from the rough end of the peninsula to the smooth, from poverty to prosperity. From one person to another entirely.

'I do live here, actually,' Marella says. 'On the outskirts, by the Mooney Waters road sign, so I've just scraped inside the boundary! I'm in the Tasman Apartments. You know, the tall ones on the roadside.' If Esperance had a rough end, this would be it – the busy road on the way out of town, on the border with Mooney. The one and only highrise, objected to by all Esperance residents except the ones that live there.

'It's not quite as picturesque as the other parts of Esperance,' Marella continues, reading my thoughts, 'but Rocky and I love it nonetheless.' She pulls herself upright as she speaks, straightens her back, her shirt straining at the buttons.

'I lived in Shivers Beach for a long time,' she continues, 'but it became hard to commute. I would have stayed there if the drive wasn't so long in the mornings.'

I nod, sympathetically, but I can't see any merits to living in Shivers Beach, which is why I got out. I had to, otherwise I would have stayed hopeless, sucked into a dreamless, futureless void. The same six hundred people from birth to death, give or take a few additions or subtractions thanks to the circle of life. The same midwife married to the funeral director. She sees you in, and he sees you out.

'Have you lived here long?' Marella asks. 'You seem' – she looks at my high-necked chiffon dress and the designer bag perched on my lap – 'quite at home here.'

'I am,' I say. 'I moved here when I was twenty-four. So it's been eighteen years.'

Eighteen years since I was that girl with the get-out clause. Twenty since I met Piers, who thought it was an act of rebellion to date a girl from Shivers Beach, even if she was bookish and clever. But I wasn't the kind of girl Dr and Mrs Ernest Denton expected their only son, training in obstetrics no less, to bring home. And it stung even more when Piers declared that he was in love with me. There were rows, huge rows. 'An obstetrician married to a cheap tart from Shivers Beach?' is one insult that stuck in my mind. Or, from his mother, 'What about if you decide to have *children*?' As if to procreate with me would be to sully the family bloodline. This is all twenty years ago, and Piers' parents are long gone, but it would be a lie if I said I don't think back to those days sometimes, and how much it hurt to feel inadequate.

'Do you go back much, Lottie?' Marella asks.

'To Shivers Beach? No I don't. I mean, I can't remember the last time . . .'

'You don't have family there, any more?'

'No, no I don't. Our parents are dead.'

'I'm sorry. Life has certainly changed for you over the years, hasn't it? And for Shelby.'

I shrug. 'I suppose it has.'

She regards me with concern. 'It was terrible the thing that happened to Shelby . . . on the beach. I remember it very clearly.'

I shift in my seat. 'Gosh, is that the time? I've got to pop into the dry-cleaners after this, so I'd better be off.' The fact is, I have all day to pick up Piers' work suits, but I need to get out of here now. My neck is starting to itch in this high collar. I begin to scratch, fingernails making sharp contact with the delicate skin underneath the fabric.

'Of course,' she says kindly. 'I didn't mean to pry.'

'No, no it's fine.' I stand up, but my legs have gone weak and I feel dizzy, a little anxious.

'I'll be in touch about the role.' Marella smiles. 'Good luck.'

I don't really know what she means by that, but it sounds very final, so I'm not under any illusions that she's about to hand me a tabard and put me to work alongside the elderly man sorting books at a snail's pace on the vast shelf that lines the front wall of the shop.

As I turn to leave, I notice a book with a torn spine at the end of the row of books, hidden between self-help tomes. It's a copy of Daphne du Maurier's *Rebecca*. My hand instinctively fingers the spine, touches the gold embossed title like I'm reading braille.

'My favourite book,' I say to no one.

Marella looks surprised. 'Really? Mine too.'

'Lovely.' I smile. 'Is it an early edition?'

'Yes, it's the tenth or eleventh imprint, from 1940. The British version, published by Victor Gollancz. Would you believe it was donated by Shivers High School? They had it in the library for years, apparently.'

'They did. That's where I first read it.'

'Me too.'

'Would you mind if I take a look?' I ask.

'Please do.'

Marella pulls the book gently from the row and hands it to me. I lift it to my face, close my eyes as I breathe in the scent of its pages, the faint aroma of vanilla from the broken-down lignin in the wood. I open the cover and turn to chapter one.

'"Last night I dreamed I went to Manderley again . . ."' I read out loud.

Marella smiles. 'It really is the best opening line of a book ever.'

I nod. 'It is. I don't know what it is about *Rebecca*, but there's something so beautiful about this young woman who is so dramatically out of place in her new world, trying so hard to fit in among all that opulence. It's just so poignant. I must have read it twenty times.'

I look up at Marella and our eyes meet, as if there's an understanding of some kind. She goes to say something and stops. Then she starts again. 'Would you like to take the job, Lottie?' she asks. 'I mean, the role is unpaid, as you know, and it can have its challenges. But it is yours if you would like it.'

I smile at her, notice the watery pull of her green eyes.

'Yes,' I tell her, my shoulders dropping. 'Yes. Thank you. I would like that very much.'

'Great,' she says. 'The position is twice a week, as you know. Hours would be negotiable – although not for me, I'm often here late into the evening, sorting things,' she smiles. I realise then that she doesn't have anyone at home – it's just her and the dog. Marella and Rocky.

'You could do school hours, say ten until three, if that works? How are you fixed for this afternoon? Would you like to come back after you've done your chores, you know, as a sort of trial? To see if you like it?'

'Oh, um . . .' It's all a bit fast. I have the dry-cleaning to collect! I'm starting to feel a little overwhelmed.

'It would just be for a couple of hours, you know, to see how you go. We're really under the pump since we lost Marjorie.'

I take a deep breath. I can do this. *I can!*

'Sure,' I say. 'Of course.'

'Wonderful!' Marella claps her hands. 'But Lottie, you might want to change into something a little less . . .' She searches for the word '. . . *fashionable*. You don't want to get your nice clothes ruined. Jeans will do.'

'Okay!' I reply. I don't own a pair of jeans. 'I mean, I'm sure I'd be fine in this, I—'

'It's also important we don't make the clientele feel uncomfortable,' Marella adds. 'So the less, um, *glamorous*, the better.'

'Noted,' I say, as I rummage around in my designer quilt bag for my car keys. They drop to the floor and I squat to pick them up as Marella watches from the front door. I give her a wave and nod as she retreats inside.

When I get in the car and switch my phone on, there's a voicemail from Shelby. I click the little black triangular 'play' icon on my screen and wait for my sister's lazy, sarcastic drawl to bounce off the leather upholstery. She always sounds like she's at the tail end of a cold. It's just another thing that adds to her allure. In the Shivers High yearbook, her entry read:

SHELBY BRENNAN
Also known as: Latto's Girl.
Most Known For: Ice Queen stare, sexy voice.
Most Memorable Moment: Coming back from the dead.

She takes a deep breath before she starts, like she can't be bothered. '*It's me,*' she says, as if she needs an introduction. '*Not sure if I'm going to make it to cheese and wine tomorrow. Don't ask me why. You don't need to know everything. Oh, and if you're doing laps at the reserve tonight, keep an eye out. Some pervert flashed me in the clearing – heavy breathing and stuff. Sounded like he was jerking off!*' A throaty laugh. '*I suppose I should put a warning on the running club group chat but God, it's so lame. Plus, if someone did stab Carole Latimer it probably wouldn't be a bad thing . . .*'

She doesn't say goodbye, just hangs up.

I'm so glad Marella has gone inside and isn't waving me off or anything, because I am struck by a sickly wave of panic and I can't seem to remember how to start the engine. But I have to, because the heat inside the car is nauseating. The wheel burns to the touch. But the pummelling of the cold air doesn't help a jot. I cannot explain it, but the image of a naked man in the bushes, looming over my sister, is bright and vibrant, almost real. I get this sometimes, it's a twin thing. Visions, as if I'm looking right inside Shelby's head. Mostly they're dreams, but sometimes they come when I'm awake, never benign, always terrifying. We were born just an hour apart, she came out fearless and I got the double dose of the anxious gene. The gene that's prone to catastrophising, but which sometimes, just *sometimes*, gets it right.

I close my eyes and exhale, empty my lungs for seven long seconds, breathe in and hold it for five, then push the air out forcibly through my mouth with a whoosh. I do it three times, until I feel my heart rate start to fall, like it does in the moments after I've finished my laps of the running track, until the wave of anxiety leaves my body. Then I straighten my back, wipe my sweaty palms on the chiffon of my six-hundred dollar dress, and let out the clutch. My hands are still shaking as I pull out into the thick afternoon traffic and tell Siri, 'Call Shelby.'

But it goes straight to voicemail, like it always does.

TUESDAY

Chapter Three
Freya

Sometimes it's a hard run, sometimes it's easy. It's hard when I'm hungover, if I'm coming down with something, if I'm feeling miserable about my domestic arrangements. But recently, it's been easy. As if my adrenaline's woken up and is flooding my body with fuel. I feel alive. Tonight's is shaping up to be a good run. A nondescript, start-of-the-week night, but an unusually energetic me.

Tuesdays are reserved for the hardcore amongst us – Tino, Shelby, Carole, me – but tonight, Piers has decided to put in an appearance. It's rather awkward because he's not particularly fit. You'd think he might be with all that pulling out of babies from bodily cavities, but it isn't the case. He is bent double by the toilet block clutching his side as I step onto the track.

'You okay, Piers?' I ask. He looks super stressed whenever I see him these days, but of course Lottie won't tell me what's going on. She's one of those wives who's loyal to a fault.

He glances up. 'Freya! Hello,' he says, his face burning red and his floppy hair slicked against his forehead, a sort of flushed Hugh Grant circa *Four Weddings*. 'Gosh it's hot today. Rather too hot for a run. I think I might have overdone it! I've got a particularly nasty stitch.'

'Can I get you some water?' I ask, wishing I hadn't bumped into him.

'No, I'm fine thank you,' he says, throwing out the mild-mannered gentlemanly aura he likes to pretend he has, even though I know different. Last time she had a few drinks, Lottie told me Piers shouts at her, criticises her constantly. No wonder she is permanently nervous. But she won't hear, or say, a bad thing about him, at least when she's sober. 'Enjoy cheese and wine tonight!' he says.

'Will you be at home?' I'm hoping he won't be. Lottie is never herself in front of him. It's like she retreats into her shell when he's there, like she hides herself away.

'No,' he says, 'I have a prior commitment with Isobel. Daddy and daughter time.'

I smile and nod and jog on. Piers is right, the heat is intense. The humidity has been building stealthily, threatening to suffocate, teasing with news of a storm at the weekend and floods that none of us want to admit we are holding out for. The weather can be so extreme on this peninsula – when it rains you wish for heat, but when it's stifling, you crave the wet.

I glance around the track. Shelby is not here tonight, which is no issue. We never acknowledge one another when we're running. She stares straight ahead, chin inched slightly up, her arms set in a march, the muscles taut, her ponytail trailing behind her. Not so much arrogant as conceited. Haughty. Oozing self-confidence.

Tonight, it is just myself and Carole. No Tino – yet. Carole treats the running club more like a 'see and be seen' event in her calendar rather than a means to cardiac fitness, which is why she is leaning against the water fountain, one toe arched, like she wants people to think she's with the Sydney ballet. In fairness, she could be, she's that skinny. She's one of those women whose life depends on retaining her slender physique and she will despair to the point of depression if she ever loses it. I know she wholly disapproves of my curvier size 12 shape because of the way she always looks me up and down in my running gear, like she wants to say something. She's never commented directly, but she does sometimes say things like, 'I bought this Marc Jacobs top but it's *huge* on me. Freya, would you like it?' and I've seen her subtly pull the chip bowl away from me when she's hosting cheese and wine. One thing I know she *does* envy of mine is my hair. It's a naturally dark, auburn colour and is thick and shiny, while hers is retriever-blonde but thin as anything.

Today Carole is wearing her fluoro top and a pair of skinny black running pants, her hair scraped back in a high pony. The tops are something else. She made us all buy one when she started the running club, and charged us four hundred dollars each, because they're made from some revolutionary anti-sweat fabric and have a built-in bra and step counter. The proceeds went to charity apparently. Personally, I couldn't give a toss about the step counter, but Carole gets pissed off if you don't switch it on, because it's 'not fair on everyone else'. She says it's 'motivational' to see how everyone is doing, which is quite blatantly code for 'nosy' and 'competitive'. She's the fastest, you see. She and Shelby. She pretends she doesn't care about winning, but I've seen her speed up when she's next to Shelby, giving it everything she's got just so she can say she was three seconds quicker.

I'm several laps in when Carole looks up from her smart watch and sees me. She hasn't yet noticed me pass her. She holds a hand up and waves at me like she's flagging me down for a random breath test at the side of the road.

'Freya!' she calls. She squints at me under the orange glow of the floodlights, rosebud lips pulling up skin that's losing the battle against gravity. Her forehead, which she has jabbed four times a year at Esperance Aesthetics, is taut and shiny like the skin on an angry boil. She must keep Sephora in business in blotting sheets alone. Don't get me wrong, I don't *dislike* Carole but, like an irritating case of athlete's foot, she has been in my life since high school and I've had to learn to live alongside her. We've built a sort of mutual fondness, in a Stockholm Syndrome kind of a way.

Carole came into my life when I was a teenager. After five years at Shivers Beach High, my dad got a massive building contract and we went up in the world. Or rather up the peninsula to Mooney Waters. It was decided I would finish my education at Arlingford Ladies College and Carole was in my class. After a year of hell as the poverty-stricken interloper, Carole stopped bitching about my humble roots and started asking me to help her in geography. She certainly never mentions my upbringing now, and she can't really, considering her husband and her best friend, Lottie, both came from the rough end of the tracks too. She doesn't seem fazed about it, although I have seen the way she flinches if Max happens to drop a vowel. But when it comes to the crunch, Carole doesn't care if it's old money or new money, because it still smells the same and it still buys the same designer things. Carole likes money a lot. You can tell because she says things like, 'Ugh, it's so uncouth to talk about money', and then bangs on about how much she spent on her latest spree at the Chanel beauty counter. And if Carole likes the stuff, then Max *adores* it. He shows off his wealth at every opportunity, like he's got a point to prove. And I guess he has, given his background.

What Carole *can't* deal with is the fact that Lottie, Shelby and I all hung out with Max all those years ago in Shivers Beach, back in the days when his accent was all 'gudday maaaate', and he wore his southern cross tattoo with pride. These days, the faded remains of the tatt are tucked away underneath a designer suit and his rising inflection steamrolled right out. Their daughter Olivia is at Arlingford while Otto, their son, is on the waitlist for a boys' high school that costs more per year than the value of Max's own childhood home. But that's the way he likes it. I mean, really, it's a marvel how the man has reinvented himself. Though I suppose we all did, all of us from Shivers Beach. Every single one of us leapfrogged across the Monopoly board, out of jail and straight to Mayfair. All of us with the gumption and the drive to get out, to leave the people we were behind: the nobodies, the chavs, the bogans.

I stop beside the water fountain, feeling my breath coming thick and fast, my heartbeat skipping over itself. It's exhilarating to feel my chest pound like this. It reminds me I'm alive. Forty-one years young. A dribble of sweat chases itself down my neck and settles in the clavicle of my throat.

'I'm *so* sorry,' Carole's hand is at her chest, faux concern strobing from pinprick pupils. 'I didn't mean for you to stop.'

'All good,' I puff. I bend over to catch my breath and my ponytail swings between my knees like a pendulum. The heat is stifling even though the sun has set.

Carole looks me up and down. 'How *are* you, Freya?'

'Er, good?' I saw her last night on the track. 'And you?'

'Great!'

'You're late tonight,' she tells me, studying her Apple watch. 'It's seven thirty now and you're only just starting?'

'You *are* observant,' I smile thinly. 'It's cooler at this time.'

She nods nonplussed and looks at her nails. 'Shelby has been running late, too. I mean, I never see her at the usual time any more. In fact, I haven't seen her for a few days.'

She's fishing. Carole likes to know Shelby's movements, to keep her tracked.

'What's she been up to?' she asks.

'I don't know Carole. You'd have to ask her.'

'I mean, they never run together, Tino and Shelby. Don't you think that's *strange*?'

'Strange?'

'Yes. That she doesn't run with her own husband, even though they both come down here on the same nights?' She gazes out across the field.

I don't tell Carole that Shelby and Tino's marriage is all but over. KO-ed. Living together but sleeping in separate beds, according to Lottie. I'm sworn to secrecy because Lottie says it's Shelby's news to tell. But even if I did feel like telling anyone, it certainly wouldn't be Carole. Carole is about as discreet as a mariachi band.

'I don't run alongside *my* husband.' I shrug.

'Yes, but Bernard's too—' she stops.

She is going to say 'old' and to be fair to her, she's not wrong. Bernard is sixty-eight and isn't exactly spritely. He was when we met sixteen years ago. Back then he was doing Ironman competitions and marathons and stuff. These days, it's all jigsaw puzzles, glasses of single malt and high-waisted pants (in a non-ironic fashion). I'm struggling with it, if I'm honest. It's like watching your favourite chocolate bar melt right before your eyes – what was once perfectly formed and delicious, now unrecognisable, unpalatable.

'Say what you *really* think, Carole,' I say.

She shrugs. 'No offence!'

Carole doesn't ask anything more about Bernard, which is a relief (previous questions have included: 'Do you ever worry he's going senile?' and 'Can he chew Mentos or will his teeth come out?', both accompanied by her trademark snort). Nor does she ask after my godawful stepchildren, Allegra and Felix, who are surely plotting my imminent demise because they hate me so much. Every time we see them, they hum the Kanye West track 'Gold Digger'. Allegra, who's twenty-four but acts like a spoilt kid, begins the song, and then Felix, who's two years younger, takes over. I do wonder if we'd had our own kids would Bernard's satanic spawn be a lot more interested in hanging out with their wicked stepmother, but we don't. Bernard didn't want them and I never had the inclination, until recently.

'Don't you think it's strange,' Carole continues. 'Shelby and Tino . . .'

'I don't *know*, Carole,' I sigh. 'Like I said, you'd have to ask them.'

'Why would I? I don't *care*,' she chirps brightly. 'I was just making conversation.'

We glance over at Tino, who has appeared on the far side of the track. You would have thought that husband and wife *should* be together tonight because it's Shelby's birthday. Shelby's today, September the seventh, and Lottie's tomorrow, on the eighth. They were born either side of midnight. Twins that couldn't be more different: one subtle and timid, the other striking and aloof.

Carole turns another nonplussed smile. 'Look, it's no biggie, but the reason we run at the same time is because of safety in numbers,' she says. 'It's just a rule of the running club.'

Before I can make a quip about the non-existent crime network in Esperance, Carole turns to the opposite side of the park, fixing her gaze on the far side of the field. The object of her attention wears navy shorts and a white running top with a tick on the right pec. Dark blond curls tumble into his eyes and he brushes them away with an unfathomably large hand, before dropping for some push-ups: one, two, three, four, five, six, seven. He is unusually handsome. Broad, tanned, masculine – not unlike Max, really. Same colouring. I don't blame Carole for striking a pose at the fountain. I pull my long hair loose and shake my head so it falls about my shoulders, and maybe the movement catches his eye, because he jumps up and looks over, first at Carole and then at me. Carole flushes pink and looks away quickly, leaving me to do nothing but offer a smile and a small wave. I touch the pool of sweat in my décolletage with my fingertips and turn back to Carole.

'So . . . how is Max?' I ask. I always ask. I'm fond of Max, have been since school.

'Wonderful. He got yet another promotion yesterday, actually. He's senior vice president now.'

'Great,' I smile. Max has worked for Carole's dad Graham since he first started dating her, like a million years ago, so it's no big surprise he's climbed yet another rung on the nepotism ladder.

'Obviously it means a *lot* more money . . .' Carole adds. At this point, I'd like to tell her that Max borrowed two hundred bucks from me to buy a bag of ecstasy pills when he was seventeen and never gave it back, but I imagine that would go down poorly.

'So yes, Max is *very* well.' She twists the diamond on her ring finger. 'We're great, you know, *great*.' She is no longer talking to me, but to the sprawling fig tree over my shoulder. She straightens up. 'Right then! I'm going to do one last lap. I'll sprint ahead so you don't have to try and keep pace with me. See you at Lottie's.'

'Bye,' I sing to her sinewy back, flipping her the bird discreetly.

I hear the scuff of a trainer on the track behind me, and when I turn around I'm face to face with the man with the curls. His eyes are black, like dark chocolate, and he has a tiny scar on his top lip that winds a path through his stubble.

'I won't tell her if you don't,' he says.

'I'm sorry?'

He flashes me his middle finger and smiles. 'The little message to your friend?'

I laugh. 'Friendship politics. She's high maintenance.'

He gives me the side eye. 'You look familiar. Do you run here often?'

'Is that the running equivalent of "do you come here often?"'

He laughs and his eyes crease at the sides. This guy is so freaking attractive.

'That sounded pretty lame, didn't it?' He laughs again. 'I'm not very good at this.'

'I run here most days,' I offer. It's not my finest work, but I seem to be a little tongue-tied. It's been a while since I've spoken to a man about something that doesn't involve a) the weather, b) the television schedule or c) if I happen to have seen the corner piece of the 1,000-piece jigsaw of the Sistine Chapel.

A smile dances on his lips. 'I like a girl in fluoro,' he says.

I cringe internally. However, on the plus side the word 'girl' makes me feel fifteen years younger. The sad fact is, having an older husband can make you feel a little like you've got one foot in the grave. You see wrinkles more keenly, feel age descending rapidly as you sit together on a bottle-green Chesterfield sofa each night watching true crime documentaries.

I glance across the park at Carole with her back to us as she runs into the wind.

'So you're a five-times-a-week girl, are you?' the stranger asks.

I feign shock, my hand on my chest, but smile. 'Sometimes. What about you?'

'If I have the energy.' He winks. 'I'll be here on Thursday night.'

Why does it sound like an invitation? I smile, bite my lip.

'See you then,' he says. 'Enjoy your run!'

Then he steps forward suddenly and leans in, touching my hair. 'Sorry,' he says, 'you had a leaf caught . . .' He shows it to me. He is so close I can smell the chewing gum on his breath. I smile and step back instinctively. Touch my hair where his fingers just were.

He grins. 'It's Luca.'

'I'm sorry?'

'My name,' he grins. 'It's Luca.'

'Hi Luca.' I smile. 'I'm Freya, but you can call me Rey.' No one's called me Rey since primary school, but he doesn't need to know that.

He looks amused. 'Hi, Rey,' he says.

I grin like some love-struck teenager and watch him run off ahead. He only turns back once to look at me, and then heads off the track and presumably towards home.

After he's gone, I tie up my hair and set off again. But as buoyed as I am by the encounter with Luca, I don't want to run alongside Carole, so I decide to head a different way back, towards the border of Esperance and Mooney, past Esperance Prestige Motors, the artisan bakery and Only Organic – the alternative and longer route to Lottie's. The orange glow of the streetlamps light my way.

When I get to the car showroom, I glimpse Max inside, admiring a shiny red Maserati that's sitting resplendent in the centre of the space. He fingers the bonnet, smiles and steps back into the shadows. I smile too, thinking about the Holden Commodore he used to drive at high school. The manual car with the dodgy gear stick and the broken air-con, a heat trap on forty-degree days in Shivers Beach. I look away, but then see someone else from the corner of my eye. Another woman in running gear slipping in through the back door of the showroom. She taps Max on the shoulder and he turns. He steps into the shadows towards her as she leans up to greet him – a peck on the cheek? Or something more familiar?

She stays on tiptoes slightly too long for a mere greeting, and it's a pose I've seen before. I've seen all of it before. The legs, the hair, the tan: they're all so familiar. It's Shelby.

She turns and looks out of the window then and that's when she sees me watching her. Our eyes meet as her arms hang around Max's neck and she gives me the very smallest of smug smiles before she turns back to face him.

Chapter Four
Shelby

Before

Latto is ten minutes late. The strap of my schoolbag digs into my shoulder, so I chuck it on the ground beside the bus stop, hear my textbooks land with a splat. He's got two more minutes, then I'm going. The arm of my cardigan has a hole in it, and I circle an angry biro line around the circumference, making a navy ring on my arm, a temporary tattoo. Graffiti decorates the Perspex window of the bus stop, words scratched in with knives. I study them and find my name. *Shelby Brennan gives good head,* says one. You bet she does! I chew on the two pieces of Juicy Fruit gum in my mouth, stretch them with my tongue then suck in with a loud pop.

Directly across the road, two rusty bikes lean against the crumbling brick wall of the church, where a sign printed with an arrow reads 'Shivers Beach Soup Kitchen This Way!' The church is the filling in a sandwich of yellow fibro cottages with chicken wire gates, painted canary in the 1960s when they were built, now a sickly jaundiced colour, like a smoker's fingers. It's autumn, but still the grass is peanut-butter brown, shrivelled and unloved, the texture of Rice Bubbles underfoot.

Two buses have already passed. One more and I'm leaving.

I give the evil eye to a year 7 kid who's staring at me with his mouth open as he passes me on the footpath, pubescent longing all over his face. They all stare at me like that, like they're terrified of me. He meets my eyes and his skin glows puce. I laugh and shake my head as if to tell him 'fat chance!' and pull my Discman out of my bag, arrange the spongy headphones on my ears.

When I look up, there is Latto striding towards me, his rucksack flapping on his back, like he couldn't give a shit. But even a boy like Max Latimer looks stupid holding a regulation school bag. My stomach twists with disgust. I haven't decided about him yet.

'Shelby Brennan,' Latto says, voice deep, and my mind is made up. He bends over to catch his breath. God he is hot: hottest boy in the school, bar none. But then, aren't I the hottest girl? That's not arrogance, it's a fact. I can't help it, can I?

'Surprised you waited,' Latto says. 'I'm later than I said.'

He takes two smokes out of his pocket, lights his own, and then lights the second from it, even though he has just used a lighter to spark up the first. He hands it to me. It's an arrogant gesture, assumptive. How does he even know I smoke? But I take it from him, lift it to my lips and watch the orange tip flare with life as I suck in.

'You been waiting since after school?' he asks.

'Just got here,' I lie. 'Had some stuff to do. Thought I'd missed *you* for sure. I was gonna leave.'

He nods.

'Glad you didn't,' he says.

I take a deep drag on my cigarette. Cancer sticks, Lottie calls them. Miss prim and proper.

'So why are you late?'

He shrugs. 'Detention ran over. Lincoln wouldn't let me leave. Wanted to drag out the punishment as long as he could.'

I imagine Mr Lincoln, the deputy principal, standing at the blackboard tapping the little stick of white chalk on the black surface over and over again. He always does it. It's a form of torture.

'Lincoln's a dick,' I say. 'What did you do?'

'What did I do? I stayed till he let me go, of course.'

'No.' I smile, take a drag. 'What did you do to get detention?'

Latto's face is tanned and his golden hair recently shaved. He turned seventeen a couple of months after me. We all went to his party at Shivers Beach and got blind drunk round the fire pit. Latto spent that whole night staring at me across the flames and blowing smoke rings. He wasn't the only one. They all look at me, all the boys.

'Smoked a spliff on the soccer field. Lincoln found me at recess.'

He looks away from me, runs his hand across his scalp like he is looking for hair to ruffle and he's forgotten he's shaved it off.

'You know how he gets. "Max Latimer! Give me that hand-rolled cigarette NOW!",' he mimics. 'Bet you he smoked it after I handed it over.'

I smile. 'I thought you were one of the smart kids? I heard you ace every test you sit.'

'I do,' says Max. 'Doesn't mean I don't like to enjoy myself, though.'

'Fair enough.' I shrug. 'Got any dope left?'

'Yeah. I've got to go deliver a bag to some rich kid in Esperance,' he says. 'Keep it to yourself though, I don't wanna get expelled. I need to do well in the HSC so I'm not stuck here all my life. I'll get a place at Sydney Uni if I get a good enough score. Anyway, I thought you could come to Esperance with me. That's why I said to meet at the bus stop. Then we can go smoke on the dunes.'

'I don't know if I should come with you,' I say. 'I heard you shot a possum with your dad's air rifle. You could be a psychopath!'

He laughs. 'I shot a possum because my brother clipped it in the car. I didn't do it for a laugh. It wasn't fun. Talk about the Shivers Beach rumour mill.'

'You haven't got a shotgun in there, have you?' I nod towards his pocket.

'Nah,' he says. 'I'm just happy to see you.'

I smile. I can't help it.

I've never been to Esperance before, because even though it's only forty minutes' drive away, it's a different world. Before he died, Dad used to slate it. 'Full of entitled dickheads who make a mockery of the hard-working Aussie battler,' he said. But I've heard about the beach with its rolling dunes, because Lottie went to Esperance with the church group when she was trying out for the God squad a couple of years ago. She said the dunes were like mountains – the houses too. 'They're massive, Shelby! Mansions!' she squealed. 'I'm going to live there one day.' I was like, 'Yeah, Lottie, good luck with that!'

I shrug and look up at Latto. He's a good foot taller than me.

'Sure,' I say. I told Mum I'd be home for dinner, not that she'll notice. 'Let's do it.'

Latto nods down the road and says, 'Bus's here,' so I grind the stub of my cigarette under the rubber sole of my black school shoe, blow the smoke out of the corner of my mouth and climb aboard with Latto, all six foot something of him close behind me and the smell of Lynx deodorant wafting off him. We sit down side by side, and his knees push against the seat in front, his grey school shorts riding up to show thick, hard thighs. I want to touch them. I cross my legs and see him glancing down where my skirt has ridden up. But I don't want him to think I'm a dead cert, so I wriggle the material down an inch. Our bags snuggle on the floor together and our bodies jiggle separately as the bus rolls down the peninsula from the rough end to the smooth.

Out of the window, the piss-yellow façades of the houses seem to slowly brighten, like a dial being turned up, until we're on the border of Mooney Waters and Esperance and they're crisp white. Even the sun-ravaged grass seems to wake up as the bus throttles forward, turning from brown to yellow to olive to vibrant emerald the further we travel, through Nash Lake and then Boorie Point as if the rain has chosen only this prosperous end of the coast to nurture. The streets neaten up, from haphazard and lazy to a simple and orderly grid formation. They have pretty names like 'Jasmine Street' and 'Violet Road'. The cars have upgraded too – no more battered UTEs with brown masking tape holding on the bumpers or wing mirrors hanging on by a thread. As we rattle into Mooney and then finally, Esperance, the polished round badges and emblems on shiny blue and white bonnets denote BMWs, Mercedes and Porsches.

'Wow,' I say to Latto.

He nods. 'Nice, huh?'

We grind to a halt on a road called Esperance Parade. The bus lets out a frustrated sigh as the doors open. We step off and taste the clean air – because everyone's richer here, they get better air quality too. A middle-aged woman wearing a pink suit with two little gold Cs joined back-to-back walks past me. Her bag has the same logo. She looks me up and down with her pointed face, then Latto. There is a ringing from her bag, and she pulls out a mobile phone and flips it open.

'This is Rosemary Parkes,' she barks into the receiver as she bends down to get into a shiny silver car. Even her name reeks of wealth.

Latto grabs my hand and leads me down a road that's flush with the beach. It's like something out of *Beverly Hills 90210*, all clipped hedges and flourishing pink bougainvillea and sprinklers showering vast green lawns. The house at the end is immense – a huge weatherboard Queenslander hugged by a balcony, and a giant fig tree that sits stately in the garden, branches sprawled out like an umbrella, shading the meticulously clipped lawn from the last of the afternoon sun.

Latto hovers at the gate, smooths his nonexistent hair, tucks in his shirt, and takes my hand. He intertwines his fingers in mine and walks up the path. I'm too in awe of my surroundings to object. This place is insane. The front door is the size of my bed. It doesn't have a bell but a knocker. He raps it a couple of times, looks at me and smiles.

A girl, who must be our age, answers. She is tall with almost white-blond hair and pretty in a rich kind of a way with freckles dotted across her nose. She is dressed in a baby blue short-sleeved shirt with 'Arlingford' stitched under a crest, and school tie with a plaid blue skirt. The shiny gold badge on her shirt says 'Prefect'. Her vowels are neat, her accent almost English.

She looks up at Latto with fierce blue eyes and smiles. Glares at me.

'Hi Max,' she says and blinks a few times. 'Good timing, my mum just left.'

'Great,' Latto says. 'Here you go.' He hands her a zip-lock bag.

She glances ahead and to the left then the right, to make sure no one sees her take a bag of drugs from the scruffy looking hoon in the Shivers Beach High School uniform. Then she slips her hand inside the bra that she barely needs for her bee-sting tits and pulls out fifty bucks, all the while looking at Latto. She hands it to him and pockets the bag.

'Thanks, delivery boy,' she says. Max smiles and looks at his feet.

I feel a hot sensation in my chest and I don't like it.

'It's great doing business with you,' Latto says and I notice he's tidied up his accent. The girl watches as we turn and retreat up the gravel path.

'Come in for a smoke next time, Max?' she calls after us, loud enough for us to hear, but not loud enough to tarnish her – or her parents' – reputation with the neighbours.

What she means is, 'Come in for a smoke when *she's* not with you.'

'Sure,' Latto calls over his shoulder. He doesn't take my hand this time, so I take the liberty of grabbing his, so that she'll see, and then I turn around and give her a victory smile.

When we're around the corner and on the downhill walk to the beach, Latto lets go of my hand to get out his box of Rizlas, ready for our own smoke.

'Someone has the hots for you,' I say.

'Her?' he says. 'Nah.'

I laugh. 'You don't have a clue, do you?'

He smiles. 'Hardly. Anyway, I'd never go there. Way too rich for my blood.'

'Who is Little Miss Entitled, anyway?'

'I dunno,' he says. 'Carole or something.'

The dunes are still warm from a day of sunshine and we settle ourselves between the tufts of marram grass and look out to sea. Latto pulls a bag of Pringles from his school bag and pops the cap off.

'How long have you been selling weed?' I ask.

'It's not me. My brother does and gives me a cut if I come down to Esperance. His motorbike doesn't always make it so I do it for him. I like it, you know? The beach down here is pretty neat.'

He twirls the end of the spliff like a liquorice twist and sparks up the lighter, has a drag. 'Sometimes I bring my board.'

'You surf?'

'Course,' he says. 'I know it's intense down here, like rich and everything, but when you're in the water waiting for a wave, it doesn't matter where you're from, Esperance or Shivers Beach. The sea doesn't give a rats how much cash you've got and what you drive around in. We're all humans when we're in the ocean. We're all vulnerable.' He laughs. 'Prisoners to a higher power. You see what I mean?'

'Yeah,' I say, because it makes sense to me.

I wait for a minute and then I tell him, 'I'm gonna die in the sea, so . . .'

'What?' Latto sits up. 'Why'd you say that?'

'It's a hunch my sister has.'

'How does she know?'

'She sees things. Dreams them. It's a twin thing. She reckons she's dreamt I'll drown.'

'That's intense.' Latto passes me the smoke. 'So she told you about the dream?'

'Yeah.'

'Why didn't she keep it to herself?'

'Dunno. She has all sorts of shit going on in her head, Lottie. She's . . . complicated, a bit messed up, I guess. But she swears by the twin thing.'

'So don't you swim, then?'

'Can't. Never learnt.'

'You should learn.'

'Nah.'

Max grins. 'It might help you one day.'

I shrug and it's quiet for a moment.

'I hope you don't,' Latto says.

'Don't what?'

'Drown.'

'Yeah,' I laugh. 'Me too.'

'Seriously, though. I love this place,' he says. 'Who says I can't come here, just 'cos I'm not loaded? Who said it was exclusive? This beach is as much mine as it is theirs.' He nods his head behind him, to where the mansions of Esperance dot the coastline, each front yard a chocolate-box scene. 'Who says they're better than me? I'll have a house here one day and they can all eat my shit.'

He exhales and I take the spliff from him and take a deep drag. He is right, though. Esperance isn't like the rest of the peninsula. It smells of prosperity, of hope. Things are possible here, achievable. I can see what Latto means. Or maybe it's just the smoke.

'The guy that owns Esperance Prestige Motors is from Shivers, went to Shivers High. If he can get out and make something of himself, why can't I?'

I pass back the rollie. 'If I get here first, you can be my pool boy.'

'You can't get a pool if you can't swim!' He looks into my eyes and his smile fades, and I know he's going to make his move. I can tell because so many boys have looked at me that same way.

'God, you're beautiful, Shelby Brennan,' he says.

I smile.

'Heard it before?'

'Couple of times.'

'That's 'cos it's true.' He cocks his head, studies my face. Then he leans over and puts the palm of his hand on my cheek. Instinct makes me rigid, my neck straighten. But Latto is not deterred. His grip is steady as he pulls my face towards him. His hand is strong, so even if I wanted to resist, I couldn't. But I don't. He pulls me to *him* – he doesn't move towards *me* – and places his mouth on mine before confidently parting my lips with his tongue. I have never had a boy kiss me like this, so assertively. Every single kiss before him came from nervous, flaccid tongues, every touch made with fumbling, sweaty hands. But this boy acts like he owns me. Still, I keep my body erect, push back into the kiss with force, show him that he won't overpower me, that I have the control. Even as every urge tells me to let my shoulders slump and my head tilt back, I do not yield.

Until, eventually, I do.

Chapter Five
Carole

I see Lottie through the glass windows that border her colonial-style front door. She's plumping cushions like she is window dressing at Pottery Barn and is wearing a godawful floral number with a high neck and billowing sleeves. I've told her a million times this style does nothing for her, but she always says the same thing: 'I'm pale and I blister in the sun, so it's just easier to cover it all up.' I've given up telling her, so now I simply push her in the direction of designers who create maxi-wear that doesn't resemble a six-man tent. I mean, if you're going to dress like a 1980s Sunday School teacher, at least have a Camilla tag sewn in the back.

It's my personal opinion that Lottie dresses so demurely because Piers likes to keep the goods under wraps, but of course it isn't my place to comment. It's just a shame, really, because in her running gear, Lottie is a siren – slender with a tiny waist and a generous C-cup chest. Half of Esperance would kill for that body!

She looks up from her cushion-plumping and beckons me in with a wave, so I climb the balcony stairs to the welcome mat that says '*family*' in a tacky cursive black font and let myself in. The Denton house is undoubtedly beautiful, although somewhat dated. It is called Oceanview, which is rather ironic if you ask me, since you'd need a telescope to see the ocean from the master bedroom window, although the way Piers casually drops it into conversation, you'd think the house sits on stilts in the middle of the South Pacific. He's even got Lottie convinced they have ocean views, which says a lot about her ability to be led by Piers.

I am immediately greeted by a cool blast from the air-conditioning, a waft of lavender and geranium permeating from a diffuser on the hall table and a rather unappetising smell from the oven. The interior is pristine as usual. Cushions sit angled on the sofa with a neat karate chop in the top, so they look like a row of Chinese fortune cookies, or a chorus line of synchronised swimmers in a sequence of pastel grey, pink and mint. A collection of candles in various jars and ceramic holders sit neatly on the mantel, alongside a row of stylish black and white family photos: Lottie with Piers, Piers with Isobel, and of course the three of them together. Isobel looks miserable in every snap. Gosh, she's a sourpuss that one, scowling out from the monochrome like she thinks she's a supermodel. The same self-satisfied smirk as her aunt Shelby.

'Come on through,' calls Lottie.

'Just taking off my shoes!' I open the hall closet to drop my trainers in and am greeted by rows of dry-cleaning in transparent plastic sheaths. They're all Piers' work shirts and suits. Lottie does two runs to the dry-cleaner a week, like the perfect little housewife she is. A veritable *Sex and the City* Charlotte. Hannah does it for me, God love her. Why struggle when you can outsource? Bless her, she even dropped off some of her frittata at Lottie's earlier so I wouldn't have to come empty-handed.

'Hello, darling,' I say and kiss Lottie on both cheeks, French-style.

'It's so good to see you,' coos Lottie.

'You're so flushed,' she says. 'Have some water.'

'I've drunk plenty,' I tell her. 'Crack open the prosecco!'

She smiles and turns to the fridge, littered with photos, all stylishly placed. In the centre is Lottie and Shelby in black and white. Lottie is smiling like she can't believe her luck that her sister has deigned to take a selfie, while Shelby pouts. Being twins, the two of them have similar facial features of course, but the way they style themselves sets them apart. Shelby's dark, chocolate-brown hair is lightened with a full head of highlights (but when her roots come through you can totally see she's on the mousy side, like Lottie), and her brows are big and bushy. She contours her cheekbones with blush to make herself look more angular, dyes her lashes black and always wears the same fuchsia lipstick, except when she goes out out – that's when she goes for slutty postbox red. Lottie, on the other hand, wears her brows irritatingly thin, despite my suggestions she fill them in (sperm brows are so 1990s), and doesn't bother with contouring or lip stain or lash dye. Plus, her constant worried expression has not been kind to her in terms of forehead lines.

Lottie wiggles the cork and lets out a little gasp as it flies up and hits the lampshade. 'Oooh,' she says, as if speaking to a child. 'That was a fizzer!'

'Quite,' I say.

The front door shuts with a bang and Lottie calls out, 'Hello?'

'It's me,' replies Freya.

'Freya, hello.' I look her up and down. She's lobster red, even though she's barely run anywhere. I only left her fifteen minutes ago! 'Just a short run for you tonight, after all?'

Freya rolls her eyes. 'Who needs a Fitbit when they have Carole?'

I shrug. Some people are so touchy.

'What a heavenly smell,' Freya lies, and I glare at her, because whatever is in Lottie's state-of-the-art Bosch oven stinks like rancid feet.

Lottie must have caught the exchange because she says, 'Gosh, so sorry about the pong! It's Ottolenghi!'

'Otto*ponghi*, more like,' whispers Freya and I stifle a snort.

Lottie opens the oven and slides the offending quiche onto the wooden benchtop.

'Frittata and quiche,' says Freya. 'This is turning out to be quite the *egg*-stravaganza!'

Lottie giggles at Freya's lame joke. 'Mine's vegan,' she says and wipes her hands on a whiter-than-white apron that says, 'Le Cordon Bleu, Paris' on the front. She did a cooking course there three years ago, and it blows my mind how she has managed to keep the apron so clean. But then, that's just Lottie: the perfect housewife. She thrives on being a Stepford wife – although she's so perpetually frazzled, she could probably do with some help. Not that I'll be sharing *my* Hannah of course. I won't even let anyone meet her. It's like babysitters – you should never pass on their number, or before you know it, they'll get nabbed by someone else.

'Take a seat.' Lottie smiles. She fumbles with the wrapper on a triangle of creamy brie and then slides it next to the quiche. Then she takes out a cheddar, a Danish blue, a jar of vegan cashew spread and some goat's cheese. Evidently Lottie is trying to put us all in a cheese coma. Or at least give us weird dreams – maybe to make her feel better about her own.

'How was your run?' she asks.

'Fine,' I say. 'Lottie, how many people are you feeding?'

Lottie looks alarmed. 'I know, but we all have such different dietary requirements,' she stutters.

Freya shoots me a glare that says, 'don't wind her up', and gushes, 'It's a lovely spread, Lottie – it caters for all of us.'

We all have intolerances, you see. Freya is keto right now, so she eats the kind of canapés that are so creamy and laden with fat you gain five kilos just looking them, but because she's not touching carbs ('hold the crackers!') the weight is falling off her. Her keto breath is revolting though, so personally, I couldn't do it.

Lottie avoids meat and dairy as much as she can because her kinesiologist told her animal products exacerbate her anxiety. Apparently they hang around in your gut and produce bad bacteria which affects your entire system, including your head.

My own diet is less a fad, more a life-threatening allergy. If I eat anything that's had so much as a staring contest with a peanut, I'll go into severe anaphylaxis. When I was twenty-one, I went into cardiac arrest in a Thai restaurant in Melbourne because of an incident with some rogue chicken satay. It is a total bore, but it doesn't rule my life. I just have to be very, very careful – and so does everyone else. If I decide on an impromptu catch up of a morning, I have to check the person I'm meeting hasn't had peanut butter on their breakfast toast, otherwise an air kiss could prove fatal.

Shelby eats anything and everything with greedy gusto, it's terribly vulgar. I can't imagine how she keeps her figure, which isn't bad I suppose (perhaps a little wide on the hips), considering how gluttonous she is. I imagine she has some foul gut bacteria going on – it's probably what makes her so unhinged. But that's her business I suppose, isn't it?

'Ugh.' I fan myself with my hand. 'Sweating like a bitch. Is your sister coming tonight?'

The fact is, I need to know if I'm going to have to make nice with Shelby this evening. Trust me to find a best friend whose sister is obsessed with my husband, just because he happened to finger her a couple of times behind the bike sheds when they were at school.

'I don't know.' Lottie pulls at her gaudy rose quartz pendant, which she swears helps with anxiety, even if it doesn't help with aesthetics. 'It's *her* birthday, so I'm not really sure. I mean, I invited her, of course.'

'Shame!' I inspect my nails. 'She doesn't seem to realise it's your birthday, too, does she?'

'Technically it isn't my birthday until tomorrow,' she says apologetically. 'I mean, I don't mind in the slightest. Shelby doesn't really do birthdays – you know Shelby!'

Unfortunately I do.

'If she doesn't come tonight then I'm sure I'll see her tomorrow!' Lottie says, only convincing herself. She offers us a bright smile, but I catch it fade in the reflection of the shiny oven door as she pulls out a tray of baked kale. She knows Shelby couldn't give a toss about her birthday, because Shelby only ever thinks about Shelby. Last year, she went away to Byron Bay to a spa to celebrate, and, even though she was still in the same state, she didn't bother to call Lottie the next day.

'Anyway,' says Lottie. 'She promised she'd come to mine on Friday.'

'Friday?' asks Freya, chowing down on a slice of brie.

'Yes!' sighs Lottie. 'Don't you remember? Piers is cooking a birthday dinner for me and you're all invited.'

The idea of Piers cooking is frankly a touch alarming, but I wouldn't miss my best friend's birthday dinner for the world.

'Of course,' I tell her as I pour myself another prosecco.

I feel my body relax into the chair as the second glass works its magic, but just as I'm settling in, the door flies open and there she is with her contoured face and her fake lashes and the injectables she denies she has.

'Shelby,' sings Lottie with an excited clap of her hands. 'You're here!'

Chapter Six
Freya

Shelby strides up the hallway, hips swinging like a Newton's cradle, long hair flowing behind her. Her skin is flawless, dewy. Even though we all see her day-in, day-out, her beauty still catches my breath sometimes. She conjures the same power as an electrical storm, causes as much damage.

Lottie reaches out for a hug, and as she does, Shelby turns her back, leaving Lottie hanging.

Carole's back has straightened like someone's put a rod up her bum. She pushes her hair off her face and glances at herself in the mirror, preens herself for the contest.

'Where did *you* pop up from?' she asks Shelby. It's the polite version of 'look what the cat dragged in'.

'Hello, *Carole*,' Shelby says, but doesn't look at her. Her voice is croaky, yet chocolatey. Over the years it has deepened, gathered in throatiness. A smoker's voice, without the cigarettes, but possibly cultivated by all the wacky-backy she smoked on the dunes when we were teens.

Carole's eyebrow raises as much as it can with all the Botox.

'Happy birthday,' she mutters sourly. Carole detests Shelby, not just because she dated Max, but because Shelby plays up to it. She acts like she knows something about him that Carole doesn't, like she'll mention Max in passing over drinks or refer to him as Latto. Carole *hates* that. She has this vein in her neck that pulses like crazy when she's annoyed, and there is always a ton of vein action when Shelby's in the room – particularly when she hears Max referred to by his former nickname. Seeing Shelby and Max together on the forecourt at Esperance Motors tonight has made me understand Carole's paranoia a bit more. The way Shelby stood on her tiptoes and tilted her head back, the way the greeting lingered. It seemed far too intimate for just friends. Or maybe I'm reading too much into it. Either way, I feel a bit sorry for Carole, even if she is a stuck-up cow a lot of the time, because Shelby has this sense of entitlement, this idea she's just better than everyone else. She's a typical school bully, reducing everyone she mixes with to a state of paranoia. Even someone as self-assured as Carole.

Shelby pulls her running top over her head so that she's standing in her sports bra, her stomach flat and taut, and hangs it on the back of one of Lottie's rattan bench stools to dry. Eventually, she clocks Lottie looking at it and says, 'You'd like me to get that off your chair back, wouldn't you?'

Lottie shrugs and tells her, 'No, it's fine,' but spends the next few seconds looking at it with a sort of anxious expression on her face. Shelby leaves the top where it is.

'You shouldn't run after dark on your own,' Lottie says, staring at the vegan quiche she's made, which *really* stinks (thank God I eat dairy, is all I'm saying). 'Not while there's a pervert hanging around.'

'Get a grip!' Shelby snaps. 'We're hardly in Bogota, are we? I only told you about it so you could pass it on to the dipshits who run along with earphones in after dark.'

She means Carole. Carole is one of those dipshits.

'What happened the other night?' I ask. 'With the flasher?'

Shelby looks annoyed that I deigned to speak to her. 'Not a lot,' she says. 'He opened his jacket, stroked his pathetic excuse for a penis and then ran off. Hardly a big deal.'

'What did he look like?' asks Lottie. 'How old was he?'

'I didn't ask for his driver's licence,' snaps Shelby. 'I don't know, do I? His face was hidden. It was his dick that got the full glare of the street lamp, unfortunately.'

'Couldn't you tell from *that*?' asks Lottie.

'Funnily enough, I didn't study it in detail.'

Carole's jaw tightens. 'And *this* is why we run in a group,' she hisses. 'For safety.'

Shelby ignores her, like she always does.

'So why weren't you running on the track?' Lottie asks Shelby.

'I took a different route.' Shelby picks up a cracker and scoops hummus onto it. 'Put that on your app, Carole!'

Lottie eyes Shelby from the opposite side of the kitchen bench. 'Which route did you take?' she asks.

'Seafront. My, aren't we nosy tonight?'

She reaches up to get herself a glass from the top cupboard and fills it with prosecco. Her lipstick is freshly applied, and she has sand in the back of her hair. As she reaches up, a dusting drops onto her bare shoulders. She sees me clock it and smiles, brushing her skin with her hand. She takes a sip of wine and leaves a fuchsia stain on the rim.

She nods towards the stairs.

'Where's Izzi?' she asks.

'Dinner with Piers,' Lottie replies.

'Ahh, they must have gone there straight from the comp.'

'Comp?' Lottie's brow knots.

'Yeah, Izzi's dance competition was earlier. Didn't she tell you?'

Lottie looks devastated. 'She told me it was just practice.'

'Oh? She invited *me*. I stopped in at the scout hut before my run. She was incredible.'

'She didn't tell me she was competing!' Lottie looks like she might cry. 'Why didn't she ring me? Why didn't *you* ring me? I would have rescheduled tonight . . .'

I glance at Carole and grimace. This is classic Lottie and Shelby – Shelby dropping a bomb and then acting like Lottie is overreacting to the scattered debris.

'Chill out,' says Shelby. 'It's not a massive deal. Go to the next one.'

Lottie's mouth twitches. She pulls the tea towel taut in her hands until her knuckles whiten, and then after a moment, she lets it slacken. Carole bites into a carrot stick and the crunch is as loud as a car crash on a quiet road.

'At least tell me you took some photos?' Lottie asks.

'No, why would I?'

Lottie's face is red. She turns away from Shelby to face the oven.

'Sand running is *great* for your calves,' I say, in a bid to defuse the tension.

'Disagree,' says Carole. She picks up a celery stick this time and buries it, to its waist, in beetroot hummus. This is about as much as she'll eat tonight – she pretty much survives on air. Gaining so much as a kilo would be a fate worse than death for Carole. 'When I was sand running last year I had calves like a *man*.'

She glances at Shelby's legs. 'Not that I'm saying *you* have big calves, Shelby.'

Carole can't say anything to Shelby that isn't passive aggressive. But the older we get, the more the aggressive outweighs the passive. Maybe that's because Shelby looks the way she does, and Carole's starting to appear a little rubbery, with all the fillers and stuff.

'I just think that if you're not careful, you'll end up going down the fat calves route,' says Carole. 'And no one wants great big Henry the Eighth legs, do they? Legs like a Christmas ham . . .'

Shelby looks up from her phone. 'Thanks for the advice, Carole,' she says. 'Where did you do your exercise physiology major, again? Oxford, wasn't it?'

'Just common knowledge,' smiles Carole.

'Wouldn't ham legs be, like, massive thighs and *tiny* calves?' I ask. 'That's how a ham looks.' I get out my phone and google 'Christmas ham' and show everyone the screen.

'Whatever,' says Carole. 'You know what I mean.'

She watches, disgusted, as Shelby loads up a cracker with cheese, prosciutto and quince paste and puts the whole thing in her mouth. Shelby smiles at her as she chews. When she's finished, she licks her lips like she's in an adult movie, and says, 'How's *that* for the calves, Carole?'

Carole rolls her eyes and looks away.

'Talking of legs, yours look *incredible* in those pants, Carole,' says Lottie, in a transparent bid to prevent World War Three.

'Don't they?' Carole chirps. 'Max *loves* them. Every time I wear them he tries to bend me over the drying machine. It's *so* tedious!' She glances at Shelby.

'Henry the Eighth,' I muse. 'Now *there* was a sexy man. There are some really hot dead men. Have you *seen* a photo of Ned Kelly? They don't make hipsters like that any more!'

'You obviously haven't been to Byron Bay,' says Carole, fanning her chest with Lottie's copy of Jamie Oliver's *Fifteen Minute Meals*. The rain hasn't yet broken the humidity, and even Lottie's air-conditioning, which is cranked up to the max, isn't helping.

'Okay, who would *you* choose then, Carole?' I ask.

'A young Robert Redford,' she says. 'He reminds me of Max.'

Shelby lets out a laugh that sounds like 'yeah right'.

Carole's head whips round. 'What about *you* then, Shelby?' A tiny fleck of her saliva lands in the beetroot hummus and Lottie retreats with her carrot stick.

'I'd have to say Max ...' Shelby replies, and Carole's pupils widen like ink on a blotter. She's doing what she always does. She plays on people's insecurities, toys with them.

'Oh,' Shelby fake laughs. 'Not *your* Max, Carole!' She makes speech marks with her fingers when she says the word 'your' and then lets her hands drop. 'Oh that's *so cute*! No, I meant Max in the film of Lottie's favourite book, *Rebecca*. Who played him, Lottie?'

'Laurence Olivier,' Lottie says obediently, her eyes darting apologetically towards Carole.

'*Rebecca*?' Carole scoops hummus on a snap of gluten-free crispbread. 'Never heard of her. And Laurence Olivier? Too foppish by far. You two have *such* questionable taste in men!'

She evidently doesn't realise the irony of what she's said.

'Anyone else for a top up?' Lottie waves the bottle around a little maniacally.

The doorbell rings and she puts the bottle on the kitchen bench and runs down the hall, almost tripping over the colourful fabric of her dress.

'Shelby,' she calls behind her, 'can you top everyone up?'

Shelby tops up her own glass and puts the bottle back in the fridge.

Lottie's happy voice trills down the hall. 'Hello! What a lovely surprise,' she chirps.

'Hello Lottie! I hope you don't mind me interrupting,' a masculine voice replies.

It's Tino.

'You're *kidding* me,' says Shelby. She gets up from her chair and begins to walk towards the door as if to usher her husband out of it. But Tino's legs are longer and he is already at the kitchen bench. I look in the mirrored splashback and check my hair. Tino is just one of those men who make you want to look good because he's so attractive himself. Tall, dark and . . . you know the rest. But then again, all of them are handsome: Tino, Max and even Piers, in a preppy, boarding school sort of a way. And so they all should be, because male or female – you can't be ugly living in this town. It's as if aesthetics are taken into account when you're signing over your millions on a property contract.

Lottie twitters away. She *loves* Tino, and by all accounts she is gutted he can't make it work with Shelby because she thinks he is so good for her, that he calms her down and the rest. But Shelby's too tricky to make it work with anyone. The man deserves a medal for dealing with her. She treats him like something she trod in.

'Hello ladies,' he says.

He turns to Shelby and says, 'Shelby.' It's all very awkward.

'I knew you'd all be here,' he says. 'I just found this in the park and thought it might belong to one of you.'

He puts his hands in the pocket of his running shorts and pulls out a delicate gold bracelet. *My* gold bracelet. I hadn't noticed it had fallen off.

'That's mine,' I say and reach out to take it just as Shelby turns her back to him and opens the giant silver door of Lottie's fridge.

'Thank you so much, Tino.'

He looks over at Shelby's back, then smiles at me and gestures for me to hold out my wrist and so I do, letting him fix the clasp. It's surprisingly intimate having another man touch my wrist, and strangely arousing that it is Shelby's husband touching me. My skin feels like it might be flushed.

'My pleasure,' says Tino. 'I thought I recognised it.'

He turns to his wife. 'Shelby, can I have a word?' he asks, nice and cordially.

Shelby looks at him and does not smile. 'Not now,' she says.

'It won't take long . . .'

'*Not now,*' she repeats and turns away from him.

Tino holds his hands up. 'Right then, I won't hang around. I don't want to interrupt this lovely gathering any longer. Lottie, the quiche looks absolutely delicious.'

'Please take some,' says Lottie, picking up a knife, but Tino pats his stomach.

'I'm all good,' he says diplomatically. 'I've already eaten.'

Lottie goes to follow him.

'I can show myself out.' He smiles. 'Thanks, Lots.'

He runs a hand through his hair as he walks along the corridor towards the door. I feel so bad for him. He is honestly such a nice guy, and attractive too! Shelby seriously needs her head read.

'What was that about?' Lottie asks once the door has closed.

'He's so needy. It's like having a puppy follow you around.' Shelby drains her glass. 'A bit like Freya was at school.'

I feel my skin flush. 'Is that how it was, Shelby? I don't remember,' I mumble. I immediately wish I'd come up with something better, but somehow I always revert to being fifteen and spotty again when Shelby says something like this. I take a giant slug of my wine.

'Why did Tino really come over?' asks Lottie. 'It can't be the bracelet. He could give that to you to pass along.'

'He's checking up on me, obviously.' Shelby inspects her nails, painted bright red. 'Wants to make sure I'm not doing something I shouldn't.' There is something smug in the way she says it, like she is indeed doing something she shouldn't.

'This *weather*,' sings Carole, who is fed up of Shelby hogging the limelight. 'It's so stifling! I'm going to be almost relieved when the downpours start.'

'You won't say that when your hair is frizzing in the rain,' I say. 'Peninsula's going to cop a thrashing on Friday night. They've told everyone in Shivers to sandbag their homes.'

'Sandbags probably cost more than the houses,' Carole laughs, then looks at Shelby and feigns innocence. 'No offence.'

Lottie wraps her arms around herself. 'Something bad always happens when there's a storm,' she says. 'It makes me nervous. They're a bad omen.'

She's not wrong. Last year, the body of a spear fisherman washed up on Mooney beach in the storm, and a couple of months later, a fifteen-year-old boy got swept off the rocks at Boorie Point during a mild cyclone. The peninsula doesn't have a great history with storms.

'I guess we'll know by Saturday if something awful is going to happen,' says Carole, and four hands wander contemplatively towards the food platter in the middle of the wooden benchtop. Carole sticks her half-eaten carrot in the beetroot hummus.

'Ugh, Carole, did you double-dip that?' I ask. 'That's the number one cause of food poisoning in bars, you know.'

'I think that's peanuts,' says Lottie, apologetically. 'Nuts in bars have more germs than there are on your phone.'

'I'd be dead if I ate a peanut,' Carole says, lifting a compact mirror to her mouth and digging out beetroot residue from between her teeth with the nail of her little finger.

'Satay, anyone?' murmurs Shelby.

'So Lottie, how was your interview?' I ask.

'Interview?' Shelby looks up from her phone. 'What interview?'

'For the job at St Paul's. I did mention it to you, but it's no biggie.' Lottie shrugs.

'Oh, that,' Shelby says. 'Spit it out. How was it?'

Lottie glows pink. She doesn't like to be the centre of attention.

'It was *great*.' She spreads vegan cheese on a gluten-free cracker. 'I got the job, so I ended up working there in the afternoon. Marella, the manager, is just so kind, and . . .'

'That's wonderful Lottie!' Carole cuts her off. 'I'm *so* pleased for you. It's so incredibly important to give back. I wish more people bothered.' She looks at Shelby again.

Then she says, 'Anyway, in other news, Max's Maserati MC20 has arrived! The one I ordered for our anniversary. He's beside himself with excitement. We're picking it up at the weekend. I'm going to ask the garage to put a giant bow on it. Maybe I'll even sit in the front seat naked! He'd *love* that . . .'

'Your arse all over his new leather?' Shelby says. 'Doubt it.'

Carole ignores her. 'Max was first in line at Esperance Prestige Motors! Top of the list. There are a thousand people waiting, and we got lucky. Can you believe it?'

'Wow,' says Lottie. 'Who did he have to screw to get to the top of *that* list?'

Her mouth drops open as she realises what she's said. Shelby does the accounts for Esperance Prestige Motors.

Shelby's eyes sparkle with amusement but she doesn't comment.

Carole mutters something under her breath and downs the rest of her glass.

Half an hour later, it's just me, Lottie and Carole. Shelby has evidently tired of us all and has gone home on a high, having won the latest round of her lifelong face-off with Carole. Lottie is frantically cleaning glasses, while Carole takes them back out of the cupboard and refills them with varietals of wine. Since the Esperance Motors comment, Carole has gone from tipsy to completely blotto. She drags me outside for a cheeky menthol cigarette in Lottie's garden. Lottie won't let anyone smoke in the house because Piers is so anti-smoking ('He's a medic. He won't condone carcinogens', she says. Which means, by default, Lottie won't either). I'll happily admit to enjoying the odd ciggy, but Carole maintains the public façade she doesn't smoke, and feigns shock that she always happens to have a packet of menthols on her. Still, it's oddly bonding in a weird way.

'Where did you stash them tonight?' I ask. 'In your running pants?'

'God no!' She sparks up. 'Behind Lottie's compost bin. I leave a box there.'

We smoke in silence for a minute before Carole grabs my forearm out of nowhere and squeezes it. 'What the . . . Get off me, Carole!' I say, pulling my arm away. 'That hurts!'

She releases her grip. 'I'm sorry, it's just . . . Do you think Max loves me?' she asks. 'I mean, *really*? You don't know how hard it is to be married to a man with . . . with *history*.'

'Of course,' I say. 'We all have history!'

But the truth is, I really don't know the answer. I know what she's really asking is whether I think there's anything going on between Max and Shelby. She doesn't necessarily mean physically, but a feeling, a flame. It's the same whenever Carole is drunk, but if anyone tries to bring it up when she's sober, she laughs it off – 'Ugh,' she'll say. 'As if Max would ever go *there* again.'

I wait for it.

'But, Shelby,' she starts. 'Shelby's so smug! Do you think . . . ?' She takes a deep drag, exhales and looks directly at me. 'Do you think she's still after him?'

'Oh Carole . . .' My mind flashes back to the garage forecourt – to the sly smile Shelby gave me as her arms hung round Max's neck. Like she was trying to tell me she was up to no good. Like she wanted to be discovered. But how can I explain the significance of a smile to Carole? It isn't *proof* of anything. 'I really don't know . . .'

Carole straightens up, eyes wide. 'You know something,' she snaps. She pushes my sternum with her index finger. 'What do you know?'

'Nothing!'

'You're lying!' she says, eyeballing me. 'Freya! Tell me what you know, immediately. Please! I'll . . . I'll *pay* you!'

I sigh. 'You don't need to pay me. Look, it's probably nothing, but I did see Max at Esperance Motors tonight, on the way here . . .'

'And? He went to look at the Maserati.'

'The thing is. . . he was there with Shelby.'

I don't know why I'm getting involved. But the truth is, I feel sorry for her. Because everyone knows Shelby is obsessed with Max, and that Max enjoys this fact immensely. He might play the doting husband, but I've seen the way he looks at Shelby when he thinks no one else is watching. As if he's longing for something he can't have.

'She does work there,' slurs Carole. It's as if now I'm giving her evidence of a potential indiscretion, she doesn't want to know. She'd rather keep her blinkers on, which she always seems to do when it comes to Max and Shelby.

'Of course. But I did see Shelby lean in to—I regret the words as soon as they're out. They're only going to fuel Carole's deep-seated paranoia.

'To what?'

I look at my feet. 'To *greet* him. A kiss hello, you know?' I shrug.

Carole moves in closer.

'So what was it? A kiss or a greeting?'

'I don't know,' I say. 'I couldn't really see. Perhaps you should talk to Max.'

'Max? Why? What has he done? She leant up to *him*, didn't she?'

I don't reply. I don't know, is the answer.

'Max wouldn't do anything with that tramp – he knows I'd cut him off if he did! Anyway, spit it out. What exactly did you see?' Carole's eyes are wild.

'Um, well, it *could* have been a kiss.' I regret the words immediately. 'But of course, I could be wrong.'

Carole's face turns puce and her nostrils flare. 'Fucking *Shelby*!' she screams, squishing her cigarette into the ground with a rough twist of the point of her running shoe.

Inside the kitchen, I see Lottie's head swivel on her shoulders at the sound of Carole's outburst. She eyeballs us, wondering if she actually heard what she thinks she heard.

'Shhhhh!' I snap, and raise a jolly hand to Lottie to show her we are having a gay old time outside and definitely not talking about Shelby, and Carole's imminent plan to exterminate her. Lottie grins and looks away just as Carole smashes her crystal champagne flute angrily into the platform of Piers' sandstone bird bath, the shards settling like deadly crystals at the bottom of the watery pool.

'I'm telling you,' Carole snaps, fixing me with a stare that can only be described as demonic. 'That toxic little narcissist is going to get what's coming to her. Just you wait and see!'

Chapter Seven
Carole

Max is in bed when I get home.

'Carole?' he calls from upstairs.

Every part of me wants to burst in through the door and confront him, to ask him what's been going on with Shelby. To tell him what I've just been told by Freya and demand he refutes it. But I need to digest the information, to think it through. Would Max really cheat on me? *Would he?* Would he really risk everything we have together for someone so rough and unrefined? And that's what she is, because when Freya and Lottie and Max all bettered themselves and slipped seamlessly into their affluent and sophisticated new world, Shelby kept the rough edge. The rough edge, only now with designer clothes. Uncouth, unpolished.

'Carole?' Max sounds confused.

'Just . . . a moment!' I may have sobered up a little, but I'm still drunk enough to cause a scene.

'Can you bring me up some water?' Max calls, oblivious to my inner turmoil.

I don't reply. Reaching up to the overhead cabinet I notice my hands shaking. It's as if Shelby is laughing at me in the reflection of the glass as I slide it towards me. Her mocking eyes, the way she flicks her hair as if she's better than everyone. All big volume and caramel lowlights, done at the cheap salon in Mooney Waters.

I climb the stairs, hands trembling and water spilling onto the oak balustrade, ready to study my husband's face for the truth or a lie. I know him so well. Don't I?

I pass Olivia's bedroom first, and for a moment I pause to gather strength. My teenager, my prodigy. She has kicked off her duvet and is sprawled belly down, like a starfish. I kiss her head and pull the quilt back up to her waist, closing the door so she will not hear the scene that I am about to make. Otto, next door, is snuggled in the fetal position under a blanket and a quilt beneath it. I kiss his temple, feel the warmth, a taste of salty sweat and pull his covers back. This is the way it has always been. Otto always loves to snuggle, to stifle himself with blankets until he bakes. Olivia, like Max, hates to overheat. Always dressed sparsely, even in the winter. Hot blooded physically, but not emotionally. Relaxed to a fault, almost horizontal, until the moment she snaps and hell is unleashed. There's always a single shocking minute of unbridled rage until her temper cools a little and she turns contrite. It's the same with Max.

I stand in Otto's doorway for a moment longer before taking a breath and turning towards the master bedroom.

Max sits up in bed as I come in, his phone in his hand. 'Hey. Good night?'

'Who are you texting?' I try to make it sound breezy, like I don't care, but my voice gives me away.

'Just Piers,' he says, studying my face. He has heard the tremor in my voice.

'Why are you texting him?'

'I'm arranging to go round for a beer sometime.' He puts his phone on the side. 'Are you okay? Did something happen at Lottie's?'

'I'm fine.'

I go into the en suite bathroom, shut the door. I wash my face, look at myself in the mirror. See the hatred in my eyes for that woman, watch my pupils narrow to dots. That vile, despicable woman who won't leave my brain. That woman who's still infatuated with my husband even though he dumped her for me over twenty years ago. The same woman who is married to an amazing man, a man she treats like shit because she treats everyone like shit. A woman who has her own husband, but is still obsessed with mine!

Take a breath, Carole! I throw cold water on my skin. Try and talk myself round. *You are worked up. You need to calm down. You are home with Max and Max loves you.*

I open the door and see him there, his phone back in his hands. It isn't the face of a man texting a lover, it is the face of my husband, hair messy and reading glasses on his nose. The man who has shared my bed for twenty years. Perhaps I should give him the benefit of the doubt when it comes to her. Perhaps I need to acquiesce, to remind myself that, just because she wants him, it doesn't mean he wants her. After all, Max doesn't like things that are cheap.

He chose me!

I walk back into the bedroom and climb into bed, turning my back to Max. I wring my hands tightly together with hand cream, hurting my own knuckles with the force.

Max puts his hand on the small of my back, his phone face down in his lap. *Face down.*

'Carole, what's wrong?'

I want to play the doting wife, the wife who's never jealous, the wife he wants me to be.

But I have to know.

'Did you go out tonight in the end?'

'No. I just watched TV. Why?'

'So you didn't go and see the car?'

Max pulls his glasses off his nose. He looks confused. 'You know I did. I told you yesterday I was going to pop in there.'

'You just told me you didn't go out.'

'Walking to the end of the street to see a car in a showroom window isn't exactly going out, is it? I didn't think it was worth mentioning.'

'Did you go inside the showroom?'

'It was open, Carole. Of course I did!'

'Did Shelby let you in?'

Max turns over in bed.

'Not this again,' he says with a sigh.

'Did you arrange to meet her?' I ask. I am trying not to sound desperate. 'Because if there's anything going on Max, I swear I will make you leave right now in the clothes you're wearing.'

Do I mean what I'm saying? Yes! No! *No* . . .

'What?' he turns back to me. 'I just told you I went to see the car. The car you bought me *for our wedding anniversary*!'

I scan his eyes for evidence of infidelity, but they do not yield any information.

He sighs again. 'I got there and she was just leaving her office to go for a run. She waved at me, and beckoned me in.'

'A wave?' I squirt more cream on my hands, pull at my fingers until they hurt.

'Yes, a wave. Have you got spies out?' Max smiles thinly.

'Freya saw you.'

He turns to plump his top pillow and sits up a little. 'Freya *saw* me?'

I nod.

'She saw you kiss her.'

Max's left eyelid twitches just a fraction. 'Kiss her?' he laughs, but it sounds hollow. 'How ridiculous! I greeted her. I kissed her on the cheek, or maybe she leaned up and kissed *me* on the cheek, I can't remember. Like I said, it was a quick greeting. A hug or something.'

'You said a wave.'

'Christ, Carole! A wave or a hug, does it matter? I've known the woman since we were at high school! I'm hardly going to blank her, am I?'

He turns to face me. 'Are we really back here again, Carole? Are we?'

I chew on the skin on the inside of my cheek, feel the warm metallic taste of blood.

Max leans into me. He touches my cheek with his hand, strokes it lightly. The gesture is so intimate, so honest.

'Darling,' he says, his voice soft. 'Please don't start this again. Shelby and I are old school friends, that's all. You know how overfamiliar she can be. She does it to get attention, you know that.'

Yes, yes I do know. Overfamiliar, inappropriate, *desperate*.

'You're only reading into this because we dated. You know it's not rational. I promise you, there is nothing going on between us. She was my girlfriend two decades ago! I was a kid back then.'

He smiles lightly. 'Come on, hmm? I'm sure if you had your first love living in Esperance, I'd be jealous as hell, but you really don't need to be.'

You were my first love.

He leans in and plants a gentle kiss on my lips. He doesn't close his eyes, and nor do I, so our eyes lock, stalemate. Eventually, I close mine, submit to the kiss.

Max pulls away first. 'Right, is this subject closed then?' he asks, like he's talking to one of the kids.

I shrug, then nod, conceding victory. But there's one thing I need to ask. 'There was a text on your phone this morning. It said "Latto, we need to . . ."'

'You looked at my phone?' he sounds annoyed again and I don't want to push it.

'You . . . you left it on the table. I didn't unlock it, I just saw the message on the screen.'

Max exhales deeply and I see a flicker of something on his face, something like panic, or annoyance.

'It was from Piers,' he says. 'It was the text I'm finally replying to now. He messaged to arrange a beer sometime soon. "Latto, we need to organise beers." It's taken me until tonight to get back to him. I've been flat out.'

'But it wasn't Piers' number,' I say.

'Maybe it was his gynae phone, I don't know. I am terrible at storing numbers, you know that. I still haven't stored your dad's number and he's my father-in-law.'

And your boss.

'Just . . . be careful,' I smile, all breezy. 'You know Daddy would cut you off if he thought you weren't doing right by me and the kids.'

Max looks at me, annoyed.

'What exactly are you saying, Carole? Has anything I just said sunk in?'

'Oh Max, I'm joking.' I smile.

It was *a joke! So why did it feel a little like I was issuing a warning?*

'Come here.' Max pulls me to him. 'You're my queen. Not Shelby, just you.'

I sigh and the relief tastes sweet, like maple syrup. He wouldn't lie to me. I relax into him, hear the steady beat of his heart. I close my eyes. He is still my Max. My protector. He would never do anything to hurt me, I know he wouldn't. I should not have listened to Freya. Freya with her tedious meddling!

I turn out the bedside lamp and lie back, let my mind wander to the first time I saw Max and Shelby together as a couple, walking down the pathway of this very house. Max with the bag of weed in his pocket, in his Shivers Beach High School uniform, and Shelby clinging like a limpet to his arm, her school skirt rolled up almost indecently. I remember the look in her eyes as she took me in – as she weighed up the competition; then the way he looked at me, how it was so much more intense than the way he was with her. That's how it's always been – me with the upper hand and Shelby scurrying behind him, trying to be seen. As if she could ever break the bond we have, Max and I, husband and wife, parents of our beautiful children. As if she could do anything that would take away the years we have devoted to one another: a wedding, fourteen anniversaries, two births, a family business! I've been stupid, so stupid.

Max's phone lights up on the bedside table and I do not flinch. He doesn't move to turn it over either to see who is messaging him. This assures me further he has nothing to hide. So I make a private vow that from now on, I will trust my husband implicitly. Because if you don't have trust in a marriage, then what do you really have?

'Listen, Shelby is crazy, you know that,' Max says in the darkness, as a final pre-sleep comforter. 'And even if she wasn't, why would I ever go there again when I have you? You are all I need. You and Olivia and Otto.'

He leans towards me and kisses me gently on the lips. I raise my arms for him to pull my silk slip over my head. I crave the closeness we always have after we've made love. Max obliges. He kisses my neck and my shoulders and moves down to my breasts until I am flooded with desire for him.

'I love you so much,' I tell him as we begin to move. He doesn't respond.

'Max?' I whisper in his ear. 'I *love* you.'

'Yes, yes, you too,' he mutters impatiently into my hair.

Chapter Eight
Shelby

Before

Lottie stands with her hand on her hip in the doorway of the bathroom. Her bare foot taps on the brown linoleum tiles, bubble gum pink varnish on her toes.

'How are you going to explain this one to Freya?' she asks.

I pick up my Covergirl eyeliner pen, look at her in the mirror as she stands behind me, her face etched with disapproval, then lean forward and close one eye.

'Shelby? Are you listening? How are you going to explain this to Freya?' Lottie is angry, but she doesn't shout.

'Explain what?' I ask my reflection. My hand is steady as I draw a line on my eyelid, above the base of my lashes, and sweep it out at the side.

'You know what I'm talking about.'

'I don't. So spit it out.'

'You know Freya is crazy about Max Latimer,' Lottie snaps. 'I'm her best friend and by default that makes you her friend, too. How would you like it if I started dating someone you liked?'

'You wouldn't.'

'I might.'

'Wouldn't happen,' I say, because the idea is stupid. We're hardly in the same pool.

'Anyway, we're not talking about me,' Lottie says. 'We're talking about Freya.'

'She should have made a move on him if she likes him so much!' I study my eyes from the sides, turn my head one way and then the other. Perfect. 'Anyway there's no chance of that happening because he's not into her.'

The thought is laughable. Freya Morton with her gangly legs and her metal mouth and the angry red acne that matches her hair? Latto wouldn't look twice at Freya!

'Besides Lots, I'm not going to hang back because she has a stupid crush. She's had a crush on half the school at one point or another. Do you want me to avoid all the boys she's listed in her Hello Kitty diary?'

'Now you're just being mean.' Lottie is stony-faced.

'Mean? What about how *I* feel?' I put on the hard-done-by voice. 'Freya batting her eyelids at my boyfriend . . .'

I know I'm being a cow, but I can't help it. It's fun. Lottie sucks up the information I've given her like Fanta through a straw.

'So Max is your *boyfriend* now?' she asks.

'Maybe.'

'Have you slept with him?'

'Maybe.'

Lottie sighs. 'You should really consider other people's feelings. You can't bulldoze people.'

'Oh lighten up, Pollyanna!'

Lottie's face reddens with fury, but as usual, she swallows it down.

'If you must know, I haven't slept with Max – yet,' I say. 'And anyway, Freya can suck it up. She's moving to

Arlingford with the rest of the snobs next term, so she can pick out some preppy dickhead from Esperance. She won't remember Latto's name in a few weeks.'

'I'm telling you, she will be so upset.' Lottie peels off her jeans and turns away.

'She'll get over it.'

My sister climbs into the shower, lets the water pummel her back. I watch her fists clench and unclench by her sides, her knuckles white against the pink flesh of her thighs. It's what she does when she's angry. She rarely lashes out. Except that one time she did. The time she lost it and the accident happened.

When it comes to me, Lottie alternates between frustrated and fearful – frustrated she can't control me, and afraid for the same reason. She worries I'm going to do something stupid like OD on party pills. That I'm going to live fast and die young, then leave her in Shivers Beach to rot alone. That would be her idea of hell.

Lottie drags a razor roughly over her shin and nicks herself. Blood trickles in a pink river over the bone of her ankle. She watches it wash down the plughole.

'Who are *you* shaving your legs for, anyway?' I ask.

Boys don't flock around Lottie. They always look at me first. She is a copy of what our mother has become: frail and pallid, her thoughts intricate like a maze of underground tunnels. 'If we hadn't all seen them being born, you wouldn't believe they were twins,' Nana Sue used to say. Two babies, grown side-by-side in the womb, yet from two entirely, almost genetically opposing eggs and sperm. 'Shelby got the beauty and Lottie got the brains.' The bookish brains, sure, maybe, but not the street smarts. Such different twins that we have different birthdays, our arrival like two ends of a bridge, straddling midnight. Two birthday parties, never one. We never once wanted to celebrate together after the age of five. My choice, not hers.

Lottie stands on the springy fake-tiled bathroom floor that still smells of Dad's cigarettes four years after his death and dries herself. Her shin is still oozing blood. I pass her some loo roll to stick on the cut, then pull on my jeans and a tank, open the bathroom window.

'What are you doing?' She is panicked, her wet hair dripping in a pool on the floor.

'Going out.'

'Where?'

'Just out. With Latto.'

I spray Tommy Girl on my chest and in my hair. I carried out the perfume from Shivers Beach pharmacy under my denim jacket when I was buying sanny pads and the checkout guy was none the wiser. He was so embarrassed bagging up the towels, he couldn't look me in the eye.

'Where are you going?' Lottie asks.

'Dunno. To smoke on the dunes, probably.'

'Not to Esperance again?'

'Probably. Why?'

'It's miles away, Shelby.'

'We're going on the bike.'

'His brother's motorbike?' Her eyebrows knot.

'Yep. So what?'

'Is Max making you go?'

I laugh. 'Making me? As if!'

'My God, Shelby.' Lottie's voice is a whimper now. 'What am I meant to tell Mum?'

Mum's like Lottie, nervous about everything since Dad died. She watches game shows every single night in the dark and jumps at her own shadow. Before we lost him, she was fun and feisty and energetic. That side of her died with him. Her soul died when Dad's car wrapped around the tree.

'Tell her I went to bed early.' I shrug. 'I dunno.'

'I'm not covering for you!'

'Then forget you saw me leave,' I hiss. 'Lighten the hell up. We're seventeen, we're meant to climb out of windows.'

I pull my body weight up onto the sink.

'Turn around and look the other way,' I say as I put my feet through the window. 'And then you won't have to lie to anyone, Miss Prissy Pants.'

But like a car smash on the highway, my sister can't look away, and I see her watery blue eyes flicker with anger she will never vent as I clamber out of our one-storey fibro bungalow and land softly on the parched earth below, creeping past the living room window where the tiny box of a TV throws out canned laughter and ugly sepia light.

The dunes are empty at 8.30 p.m. In Esperance, kids don't throw impromptu parties or make fire pits in the sand like in Shivers Beach. The beach has been raked in the last few hours, and the pattern is only broken by the odd footprint of man and dog. Latto and I smoke a spliff, drink two cans of cider each, and then it's down to business. We both know why we're here.

Max pulls my top off, undoes my bra with one hand. He has the other free, but he wants to show off that he can do it one-handed. Then he shoves his hand down my jeans and rummages around a little, finds the sweet spot and my body yields unwittingly.

'I brought a Johnny,' he says, unwrapping a little foil packet. It's all a bit awkward on the sand, and his body is heavy on top of me, but I guess it's kind of romantic with a starry blanket overhead. I fix my gaze on the brightest one (Sirius A, isn't that what Mr Lincoln said?), watch as it winks at me in time with the movement of Latto's hips.

Eventually I close my eyes and go with it, let my body move how it's meant to and I feel something that might be love. Afterwards, Latto rolls off me and we stare at the stars, each catching our breath. He takes out two cigs and lights one off the other, like he always does.

He takes a drag. 'You done that before?' he asks on the exhale.

'That's for me to know,' I say coyly.

'Thought so. How many times?'

'Not saying.'

'You knew what you were doing,' he says.

'Yeah, well.'

'Go on, tell me who you've done it with. Jason Simmons? He said so, but . . .'

'He wishes.' I smile.

Latto laughs.

'What about Theo Alexandrou? He said you gave him head.'

'Whatever.'

Latto laughs. 'Maybe it's better I don't know.'

'What about you, anyway? I hear Freya Morton likes you.'

Latto doesn't laugh, like I expect him to.

'Freya?' he asks. 'Yeah, I've kissed her before.' He is matter of fact.

I feel the hairs on my neck stiffen. 'You pashed Freya Morton?'

'Yeah.'

'For a bet?'

Latto looks at me weirdly. 'No, not for a bet.'

'Didn't know you liked redheads.'

'I don't usually, but she's kind of cute, I suppose.'

I feel the burn of rancid acid in my chest.

'When did this happen?'

'Dunno, a few weeks ago. We were in study group together and I walked her home.'

We're silent. I don't care about Freya, like *really* care, but even so I feel like I'm struggling to swallow a hard ball of nothing. I want to ask if they did more than pash, but I don't want to look like I'm desperate.

Latto looks up at the stars, his hands behind his head the way men always seem to lie on TV after they've screwed.

'Are you still into her?' I ask. 'I mean, it's cool if you are.'

'Nah. Not any more.'

'Did you come here with her?'

'To Esperance? No, don't be daft.'

Silence again. In front of us the waves crash on the shore and dissolve into the sand under the watchful eye of the crescent moon.

'Have you done it with many girls?'

'Six or seven.'

Which is it? Six or Seven?

'Stud.'

'Feels weird to talk about this, hey?' Latto says. 'Right after we've . . .'

'Yeah,' I say. 'I don't *care.* That's not why I'm asking. It's just I know Freya, so I wouldn't want to feel like I'm doing the wrong thing by her. Girl code, you know?'

'Then don't tell her.'

'Don't you want people to know about us?'

'Yeah, course I do. You're the hottest girl in the school!' He laughs and my skin feels warm. 'But you're the one saying you don't want Freya to get upset.'

'This will get out anyway.'

'All right, if you want us to call it quits because of her, then I'll understand.'

What is he saying? That he'd be happy to let me go? Am I that *disposable?* Aren't there a hundred boys at Shivers Beach High waiting to take his place? I look down at Latto, the square cut of his jaw, the shaved head. He is different, he means something. It's making me feel . . . shitty. Then it hits me, like it always does. The refusal to be vulnerable, to be hurt. I can either take control of this, or let it own me. I straighten my neck, shake the hair from my shoulders. *That will never happen.*

I stand up, pull on my jeans and shirt, and take a cigarette from the pack that lies next to his naked hip. He looks smaller from above, so much more vulnerable without his clothes, his wet cock lying flaccid to the right. I stub out my smoke and pick up my bag.

'Right, I'm off,' I say. 'See you around, Max Latimer!'

I stride off towards the clearing that leads to the reserve and beyond it the bus stop which will take me back home, up the coast to Shivers Beach. I'll look like I'm too keen if I ride home with him on the bike, even though I want to.

Latto is obviously surprised. He lies there and watches me go, but after a moment, I hear him get up, hear the jingle of his belt as he scrabbles to pull on his jeans, the squeak of his feet in the sand as he slides around for his thongs.

'Wait up, Shelby,' he calls, and hurries after me like a lost dog. I smile to myself. When he catches up, he nudges me with his shoulder.

'So, do you want to go with me, or what?'

'Go with you?'

'I mean, do you want to be my girlfriend?'

I shrug. 'Sure.'

'Yeah?' Latto grins.

'Whatever, yeah.' I shrug again. 'Why not?'

He interlaces his fingers with mine. 'Okay, Shelby Brennan, it's official,' he says. 'You're mine now.'

He squeezes my hand a little too hard. 'Listen,' he says, 'if we're together then I don't want you going with anyone else.'

'I'll try,' I say, and I let the warmth wash over me like bath water.

It is one in the morning when I get home and Lottie is still awake, reading. She can't sleep if I'm not there. She sighs with relief as I tiptoe through the door of our stamp-sized bed-room, with its two tiny single beds. The aisle between them is less than a metre wide, and usually chaotic with clothes and make-up, mostly mine since Lottie doesn't like mess. Her bedside table is neatly organised with books. There's *Rebecca* and *The Canterbury Tales*, because we're studying them in English, a browning Polaroid of us when we were six or seven in matching corduroy pinafore dresses, and a Body Shop watermelon lip balm. On the wall behind her headboard is a poster of James Van Der Beek. I have one of Anthony Kiedis from the Red Hot Chili Peppers. Says it all, really.

'Thank goodness,' she says. 'I was worried about you.'

'Why?'

'You go on a motorbike for a joyride down the coast in the middle of the night with someone who may or may not have a licence, and you expect me not to worry?'

'My God, Lottie, relax would you?'

I pull off my jeans and leave them on the floor. Lottie looks at them and at me, her face aching with exasperation. She doesn't say anything, just turns away from me towards the wall, staring at the psychedelic wallpaper.

'Look, I made it back, didn't I?' I hiss.

She turns around. 'So, how was it? Did you and Max, you know . . . ?'

'Yeah.'

Lottie whips back around.

'Really?' Her eyes light up. 'Oh my God.'

'It's no big deal,' I tell her, although my body is coursing with the adrenaline and I still feel tender down there. 'It was just sex, you know.'

'Did you use a . . . ?'

'Get stuffed! Of course we did.'

Lottie stares at me in wonder.

'Look, I didn't mean to have a go at you about Freya,' she says. She sits up on her knees on the bed. 'So?'

'What?'

'What did it feel like?'

I could tell my twin everything as she looks up at me expectantly. I could confide in her, tell her it was weird, sore, emotional. I could offer her the closeness she craves, the companionship. But I can't, not since the accident. Not since Dad died. Besides, I'm not a girly girl who wants to pour out secrets and share first kisses and copies of *Girlfriend* magazine. I never have been.

Lottie leans forward. 'So? Did you like it? What was his . . . *thing* like?' Lottie persists.

'His *thing*? Have you been reading *Sweet Valley High* again?'

Lottie sits back.

'Big,' I say.

'Really?' Her eyes widen. 'Like how big?'

'Would you give it a rest?' I snap. 'It was just sex. Go to sleep.'

Lottie's shoulders drop.

I wait in silence. If she asks again, I might tell. But she switches out the light, and as we lie in our parallel beds and stare upwards, all I hear is the deafening sound of our breathing in the dark.

WEDNESDAY

Chapter Nine
Lottie

I wake up late, fuzzy after cheese and wine. Piers is sitting up against the headboard, studying his phone in bed beside me, a deep frown on his face. I watch him silently, my head facing towards him on the pillow. Our money troubles have aged him. His skin is dry and jowly, his eyes underlined with dark, fleshy circles. Piers works so hard for our family, and to see him flooded with fear about not being able to pay our daughter's exorbitant school fees gives me a renewed feeling of angst.

He starts when he sees I'm awake.

'Good morning.' His voice is flat. 'Happy birthday. Did you sleep well?'

'Like a dream,' I smile, even though my sleep was fitful, as it usually is when I'm anxious, when something is happening in my world that is beyond my control. I stand up, flatten my bedhead with my palm and duck into the bathroom to brush my teeth – I don't like Piers to see my bedhead or smell my morning breath. Sometimes he likes to make love in the morning, but judging by the expression on his face, I don't think this morning will be one of those occasions. I make him a coffee using the Nespresso machine we keep in the walk-in wardrobe next to a tiny bar fridge, pass him his espresso, and then slide back in beside him under the sheets. It is a morning ritual we have, come rain or shine. It doesn't matter that it's my birthday.

'Present and card are coming later tonight,' he says and kisses my forehead distractedly. He has forgotten to get both, but that's okay. He's been so stressed.

'Sounds lovely,' I tell him and he smiles flatly.

'Isobel?' he calls. When there is no answer, he puts a foot out of bed and yells, 'Isobel! What the hell is she playing at? *Isobel!*'

'It's okay, darling,' I say, my hand on his thigh to calm him. I must remember to speak to Isobel about being sensitive around her father at the moment, remind her not to wind him up. To come when he calls.

Isobel wanders in, all tousled and sultry. She looks so disdainful, so *contemptuous* that I feel a strange and unnatural flash of hatred, just for a fraction of a second, and then immediately berate myself for it. *She doesn't mean it*, I tell myself. *She's just a petulant teenager. They're all like that. I'm sure I was like that, too. Shelby certainly was.*

'Yep?' she asks.

'Don't you have something to say to your mother?'

She looks confused, then she twigs. 'Oh yeah, Happy birthday!' she says before turning to leave again. 'I'll give you your card later, okay?'

It seems to be a theme.

'Sure.' I pull my lips up into a smile which I hope looks sincere.

Isobel struts out of the room, her hips moving in exactly the same way as Shelby's do. A kind of careless sashay.

Beside me, Piers sighs and clicks his knuckles.

'Penny for them?' I ask, even though I know what he is thinking about.

He doesn't answer.

'I tried to talk to Shelby again . . .' I begin.

I think back to last night, how I'd run after Shelby as she was leaving and asked her about the money. 'Shelby, please can we . . .' I stuttered. 'We need you to help us with the money thing, Piers and I.' I knew right away that I'd bungled it, messed it up.

'Not tonight,' she'd snapped, pulling the door closed. The accountant who didn't want to talk about money.

I'd stopped the door with my foot, in an uncharacteristic show of desperation.

'Please, Shelby,' I pleaded. 'We need your help. That money is rightfully *ours*!'

'No!' she'd hissed and turned on her heel, disappearing into the night.

Piers throws the duvet back. 'Can we stop talking about it?' he snaps. He stands at the foot of the bed in his pyjama shorts, his stomach slightly bloated, rounding. I feel terrible for mentioning it again. He folds himself into a calming downward dog. He doesn't like to be reminded about what's going on, and I understand that. It was an awful lot to lose. And I mean an *awful* lot. Which is why I need to know.

I try a different tack. 'Will you be seeing Dr Finch again?' I ask.

Dr Finch is a renowned hypnotist in Esperance. She costs four hundred dollars an hour, but she is meant to work wonders with all kinds of emotional issues. Obviously I didn't tell Piers this explicitly, I just suggested that she might be able to *relax* him a little, open him up.

He sighs. 'No I won't. She didn't exactly solve anything the first time, did she? It'd just be pissing more cash up the wall.'

I pat his hand sympathetically. I'll have to think of another tack. I'll wait until he's a little less frustrated.

'Should I shower first, darling?' I ask. 'Or would you like to?'

Piers nods. 'Go ahead.'

I've only been under the water for a minute when I hear Isobel's voice outside the door. 'Can you hurry up, please?' she snaps. 'My shampoo's in there and I'm going to be late for school.'

I bite my lip. I wish my own daughter didn't speak to me with such disrespect, but I can't tell her not to, or she'll hate me even more.

'One second, darling!' I call as I fluster about trying to work out which shampoo is Isobel's. Ahh yes, the one for thick hair – just like Auntie Shelby's. It could be twenty years ago, in the fibro cottage in Shivers Beach, and Isobel could be Shelby, shouting for shampoo out-side the bathroom, issuing orders that I would willingly obey. I hurry to finish my shower and wrap my hair haphazardly in a towel, in a rush to do my daughter's bidding.

'How was dance last night, darling?' I smile at her from the doorway of the bathroom. 'You didn't tell me it was a competition!'

'Forgot.' Isobel shrugs.

'I would really have liked to see it.'

'Why? Dad and Auntie Shelby came instead.'

Of course Auntie Shelby came instead! Shelby and Isobel get on like a house on fire. They have that special friendship, and I can see why. They're so similar, and even though I carried Isobel in my belly and gave birth to her over nineteen painful hours, I sometimes wonder if she wishes Shelby were her mother instead of me. Last week, at Mooney Mall, they walked ahead of me, their arms entwined like paper dolls, both in tiny denim shorts and white T-shirts with their brown, chocolate-coloured hair tumbling down their backs, feet perfectly synchronised. I followed inelegantly behind, like the third wheel, tried to smile gracefully when an elderly woman with a trolley stopped and said to Shelby, 'What a beautiful daughter you have!' and Shelby and Isobel looked at one another and laughed and said, 'thanks' instead of 'No, no, you're mistaken, *we're* not mother and child.'

As much as I try, I can't put a foot right. I embarrass her, stifle her, needle her. I try my best not to, but I've always found it so hard to discover that delicate balance between mother and friend. I wonder if I ever will.

But I shouldn't complain. I couldn't ask for a better relationship between my child and her aunt, although I'd be lying if I said it doesn't make me a little jealous.

I smile at Isobel now. 'But darling,' I say. 'If I'd have known about the competition—'

'You are supposed to know,' Isobel interrupts. 'You're my *mother*.' I almost expect her to add 'unfortunately'. Instead she says, 'There must have been an email about it at some point.'

There wasn't. I'm sure there wasn't. 'How was it, anyway?'

'Bad. Kelly Barton did the worst round-off and sprained her ankle when she landed. It messed up the whole thing. We'll be lucky if we place at all.'

'Oh Isobel,' I say. 'I'm sure it was wonderful. No one will care about one bad round-off.'

'How would you know?' she asks. 'You weren't there, so how can you say?'

There is it is again, the anger, the disrespect. She puts her hand on her hip and gives me the same side-gaze my sister does – a gaze that's laced with repugnance and perhaps even pity.

I hold my hands up in defeat. 'You're right. I'm sorry, darling. I couldn't possibly know, but I know how good you are, that's all.'

I look at her as she stands in the doorway, hand on hip.

I know it is a terrible thing to say and I don't know how many mothers would admit this, but sometimes I really dislike my daughter. I know she is a teenager and teens are generally rude and obnoxious, but the way she speaks to me is just so venomous. She's so like Shelby with her biting comments and her vanity. Sometimes I wonder where I am going so wrong. But like any mother, I will never show Isobel how I feel – I mean, it's probably just a phase and I don't want to mess her up for life. I love her, but I don't have to *like* her, do I?

'Did you have a nice dinner with Daddy after the competition?' I ask.

'Yep!' Isobel grins up at Piers. 'Dad let me have a sip of his wine.'

I look at Piers, who is now cross-legged and meditating, which I've convinced him to try to temper the stress. Daddy's little girl gets what she wants – possibly because Piers feels so guilty about barely being there when she was younger and he was climbing up the greasy career pole. Now Isobel is older, he lavishes her with whatever she wants – or rather he *did* until recently – horse riding lessons, a school trip to Whistler, designer clothes . . . I learned the hard way not to criticise when Isobel came home wearing a Cartier LOVE bracelet recently. Apparently all the Arlingford girls have them – at least that's what Isobel told us.

'Piers,' I'd said after Isobel was in bed. 'That is a very pricey piece of jewellery for a thirteen-year-old. It might get lost . . .'

'Leave the finances to me,' he'd snapped, and turned away to indicate the discussion was over. It had felt a little like a slap in the face.

Isobel looks me in the eye and I wonder if she's about to say something kind. But my child doesn't seem to possess the warmth I've tried to instil in her. Like Shelby, she can be defensive and cold. She sighs and cocks her head to the side. 'So, are you going to pass me my shampoo or not?'

It's technically my shampoo, but of course I don't argue.

'Here you go, darling!' I chirp, and hand over the goods.

A touch of emotional exhaustion, mixed in with worry and Adele's new album on the stereo means I'm feeling melancholy by the time I arrive at St Paul's for my next volunteering shift. Marella waves at me across the carpark.

'Sorry,' she mouths as she marches towards the door of the shop with her key, even though she is not late, it's me who is early. She is wearing a red T-shirt and too-tight black pants and is holding an Aldi bag. She has to lean over a heap of plastic bags that have been left on the doorstep to get the key in the lock. 'Why do people dump things on the doorstep? How are we meant to get inside? And it's used underwear too. I mean, come *on*!'

Her hair is frizzy on the underside, evidently losing the battle against the crazy humidity.

She looks at me, senses something's wrong.

'Lottie, are you okay?' she asks. And it's genuine. Not fake, in say, the way Carole sometimes asks it. She is doing the thing where she studies my face again.

She did the same thing on Monday. The constant questioning. *Are you okay, Lottie? Do you need me to show you anything? Are you sure you don't want a slice of carrot and walnut cake – it's homemade! Did something spook you – you seem a little jumpy? If it's Rocky then don't worry, his bark is worse than his bite! Would you like to go for lunch next week? My door is always open if something is on your mind and you need to talk!*

I don't tell her what's on my mind today, of course, because how do I say, without sounding like a psycho, that there is a catalogue of things: my daughter didn't write me a birthday card, my husband forgot to get me a gift and that we are facing an alarming financial issue; and that, on top of this, I have an irrational fear that my twin sister will . . . how do I even say it? *Die?* How could I possibly admit I have prophetic dreams, almost nightly, that bad things are going to happen? That most of the time I simply worry about *worrying* and about how, if I do it too much, it could make me sick, give me cancer. How could I confess I am only doing this job to escape having so much time on my hands to think?

But here is the strange thing, Marella does make me want to talk about it all. She has this voice that is really kind, that pulls you in and makes you want to divulge your deepest fears. And my goodness, I need that sometimes: genuine smile and a hand over mine. The ear of a person who takes me back to my old world, like a comforting old sweater – not one I'd want to wear forever, but still. Yet, despite this urge, I can't quite bring myself to tell her. Golly, where would I even start? She'd think I was crazy.

So instead, I say, 'I'm fine thanks. Just fine!'

'Holy moly!' she exclaims. 'It's your birthday today, isn't it? I'd forgotten. Please forgive me. Wait there . . .' She runs into the office and comes back sweating, holding a parcel in her hand. 'This is for you!'

I'm touched, so touched. 'Thank you,' I say. 'Can I open it?'

Marella nods. 'Of course!'

I peel back the cheap thin wrapping paper and inside is a multicolour kaftan from Zara.

'Oh,' I say, 'it's lovely.'

'It's from here, from inside the shop,' says Marella. 'I paid for it of course. I thought it would suit you.'

'It's lovely,' I say. And I mean it. I just won't tell Carole it's not designer.

'Pleasure,' says Marella.

'So,' I ask. 'What do you want me to do today?'

'How about you sort through this stuff on the doorstep? Bin the items we can't sell, like stuffed toys and the underwear – just pop them in the skip outside. Then price up the rest. Just like you did on Monday, really. Ask me if you think something's valuable, or put it into Google or eBay to find out what it is worth. You'll be working with Ron.'

'Ron?'

'Yes, the elderly chap who was here on Monday.'

'Oh,' I say. 'Right.'

Last shift he didn't say much, just bumbled around in his brown pin-striped suit, picking things up and putting them in the wrong spot. I must have spent an hour rehoming them in the right sections of the store.

'Ron is a lovely old chap,' says Marella. 'He has dementia though, so you have to be patient with him. He likes to pop into the changing room and put all sorts of outfits on, bless his cotton socks. He's a great big softy and it's all very amusing, provided he remembers to put his pants back on!'

I smile and consider that it might be a good day after all.

At twelve thirty, Marella suggests we go out for a birthday lunch, and as we're walking a few shops down to the sushi bar, I pray we don't bump into Carole. I just know she'll judge Marella for dressing like she's behind the counter in McDonald's and make some snide comment about the new white jeans I got online at Marella's request ('Oh look, it's Liz Hurley!') so I'm ashamed to say I scurry a little with my head down. Thankfully, I have a very casual relationship with my veganism, because a cucumber rice roll won't cut it today. I order a single chicken katsu roll with iceberg lettuce instead and vow to go animal-free again tomorrow.

Marella unwraps one of her three rolls and takes a hearty bite.

'What have you got in yours?' I ask.

'Chilli tofu,' she says. 'I'm vegetarian.'

I'm a bit taken aback.

'Really?'

'Why's that such a surprise?'

'I just didn't . . .'

'Why? Because I'm a little overweight and vegetarians are supposed to look like you?'

'No, it's just I didn't realise . . .'

I look from the floor to Marella's face. She is grinning at me.

'I'm teasing,' she says. 'Lottie, are you all right? You seem a little . . . *jumpy*.'

I smile. 'I'm fine. Super fine,' I tell her. 'Just a little peckish, I think.'

'Listen,' she says. 'I don't know what's up, and I hope this isn't out of place, but if you ever want an impartial ear, that's what I am trained to do.'

'Trained?'

'Yes, Lottie. I'm a psychologist, by profession. I'm *Doctor* Marella Wright, technically. But I needed a change of career after working for so long with trauma patients. I happened to know one of the chaplains from St Paul's and he recommended me for this role. So yes, I'm a proper psychologist turned shop manager.'

'Wow,' I say. 'That's impressive.'

'I like helping people, that's the crux of it, even if it does sound a little trite. Often you get people who don't want to be helped, but I'm there for the ones who do. It is the biggest thrill doing something for somebody else. St Paul's is an open house. Anyone can come into the shop and talk to me.'

'That's great,' I say, and I mean it. Somehow, the idea of people who really need help makes my own worries seem trivial, like another luxury I don't need.

'So what I'm saying, is that unless you're about to con-fess to a crime – because in that case I'd have a legal duty to report it – you can tell me anything without fear of judgement.'

I get the urge to talk again and this time I do. I don't tell her anything about Piers and the money because my loyalty lies with him, but I do tell her a little bit about Iso-bel and how I'm gutted about the dance concert and the fact my daughter can't hide her hatred of me. I don't tell Marella I sometimes feel the same about Isobel, because mothers aren't meant to feel this way, are they?

'Gosh, you do have a lot on your mind,' Marella says. 'Try not to worry too much about Isobel, though. At the end of the day, kids are programmed to be awful to their mums, even though secretly, they love them the most.'

'That's what my friend Carole says.' I smile.

'Then perhaps there's something in it,' she says and pats my hand.

I spend the afternoon lost in alphabetising the fiction section, reordering books that Ron has misplaced. It's glaringly obvious that the poor old man doesn't have much of a grasp of the letters of the alphabet any more. By the time I get to G, I'm exhausted. Plus, Ron keeps popping into the changing room and coming out wearing strange outfits. So far we've had ski gear, a satin ball gown and his birthday suit, which was a little awkward. Thankfully, Marella found some men's underwear from the bag that was left on the doorstep, because goodness knows where Ron has left his.

When I broach the mixed-up fiction with Marella, she says, 'Poor Ron, he's fading fast. I keep him on because he loves it here so much – plus he is a whizz at identifying antiques. He used to be an expert for a famous London auction house, apparently. Give him a vase or some crockery and he'll identify it on the nose. You should try it, he'll get it within five years, I promise, even if it's from the Ming dynasty. Just incredible. I mean, he can't remember the names of his children, or where he's left his clothes, but he knows antiques like the back of his hand.'

Never judge a book by its cover was evidently today's lesson.

At three o'clock, I stick my head round Marella's door and say goodbye.

'Bye Lottie,' she says. 'Thanks for today. I'm so grateful you offered to spend your birthday with us. I hope you're doing something very special to celebrate.'

'Thanks,' I say. Marella doesn't know I'm actually celebrating on Friday evening and I don't plan on telling her, either – but when I get to the door, something makes me turn. 'I'm having dinner on Friday at my place with some friends,' I tell her. 'It's a birthday thing, if you'd like to come.' I regret asking as soon as the words have left my mouth. Carole will chew the poor woman up and spit her out.

I close my eyes, hoping she will say no, but she doesn't. Instead she says an emphatic yes and asks what she can bring. I give my standard response which is 'don't bring a thing, just yourself' and she smiles.

'I'll make sure I walk Rocky early, then,' she says.

'Fabulous.' I paste on a smile. 'Bye!'

At home, I park in the street, since Piers has turned on the sprinkler and I don't want to get doused. The front door is in the firing line from the jets, so I creep round the back to go in through the laundry, and that's when I hear both their voices.

'Please . . .' My husband's voice is unnaturally high. Through the corner of the window, I see him run his hand through his hair. 'I am *begging* you.'

Then Shelby comes into view.

'What is it, Piers?' she snaps. 'What do you want?'

My husband says something I can't hear, through gritted front teeth. His face is ruddy, like he's just back from running, and sweat collects on his furrowed brow.

'I'm sorry, but I don't *have* it!' My sister shrugs.

The conversation feels wrong, illicit. I push open the door, only seconds later wishing I'd stayed to listen. Shelby glances up at me. She doesn't look flustered, but then she never does.

'Hello, Lottie,' she says and reaches across the bench for the last apple in the fruit bowl. She bites into it with a crunch. It was for Piers' muesli tomorrow morning, that apple.

'Hi,' I say to my sister, try to make my voice singsong, light. Not like the voice of a woman who has stumbled across a hushed and private conversation between her sister and her husband. 'How are you?'

She doesn't reply, just takes another loud bite of the apple.

'What are you two chatting about?' I smile, even though I am well aware of the subject. The fact is, we need Shelby's help in recouping what we have lost.

'Just shooting the breeze,' says my sister. 'I actually popped over to see if you had my diamond earrings. I left them here last night.'

'I'll look for you,' I chirp and swallow my growing sense of unease. 'I'll let you know if they turn up.'

'Don't worry,' she says. 'I'm going out tonight and want to wear them, but it doesn't matter.' Shelby picks up her car keys and cups them in her hands suggestively. She isn't wearing her wedding ring any more.

'Stay for a while,' I say. 'For a cup of tea and a chat?' I glance at Piers.

'Wish I could,' she sings. 'Too much on.'

Shelby turns towards the back door. Piers glares at me and nods his head towards my sister twice. He mouths, 'Do something!'

'Will I see you on Friday for my . . . for *our* birthday dinner, then?' I ask. 'Freya and Carole, are coming, plus my new . . . friend from work, Marella. And Isobel of course. I have mentioned it a few times. You will be there, won't you?'

Piers nods at me, like he's telling me I'm a good girl, that I've done a good job.

'Piers is cooking,' I say, making light. 'You have to be here to see *that*!'

'I'll try.' Shelby shrugs. It is a non-committal acceptance, but it is better than a decline. And although I don't really want our Friday night celebration to turn into a financial discussion, it is a conversation we have to have, the three of us together. And what better way than in a civilised setting with a glass of wine? Perhaps it's the perfect time for Shelby to realise that we are her family, that we could really benefit from her financial know-how.

Shelby doesn't ask what she can make or bring with her, she never does. Instead she tosses the apple core into the compost bin, says, 'Bye-bye, Lottie, bye-bye, Piers,' like she's talking to a couple of kids, and walks out of the back door, leaving it open behind her, until Piers' foot eventually slams it shut.

Chapter Ten
Freya

The late afternoon traffic in Mooney Waters is hectic, and I have to drive around the lower ground floor of the car-park three times before I find a parking spot. I eventually park up between a shiny SUV with personalised plates and a battered Nissan. That's Mooney Waters for you – the bustling go-between for poverty and prosperity. Louis Vuitton just two shops along from The Reject Shop inside the shiny floored, fake-plant adorned shopping mall.

Dr Jayne Saunders is my therapist. I don't see her because there's anything wrong with me, per se. I mean, I'm not anxious like Lottie or anything. It's just what people do in Esperance. Why not sit down and talk through stuff with a professional if you can afford to? Everyone – and I mean *everyone* – has repressed trauma linked to childhood or daddy issues, don't they? I haven't worked out exactly what my own repressed trauma is, since my parents are still married and I had quite a nice upbringing as it happens, but Jayne always takes a keen interest in Shivers Beach. She's eager to know what life was like for me growing up and how I adapted to the transition between two totally different suburbs and schools. How I coped moving from Shivers High School to Arlingford Ladies' College, where money seeped from the stitching of the uniform and where I was different to everyone else. I've told her before that it wasn't too much of a hardship for me, aside from the odd bit of bullying at the start. I actually got it worse from the people who were supposed to be my real friends, the assumption I'd become a snob now I'd gone up in the world, that Shivers Beach wasn't good enough. It's ironic, given Shelby and Lottie both moved to Esperance themselves as soon as they got their meal tickets out.

Jayne's office is a street back from the beach, on Waterview Parade. It's a small, glass-fronted office with a fiddle-leaf fig in a basket and an essential oil diffuser always on the go, pumping out a heady blend of de-stressing smells. Jayne probably makes more money than anyone we know. An hour-long session costs a few hundred dollars and her diary's so full she doesn't accept new clients. More's the pity, since Lottie could do with an iron out of all of her Shelby-related issues. I know for a fact that a weekly chit-chat with Jayne is how most of the housewives of Esperance keep their sanity intact – therapy, along with a somewhat contradictory diet of excess booze and green smoothies. Excessive sin, followed by excessive redemption.

The clock on Jayne's wall says five p.m., and the second hand gives a tick that in moments of silence seems louder than the bang of a dinner gong. She consistently sits with her back to it, referring to the time on her wristwatch instead – although she always seems to know when our hour is up without looking. She's been doing it that long. Or perhaps she steals glances at her watch in the moments it takes her clients to blink. Either way, the surplus ticking must do her head in.

Jayne is tall, with hair the colour of maple syrup, and today she is dressed immaculately in an avocado-green top and a black pencil skirt. Her green eyes peer over her black-rimmed specs. They are intense eyes that beg you to talk to her, to divulge your innermost secrets. Eyes that seem to know when you're lying. She was made for this role, with peepers like that. She'd be wasted behind a checkout counter or in a call centre or anywhere where she couldn't bore into someone's soul with just a look.

She smiles at me. 'You look happy,' she says, her ring-bound notepad flat on her lap.

'I'm off for a run after this, and you know how much I love to run.'

'With Bernard?' Jayne asks.

'No, he doesn't run,' I tell her.

Jayne nods. 'Fair enough, it's not everyone's cup of tea.'

'He's not as fast as he used to be.' I attempt a smile.

When I first met Bernard sixteen years ago, he was what you'd call a silver fox, with salt and pepper hair, a square-cut jaw and sparkling eyes. He was in his early fifties, a successful barrister with numerous winning cases to his name and a father to two young children. I was a twenty-five-year-old legal secretary, or I was hoping to be, and had arrived at his chambers to be interviewed for a job. By then, Lottie had already married into money and moved to Esperance, and Shelby was engaged to Tino. I'd been hoping desperately to meet my own Prince Charming as I perched on the warm leather seats of upmarket bars.

'That's Bernard Harrington,' Shauna, the receptionist who'd facilitated my interview, told me. 'The man you're checking out. Super-hot for an old bloke . . .'

'I'm not checking him out,' I lied.

'I won't tell,' she said. 'Looks like George Clooney, doesn't he? Loaded, too.'

'Loaded?'

She leaned forward conspiratorially. 'Rolling in it. He's a top barrister. He defended the guy who got off murdering his wife, you know, the Pinder case?'

'Really? Wow.' The Pinder case had been the most high-profile murder case in the country two years before. A man was accused of burying his wife in the garden during patio renovations. She was found buried all right, but the husband got off by pleading he was a battered husband or something.

'He's *very* well respected,' Shauna continued. 'Lives in Esperance in some massive mansion, apparently. *And* he's single. Divorced a couple of years back.'

I cocked my head to look at the man in the bespoke navy suit. He was tall and undoubtedly handsome. Sexy even, the way he stood upright, nodding as he spoke to a female lawyer in the doorway to her office. I watched the way the woman touched her hair self-consciously as he spoke to her. The way he gesticulated with his hand to make his point, the way he nodded earnestly. I watched him as he stood back to let her through her office door first, but not before turning to give me a thorough once-over.

'Do you know each other?' asked Shauna. 'He's staring at you.'

I shook my head but wondered if somehow our paths *had* crossed before.

I started work a week later, and the same day, Bernard Harrington walked past my desk and said, 'Good morning, Freya,' eyeing up my cheap blue pencil skirt and white, frilly blouse. I didn't know how he knew my name. The third time, he stopped at my desk and said, 'Thank Christ you work here. This place could do with some colour. We're such a bunch of old farts.'

I found myself laughing. 'I aim to please!'

'You *are* very pleasing. How about you join me for a quick lunch?'

A quick lunch at a swanky eatery in the City turned to a six-hour working lunch; the 'working' lunch turned to dinner; dinner turned to a wine bar; wine bar turned to sex; sex turned to long, boozy weekends on his yacht in the harbour, and ultimately, those weekends became month-long stints at his mansion in Esperance, where I'd catch up with Lottie when we took a break from the bedroom. And the man had stamina! Bernard loved that I had a best friend who was happily partnered to not only an esteemed local, but one he played rugby with, no less. He didn't give a shit where I came from, because I was young and pretty and I looked the part.

His ex-wife said he was having a midlife crisis, that I was a gold-digger because Bernard rapidly replaced every single pleather handbag in my wardrobe for a bona fide designer one. Because he swapped my cheap, gold-plated costume jewels for real ones. My friends told me how well I'd done, joked about my sugar daddy. But it wasn't like that. By then I'd fallen in love with the man: with his confidence, his success, his almost fatherly nurturing of me. He adored me, and I let him. He needed someone to spoil and I needed to be spoiled.

Bernard proposed outside Tiffany & Co. on Fifth Avenue in New York when I was twenty-five and he was fifty-two and I said yes immediately. I cried as he slipped the emerald-cut diamond from the little turquoise box on my finger and told me he would love me and look after me forever. And we were happy for the first few years, we truly were. I would skip down the stairs in the morning to make him breakfast before work and he would pour me a rosé when he got home. We had fun together, we made one another laugh.

But five years into our marriage, Bernard started to age. He would come home from work and turn down the music; order a cab home from the bar when the evening was just getting started; ask me to put on a longer skirt for the Law Society dinner. He'd suggest cosy nights in with a movie instead of swanky restaurant dates, pick walking the dog over going out. And the change was rapid: one minute it seemed he was still young and energetic, the next he was full of aches and pains and sore hips and a tender back and rampant halitosis. And I wasn't ready for it! I wasn't ready to get old! I'm still not ready.

'You love him, though!' Lottie had said when I first lamented that the age difference was starting to show. 'Isn't that all that matters?'

'Yes,' I'd replied. But I'd felt like the then Prince Charles in his engagement interview when he said, 'Whatever "love" means.' The truth was, I *had* known what love meant, because I'd felt it before. I'd felt it when I was sixteen and I'd fallen in love with Max Latimer: I'd felt it so intensely I'd thought I would die from it. Love that was euphoric, until it was no longer requited and then the pain cut like a knife through flesh! Heartbreak that early can ruin a person for anyone else, and that's what it had done for me.

Jayne rolls her head a couple of times to the right. I wonder if she does that with Carole, braces herself for the onslaught of emotions with a roll of the neck. It must be hilarious for her, because presumably Carole has told her all about me, about the others, about Shelby and how we all dated Max when we were teenagers. I've certainly told her about *my* history with Max, and how weird it is that we're all here in Esperance, living our best lives together, coexisting like tadpoles moved from a murky, muddy pond, and rehoused in a glass jar filled with crystal clear water.

Today she asks what I'd like to talk about, and when I say I'm not sure, she suggests we revisit school and peel off the layers of my childhood friendships like an onion.

'Shall we start?' she asks. She opens my file, takes a lady-like sip of her black coffee and then looks up.

'I'd like to go back to Shivers Beach today,' she says. 'Let's talk about your relationship with Shelby.'

'My relationship? You make it sound like we're having a bit of ooh-la-la!' I laugh nervously.

Jayne doesn't.

'Um, we're not,' I quickly point out.

Jayne nods. 'I know that, Freya. What I would like to discuss is the very . . . interesting dynamic at play, with you and Shelby and Lottie. I'm keen to see how it affects you. How about we start with you simply telling me about her.'

'About Shelby?'

'Yes. Go ahead.'

I don't see how it's particularly relevant, but the fact is, I'm paying the woman, so there must be a point to it. Unless she's obsessed with Shelby, like the rest of the world. It wouldn't actually surprise me.

'Shelby is Lottie's twin as you know, and Lottie's my best friend from childhood, so that's how we've ended up in the same circles of friends.'

'Right, so what you are saying is that you are mainly friends with Shelby because you have to be, and not because you want to be.'

'True,' I say.

'Weren't you friends in school?'

'Not really.'

'Why have you never warmed to her? You must be quite similar characters if you're both so close to Lottie.'

'I'm not sure Lottie would have chosen Shelby as a friend if she wasn't her sister, to be honest. Shelby's confident, complicated, selfish. And self-absorbed, very much so. Lottie . . . well she's gentler, kinder. She worries about things.'

'Who are you most like?

'Out of Lottie and Shelby?' I ask. I think of Luca and Bernard and of what I'm doing to my husband behind his back. 'Shelby, I suppose. In terms of confidence, at least. But without the arrogance, and the sense of entitlement and the inbuilt drama . . .'

'Have these similarities made you competitive, do you think?'

'Maybe.'

'Always?'

'Since high school, I guess.'

'Competing for Lottie?'

'Yes in some ways, but mainly . . .'

'Go on.'

'For boys.'

'Boys?

'One specific boy, actually.'

'Go on.'

'I mean, it's ancient history now, but I dated Max – as in Carole's Max – at school. He ended up sort of breaking my heart, dumping me for Shelby.' *Breaking my heart into a thousand pieces, so it that it wasn't put back together right.* 'But it wasn't a big deal.'

Jayne taps her notepad with the end of her pen.

'Were you in love with him?'

'I was sixteen . . .' I say, dismissing the reality of what I felt all those years ago.

'Sixteen is not too young to fall in love.'

I shrug, look at my hands.

'So, were you?' she asks gently. 'Were you in love with Max when he chose Shelby?'

The question feels uncomfortable, the delving has gone too deep. But I'm in up to my waist now, so I tell her the truth. 'Shelby *stole* him, technically.'

'I'm sorry?'

'I mean, it was more a case of her stealing him, than him choosing her.'

'Right, I see. But regardless, there was an overlap?'

'Yes.'

'And Shelby knew you were fond of him?'

'Lottie told her I was.'

'And you were heartbroken by this?'

I nod. *Affirmative.*

'Was it a serious relationship?' Jayne asks.

'I thought so,' I tell her. 'But Max didn't.'

I look at Jayne and realise that I may as well be honest – after all, I am paying her, and what's the point in having a therapist on a monthly retainer if you lie your way through the session? Jayne can't tell anyone. She isn't allowed.

I sigh. 'I lost my virginity to Max,' I say. 'On the sand dunes at Esperance. He took me there one night and told me he was falling in love with me. It felt right.'

Jayne nods. 'So it was a proper relationship you were in, then, when Shelby came along.'

'I thought so,' I say. 'I was only a kid, but I was in love with him. I know everything is so much more agonising as a teenager, but I remember wanting to die when Shelby started seeing him. That's first love for you. It's always painful, isn't it? No one ever won against Shelby Brennan, so I chose not to put up a fight and I tried to move on. I forgot about it all when I started at Arlingford.'

Jayne regards me with squinty eyes. She picks a fleck of white fluff off her black skirt and drops it to the floor.

'Anyway, Carole ended up with Max, didn't she? So I suppose Shelby did lose in the end.'

'Lose?'

'She lost Max.'

Jayne looks pensive.

'What word would you use to describe how you feel about Shelby now?'

I pause. 'Strongly dislike.'

'Is "hate" too strong?'

'Isn't that what "strongly dislike" means?'

'It's a rung up,' Jayne says.

'I suppose I do hate her, if I'm honest,' I tell her. 'But not because I'm traumatised by Max dumping me for her when I was sixteen.'

Jayne's head cocks to the side. 'Then why?' she asks.

'I hate her because she never apologised for it, not even as an adult,' I explain. 'She is incapable of empathy, kindness or remorse. I truly believe that if she took me to one side and said to me, "Hey Freya, I treated you badly when we were kids, I'm sorry", it might go some way to diluting the resentment I have for her, but her attitude is so unapologetic. Like everything is hers for the taking. So yes, I'm resentful. I mean, it's not the kind of resentment that is omnipresent, but it *is* there, and sometimes Shelby will do something that will make it flare and I will detest her for it, possibly irrationally, I don't know.'

'Such as?'

'Such as belittling Lottie. Lottie is a shell of the person she should be because Shelby manipulates her. She pushes her away, then pulls her back in when she needs her again. She leaves everyone flailing in her wake and it's always been that way. She's self-absorbed and she's selfish and she's easy to hate . . .'

I feel my face flush as the words tumble out.

Jayne looks at me expectantly, but I don't have anything left to say. I feel I've summed it up succinctly enough. Jayne scribbles something on her notepad and looks up with a shuffle of papers.

'That was good, Freya,' she says. 'I feel like we've really got somewhere today. We'll revisit this next week and try and uncover some more of those feelings.'

I smile and get up to leave, feeling a little like Pandora's Box. All these emotions have been locked away for so long. What will I do with them? Where will I store them all now?

Chapter Eleven
Shelby

Before

Freya and I sit side by side at a thick wooden bench in the chemistry lab.

'You playing netball tonight?' I ask.

Freya jumps, like she's surprised I'm talking to her. She has pretty much avoided me since she found out about me and Latto three months ago. She puts a pair of plastic goggles over her eyes and buttons up her lab coat.

'Yeah,' she says.

'We're playing Arlingford,' I tell her. I don't know why I'm making conversation with her; I guess I feel bad about what happened or something.

'I know,' she says, frosty as anything. 'I saw.'

'You'll be in their team soon,' I say. 'Arlingford's.' It's all everyone's talking about at school, how Freya Morton is moving to the posh school in Esperance because her dad's rich now.

'From next month,' she says.

'They're lucky to get you in Goal Attack.'

'Thanks.' She shrugs. She scribbles over the sentence she just wrote about distillation, even though there's a rubber in front of her. Her hand moves back and forth angrily, until there's a thick, shiny lead line on the paper.

When Freya first found out about Latto and me, it was the Monday after we'd slept together at the dunes. Kylie Baker asked me outright, at recess, 'So, are you and Max Latimer together, then?' and when I said, 'Yeah, I suppose', Freya went bright red, like she was holding her breath, and scurried off down the corridor, Lottie running after her.

'Maybe I shouldn't have asked that in front of Freya,' Kylie said. 'Looks like she's devo. Didn't they have a thing for each other?'

'What, does he have a name tag on him?' I snapped. '"Property of Freya"?'

Kylie recoiled. 'No, but . . .'

'So shut up then. They weren't an item or anything.'

'Sorry Shelby,' she mumbled. 'My bad.'

Freya pretends to focus on the meniscus line on the measuring jug.

'You playing Goal Attack tonight?' I ask.

'Yep,' she says. She is conflicted. She hates me, but she is scared of me. She doesn't want to make an enemy of me, yet she despises me for taking Max. She chooses to give in to the fear. 'I was going to play defence, but Coach Driscoll moved me.'

'Driscoll knows you're good.'

'Lottie's a sub,' Freya says.

Lottie is always a sub. She isn't great at team sports. Always gets picked last, always the one on the subs bench, but she still puts herself forward for the teams.

'Should be a good match,' I say.

The bell rings and Freya gathers her folder, and we walk side by side down the corridor. That's when I see Latto coming in the other direction. He grins big and holds out his arms.

'Hey babe,' he says and bends down to kiss me. I let him kiss me for a few seconds before I pull away and indicate we have company.

He catches on. 'Oh, hi Freya,' he says. He looks awkward, because he knows she has a thing for him.

'Hi Max.' Freya glows scarlet.

'Where are you two off to?' he asks.

'Just netball,' Freya mumbles, trying to keep her top lip over her metal braces.

'Good luck,' he says. 'Who are you playing?'

'Arlingford,' I say.

'Ah right,' says Latto with a shrug. 'I'll come and watch.'

We walk in a row of three down towards the gym, until Freya turns around and says, 'I left my textbook in the lab,' which is a lie because I can see she's slipped it inside her black lever arch file.

Latto stands next to Lottie to watch the game. Although Lottie *is* technically a sub, she never plays if we can help it, because she's so crap. Coach Driscoll makes us gather round for a pep talk, and out of the corner of my eye I can see the Arlingford girls file out of a pristine white bus with 'Arlingford Ladies' College, est. 1901' painted on the side in red. The girls are as perfect as the bus – shiny and polished, with spotless white Aertex shirts and blue skorts, hair braided in French plaits or pulled into high ponytails. The fourth girl to exit the coach looks familiar, with her shiny blond hair and turned-up nose. She looks around her at the netball court, with its high wire fence full of holes and its tired asphalt. The white court lines are worn, their colour faded in the oppressive heat. Her nose wrinkles as she sees the grey outline of the school beyond it. She turns to whisper to the girl behind her, and they both snigger.

Then I realise. She's the girl who answered the door at the house in Esperance, when Latto dropped off the weed: Carole.

The Arlingford PE teacher blows her whistle, and the girls file in for a team talk. They probably want to get started as soon as possible so they won't have to hang around on this shitty court. I watch Carole survey the grounds, and clock Latto on the perimeter of the court. He doesn't see her at first but then glances across and catches her eye. She smiles, waves and shrugs her shoulders. 'What are you doing here?' she mouths.

Latto nods towards me, and Carole follows his gaze. Our eyes meet, but she doesn't smile, just looks me up and down, taking in my second-hand netball skirt and the Aertex shirt that's been through the wash with a black sock a couple of times too many. Her eyes narrow and she looks away, and I think to myself, *Game on!*

We win the first half effortlessly, scoring 10–8, and it's awesome when Carole gives me the stink eye as she drinks from her Evian bottle on the sideline at half-time. But then it turns around in the second, and Arlingford gets dirty. I'm about to pass to Tracey Brogan at 10–9 when Carole's arms dart out in front of me, her slim body jumping in front of mine. I push myself forward to get her out of my way and reclaim the ball that's rightfully mine, but my shoulder connects with her ear and one of her diamond studs rips clean out.

Carole howls and clutches her ear.

'My earring!' she screams. 'You ripped it out!'

She swings her body round to the ref and points at me. 'She . . . she . . .' she begins, grabbing at her ear. Blood drips through her fingers on to her vest and the pristine white collar of her sports top.

'Sorry,' I shrug, even though I'm not, and I'm sure my tone corroborates this. 'It was an accident. Accidents happen.'

'It wasn't an accident,' snaps Carole.

Freya pitches up beside me but doesn't defend me. I give her a quizzical stare and mutter, 'Thanks for nothing!'

'I'm sure it was an . . . accident,' stammers Freya.

'My earlobe's ripped to shit!' Carole snaps.

'Language,' says Driscoll, who's also playing ref. 'Put a plaster on it and play on.'

'But it's pouring blood,' cries Carole.

'Okay, we can't have bleeding on the court,' says Driscoll. 'Substitution for Arlingford!'

'I can't come off,' Carole bleats. 'We don't have a sub! Nikki Combs sprained her ankle running for the bus and Verity Adams has a migraine!'

Miss Driscoll looks at the Arlingford coach.

'You can borrow our sub,' she shrugs. 'We only have two minutes left and it's a friendly. Lottie Brennan, put the Goal Attack vest on, please.'

Lottie stands up. 'But . . .'

'*Do it,*' says Driscoll.

Carole tugs off her bloody vest and slams it into Lottie's chest. Lottie takes it and slips it over her grubby Shivers Beach sports Aertex.

'Play on!' shouts Driscoll, as Carole rummages around in the first aid box.

Lottie walks on to the court like a six-year-old walking on stage to read something in front of the whole school, but once the whistle blows, she is transformed. She lunges forward like there are springs in her feet. She ducks, dives, pivots, catches and throws.

'To me! To me!' shouts a dumpy redhead, holding her arms out. Lottie throws the ball to her new teammate, who scores. 'Yessss!' the Arlingford girls squeal, and the score is 10–10.

There is only a minute left, and I get a clear run for goal so I leap forward to catch the ball from Freya, and that's when I see Lottie. She is running towards me, her eyes glazed with determination. It almost stops me in my tracks, which is probably why I don't react quicker as her foot juts out in front of my shin and my legs give way beneath me. I slide across the tarmac, my leg grazed along the length of my shin. I clutch it with my hand as Freya appears beside me.

'Shit,' Freya says as she watches red dots spring to the flesh where my skin has been removed.

'Oh dear,' says Lottie. 'I'm *so* sorry!' Although there is something in her tone that hints more at exhilaration than regret. It's Freya who hauls me up.

'I can manage,' I snap, and Freya looks like she might cry.

'Play on,' says the ref, as Carole takes her place back on the court.

Arlingford win the match 10–11 with Carole popping the ball into the net in the last thirty seconds. She leaps up and high fives one of her teammates and that's when I notice Latto watching her from the other side of the court, his eyes running up her body like fingers on a piano.

After the match, Lottie runs after me.

'Are you okay?' she asks.

'Fine, no thanks to you.'

'It was an accident,' she says.

'Was it? Because it looked like a foul to me.'

Lottie puts her hand to her chest. 'Of course it was an accident,' she whimpers, doe-eyed. I turn away from her and she slopes off towards the changing rooms.

Latto appears and puts a hand on my bum.

'Well played,' he says.

'Would have won that one if it wasn't for your mate Carole.'

He laughs. 'She's not exactly my mate.'

'Good, because she's a bit of a bloody idiot, isn't she?'

'Come on, she's not that bad.'

'Did you see her earrings? Why the hell would you wear those to play netball? Diamonds?'

'One day I'll buy you some of those,' he says and takes my hand, swings it. 'When we're rich.'

'You're confident.'

He looks at me, dead pan. 'I've told you, it's my big life plan, Shelby. I'm not gonna live and die in this shithole forever.'

'You must like *something* about Shivers,' I pout.

He takes the bait. 'You know I do,' he says. 'What I mean is I don't want to end up like my old man, sitting around

drinking VBs and getting a gut on me. I want a nice house
and kids with good prospects. I don't want to be on Struggle Street forever. Otherwise what's the point? And I can
do it, I can get out of here because somehow, I'm smart.
I'm already revising like a proper nerd. There's only a term
left until the HSC.'

I nod. I can't properly imagine a world beyond Shivers
Beach, a world of opportunity and shiny cars and diamond
earrings and restaurant meals.

'And how do I fit in?' I ask. I don't say it in a needy way,
I keep it casual. But my heart is thumping so loudly in my
chest I wonder if he can hear it.

'I want you to get out of here with me, don't I?'

'Yeah?'

'Yeah.'

He doesn't elaborate because he doesn't need to, and that
makes me feel scarily vulnerable. I switched off my emotions after Dad died because feelings hurt too damn much,
but now I'm back at square one. This guy is like a new drug
pounding through my veins that I can't live without. I *need*
him as much as I want him. I'd die for him. Die without him.

'What about Carole?' I ask him.

He looks down at me and laughs. 'Carole? Trust me,
you have nothing to worry about!'

'You swear?' I ask, because I've got to know.

''Course I swear,' he says, and the smug look he gives
me suggests he knows he holds all the cards. 'Now let's get
the hell out of here.'

And I don't know whether he means the school gym, or
Shivers Beach in general.

THURSDAY

Chapter Twelve
Carole

Only Organic is busier than usual and I'm struggling to be patient with the hideous toddler and primary school brigade who seem to have descended before the early morning school bells ring. Haven't they heard of online shopping? Thank God Olivia and Otto walk themselves to school. I would never dream of dragging them through this pushy rabble!

It is only 8.30 a.m., but the heat is already stifling, and the cool air inside the shop is a welcome haven – especially by the meat counter.

I pick a large organic eye fillet and a ready-made truffle mash. Max loves nothing more than a steak for dinner, and tonight I will treat him to a lovingly prepared, homemade meal. It's a gesture to say I fully trust him, an apology of sorts for accusing him of dallying with *her*. Discussing Shelby has only made us closer. My husband has looked me in the eyes and told me I have nothing to worry about, and I believe him. Perhaps any other woman might roll her eyes and consider me deluded – the naive housewife with the impossibly handsome husband and his apparently 'alluring' ex – but I know Max and I trust him. And, like I said, without trust in a marriage, what exactly do you have?

I'm inspecting the back of a packet of organic dark chocolate brownies for nut traces when I hear an unfamiliar voice behind me.

'*Carole*? Carole Latimer?'

The woman is overweight, at *least* a size sixteen, and horribly unkempt. Her red top strains across an ample bosom, giving a flash of a gaudy maroon 'lace' bra likely bought in the sale at Kmart. She is grinning at me like the village idiot.

'Yes?' I look around from left to right to ensure there are no witnesses to this invasive encounter.

'Marella,' she says, her chins falling over themselves. 'From St Paul's.'

'Um, do I—?'

'I work with your friend Lottie!'

'Ah, yes!' I turn away to study the nut content of a cara-mel slice. I am not interested in discussing how this woman may or may not be acquainted with someone who also happens to know me. It's of no consequence. It doesn't mean we need to be friends.

'Delighted to meet you,' I say.

'Jeez,' she says, in a strong regional accent, 'it's so pricey in here. I only popped out for some more teabags for the shop, but perhaps not – eight bucks for a box of English Breakfast!'

I stare at her in disbelief. Eight dollars is *cheap* for organic, fair trade tea!

'Is there a discount section?' she asks. 'You know, with the use-by dates almost up? I often find a bargain there.'

I clear my throat discreetly. 'I'm not sure I . . .'

'Over there,' says a mother with a snot-nosed child in the front of her trolley. 'Right near the fruit.'

'Oh thank you,' says Marella. Then she looks at me. 'Good to see you again, Carole. I'd better get to the shop. It's almost opening time!'

I watch her waddle off and wonder to myself what on earth she meant by 'again'.

Once I'm done, I drive into the centre of Esperance and park by the sea front – I need to make a stop at White Bloom Flowers to pick up my seasonal arrangement for the marble console table in the hallway. Flowers on the console transform the house, add a touch of opulence and they are always a talking point for anyone who comes to the door. I call the florist every week to place an order, and I usually pick them up myself. The delivery staff can be shoddy and I can't abide squashed peonies.

Max calls me as I emerge from the florist's with my large arrangement of hydrangeas, peonies and lilies. I have to juggle a little to get the phone to my ear.

'Are you home on Friday night?' he asks.

'No darling,' I say. 'You know it's Lottie's birthday dinner. Why?'

'I've said yes to drinks with a couple of the guys from golf, just for an hour or two.'

'Olivia will be home, I'm sure she can mind Otto for a couple of hours. I'll only be down the street if they need me.'

'Great,' he says. 'I'll see you later.'

I don't want to ring off.

'Are you busy? Time for a coffee if I pop in?'

'Not possible' says Max, like I'm a colleague on the trading floor. 'It's so busy in here today. Sorry Carole.'

'Okay. I love you,' I tell him.

'Yep,' he says, because he never says anything affectionate when he's at work – it's such a male-dominated arena. 'Talk to you later.'

I smile to myself as I walk towards the car. Things are okay. Max doesn't seem too bothered by my questions last night. Everything is as it should be.

That's when I see her. *Shelby.* She is wearing denim shorts and a vest top. That tatty old Chanel quilt bag she drags around with her everywhere is slung over her shoulder and there are a bunch of papers poking out the side, and for a moment, she looks just like Lottie. But her walk is way more confident. She strides, head high, like she owns the world. Her shorts are so short, you can see a hint of a tanned buttock underneath, which is most unbecoming on a woman her age. When she lifts her arm to push her hair out of her face, I get a glimpse of her stomach. It is taut, perfect – the stomach of a woman who hasn't been ravaged by childbirth, who doesn't have a sac of loose skin hovering above her bikini line with a white, wormy roadmap of stretch marks.

She walks along the path towards St Paul's, even though she must know Lottie doesn't start work until ten. It looks like she's there to shop. Well there's a turn up for the books! Shelby Massini gets her clothes second hand! Who knew?

I don't know what possesses me, but I move to one of the thick-trunked pines on the opposite side of the road, hiding behind it and watching as she enters the shop. I'm so close I can hear the little bell ring on the door frame as it opens. On the other side of the large glass windows, she peruses the racks of clothing, holding things up against her body. The large woman who I now know to be Marella, fresh from her quest to find cheap teabags in Only Organic, is in the window, dressing a mannequin in some tasteless-as-all-hell outfit and hasn't acknowledged the shop's latest visitor, but now turns around and sees her. For a moment, there appears to be a rather icy stare-off between the two women. Marella stands with her hands on her hips with an angry glare, and Shelby makes a gesture that looks like an apology, but one given begrudgingly.

Shelby shrugs and lifts up her hands and eventually, Marella sighs and points to her office at the back of the shop. Shelby follows her in and shuts the door. I don't know what I'm thinking but I run across the road and down the side of the shop, hidden by my giant bunch of flowers, and lean against the wall next to the window of the office, a little open slit halfway along the alleyway. I strain my ears to hear, snuggling between the two large clothing donation bins that line the lane. I can't hear a great deal, aside from muffled voices, however much I stand on my tiptoes. Then one voice comes closer to the window.

'It's hotter than hell,' says Shelby. 'I'll close the window if you put on the aircon.'

It's not a request so much as an order.

Marella does not speak, but I hear the shrill beep of the air conditioning unit being switched on. Marella is clearly falling into line like everyone does when Shelby asks them to do something.

Shelby's red fingernails grab the handle of the window and begin to drag it shut. And, just three inches from the top of my head, she speaks, loud and clear.

'I'm here because I need you to keep a secret for me,' she tells Marella. 'And it's big.'

Then she pulls the window shut with a bang.

Chapter Thirteen
Freya

They say you shouldn't wish time away, but I can't help it. The minutes tick by at a snail's pace all day long as I go through the motions of laundry and shopping and admin. Even a trip to the nail salon in Mooney seems to drag. Until seven o'clock, of course, when time speeds up exponentially and I find myself rushing to get ready for my sacred hour on the running track. He said he'd be there on Thursday night, didn't he? My stomach twists at the thought of seeing Luca again.

The air is sticky, but still the floodlit track is bustling. Runners pant their way round, sweat dripping down their faces and shoulders, cheeks flushed and ruddy.

In the distance a hand raises, waves at me, and it takes me a moment to register it is Lottie. She smiles and jogs towards me, the green fluoro stripes on her top winking in the semi-light, and I feel a sinking in my belly. How am I meant to flirt with Luca when I have Lottie tagging along? She is out of breath when she reaches me and leans forward, her hands on her knees.

'I knew you'd be here,' she gasps. She leans in and gives me a gentle hug. 'I called Bernard. Hope you don't mind, but I decided to join you. I have been so lazy the last couple of weeks and it's all piling on here!'

She pats her stomach. 'Can't be getting love handles! Piers would have a fit. Plus, Carole is stressing out big style about none of us recording our laps. Shelby hasn't done it once! So, can I join you?'

'Of course!' I paste on a smile. 'What a lovely surprise.'

'Got to get some laps in before the weather turns,' she says. 'Although running in this heat is pretty intense.'

'Yes, there is that . . .'

'Are you okay?' Lottie asks. 'You seem a bit distracted. How was your session with Jayne?'

'Fine,' I say, scouring the reserve for a sign of Luca. I have no guarantees he'll be here, but I'm hoping he'll show up. I glance over Lottie's shoulder as she bends down to touch her toes. I spot him at the far end of the reserve and my stomach lurches in anticipation. I turn back to Lottie. 'You know, the usual stuff. Wanting to talk about Bernard, mainly. I don't know why.'

Lottie nods. 'If it helps, then it's wonderful.' She turns to her left, ready to run clockwise. I glance at Luca. He has spotted me and gives a discreet little wave. I can't wave back without Lottie noticing, so I risk a grin back at him instead.

'You okay?' Lottie looks at me. 'What are you laughing at?'

'Nothing,' I say. 'Just a cute dog over there.'

Lottie doesn't respond.

'Right.' I point in the other direction. 'I'm going this way today, I think, so I'll catch you later?'

Lottie always goes clockwise. She gets unsettled if she does something in the wrong order. On any other occasion I'd be happy to run with her, but tonight I really need to shake her off.

'What do you mean you're going that way? Why?' she looks around but can't see anything.

'I just prefer to run that way.'

Lottie looks confused and then she smiles. 'Ah, I get it. You don't want to chat on your way round.'

'You got me.' I smile.

'Okay, so I promise not to talk. Come on, then.'

'But . . .'

'But what? Don't you *want* me to run with you?'

Oh God, this isn't going the way I'd hoped.

'Don't be silly,' I chirp. 'Why wouldn't I? I just thought you might come out in hives if you go the wrong way.'

Lottie laughs. 'I'm not *that* OCD.'

We set off, running against the grain. Lottie apologises to every man, woman and dog she confronts on the path. When we get to the giant pine tree with the peeling bark at the far side of the reserve, I look up and around for Luca, not realising he is running directly towards us. I push my hair out of my face. He smiles when he sees me and slows his pace. The fact he stops means Lottie and I have to by default.

'Ladies,' he says.

'Oh, hi!' Lottie says when she sees him. There is a smile on her face, a smile of recognition. She touches her hair nervously. 'Where's . . . ?' She does a 360-degree turn looking for the woman he *should* be with.

'I'm alone tonight,' Luca says.

'Oh right. Is she . . . ?'

'At home,' he says. 'She ran this morning.'

Lottie nods.

You see, Lottie knows who Luca really is. And so do I. We have all known one another for years. We know each other's spouses. We have been inside each other's homes for barbeques and cocktail parties. The fact is, Luca and I have undressed one another in our minds' eyes in front of our respective partners over and over and over, like two pressure cookers waiting to explode, two whistling kettles, shuttles flaming underneath, fierily anticipating launch. And that's why we have to keep it secret, and that's why we have pseudonyms for one another. His is Luca and mine is Rey. As Luca and Rey, we are no longer the people we always were – the people with messy, intertwining pasts – but different people, *new* people. Two individuals who truly *see* one another.

I look up at Luca and smile. He winks at me and I bite down on my grin, and that's when Lottie turns around. She catches the tail end of the look between us and seems momentarily confused. Then she blinks whatever inappropriate thought has popped into her mind firmly away, as if she's imagining things.

'Great to see you,' she says to him as she pulls on my arm. 'We're doing laps, so we'd better get on. Come on, Freya.'

I shrug at Luca and follow Lottie, annoyed at the missed opportunity, but glad to have been at the receiving end of that sexy smile.

Lottie glances back at him as we jog on, while I keep my eyes forward. She looks at me.

'What?' I ask.

'Nothing,' she says. 'He was a bit flirty, that's all. Mind you, he always is with you.'

'No he is not,' I protest, but the thought makes me feel insanely good.

'He was looking at you really weirdly.'

'He was not! God, Lottie, you should be a novelist or something – you see the drama in everything. Poor man, being slandered like that.'

She laughs and it makes me laugh too. Lottie is beautiful when she laughs. She doesn't do it often, on account of her perennial anxiety, so it is good to see. But like the sun, the momentary flash of splendour is behind a cloud again within a mere second.

'I don't know what's going on with me at the moment,' she says. 'Shelby is playing up. I'm thinking all sorts of irrational thoughts.'

'What do you mean?'

'She's just . . . I can't put my finger on it. She's being vague. It's making me worry about her. She insists on taking these weird running routes. Yesterday she went out at ten at night, according to the app, which she never usually bothers to use. It makes me really worried, that's all, especially when there's a pervert hanging around.'

'No one else has been flashed, have they?' Not since it happened to Shelby, and I wouldn't put it past her to make the whole thing up just to get Lottie in a tizz. In fact I wouldn't put it past her to use the app just so Lottie will worry about her being out late.

'Yes,' says Lottie, shattering my theory. 'The woman with the curly brown hair who works behind the counter at Only Organic. You know, the fruit and veg woman? She saw him yesterday, and apparently he was touching himself . . .'

'Gross,' I say.

'I know!' says Lottie. 'So you can see why I'm worried.'

'Look, if anyone can look after themselves, it's Shelby,' I tell her. 'I do think perhaps you're worrying for nothing.' I don't mean to be flippant, but this conversation has replayed over and over the last two decades, and frankly, it's still as tedious as it was back then. It might be easier to stomach if Shelby was more likeable.

Lottie sighs. 'Maybe you're right,' she says. 'Anyway, you don't want to hear about all of this again, do you?'

I don't reply, which I think is enough to confirm that I concur.

'Only one more lap for me,' she says brightly. Thankfully she hasn't caught on about Luca – she is too frantic in her own head. 'I need to get home and make Piers' dinner. Beef Wellington tonight. How seventies is that?'

'Why do you always cook him meat when you don't like it?' I ask. 'I'm sure you could find a nice vegetarian alternative.'

'He works hard, Freya,' says Lottie. 'He deserves a good meal on the table.'

'You're Wonder Woman, Lots,' I tell her, because she is, putting up with Piers. 'Now stop talking to me, I'm out of breath!'

We run another full lap, and as Lottie turns to the clearing to take the shortcut to the road I shout after her, 'Don't worry about Shelby!' and I think to myself that if Hallmark made a greeting card with those exact words, I'd have kept the whole board in dividends with sales from that single product alone.

Twenty minutes after I get home, Luca texts me, because he's had my number all along, of course – for about fifteen years, actually.

That was fun, but when are we going to get some alone time, Rey? he writes. Then a moment later, a second message pops up. **Tomorrow in the clearing, far end. 7.30?**

I bite my lip, feel the goosebumps spread across my skin, a jolt of electricity from my belly downwards, the excruciating tug of desire. Is this really happening? I figure I can meet him and then head straight to Lottie's after. I begin to type, my fingers pounding the keys. **Yes,** I tell him. **I'll be there.**

Chapter Fourteen
Lottie

Piers comes home at eight o'clock on the dot. I can usually make out his mood from the way he pulls into the drive. If the wheels of the Porsche slide in softly, he's in a good mood. If I hear pop music blaring, even better. If there's a screech of the tyres and classical music on full pelt, I know not to ask.

Tonight Piers' car swerves into the drive and the wheels scream to a halt, and I feel my blood pressure begin to rise. I busy myself wiping the worktop and arranging the tea towel in perfect symmetry over the oven handle. I need to keep the house immaculate so he isn't riled, because when a camel's back is weighed down, it only takes a straw to break it.

Today Piers has had a session with Darla Reynolds, a psychic medium and fortune teller. I booked him an appointment in the hope it would help and used my personal savings account (Carole made me open it – she says every woman should have one, just in case the worst happens – meaning infidelity or divorce, or if you have to flee your husband for any reason with your kids. 'You should have enough in there to buy a car,' she says). Darla teaches Psychic Studies for six months a year at the London School of Economics, so she's the real deal. Leanne Markham, the mother of one of Isobel's friends from Arlingford told me that she saw Darla after her father died and Darla picked up straight away that he was in the room, was called Martin and had a tendency to fall asleep during *Antiques Roadshow*. Darla even knew the names of Leanne's grandparents – the ones she'd never met.

Piers was reluctant to take the appointment at first, but I persuaded him in the hope Darla might be able to shed some light on things, to help Piers recall the information we so desperately need to access the Bitcoin account where our nest egg sits, untouched, for a rainy day. The harsh fact is Shelby is the only person who has access to the account, the only one who knows the login details, although she swears she doesn't and that she never had them in the first place. '*She* has the password, *she* has the information at her fingertips!' insists Piers.

That's why Piers is so vexed. That's why he wants to shake Shelby and tell her, 'Think, *just think*!' And I'm an anxious spectator, a fearful fence-sitter. I know Shelby can be manipulative and harsh, but she isn't a thief. She wouldn't intentionally withhold our money, even if she does tease Piers in that easy way she has. This is one thing I'm certain of – because despite her flaws, Shelby has never really cared about the money.

I brace myself as I hear the key turn in the lock. I always wait for Piers to call me during work hours (he doesn't like to be interrupted when he's with patients), and he hasn't called today. It doesn't bode well.

I wait in my pinafore at the end of the hallway.

'Piers?' I ask as he walks in through the door and strides past me.

'Hold on,' he says and races past me to the office. It appears he is not angry, but excited, wired. I follow him.

'How was Darla?' I ask.

'*Wait!*' He holds up his hand for me to stop talking.

'Did you find what—?'

'Be quiet,' he snaps. 'I think I remember. She reminded me. The letters. She took me back to that night, with Shelby, and I remembered the letters.'

I look up at him. 'You remember your password?'

He types 'CryptoWallet' into Google and taps his fingers on the desk impatiently as he waits for the login page to load. He quickly types in his wallet ID, which is my email address, but his fingers are shaking so much he has to do it four times.

'Slow down, darling,' I tell him. '*Slow down.*'

He breathes in deeply with his eyes closed, cracks his knuckles and my heart begins to beat like I'm on a roller-coaster that's about to drop.

Piers types in a word that I can't make out, followed by six numbers.

We wait for what seems like forever as a circle spools in the centre of the screen. A drop of sweat from my husband's brow lands on his blotter, and he wipes his palms on the tweed of the bespoke suit from London's Savile Row that I will take to the dry-cleaners when I go on Saturday.

Then a notice pops up: 'Password failed!' In a smaller font underneath, it declares: 'You have one more attempt before your Bitcoin account is permanently locked.'

Piers grabs his hair with his hands and pulls, lets out a scream that's part anger, part anguish. One more attempt.

We have used nine out of ten already. In my eyes, we lost the money around the fifth attempt, but Piers has held out hope.

'One more lifeline,' he says and it sounds like a whimper.

One more chance before we are locked out forever.

One more failure and we are locked out of eight million dollars. *Eight million*. That's how much a three-thousand-dollar investment, twelve years ago – a gamble on a brand new crypto currency back in 2011 – has gained us today. The life changing 'what-if' that's tearing my husband apart. The means to repay our debt and clear our entire mortgage. To school Isobel and send her to university wherever in the world she desires. Financial security until the day one of us dies.

Piers puts his head in his hands.

'Piers,' I say. 'Please darling!'

He looks up, wipes his eyes.

'We will speak to Shelby on Friday. We will beg her if we have to,' I say.

'What's the point?' Piers cries. 'She's not going to give it to us!'

'Perhaps she really doesn't have it,' I say.

'She has the password.' Piers' voice is shaky. 'She pretty much told me other day in the kitchen.'

I can picture Shelby standing there, by the fruit bowl, telling Piers, 'Maybe I do, maybe I don't!' Studying her nails. Shelby, the accountant of the family. The code breaker. The holder of the password. The secret keeper. The *thief*?

'She's teasing you. She loves to do that.' My attempt to play devil's advocate sounds desperate, even to me.

'I am *telling* you, she is not!' snaps Piers and I flinch. 'She alluded to keeping the money. "Finders keepers, Piersy Boy!" she said. This is not a joke to her!'

'If she had the login details she would have cashed it in by now,' I say. 'She's bluffing!'

'What if she isn't?'

I feel my stomach lurch, my heart begin to race, the panic about to come flooding to the surface, drowning me. Then there is a burst of anger. Why isn't Shelby even *trying* to help us? Why isn't she even looking for ways for us to access this money? I feel a stab of hatred towards my twin.

'We could . . . offer to share it with her,' I say. 'See what transpires?'

Piers laughs. It's a bitter, desperate laugh. 'She won't share it. She is evil, Lottie, *evil*.'

'No,' I say. 'No, don't say that! She's my sister, Piers. *Please!*'

He bangs his fist on the desk so hard that the black and white framed photo of Isobel as a baby falls forward and the glass cracks down the middle.

'She's a bitch!' he shouts.

His head falls into his hands and, to my surprise, he starts to crumple, to cry. His body is bent over the desk while I stand beside him in my French cooking apron.

I turn to him, my body suddenly upright, my role as carer kicking in.

'Pull yourself together, Piers,' I snap in a voice that isn't mine.

His head shoots up at the command. He wipes his eyes and nods.

'We will talk to her tomorrow,' I tell him, as if he is a small child and I am the adult decision-maker. 'We'll do it when everyone else has left. She'll see reason, I promise.'

Piers wipes his eyes and nods again. Then he puts his head on my stomach as I stand beside him and lets me stroke his hair.

'Shhh,' I tell him as I stare out of the window and into the darkness. 'It's all going to be okay.'

We eat dinner in silence and when we go to bed soon after, it takes me ages to get to sleep. In the end I get up and go downstairs to get some water, and pop in some magnesium powder. I can't take sleeping tablets because I'm scared I won't wake up and then where would we be, Piers and I? Where would Isobel be?

When I finally fall asleep, it is fitful, like the beginnings of the worst nightmares always are. First comes flashes of the dream I've had since I was fifteen – me, in the car with Shelby and our dad. Dad and Shelby singing an Elton John song together, laughing as they get the words wrong. Me, in the front seat, feeling jealousy whirl like a tornado as I listen to their laughter. Hearing the screech of tyres as the car veers into the path of the ute on the other side. Then, in my dream, I am no longer in the car, I am at Esperance Reserve. Shelby – although sometimes her face seems to merge into Isobel's – is in the clearing behind the running track wearing dark activewear. She is lying back on the springy mulch with a man standing over her. His face is dark, his features blurred to obscurity. He stands above her and Shelby grips the earth, scrabbles with her feet to back away from him. She screams soundlessly with empty lungs, as joggers pass by, clueless, just feet away. But she can't get up, and there is no time to even try, because there are hands round her neck and she struggles until she is lifeless and staring up, up into the moonlight.

When I wake up, I am covered in sweat, and utterly shocked by the first thought that creeps into my mind: Shelby can't die, we need her! She is the only one who can access the money – our money! I bask in guilt as the sun rises, blood red, for putting thoughts of the money ahead of the safety of my own sister.

FRIDAY

Chapter Fifteen
Freya

Lottie wafts apologetically up the hall in a flowing kaftan of some kind.

I jump about three metres high. 'Lottie! You frightened the life out of me!' I laugh.

It's eleven in the morning, and I'd forgotten she was popping round.

'I'm so sorry,' she grimaces. 'I should have knocked.'

'Come on in!' I lead her through into the kitchen

Her eyes fill with tears as places her bag on a bench seat.

'What's wrong?' I ask. 'Has Piers upset you?'

'No!' she whimpers. 'I just wanted to hear a friendly voice.'

'Are you sure he hasn't been calling you names again?'

Lottie's brow knots. 'You make it sound like he's verbally abusing me,' she says. 'It was just that once, and I wish I'd never told you.'

The fact is, it wasn't just once. Most times Lottie gets drunk, she confesses that Piers has shouted at her and called her a name ('But it's never anything too bad, I mean, I *was* being a total bitch!'). But when she's sober, she likes to maintain he is the perfect spouse.

Anyway, whether she wants to 'fess up about Piers or moan about Shelby, I'm here for it.

'Grab a seat and I'll make us some tea,' I tell her. 'I'm sorry about the mess.'

Lottie sighs, surveys the black marble kitchen benchtop, covered in a blanket of papers bearing the logo of Bernard's firm Harrington, High & Holman (HHH). Bernard is working on a high-profile case which he can't talk about, which is fine with me. Papers litter the house: piled on the arm of the sofa, on the bathroom floor, beside the bed. It's the way he works. I used to find the chaos of papers endearing. Now it irks me to high heaven. I sometimes want to bundle them all up and stick them in the fire pit in the back garden.

'Right,' I ask my friend. 'What's going on?'

Lottie sniffs and she looks from left to right, as if she's expecting Bernard to emerge from under a sofa cushion or from behind one of the framed Ken Done originals on the wall. 'It's just . . . I had one of my dreams again.'

She isn't talking about a dream where she loses all her teeth or is sitting her exams and has forgotten everything she ever learned. She's talking about the vivid dreams she gets about Shelby, the ones she calls 'visions' because she swears they come true. She has them rarely now, but they freak her out. Personally, I have no evidence they actually come true, aside from what Lottie tells me and what happened when Shelby 'died' in high school. I suppose it was strange the way she described Shelby walking down the sand to where the waves crashed on the shore and walking confidently into the rip. And then later, those schoolboys dragging her limp body out of the water and pumping her chest until her ribs broke. But that could have been one giant coincidence. If I'm honest – and I'd never say this to her – Lottie's dreams seem nothing more than a figment of one very active imagination.

'Go on,' I tell her.

'Freya,' she says, 'it was so real. Just like the dream I had, you know, at school on the beach, before that night. Before she went in the water . . .' She trails off.

'What happened this time?' I ask, my hand on hers. It feels cold to the touch.

'She was dead in a ditch, with a man standing over her. She'd been hit or strangled or something.' Lottie purses her lips and exhales slowly, as if she's trying to stop herself from panicking.

'Who was the man?'

'I don't know. I couldn't see his face. But it was real, Freya. *Vivid.* I can't talk to Piers about it. He thinks it's rubbish, and besides, he has a rather worrying financial matter on his mind . . .'

'Anything you want to talk about?'

'No,' Lottie sighs.

Like I said, she's not the kind of wife to betray her husband's confidence, even to her closest friends.

'I would,' she says on cue, 'but I don't think Piers would appreciate it.'

'Come on,' I tell her and pull her in for a hug. 'Shelby will be fine. And so will you. All this talk of a flasher in the park is probably heightening your anxiety, that's all it is. And whatever's going on with Piers is just exacerbating it. I promise, you have nothing to worry about.'

Lottie's shoulders drop. 'I know,' she says. 'You're right. I don't know what's going on with me at the moment. I just have this horrible sense of . . . foreboding.'

'Then phone up Jayne Saunders' office and see if there's any way you can sneak on to her list. Or try the woman in Mooney. Katie someone. I swear, it's the *best* tonic.'

But I know she won't. Lottie pushes her chair back and gets up. 'To be honest, Freya, Piers doesn't really like the idea of me seeing a psychologist. He's nervous people will think I have emotional issues.'

'Then don't tell him.'

Lottie looks shocked. 'I couldn't *lie*. And anyway, he'd find out about it. He gets an alert on his phone whenever I spend money.'

'It's not lying, it's just not mentioning. There's a difference. And I could lend you the cash if it would make things easier,' I say. I feel sorry for my friend, always needing permission, trapped at home.

'I'll think about it,' says Lottie. 'Thanks for the tea.'

I follow her to the front door. 'Please Lots, don't give it another thought, especially not today. It's your dinner tonight.'

She smiles. 'You're right. See you later on. I hope you don't mind but I told Marella about it – I think I mentioned her to you before. She works at St Paul's with me. I didn't mean to invite her, I just got carried away . . .'

This is so Lottie, to invite the random waifs and strays.

'Of course,' I tell her.

'Great! Is eight thirty okay? I know it's a bit late but Isobel has dance until then, and I don't want her to miss out on dinner.'

Heaven forbid bratty Isobel should feel excluded. The girl is a carbon copy of her aunt.

'Eight thirty is perfect with me,' I tell her.

It means I can fit in a good hour with Luca first.

I prepare as much as I can for my hour of fun, considering I'll be wearing activewear. I put on a slick of lip gloss and mascara and pull my hair up in to a sleek high ponytail.

On the way to the running track I pass Carole's house and wait for the sensor light to beam out at me like I'm a criminal, but it doesn't come on, so instead I slow down and gaze in through the living room window. Carole is holding a glass of wine in her hand, her running gear still on. She looks upset. Her hair is wet against her head, slicked back with sweat. It's so on brand for Carole to go for a run and then binge-drink French reserve when she gets back.

I pass the rest of Esperance's biggest-ticket real estate, all perfect building clones of one another, and get to the reserve at seven thirty on the dot. The track is quiet tonight on account of the ominous clouds lurking as the sun set. It's going to pour. I pull back the branches of the side-by-side lilly pillies that line the route, and step inside the clearing. The air hums with the cool, relaxed chatter of cicadas. The calm before the storm.

Luca is leaning against a tree and looks up when he hears my feet tiptoeing across the blanket of leaves underfoot.

'Hey you,' he whispers.

'Hey,' I say, and I'm aware I sound breathless.

'Let's go somewhere more private, where we won't be found,' he says, and takes my hand.

He leads us away from the trees and down the path that will take us to the trough at the lower side of the dunes, where the sand is overgrown with silky marram grass and everything is hidden from the beach and the running track and even the clearing. The way his body twists on the path shows he has taken this route many times previously. It is a place he has gone to before, with her, of this I'm certain.

We walk for a few minutes until we're at the furthest point of the dunes, the highest mountain of sand, and then we sit in the trough at the bottom, the hidden spot that can't be seen from the mansions that line the cliff edge.

'You good?' he asks.

'I'm fine. I just . . . I guess this feels strange.'

'But a good strange, right?'

I smile. 'Definitely a good strange.'

We look at one another and offer smiles that are tinged with both nerves and desire.

I bite my lip. 'What do we do now?'

He twists the skin on the finger where his wedding ring still sits. I'm surprised he hasn't taken it off.

'I bought a flask of Tempranillo.' He smiles.

Tempranillo. It always makes me think of Shelby. It's her favourite wine. A lusty, greedy, fiery red.

Luca unscrews the lid of the flask and the muscles on his forearm ripple as he does it. He passes the Thermos to me. 'Ladies first,' he says.

I smile and take a swig, but when I face Luca again, he isn't smiling. Instead he reaches out his hand and pushes me by the shoulders onto the sand. I lie back and look at him. He picks up the flask and pours some wine into the hollow of my neck; I feel it pulsing, like a pool of lava bubbling, alive. He bends down gently and sucks the wine from my skin and my body stiffens with goose bumps.

'My God,' he whispers. 'I have always wanted you, Freya.'

'You have?'

'Always.' He kisses my skin, peels down my top, kisses further down still. Thirsty, gulping me down. His hands thread through my hair, over my face, my neck, my breasts, and mine respond, frenziedly. There is not time for long, languid foreplay. We both know that tender and loving is not what this is. It was never meant to be. It is something instinctive, animalistic. This particular flame is from a match that will burn briefly after it has been struck and extinguish abruptly, not a votive gently burning up its wax and flickering prettily even in its dying throes.

He pulls down my leggings, I yank down his shorts. He bites on my skin, breathes heavily in my ear. I pull him on top of me. He is different from Bernard: firmer, bigger. I have waited so long to feel this alive! We move until we are both groaning with the pleasure of it, and I forget where I am and the fact I am with Shelby's husband instead of my own, and when I call out Tino's real name, he laughs and says 'Shhhhh!' and puts his hand gently on my mouth to silence me, until we are both done, spent.

Chapter Sixteen
Shelby

Before

The HSC comes and goes, and I don't care much about it, not like Lottie who gets all het up beforehand. Max goes quiet the week before his first exam and I feel a bit affronted, as if he's chosen school over me. Then I try to remember what he's said about getting good grades and getting out of Shivers with me.

On the Friday night after the last exam, we go to the fire pit at the beach to celebrate. Half of Shivers Beach High are here drinking beer and smoking weed. Some of the Esperance rich kids have come to our beach too – it's like their way of rebelling against perfection.

Carole and her brother Sebastian arrive in their dad's soft-top BMW; she has her elbow on the passenger seat window and her hair is blowing behind her in the breeze. They pull into the carpark beside Shivers RSL, Eminem's 'Stan' blaring from the speakers inside. The posh kids love that song, probably because it isn't too street. It's got a non-threatening melody too.

'Why are they here?' I ask Max.

'Because Seb wanted a smoke,' he says.

'*Seb?*'

'Yeah, Seb. He's a good bloke.

'Why's *she* here, then?'

'I dunno. Maybe she wanted a night out.'

'Well I don't like her,' I say. 'I don't *trust* her.'

'You're not still sore about that netball match are you? Come on, babe, it was just a game. And in fairness, you did rip her earring out.'

Latto hangs with me for a while and then leaves me with Lottie and Freya so he can go and talk to Sebastian. Carole stands close to her brother, holds out her hand and takes the smoke from him. She looks like him, the same striking features and downturned lips. She is dressed in jeans, a white polo shirt and boat shoes. She looks uncomfortable here, on this beach, *my* beach. A fish out of water. But then she is. This is Shivers Beach, not Esperance. Even the sand is less chic here: black, volcanic rock and oyster shells cling together, which is treacherous underfoot, and cigarette stubs, bottle caps and crisp packets cling to the seaweed and the scummy brown foam that traces the shoreline.

Latto puts his can of beer to his lips and looks over at me as his head tips back. He catches me looking at him as he moves right next to Carole. He beckons me over and I ignore him. He doesn't ask again, just leans in and says something to her and she laughs. She runs a hand through her dry, stringy hair, takes the smoke from his fingers, puts it to her mouth while she looks at him and takes a drag. Blows it out still staring at him, in rings.

I turn my back to them because I don't want to see her glance over at me again with the smug eyes that say, 'Look, he's standing with me now!' And I'm okay with it until

Lottie says, 'Whoa, Latto is really flirting with that Carole girl!'

I hear a laugh and turn around to see Carole stumble forward, and Latto's arm shoot out to steady her. She falls into him. She stays there for a second too long, and then, when he positions her upright on her own two feet again, she throws her head back and laughs, her hair stumbling deeper down her back, the ends bouncing on his shoulder. She's rat-arsed. I watch them, a tsunami of anger and the fear rising inside me.

I don't know why I do it, but I do. I pull off my T-shirt and shorts so that I'm in my bra and underwear. Johnny Turretson wolf-whistles and Latto turns from the fire, from Carole, towards me. His smile fades as he sees me run half-naked to the water and into the triangular strip of surf that's illuminated silver by the full moon. He knows I cannot swim.

'Shelby?' he calls. He excuses himself from Carole with his hands up, backing away. Her own smile fades and she shrugs, lets him go, glares at me. I am wading into the surf now, feeling it smash against my calves and then against my knees, my thighs, my abdomen. The redhead from my maths class, the chubby one with the nose ring, stands next to the shore and watches as I wade in. She turns to see Latto power-walking down the sand towards me, realises there's a situation.

'What are you staring at?' I call back to her.

The water is cold, but I can bear it. I can bear it to make a point. My feet feel firm on the sand below, I am holding my own, until I am not. Until the sand ledge I am on is gone and start to panic a little, flapping to get back to where I was. I hear Latto shout, 'You're in a rip!' See a few figures running down the beach, hear Lottie scream, 'Shelby? Someone *help* her!'

Before I go under, I have got what I wanted. I have seen the look on Latto's face. I have seen the fear. I have confirmation that he is mine. He is anguished, terrified, wading with all his might to get to me, his triangular torso pressed forward in the surf, his arms marching against the current. But he cannot reach me, the waves are too strong for him.

Underneath the water, it is black, there is no air. My body flaps like a fairground goldfish emptied out of a sandwich bag onto a tiled floor, as I try to get air in my lungs before they become waterlogged, try to keep my body out of the water with my arms. But I am tired, so tired. I hear Latto shout my name and 'Shit! Shit! Shelby *no!*' before everything goes black.

This is the first time I will die. But it is okay, because after the black comes the light. The pictures roll like cine-film. Under the water, I see Mum and Dad. Dad pulling me along on my tricycle, the ash from his cigarette longer than the remainder of the stick. Dad in the car, singing 'I'm Still Standing' at the top of his voice as the freeway unfolds in front of us. The fear in his eyes as we collide with the ute. The way he looks afterwards, eyes open and blood spilling from his ear. Lottie with pigtails and a brown pinafore dress with a white polo neck underneath, smiling with two missing teeth. Me with a long plait. Mum, in rust-red flares tucking us into bed and singing songs from *The Sound of Music*, stroking our heads. Cartoons on loop on

Saturday mornings. The smell of cigarettes twisting down the hall and through the gap between the floorboards and in under our bedroom door. Lottie and I pretending to smoke with candy canes, tapping the end into a pot and giggling. Lottie and I fighting over a Barbie doll, me with the legs, Lottie with the hair, pulling at her until she breaks apart, her decapitated head in the palm of Lottie's hand, Lottie grinning the evilest of grins.

The first time I kiss Latto.

The first time I sleep with him.

His eyes. His lips. The sweet smell of his skin. The weight of his head on my stomach. It is all so vivid, so sweet, the way my brain reacts as the oxygen is taken away.

I am lying on a white papasan chair in the sun. Hot, summer sun. The kind of sun that glows orange through your eyelids. Perhaps this is the light they tell you about, the bright light they say you want to follow when you die, that wraps you like a blanket and pulls you home.

It pulls me forward like a lasso.

Chapter Seventeen
Carole

Max jumps up. 'I'm going to do a quick run before I meet the golf boys,' he says.

'What about your steak?' I ask. 'I can put it on really quickly?'

He pats his stomach. 'I shouldn't run on a full stomach. I'll eat when I get home.'

'Sure!' So much for the special meal.

Max undoes the strap of his Apple Watch and throws it down on the benchtop. He alternates his watches frequently and he has to really, since I have bought him so many: a Piaget, Breitling, a TAG. But it's his Apple whenever he's not in the office.

'Don't forget your water,' I say, handing him his Nike bottle. He nods, takes it. Then he looks me in the eyes, seems apologetic somehow.

'You know I'm grateful, Carole, don't you? For everything?' he says, and I feel confused for a second, like I should be reading between the lines.

'I know, darling,' I say. 'I love you so much.'

He smiles at me and turns away, drops his wedding ring in the ceramic pot. He doesn't like to wear his ring when he runs, either.

I go right upstairs and start the preening process. Even though it's all the same people I always see, I want to look my best for Lottie's special dinner. I unhook my black silk Bianca Spender dress from the hanging space in the walk-in and slip it over my head, shake out my hair onto my shoulders. I already have a full face of make-up on because I've been with my husband. God knows I'm not one of those women who doesn't bother in front of her spouse. I always make an effort with Max. I have since I was sixteen!

I go to check my reflection in the full-length hall mirror and that's when I see a small green flash from the benchtop. It's Max's Apple Watch. I turn it face-up out of curiosity, but the light has gone out as quickly as it went on. But I want to know who's texting him, if it's important. Unlike the iPhone, I *can* unlock this device.

I click on the new message. It's from Max's golfing chum Bryan. It says, **Of course, mate!**

I feel relieved, and guilty. Had I been expecting something else? I scroll down his list of other messages, just, you know, out of curiosity, and I see it – the unstored number from his phone – the one he said belonged to Piers.

I click open the thread. The latest message, sent just two minutes ago while I was upstairs changing, reads: **I need to see you badly. S x**

The dots jump as my husband replies to her from his actual phone (but he's running, isn't he?): **On my way to you, beautiful.**

I scroll backwards and there they are, all of them from weeks back. The 'meet me at 8' texts and the 'miss you' texts and the 'Latto we need to talk' texts. I feel the air leave my lungs, try to catch a breath but I can't. I clutch at my chest, try to quell the rapid beating, feel the blood as it floods to my face. The blood that's thick with anger and the agony of betrayal.

'No!' I scream. My fist hits the table and the skin on my knuckles splits. Blood springs easily to the spot. 'No!' I throw Max's watch against at the mantel and it catches the edge of one of our wedding photos, which falls face down onto the floorboards below.

He lied to me.

Max lied *to me! Two nights ago, he made me feel stupid for questioning him. How dare he?*

How dare she?

Who the fuck *does she think she is?*

I haul myself up, wipe my running nose roughly with my bloody hand, storm to the front door and yank it open. It slams so hard behind me that the glass rattles. I run down the road barefoot, scouring the roads and the bushes and the windows of any house with a light on.

I'm going to find her, I am going to find her right now. And the thought terrifies me, because I know for sure in this moment that if I do find Shelby Massini, I will kill her.

Chapter Eighteen
Freya

We lie on the sand for a while, side by side, listening to the deafening crash of the ocean on the shoreline beyond. Tino's bare skin touches mine, the rough back of his hand rests against my naked thigh. I like the feel of it there.

We have done what we have wanted to do for years, and it more than lived up to expectation. It was only over too soon. I know already I want more.

'Well, well, well, Freya Harrington,' Tino says. No more Rey. 'That was *really* good.'

I laugh. 'It was a long time coming,' I say.

'You're not wrong.'

We didn't plan the affair meticulously, but it was inevitable. Even when they were dating, he and Shelby, I saw the glint in Tino's eye. He was always gentlemanly – touching the small of my back on his way to the loo, or ushering me first through a door, setting my skin alight with goose bumps. Shelby didn't care, she let him be a gentleman, she let him mildly flirt because I think she thought it was amusing, watching her plaything toy with someone else. She probably thought he was doing it to make her jealous. And he did toy with me, until a few months later when he proposed to her. Luckily, by then I'd met Bernard, and I'd fallen under the spell of a silver fox with his lavish gifts and his chalet-style home a stone's throw from Esperance beach.

Tino and I saw one another at events, said hi, greeted each other with air kisses, and 'how are things?' and inane chat about houses and renovations and his work and Bernard's work. I never asked about her because I got it all from Lottie. And that was how it went until six months ago, when I visited their home on a Friday night to deliver Shelby's running club top by order of Carole, and I ended up staying for a drink.

'Shelby isn't home on Friday nights,' he told me on the threshold. 'She has a class. But come in if you like?'

Tino had drunk a few already and I quickly caught up. We laughed and flirted, drank gin and then drank some more. We were suddenly on one another's sexual radar once again.

'You've always been such fun, Freya,' he told me, and when he kissed me on the cheek to say goodbye, his lips lingered on my skin a second or two too long. I felt my body flood with heat as I breathed in the boozy scent of his warm breath.

The following Friday, he sent me a text message. Bernard was in his study, organising his law periodicals, his bifocals perched on the end of his nose. I was sitting in front of a crappy TV police drama, bored out of my skull.

Come and keep me company. I need a drinking buddy – purely platonic, it said – and by virtue of mentioning that it was platonic, showed me it wasn't. And so I went to see him and we drank and talked and flirted.

And it went on. Friday nights, when Shelby was out, I'd put on my running gear and jog to Tino's, stay for a while and come home. Nothing physical happened in those first weeks, although the tension in the air suggested it was going to.

'It's over with Shelby,' he told me on one of the last Fridays. 'It's been over for a while. Separate beds.'

'I'm sorry,' I told him, even though I wasn't.

'Don't be,' he said. 'I couldn't give a shit.'

He'd been pushed to the limit, learned through the school of hard knocks: the put-downs, the abandonment, gaslighting. She'd done to him what she'd done to everyone else.

'In another world, if we were other people, we'd be together,' he continued. 'There'd be no Shelby or Bernard in the mix.'

I hadn't been shocked by what he said, because it was true.

'Why don't we try it?' I said. 'Be other people.'

And so Luca and Rey were born and officially met on the running track. A fantasy which eventually reached its climax (quite literally) on the dunes. And the tension had been like nothing else. When I saw Tino with Carole that day, as I saw her watching him from the water fountain – sexy as hell on the other side of the track – oh, it was palpable. Like a pressure cooker just waiting to burst. My body had responded to him in the strangest of ways: goose bumps on the skin, heat on the neck, swelling breasts, swelling *everything*. The adventure of being outside in the world, where we could almost get caught, was too much to bear. A dirty little secret with a dirty, but oh-so-satisfying ending. And I'd be lying if I said the fact he belonged to Shelby wasn't the biggest aphrodisiac of all.

Tino rolls onto his side, brushes the hair from my face a little roughly.

'I knew you'd be good in bed. I always thought you were sexy.'

Sexier than Shelby? I want to ask. But I don't. It doesn't matter, because right now he wants me more than her. That's why he is here.

'You think so?' I ask for affirmation, then kick myself for being so needy. Thankfully I said it in a flirty way.

'Yes,' he says. He traces his finger between my breasts.

'God,' he sighs. 'I want you all over again, but . . .'

He is going to say he needs to get back before his absence arouses suspicion – never mind arousing anything else. He pulls himself up with a swing of the arms, his abs bulging as he does it. I can't help but stare, it's been a long time since I've seen a body that taut and toned. I want to touch it again, because I didn't get to fully appreciate it in the frenzy. I lift my hand up, but he has already pulled his T-shirt down. He doesn't offer me help to stand, so I haul myself up and wriggle back into my yoga pants, brush the sand off my bare skin.

Tino turns and shrugs, leans in to me.

'See you, sexy,' he says, and kisses me on the lips. He doesn't offer any platitudes such as, 'you're amazing', or even a proposition: 'same time next week?' like he did on the running track. Instead he does the same as most teen boys at Shivers Beach High would have done all those years ago: he comes and then he goes, only this time without the roar of a Holden Commodore or the jangle of changing gears in his wake. All I hear, as he leaves, is the squeak of his feet on the silky sand.

'You'll be okay getting back?' he asks over his shoulder.

I nod, nonchalant. 'I'll be fine.'

I will be. I can see the upstairs of my house from here. But the upstairs of my house can't see me, not in this particular spot, in this secretive trench where the base of the dunes meet the trees of the reserve. A place where no one ever goes, unless they have something to hide.

Tino puts his phone in his pocket, winks at me and turns around. I watch him disappear into the bushes, his trainers swinging by the laces in his hands, and I attempt to reassemble myself so that when I get to Lottie's, I don't trail sand across her parquet flooring. I shake my hair out, empty the sand from my shoes, turn my socks the right way out and head towards the clearing, which is the quickest route home – the beach can be treacherous after dark when there is no silvery moon to light the way and you can't see the ferocity of the waves. As I pass the clearing, I hear the crack of a branch underfoot. The lights from the track don't reach this far, and in the darkness, it scares me a little. I quicken my pace until I'm back out on the running track. It is 8.20 p.m and I need to run home to grab Lottie's present from the sideboard on my way to her place. There is no one on the track now, except for Shelby, jogging steadily in her trademark arrogant pose, in her favourite pink fluoro shorts, her arms marching, body leaning forward. She doesn't care about the imminent storm.

I feel my phone beep against my thigh as I head across the track towards the street. I stop to read the text, hoping it might be from Tino. But it's from Bernard and it says, **Have a lovely dinner!** There are two more beneath it: one is from Lottie fifteen minutes ago telling me she has to collect Isobel from dance class and to let myself in because she'll be five minutes late (**The key's under the third plant pot from the front door!**). It's a relief because it means I won't have to burst an artery trying to race from my place to Lottie's carrying a massive bunch of flowers and her present. The second, sent half an hour previously, at around the time I met her husband for sex, is from Shelby.

Freya, she has written, and I steel myself for the coldness I know to expect when she does not use a greeting. **Your little crush on my husband is very sweet, but a little desperate, no? We all know how that behaviour ended for you at high school.**

I feel my heart plummet. **So here's a little warning,** she's written. **Stay the hell away from Tino, or I'll tell Bernard what you're up to. Kisses xoxo.**

Chapter Nineteen
Lottie

I usher Isobel through the door. 'Come on darling, I need to pop the meat on.'

She drops her dance bag on the floor of the hallway, opposite the cupboard where it is supposed to go.

'I could have walked,' she grumbles and stomps up the stairs to her bedroom. 'It's five minutes away. I'm not a kid!'

I sigh and pick up her dance bag, then head to the kitchen and pop on my pinafore ready to prepare the food Piers was meant to be cooking, before he got called out to a delivery this afternoon.

The oven is already pre-heated and I put my nut roast inside, alongside the bloody joint of beef that's been acclimatising on the kitchen bench for the thirty minutes it will cook so Piers can have it pink and bleeding. It turns my stomach. I couldn't deliver a child. I couldn't do the job my husband has done today, wrestling with a woman's flesh.

Thunder shakes the house and catches my breath, and it feels, for a second, as if the world might implode.

It was a day like this when we bought the Bitcoin – Piers, Shelby and I. A stormy, wet Thursday night in 2011. A winter evening fit for a mantel fire and a deep, plummy red wine. Shelby had come over to pick something up and I'd persuaded her to stay for a glass. Before long we got talking about Bitcoin, the new crypto-currency making headlines.

'They're the currency of the future,' Shelby said. 'You should invest.'

'Have *you*?' Piers asked her.

'Not yet,' she said. 'But I'm going to.'

'It had crossed my mind,' Piers told her. 'Do you think it's sound?'

'Trust me,' said my sister. 'I'm an accountant.'

And so we agreed. Shelby suggested using CryptoWallet because it was 'a good one, the best'. We would invest $1,500 and so would Shelby, and then we'd let in percolate in the hope it would make us money one day, which we would then split.

'Come on, it's only a grand and a half,' Shelby said, as I wavered. 'I'll do my own with Tino at some point, too.'

Piers was chomping at the bit, keen to hand over the cash. I think part of him wanted to show Shelby how flash he was with his money, how easily he procured it, perhaps so it would get back to Tino. He's always been a very proud man.

'Let's do it,' he enthused and logged on to the site.

Shelby made up the password – a really complicated one – and scrawled it on her Esperance Motors business card, of all places.

And then she said, 'Just pay my share for me, will you, Piersy? I'll pay you back!'

And she never did. That was the start of the trouble.

Freya bursts in through the door, out of breath. She is still in her running gear. She hands me some flowers and a parcel wrapped in floral paper and kisses me.

'You beat me to it after all,' she smiles. 'I had to run past my place to grab your present. No time to shower though, sorry! I figured you wouldn't mind. You've seen me in worse states than this. Where's Isobel?'

'Her room, of course. On Snapchat as usual. You beat the storm.'

'Just,' says Freya.

'Wine?'

'Yes please.'

'Red or white?'

'Red would be wonderful.' Freya takes a crinkle cut crisp out of a bowl on the table, and dips it in hummus. 'Mmm,' she enthuses, as if hummus is the most delicious thing she has ever tasted. She is a good friend, Freya.

My phone beeps and I pick it up. 'Oh,' I say. 'It's Carole. She reckons she's got gastro, so she's not coming. She must be feeling bad if she's texting and not calling.' I feel a stab of disappointment. 'Marella can't come, either – she's had to take Rocky her dog to the vet because there's something in his paw. Glass, she thinks, the poor thing. She was quite upset when she called, but I couldn't stay on the line to chat, since I was outside the dance studio waiting for Isobel.'

'Oh Lottie,' Freya grimaces. 'I'm sorry they can't make it. It's just us and Shelby, then!' Her face suggests she finds it all a bit awkward. 'I mean, I don't want to intrude on a family thing . . .'

'You *are* family!' I insist, feeling a little affronted. 'Please stay.'

'Of course I will,' she agrees, but she doesn't look thrilled at the thought.

I open her gift to try and lighten the mood. It's a set of Chanel No 5 goodies.

'Happy birthday!' Freya sings. 'Sorry the pressie's late but I figured I'd wait and give it to you at your official birthday dinner.'

'Thanks,' I tell her. 'It's lovely.' Perhaps tonight isn't so hideous after all.

The front door closes and Piers walks up the hallway towards us. He is straight from a delivery, and he looks tired, dishevelled. He offers an air kiss, French-style, to Freya and drops his keys on the kitchen bench.

He looks around and shrugs. I know what he's asking me – where is Shelby?

I shake my head discreetly.

He leans in to kiss me. 'She had better turn up,' he whispers in my ear.

Freya looks away, realising that there is some kind of private exchange going on between me and Piers. She picks up her phone and mouths to me, 'Just texting Carole!' and proceeds with her head firmly down.

Piers flings his suit jacket over the bottom balustrade of the stairs and loosens his tie with his finger. There is a large splash of rusty red blood on his white shirt. It happens often and it doesn't usually bother me, only tonight it freaks me out a little because it makes me think of darkness and the clearing and murderous men in trench coats. In reality, it's life-giving blood, but try telling that to my over-stimulated amygdala the evening after another of my night terrors.

Freya looks at Piers' shirt with a disgusted expression pasted on her face.

He looks down and frowns. 'Don't worry,' he says. 'I'm taking it off. It's on my jacket too, thanks to an emergency caesarean.' He lets out a 'tsk'. 'Blood on a ten-thousand-dollar bespoke suit – not ideal. I'll take it to the dry-cleaners tomorrow.'

Piers is only saying this for my benefit, since it will, of course, be me who takes it to the dry-cleaners.

'Occupational hazard!' I smile at Freya. 'We do have to look after this suit though – it's so precious. We got it on our honeymoon in London.'

'What Lottie is saying in a roundabout way is that she thinks I shouldn't wear it to work.' Piers smiles amiably. 'But you have to look the part in my profession.'

My husband is right, of course. Part of being an obstetrician is *looking* distinguished, even if it does mean bodily fluids spurting on you from various orifices. He unbuttons his soiled shirt and balls it up in his hands. I reach for it and take it, with his suit jacket I've collected from the balustrade, down the hall to the downstairs bathroom beside the front door.

'Don't mind me,' I hear Freya laugh from the kitchen.

'Sorry,' Piers says. 'Lottie doesn't like me wearing my work clothes upstairs.'

'No.' I grimace as I return to the kitchen. 'So what happened with the birth?'

'It was a little dicey! Head got stuck at eight centimetres, baby in distress. But it was all fine in the end.'

'Who did you deliver today?' asks Freya.

'A four kilo little bruiser called Anne-Marie,' Piers grins. 'Anne-Marie Cairns. Remember that name, because according to her father, she's going to be famous.'

'Anne-Marie? What kind of a name is that for a baby?' Freya asks.

'You should hear some of the things people call their kids.' Piers shrugs, then disappears upstairs for fifteen minutes and returns smelling heavenly in jeans and a T-shirt.

'Still no Shelby?' he asks, a little too brightly.

'Not yet,' I chirp, as if our earlier exchange never took place.

'Don't worry,' says Piers to Freya, as if Freya even cares, 'she'll be fashionably late.'

'I'm not worried,' says Freya and gulps her remaining half-glass of wine.

Piers heads in the direction of his study to fetch his glasses.

'Oh, here she is!' Shelby's name illuminates my phone screen. 'She says she'll be here in twenty minutes.'

'Twenty?' A bespectacled Piers hisses as he re-enters the kitchen. 'Bloody typical. It's ten past nine already. So you're telling me we won't eat until nine-thirty?'

I look at him with a pleading expression and tap at my phone.

'What are you saying?' Piers demands.

'That we'll wait for her,' I say. 'I mean, if that's okay?'

'Of course,' says Freya.

'No, we'll eat,' says Piers. 'I'm sick of this.'

'But I just told her . . .'

'That's her problem.'

'I'm so sorry about this,' I tell Freya. 'You know what she's like.'

'Gosh, don't worry!' Freya bats a hand, but the atmosphere has soured somewhat.

'I suppose Piers is right, there's no point in waiting.' I smile. 'Piers? Will you carve?'

Piers sharpens the meat knife vigorously and slices roughly through the beef. I can tell from the sawing motion that it is ruined. Ten minutes makes all the difference with beef.

He sits himself down at the head of the table and we eat in silence. I feel like my throat has closed. The meat is ruined and the nut roast is like charcoal.

Piers chews irritably.

There is a bright flash outside the kitchen window and Freya sits up straight. 'Wow, look at the lightning,' she says, and I am grateful for the diversion. 'The storm is coming.'

We all turn towards the window, where the rain has begun to blast the glass and run down it in torrents.

Two winters ago, I'd stood at the same window with Isobel next to me. It was a Wednesday night and the clouds were black, like iron oxide. It was before she hated me.

'Wednesday's child is full of woe,' I'd muttered.

'What do you mean, Mum?'

'It's an old rhyme,' I'd said. 'Do you want to hear?'

She'd nodded. My privileged child who would never know the cold, never know what life was like on the other side of the fence – the rusty side.

'Okay, it goes like this: Monday's child is fair of face – that means she is pretty – Tuesday's child is full of grace,

Wednesday's child is full of woe, Thursday's child has far
to go . . .'

'What's woe?'

'It's sadness.'

'Oh,' she'd said. 'That's too bad if you were born that
day.'

'Listen to the rest: Friday's child is loving and giving,
Saturday's child works hard for a living. And the child
who's born on the Sabbath Day, is bonny and blithe and
good and gay.'

Isobel had looked confused.

'Blithe and gay mean happy,' I'd told her.

'Then what day was I born?'

'Sunday.'

A flash of lightning made us both step back.

'What about you and Auntie Shelby?' she'd said.

'Actually, we were born on different days. Auntie Shelby
was born at the end of one day and I was born at the start
of another.'

'Which ones?'

'Auntie Shelby was born at 11.58 on a Tuesday night . . .'
Tuesday's child is full of grace. 'And I was born at 12.02 on
Wednesday.'

'That's why Auntie Shelby is always so happy, and you're
so sad,' said Isobel. 'Wednesday's child is full of woe.'

I remember thinking maybe that is it. Maybe it isn't
genes, but all down to the days we happened to be born
on. Maybe if I'd come out first, it would have been different. I would have been Shelby and Shelby would have
been me.

'I'm not sad . . .' I'd told her, but it wasn't true. Perpetual anxiety can't help but bring sadness.

A clap of thunder had rattled the windowpane, and I'd found myself jumping back from the window in fright, but Isobel stayed put.

'Are you scared?' she'd asked.

'A little,' I'd heard myself say. *My darling, I am scared of everything.* 'Are you?'

She'd turned to me, her eleven-year-old eyes blazing brown.

'No,' she'd said, and all I saw was Shelby. 'This is the most epic thing I've ever seen!'

Forty minutes later, Shelby is still not here. Piers puts his fork down.

'You haven't touched your food,' Piers says to me.

He is right. My plate is full. Nut roast and vegetables pushed around to the edges of the ceramic, toyed with but not eaten. 'I'm worried about her,' I say, testing his mood.

'Lottie,' Piers says with no attempt to hide his annoyance. 'Your sister will be out drinking with a friend somewhere or she'll be running and have lost track of time. Unreliable and selfish are her specialities. Please don't work yourself up.'

I feel my stomach drop. I know how hard this is for Piers. How hard it is to pretend he isn't as desperate to have Shelby here as I am, but for different reasons. How hard it is for him to act in front of Freya.

'It isn't the first time she's stood us up,' he continues, as if he doesn't care, 'and it won't be the last.'

Freya puts her hand on my wrist, the only part of me that's seen the sun lately. It's the brownest part of me. I wonder if she notices the contrast like I do.

'Shelby is fine, Lots,' she says. 'Try and stay calm.'

'She's right,' says Piers. 'Don't overreact.'

I look at him and nod, show him I understand he is playing a role.

'What about Tino?' Freya doesn't meet my eye. 'Have you called him?'

Piers picks up his phone, puts it on speaker and lets it ring. 'He's not answering,' he sighs, stating the obvious when the voicemail kicks in. 'They're probably together.'

'But she *said* twenty minutes!' I cry.

We're silent for a moment and I get the feeling neither Freya or Piers can be bothered to entertain my bubbling anxiety.

'I should go,' says Freya. 'I don't want to intrude. This is family stuff.'

'Nonsense,' says Piers at the same time as I say, 'Yes, okay.'

I offer for Piers to drive her since it's almost 10 p.m., but Freya isn't having any of it. 'I love the rain,' she says. 'I'll enjoy walking, but I might just borrow an umbrella.'

After Freya has gone, I retreat to our bedroom and try Shelby's number, but it also goes to voicemail. My heart palpitates wildly and I want to crumple into a ball in the corner of the room and rock back and forth to soothe myself. I hear Piers' footsteps on the landing and so I pull myself upright and wipe my eyes.

'Doesn't look like we'll be talking about the money tonight,' he says. He wrings his hands nervously.

'I'd settle for just seeing Shelby with my own eyes,' I snap. It's unlike me, but I can't help it.

Piers sighs and walks into the bathroom. He comes back with a brown bottle and hands me a pill.

'Have a Valium,' he says. 'And try to sleep.'

I'm tired, so tired. I know I tend to catastrophise, but this feels different.

I hold out my hand like a child being given medicine and take the pill.

'Good girl,' Piers says.

Chapter Twenty
Shelby

Before

I am dead in the water for seven minutes. Seven minutes of heaven. Cocooned in a warm blanket, snuggled away from the world.

What I don't like at all is coming back. When the voices calling my name stop being a lullaby and sharpen into focus like a bark on a soccer sideline. Lottie screams like a stuck pig, wild shrieks that turn to breathless sobs when they turn me over onto my broken ribs and let me vomit out the water from my scorched throat, hoarse from trying to stay alive. I hadn't realised I'd tried. The pain in my ribs begins to throb and ache where Turret, who's in the surf-lifesaving club, has brought me back from the dead, his massive fingers interlinked, pounding at my chest with the heel of his palm, while the fat girl from maths with the nose ring stands behind him shouting, 'Come on, Shelby! Come the hell *on!*' like she knows me. My lungs burn like fire from the water that's filled them; the blood begins racing through my blue skin once more, bringing back the colour, bringing back the redness, and the oxygen. Bringing back the life. And suddenly, I am deathly cold. My body convulses with shivers. Goose bumps coat my skin like marbles. The maths girl covers me with a towel, screams out, 'Get another one. Give me a coat – *anything*!'

Latto rubs my hand, my hair. 'Shelby,' he cries softly. 'Shelby?'

Over by the fire, Carole stands motionless with her hand over her mouth. Lottie kneels beside me, rocking back and forth with shock, saying in a manic voice, 'I dreamed this was going to happen. I dreamed she would drown. I was right, don't you see? I was *right!*'

Chapter Twenty-One
Carole

I am soaked through when we meet at the end of the street.

'Carole?' Max walks towards me with open arms, as though he has nothing to hide.

'What are you doing outside?' he asks. 'You're drenched. Your dress . . .'

The rain pummels my face, the silk of my designer dress clings to my body. I look at Max.

'I know where you've been,' I tell him.

He looks at me, confused. And then he laughs.

'So do I – at drinks,' he says.

'No, Max!' I cry. 'Stop! Please just stop it, will you? I *know*!'

He looks confused, trapped. He doesn't want to confirm it.

'I know you were with her,' I tell him.

He stares at me. 'Carole, not this again. I told you . . .'

I throw the watch at his chest. '"On my way, beautiful xo",' I spit. 'The same text you've apparently sent her every time you've played golf. Bad luck *darling* – you left your watch at home. You know, the watch I bought you, like I did every other designer item you own!'

'Shit,' is all he says. Above, a yellow flash of lightning zig-zags through the sky, followed by a bellow of thunder. I shiver.

'"Shit"?' I shake my head in disbelief. 'Not "I'm sorry, Carole" or "No, I didn't"?'

'I'm sorry, Carole,' he says, but he can't look at me.

He has confirmed my worst fear. I slap him across the face, hard. His eyes flinch but his body doesn't move. He just stares at me.

'You can say goodbye to it all,' I wail. 'Everything. The money, the cars. You're not getting a cent from me, not now I know you've been with her. You *lied* to me! You made me feel stupid for questioning you!'

Max doesn't look up.

'I hate you,' I wail and I pummel his chest over and over. 'I hate you!'

I love you.

Oh God, I love you.

That's why it hurts so much.

I want to tell him to go home and pack. To get the hell away from me. He told me I was imagining things that night after cheese and wine at Lottie's, that Shelby was desperate, a fantasist. That I had nothing to worry about. I want to tell him I will never let him see our children again, for as long as he lives, but I can't.

I just stand and cry, and let him pull me into his arms. I feel so safe there, even now, after finding out what I have, his arms are comfort. All I want is him.

But I will not play second fiddle to her. I will not.

'No,' I spit, and I push him away. I cannot prostrate myself this low. I cannot beg. Not now. Not after *her*. 'Get away from me!'

'I'm so sorry, Carole,' he says again. 'I'm so sorry.'

My throat is burning, my heart thuds out of time.

'Anyone else—' I say, my voice choking on a sob. 'Anyone else, I could have handled. But not her. Not that cheap slut . . .'

He looks at me and he reaches out to me, to offer comfort, restore calm.

But it can't be restored. Any of it. It can't be made better. I shake him off and I run.

I walk along the beach, round the rocks of the headland that turns Esperance into Mooney again. At some point I turn back, but I don't know when. I don't remember anything about walking. The wind howls, the rain lashes down. I'm soaked to the skin, freezing cold. The only warmth is the salty lick of tears as they burn in my eyeballs and run in rivers down my cheeks, stinging my face where the wind has chafed it.

Oh Max, no! Not her! Anyone but her!

At some point, I sit on the shore and I will the ocean to come for me, like it came for Shelby, but I'm not brave enough to go in. Is this what he does to women, my husband? Is this the effect he has on all of us? Why has it taken me this long to get to this point? To the point of wanting to go under? For a single moment, I understand her. I understand the teenage Shelby who wanted to sink to the bottom of the seabed on the night of the bonfire and stay there, to switch off the agony in her chest, the constant stab of hurt and rejection.

But I hate the woman she is now and I wish she was dead. I scream at the top of my lungs, try to drown out the pound of the waves with my cries. I kick the rocks until I feel the pain in my toes through the mesh of my running shoes, pound the sand with my fist, grasp it so tight my fingernails rip my palms and my nails fill with blood.

How long have I been walking? I don't even know.

I hate him.

I love him.

I hate her. Why didn't she drown? Why didn't she?

I sit and I cry some more until it is silent, just breath. I tell myself to breathe. Remind myself I am a mother. I need to be in this world, I must pull myself together. The homing beacon switches on. I need to get back to Olivia and Otto. I have to rest, to sleep. I have to kiss my babies' heads and tell them I'm sorry for . . . I can't think what. Sorry that I married their father? Sorry I didn't see what he's been doing to us? Sorry I wanted to hurt someone? Sorry I want a woman dead?

I can't climb up the cliff face in the dark, so I walk along the base of the dunes to the clearing and pull back the branches. For the first time perhaps ever, I feel a sense of unease in the midst of the trees in the pitch black, as if someone is here with me. I grew up playing in this exact spot, came here as a child and a teen, and the feeling unnerves me. I head towards the middle where the light from the running track shines orange through the trees, illuminating the path ahead. The leaves are dry, sheltered from the rain by a roof of branches. My feet crunch underfoot.

I don't see it until I reach the light. It is close to me. A foot. A foot in a peach-coloured running shoe with a white tick on the side. A slender, tanned calf in black, yoga pants leading to tiny hips, which don't quite seem level, as if this is a Barbie doll that's been twisted out of shape by a child. I stare at the hips for a minute, before my eyes reluctantly roll up.

Her tongue protrudes from an open mouth, her trademark fuchsia lipstick smudged all over her chin. Her eyes are open wide, and she stares at the night sky, her fingers set in claws in the mud. Her neck is red and bruised, grey and purple and hot pink. On the earth beside her, a single red fingernail, ripped from its bed, protrudes from the mulch. I open my mouth to scream, but only a whisper comes out. I have nothing left in me. Max has taken it all.

'Help,' I whisper, backing out onto the running track. 'Somebody . . . please . . . help.'

My heart thunders, my calves burn, my lungs forget how to breathe.

Shelby is dead. The scream when it finally comes is animalistic, shrill, like it's from somebody else and not from me.

I wished for this! I sat on the edge of the shore and I willed for it. What in God's name have I done?

Part Two: Revenge

THE FOLLOWING
SATURDAY

Chapter Twenty-Two
Lottie

It is eight days since my sister was murdered.

Eight days since she ceased to exist in the world, extinguished by a pair of hands to her neck and abandoned in the muddy earth.

I am in limbo. I am a plane waiting to take off, a refugee in a chaotic borderline, a tightrope walker caught in between two craggy precipices. I am a soul in purgatory, a tortured mind. I am one half of a golden locket, searching for its missing piece. I am a sister without a sister. A twin but a single. She is here, but she is not. She is in the air where the sun streams in through the window, one of a million tiny dust motes that dart about maniacally, performing impossibly light spirals and arabesques when they catch the light. She is in the whistle of the breeze, the wind that moves the trees. She is in the rays of the sun which has returned to Esperance, which streams in through the windows and burns the skin in only minutes. She is birdsong, a jet-stream, a rainbow. She is the glitter that dances on the ocean in the midday sun, a mirrored disco ball, flickering and flashing a million shards of light to every corner of the world.

Eight days is a long time. Time for someone to change, to be reborn. To change an anxious little girl into an angry woman. Time for me to take my dead sister's chutzpah and swallow it, take her spirit and suck it inside myself.

Eight days is a long time to lie in a bed and watch the cotton curtain flap in the breeze, watch the fabric billow out and in, over and over again.

The morning light streams in lazily, an acute triangle of yellow on my dressing table. It hits my shoulder as I sit in front of the mirror. My make-up is laid out before me, and my black dress hangs from the back of the bedroom door.

We cannot bury Shelby until the autopsy has been performed, so today we will celebrate her life with a wake. Life has run oddly like clockwork since she died: it goes on behind the scenes as I hover like a ghost on the periphery, watching yet not participating.

Carole has cleaned my house for me. She wanted to send Hannah, but Hannah's mother is sick, so she has stepped up and done it herself. I almost laughed when she turned up with yellow marigolds on, wiping, disinfecting, mopping, plumping pillows. She even cleaned the toilets, scrubbing and bleaching them without question, dusting photos of my sister with care, ignoring the fact she detested Shelby. It is quite possible that Carole *is* delighted she is dead (despite the obvious trauma of finding her), but even so, she plays the supportive friend with aplomb, which is so dreadfully unlike Carole that it's perhaps the most unsettling thing of all. It is yet another plane in my world that has shifted inexplicably, seismically. A small part of me wants the selfish Carole back, not this impostor. I can't deal with any more *change*!

As part of her support drive, Carole has sorted the flowers for today, called in some favours from White

Bloom Flowers in Esperance, where she spends a small fortune every week in order to decorate her console table.

'We want to make a big statement,' she told me. 'We'll go big on the flowers!'

'It's a wake, not a wedding,' I'd hissed when she first mentioned it, and she'd looked at me, astonished, like she couldn't believe the words had come from me, from mild-mannered little Lottie. But she shook it off, of course, because you always have to forgive the person who's grieving. When you've lost a loved one, you can say and do what you want. *It's the grief talking.*

Freya takes Isobel to school each day, toots the horn outside the house at 7.50 a.m. so she doesn't intrude on our grief. Isobel obliges, robotic. She hasn't taken the loss of her aunt well at all. She blames me. 'Why didn't you go out and *look* for her?' Perhaps what she really means is, 'I wish it had been *you.*'

Marella has taken to leaving food on the doormat. Big, family sized portions. But I can't eat. I exist on coffee. Coffee to wake me up, coffee to get me through the morning, coffee to keep me awake in the afternoon. It usually takes me months to shed a single kilo – now Shelby is dead, I have lost four.

Today we will celebrate my sister's entire life in the space of just four hours. A short life, worth just a single afternoon. And all of the voyeurs who come will say how beautiful she was, and 'what a waste of a life', even though half of them hated her, were jealous of her for what she was and what she had, which was everything.

Piers' head nudges round the bedroom door. He looks first at the bed, where he expects I will be, cocooned under the duvet. He is almost shocked to see me at the dressing table, painting on the face of a bereaved sister. My foundation is flawless, my cheeks streaked with rose pink, eyelids thick with liner and flicked up at the outer corners. Cat eyes, like Shelby used to do. It is my homage to her.

'Wow, you look beautiful,' Piers whispers. 'I've never seen your eyes look so . . . dark. You look so much like Sh—'

He stops. Looks at his feet. He is wearing socks with poo emojis, a gift from Isobel. A fitting pattern for a shit situation.

'Just checking in,' he says, his voice gentle. Now I am at my lowest, he doesn't know how to be around me. 'How are you feeling?'

I should be pleased my husband is wearing an expression that denotes something other than fear of financial ruin. Although I know he must be feeling it – a deep-seated worry about how we will get the money back from Shelby now she is dead. How we'll pay off the loan and the mortgage and the school fees if we can't access the funds that are rightfully ours. Now the password is gone forever, gone with Shelby.

'Fine,' I say, looking at myself and not him. I'm not fine. Of course I am not fine. His question was stupid. It doesn't deserve an answer any more detailed than this.

I study him in the mirror. He looks guilty – guilty he didn't take me seriously when I told him Shelby was in danger, guilty he hated her. He offers a half-smile, a sympathetic pressing together of the lips.

'Isobel is ready,' he says. 'She's pretty quiet, but I think she'll be okay.'

I nod, thread the back of a diamond stud through my ear.

'Carole is downstairs, with the florist,' he says. 'The house looks sensational. And the smell coming from the kitchen is . . . wow.' Piers hasn't lost *his* appetite. 'Tino has been very generous, considering . . .' Ah, *there* is the mention of money. Piers is evidently grateful we are not footing the bill for today. We wouldn't be able to if we wanted to. There is no money left in the pot.

'Considering?' I snap. 'They *were* married.'

Piers doesn't push it. 'Marella has done a wonderful job with the food,' he says to deflect. 'It's pretty amazing of her to come and help, to take such an interest in Shelby.'

I'd forgotten Marella was going to be here. The thought lifts me for a second. I don't always appreciate her bugging me to talk about my feelings at the shop, but at least her concern is genuine. She didn't know Shelby well enough to gather the steam to hate her like everyone else did, so I know she is genuinely sorry for my loss. Carole and Freya may feel sorry for me, but they'll chink their glasses at some point today, I'm sure. They both hated Shelby.

'Anyway,' says Piers, 'we won't run out of canapés.'

'This isn't a cocktail party, Piers!' I snap.

Piers holds his hands up. 'I'm sorry,' he says. He looks a little afraid, like he can't work out how to handle the bereaved me. He expects me to cling to him, anxious about the people in the house, but strangely, I don't feel the need for a crutch today. My anger has trumped everything, coated me with an armour of strength. It's like Shelby is *in* me. I have swallowed her bravado, eaten it whole. I am no longer scared, but determined. I have lost my sister, but gained my nerve. The funny thing is, I always wanted to be more like Shelby as a child: prettier, more confident and self-assured, popular. I wanted her vitality, her *life*. And now I have it and she does not.

'I'll be down in a moment,' I say.

Piers nods and shuts the door almost silently, as if he's closing it on a sleeping child.

I walk over and reach up to the back of the bedroom door and pull down the black Yves Saint Laurent bridesmaid dress I haven't had the confidence to wear since Shelby made me put it on for her wedding. I step into it and wrestle with the zip, but manage to pull it to the top without calling Piers back to help. It wasn't my style when I first wore it, and I'd spent the day yanking it down. But today it fits like a glove. My breasts look full, my décolletage youthful. I slip my feet into the patent Louboutin heels that have sat, gathering dust, at the bottom of the wardrobe since Piers bought them for me when we first met. Before he understood that's not the person I am, or the way I like to dress.

I fix a mesh fascinator on the side of the bun I have pinned on the back of my head, pick up the lipstick wand Shelby left on my kitchen counter two weeks ago and slather the pink colour slowly across my lips, breathing in the floral scent of the wax stick that touched her lips just days ago. I will wear it to honour my sister.

I step out onto the landing. Piers is waiting for me.

'I mean it,' he says, 'you do look beautiful. I think Shelby would approve.'

I want to say to him, 'But you hated her, just like everyone else hated her, so why do you care if she would like it or not?' But I don't. I may be numb to everyone and everything right now, but I'm not cruel.

I turn away from Piers. At the top of the stairs, the sunlight floods through the open-plan living area, bringing with it so much light that it feels like I'm in an airplane turning in to the sun. Enormous pink and white lilies in massive glass vases like a giant's urn are positioned on every surface, their scent dancing on the breeze from the open windows more vivaciously than any of the scented candles Freya has placed around the room. Beautiful, umbrella-like lilies that will live a life of unrivalled beauty for the shortest amount of time, resplendent, almost arrogant in their allure, before shrivelling up, untimely, to die, like once-vibrant butterflies.

It is what happens to everything that's beautiful.

Chapter Twenty-Three
Carole

I hear my breath pull in sharply as she walks down the staircase.

Shelby.

The silhouette is the same, the hourglass shape with the pin-thin calves and the slender arms. The profile as she turns, the confident uptilt of the head. The scowl, as if everyone owes her something, a fuchsia-lacquered pout. The irony is, that when I saw her lying there in the mud, Shelby looked more like Lottie, the pallid skin, the deep set eyes searching for answers. The look of overwhelming defeat.

Now Lottie walks down with one shiny calf in front of other, full of life. The dress clings to her body, hugs her tightly. It's the type of dress I have always pushed her to wear, the type I might never have suggested if I'd known she would look like *this*.

Max, who has been sleeping in the granny flat since I found out he cheated on me with the tramp we are all here celebrating, stares at Lottie from the other side of the room as she descends the stairs. His lips are parted, his eyes anguished, his skin deathly pale like he is looking at a ghost. The look on his face makes me want to vomit.

I turn away from him, anger bubbling inside me.

Lottie arrives at the bottom of the stairs.

'Carole!' She clasps my shoulders and kisses me on both cheeks.

'Lottie,' I say. 'You look . . .' For once, I am lost for words. *You look like your dead sister, the woman I despised.*

'Is it too much?' she asks, but she doesn't wait for my answer.

Yes, yes it is. Because you look like her, and my husband is anguished by it.

'No,' I say, not quite meeting her eye. 'It is . . . a very fitting outfit.'

Lottie seems relieved.

'The room is amazing, Carole,' she tells me. 'Thank you.'

I nod. It *is* amazing. The entire space is awash with flowers. White lilies with angry orange stamen exploding like fireworks on every surface: the kitchen bench, the coffee table, the mantel. I have done myself proud, and I look forward to the acknowledgements I will receive throughout the day. I couldn't let it be all about Shelby, could I?

In the kitchen, Lottie pulls wine glasses from an overhead cabinet alongside Marella, who is dressed in what looks like the Sass & Bide maternity dress Lottie wore fourteen years ago when she was pregnant with Isobel. Piers and Bernard have moved Lottie's pallid cream sofas back against the walls and the large oak dining table now sits in the centre of the room, with trays of nibbles – triangular sandwiches, Kettle chips and sausage rolls – and row upon row of wine glasses and bottles of beer. In the centre of the room is an A3 black-and-white photo of Shelby. She stares out from on high, follows me with those greedy, smug eyes as I make my way through the sparse clusters of mourners. Everybody's here to rubberneck at a scandal – it's not like they really liked Shelby. She treated everyone like they were a waste of her time.

It's been eight days since I found the body. The police arrived in minutes. Two young first responders, eager to see the scene of the crime, but equally freaked out by it. 'You stay with her,' one had said, nodding at me. 'I'll call Crime Scene.'

They'd called an emergency ambulance for me because the shock had made me faint, and they'd wrapped me in foil and given me sweet tea. The first paramedics didn't even look into the clearing to check Shelby for a pulse, they didn't need to.

'Deceased,' said one of the cops. 'Unquestionable. Keep the area clean for Crime Scene.'

By the time it had taken me to drink the sickly-sweet milky tea from the white, polystyrene cup, blue and white tape had been wound round the clearing, and inside, men and women in white suits and paper booties swarmed around like ghosts, snapping away with their cameras and calling out to one another, 'Over here. See this?'

The detectives from the homicide squad came next. They told me their names but I didn't register. A woman and a man in heavy jackets, unseasonable for spring but necessary in the weather. I was aware how odd I must have looked to them in a silk dress, wrapped in foil.

'I gather you know the victim, Mrs Latimer,' the woman asked.

'Yes.' I sipped my tea. 'Shelby Massini. I'm friends with her twin, Lottie. I've known them since high school.'

She nodded. 'Why were you out so late?'

Was I a suspect? Could she see how much I hated Shelby? Was I that transparent?

'I went for a walk,' I told her.

'This late?'

'I needed to clear my head. I'd had an argument with my husband.'

A scribble in a notepad.

'Apologies for being blunt,' said the man, 'but you're rather unusually dressed.'

'I was on the way to dinner when the argument happened,' I say.

'Why were you in the clearing?'

'I often go to the dunes to think,' I told them. 'It's quiet.'

The detectives looked at one another and the questions fell over themselves: 'Did you touch the body at all?' ('No, I could see she was . . . dead.'); 'What about the surrounding area?' ('No, no. I just screamed and backed away, I think. I can't remember.'); 'Did you see anyone else in the clearing?' ('No one.'); 'And you were alone?' ('Yes. Yes! I've already told you that!'); 'Do you know of anyone who might want to hurt Shelby Massini?' ('No!' *Everyone did. Including me.*)

I suddenly felt very, very scared and vulnerable.

'Can I call my husband?' I asked.

'Max,' I said into the phone, a few minutes later, my voice shaking, but lucid. 'Something's happened. I need you to come and get me from the reserve.'

I'd almost forgotten about the infidelity. Murder trumps cheating. I needed him.

'Carole?'

'You need to come,' I told him. 'It's Shelby.'

Max didn't do his usual 'Oh come on, Carole, get over it' routine.

'What about her?' His voice was urgent.

'She's dead.'

'What?' A weak laugh, like he thought it was a sick joke.

'She's dead. She's in the clearing, Max. I found her body. Max? Are you there?'

Silence.

'Max!' More forceful now. 'You need to come and get me!'

The rest of it is a blur. The sound on the other end of the line after he thought I'd hung up, a wail like that of a mother losing a child, a husband losing a wife. A guttural sob, just like when I'd seen him drag her body from the water all those years ago, his head buried in her lifeless neck. Yet another physical reaction to Shelby – like the flinch I'd spotted when he watched her walk down the aisle with Tino. Or that moment when I'd pushed Olivia out of me and he'd been so overwhelmed with emotion I could have sworn he'd murmured her name, just a whisper, but clear enough for me to hear. They were just the imaginings of a paranoid woman, he'd said. And perhaps they were.

But a paranoid woman knows exactly how much she has to lose.

Chapter Twenty-Four
Freya

Carole is holding up well considering she was the one who found Shelby's body. She is dressed to the nines with a new pillar-box-red lipstick from Sephora ('When I saw it was called Light Up The Funeral, I just *had* to have it,' she says, woefully), and her eyes are red. She holds a scrunched up handkerchief in her hand.

Something weird is definitely going on between her and Max, because they arrived in separate cars and Carole turns away from him whenever he tries to talk to her.

'How are you holding up?' I ask.

'Fine,' she snaps. 'Why wouldn't I be?'

'If you want to talk . . .'

'Oh for fuck's sake, Freya,' Carole snaps. 'Just ask if you want to know! There's nothing much to say except that I found out Max had been dipping his wick where he shouldn't, so I've thrown him out.'

'Oh, Carole!' I say. No prizes for guessing where he was dipping it.

She reads my thoughts. 'He's not the first man to cheat and he won't be the last,' she snaps. 'It's just unfortunate that the woman he's been sleeping with ended up dead.'

I glance over at Max. Does this make him a suspect?

'I really am so sorry,' I tell her.

Carole's eyes fill with tears. 'You guessed it, didn't you?' she says. 'Turns out he was kissing her the night you saw them at the garage. So he's living in the granny flat until I decide what to do. Because the ball is in *my* court, you understand,' she says.

'Of course I do,' I say, even though I know exactly how gutted she is. 'For what it's worth, I think you're incredibly brave . . .'

'Oh do shut up, Freya – I'm not in the mood for a sympathy vote today. I'm here to see off my arch-nemesis.'

I smile, because when Carole is like this, I know she'll be okay. Appearances or not, she still has that fire. I decide to change the subject.

'I think I went a bit overboard on the candles,' I say.

Carole agrees. 'They smell like toilet freshener. Where the hell did you get them?'

'Diptyque,' I say.

'Oh,' says Carole. 'They're stunning!'

She heads off to chat to her brother Sebastian, and I am left alone. I cradle my glass of wine and look around. Bernard stands by the fireplace with Max and Tino and a couple of men I don't know. Tino looks sort of dumbstruck, and it's all I can do to stop myself from going over to him and placing my hand in his; Max looks devastated, with red eyes and giant grey bags underneath, as if he hasn't slept. All of them cradle expensive whisky glasses and talk in hushed tones. The air hums with whispered speech, out of respect for the dead.

At the wakes of the elderly, you're allowed to smile and tell funny stories, unless they die in an awful way, that is, but when it's someone under fifty, it's a lot more morose. No one smiles. No one tells hilarious stories – even though there are some truly good ones in this instance. Everyone looks at their shoes, and if not theirs, then other people's – maybe because of guilt, because, after all, aren't we all voyeurs here? There can't be many people here who are genuinely stricken with grief? But we're all talking the talk, regardless. I've lost track of the number of times I've heard the words 'it's a tragedy' or 'it's such a shame' or 'she was *so* beautiful' – as if beauty is the ultimate accomplishment in life. As if being physically unattractive might make the situation more palpable, somehow. Make it less of a waste. Twenty per cent of me wants to giggle inappropriately, seventy per cent of me wants to get horrendously pissed, and the remaining ten per cent has a strange impulse to jump on the dining table and sing 'All That Jazz' from *Chicago*.

Lottie is busy chatting to distant relatives and insists she doesn't need another pair of hands in the kitchen, so I wander into the middle of the room and stop to pay my respects at the poster-sized framed black-and-white print of Shelby on its easel. The face looks back at me. The eyes are so familiar, so dark. Like a whirlpool that could suck you in; pull you down and under like quicksand. Eyes that were always full of secrets, that teased under naturally dark lashes. The smile – less of a smile than a smirk – assessing every goddamn person in the room.

An elderly woman arrives beside me.

'It's such a terrible shame, isn't it?' she says.

'Yes,' I agree. She *was* beautiful. Shame she was ugly as anything on the inside.

Piers appears as the elderly woman leaves. He stands close, so that our shoulders touch.

'How are you, Piers?' I touch his arm. 'How is Lottie?'

'Beside herself with grief. She hasn't eaten a thing. She's so exhausted she's sleeping for hours at a stretch. I couldn't get her to do that when Shelby was alive.'

'Piers, I want to help. Let me know what I can—'

'I wanted to off that woman so many times in my head,' he says, staring at the photo, 'but unfortunately for me I love my wife too much. I can't believe someone actually did it.'

'I know.' It's all I can think to say.

'I was livid on Friday night when she let Lottie down,' he says to me. 'I hated her, you know, Freya. She was unreliable, greedy, selfish. But murder?'

'We all hated her,' I say almost absentmindedly, and I realise I'd never vocalised that with anyone other than Jayne.

Piers nods knowingly and walks away and I am alone again. I turn to see if I can spot Bernard, and I spy him in the kitchen chatting to Marella. She is nodding earnestly as he talks, giving him the occasional polite laugh. She touches his hand and he puts his on hers, like he's the bereaved husband. I should really go over and check in, but it looks like the world's most dull conversation, so I head instead towards Isobel, who is sitting on her own on Lottie's white sofa. I figure she could do with some company, but I'm interrupted by Carole, who is still doing an Oscar-winning job of pretending she isn't completely cut up about Max.

'No,' she hisses, shaking her head.

'What?' I shrug.

'Lottie said not to talk to Isobel. She's a complete mess. She doesn't want to talk to anyone – you know how much she loved Shelby. She worshipped her. Two peas in a pod, those two.'

We both glance over at the photo of Shelby, feel her hard, mocking gaze on us yet again.

'It must have been terrible finding her,' I say. 'What did she . . . look like?'

'Pretty bloody average,' snaps Carole.

'I mean, did she look peaceful?'

'Not really.' Carole bites her cheek. 'She looked . . . shocked. She was staring upwards – he didn't even bother to close her eyes.'

'Or *she*,' I say. 'I don't suppose you would bother closing someone's eyes if you hated them enough to strangle them to death.'

Carole looks like she might cry. She seems to crumple, her shoulders slack. But then she collects herself, straightens her back.

'For what it's worth,' she says, 'if I die any time soon, let it be known that I do *not* want an A3 poster of me in the middle of my living room. You can see her *pores*.'

'I don't mean to be gruesome but why aren't we burying her today?' I ask.

'They can't bury her because they don't know who *killed* her. That's why we're all paying homage to *that*.' She nods at the picture on the stand.

'Poor Lottie,' I offer.

'Rocking that Saint Laurent though,' muses Carole. 'Unusually bold for her.'

We turn to look at Lottie as she stands on tiptoes and picks out another wine glass for one of the mourners. She is utterly striking – even more so than Shelby was. It's bizarre. It's like she's a completely different woman from the one we know, the one who's always dressed in a floral moo-moo and Jesus sandals. Bernard stands in the kitchen, still boring Marella with some long-winded legal anecdote. He sees me and nods.

I turn back to Carole. 'So how long is it till they can bury her, or cremate her or whatever?' I ask.

'No idea,' says Carole. 'But Esperance police told Lottie they can't put a timeframe on it because they're still waiting for an autopsy, even though we all know she was strangled. I saw it myself. Her neck was messed up.'

'So they just have to keep her on ice until then?'

'On ice?' snaps Carole. 'She's not a tray of fucking oysters.'

'Okay!' I say, hands up. 'I didn't know you liked her so much!'

We're silent for a moment.

'Lottie asked me to help pick out Shelby's casket clothes,' Carole says.

'You mean her burial outfit?'

'Yes, tops, bottoms. Even *underwear*. Lottie chose a Chanel pant suit.'

'Isn't that a horrific waste?' I lean in, lest Lottie should hear. 'To dress her in *Chanel*?'

We spring apart as Marella forces a tray of Peking duck canapés between us.

'Duck?' she asks gravely. 'It has hoisin sauce and everything.'

'No thanks,' we say in unison.

Marella holds out her right hand and balances the tray on her left. She's totally worked in hospitality before.

'Carole?' she asks and looks up at Carole expectantly. 'We met in Only Organic last week, remember? I work with Lottie at St Paul's, but I used to go to school with Lottie and Max.'

Carole's eyes fill up again.

'And me,' I say to Marella. 'You went to school with me. I thought you looked familiar. I'm Freya Harrington, I used to be Freya Morton.'

'Ah yes!' Marella chirps. 'Of course.'

'Yes, well,' says Carole briskly. 'Thank you for offering us the canapés.'

'Pleasure,' says Marella. 'Although I can't eat them myself since I'm vegetarian. Anyway, I must offer some of these to the men. Bernard over there can't get enough! See you later.'

'Ugh, hopefully not,' whispers Carole. 'I mean duck? Seriously? It has *so* many calories.'

We take simultaneous swigs of wine. I watch Marella avoid Piers as she crosses the room. She doesn't ask him if he'd like a duck pancake.

'So how exactly did you help with the outfit?' I ask Carole, keen to know how she has contributed to Shelby's sartorial outgoing.

'I gave Lottie a scarf.' She shrugs. 'Something to cover the *bruises*.' She puts a hand on her neck like she's strangling herself.

'A *scarf*?' I snort. 'I never once saw Shelby in a *scarf*.'

'She didn't usually have bruises on her neck, did she?' Carole snaps. 'And anyway, Piers said Lottie was struggling with what to choose, so I offered to help.'

'That *was* kind of you, Carole,' I say, laying on the sarcasm.

'I mean, it's the very *least* I could do. I gave her my vintage Burberry check. It's worth a lot of money.' She studies her nails. 'But you know, Freya, this horrendous situation has shown me that money really doesn't matter in the grand scheme of things.'

She twists the Cartier bracelet on her wrist and smooths down the front of her Hervé Léger dress. 'Our time here is fleeting.'

'Carole, no! Shelby *hated* a print,' I say. 'Remember that time Lottie got her a Louis Vuitton wallet with the LV motif all over it and she despised it? She would hate that Burberry scarf!'

Carole's hand flies to her chest at the idea she has intentionally sent Shelby off on her eternal outing in something that was nothing short of a sartorial catastrophe. 'No she *wouldn't*! Unbelievable, you try to do the right thing and this' – she makes a throwing gesture with her hands – 'is the reward you get!'

'A Chanel pant suit and a neckerchief,' I confirm. 'So what you're basically telling me, Carole, is that Shelby is going to be six foot under dressed like a Qantas stewardess.'

Carole's eyes are steely. She has played the last card in a friendship that was all about one-upmanship – and not only has she *played* it, but she has slammed it down on the table defiantly, the palm of her hand rigid, a royal flush.

'Well-played,' I tell her. If I could clap my hands slowly, without looking gauche, I would.

'I was trying to help,' Carole snaps. 'What do you want her to wear? A polo neck?'

'Oh Christ, no!' I reply a little too loud. 'She wouldn't be seen *dead* in one of those.'

Carole pretends her snigger is a sob.

I take myself off to the kitchen after this for a glass of water, and Marella is there making some kind of dip in the blender.

'Looks great,' I say.

'Satay,' she says.

I let out an audible gasp. Carole is seriously allergic. She'll die if she as much as sniffs a peanut. I tell Marella this and her face falls.

'Oh my goodness,' she says. 'I had no idea!' She walks to the bin and scrapes out the caramel-coloured dip and rinses the bowl under the hot tap for ages.

'Throw any ingredients away and be careful you don't reuse any of the cutlery you used,' I offer. 'Everything will need to be thoroughly cleaned.'

'Oh dear,' Marella says. 'I'm mortified.' It's probably not the best choice of words, but it's warranted. It really wouldn't be a good look to inadvertently kill someone at Shelby's wake.

'Don't worry, Marella – no harm done.' I smile and head to the bathroom for some alone time, because frankly, it's all too much.

When I get inside, I lean against the back of the door and sigh. It's all too intense. I notice the loo roll is finished, so I bend down and open the cabinet under the sink and grab a new one to pop on the holder, you know, to tidy up for Lottie.

That's when I hear the door open.

'Excuse me, there's someone in here . . .' I begin.

'Freya?' comes the whispered reply.

It is Tino. He steps into the bathroom and, on account of sheer spacing issues, we're left standing inches apart.

'Hello,' he says. 'You look *insane*.'

'Insanely good or certifiable?'

'The former.'

He pushes me backwards into the bathroom, the door still slightly ajar, and pulls me to him by the waist. He puts one hand behind my neck, holds it firm in his strong grip. His thumb rests on my windpipe. 'I've missed you,' he whispers.

Then his mouth is on me and his tongue searches for mine, brushes against my front teeth. He smells of wine and expensive aftershave. I feel my body melt into him and my tongue respond, but then I glance past his ear and down the corridor towards the kitchen. Even from the miniscule crack in the door I can see that damn black-and-white photo of Shelby, and she's still looking at me.

'Don't!' I say, freaked out. 'Not today!'

He ignores me until I push him away. 'I want to,' I tell him, 'but I can't. Not here. I'm sorry. You have to leave . . .' I actually can't believe he's got the stomach for this with that great big photo of his dead wife watching us from down the hall. Even I draw a line at sex in my best friend's toilet at her sister's wake.

'I know it's inappropriate, but I just can't help it. I just want you,' he says, but he glances over his shoulder at the photo through the crack in the door.

I push him gently away.

'Later,' I say.

He nods and takes my hand, only letting it drop to shut the bathroom door behind me as I head back down the hall.

I turn to see Lottie step out of the shadow of the study nook next door to the bathroom. She fixes me with a glare and marches back down the hallway to the kitchen. I follow her, thinking nothing more than, *Oh shit.* She ignores me when I walk in behind her, so I open the cupboard above my head, which is so big it's like the overhead locker in an Airbus A380, and prepare to clear the drying rack, so Lottie doesn't have to do it later. The glasses inside are all stacked haphazardly, and one is balancing precariously against another, so I grab the little stepladder that Lottie sits on when she hides away from life in the pantry. I step up and busy myself arranging the glasses.

'Good job,' says Marella.

'Um, Marella,' I say, 'would you mind giving me and Lottie a minute?'

'Of course,' she says, picking up a tray. 'I'll go and collect some empties!'

'Are you okay?' I ask Lottie when Marella is out of earshot.

'Fine,' she says.

'I mean, really?'

She looks at me. 'I've had better days,' she says.

'Is there anything else I can do?'

'Aside from make-out with Tino in my downstairs bathroom?' she hisses.

'I'm so sorry you saw that,' I say.

'I mean I'm hardly shocked,' Lottie says. 'I guessed when I saw you together in the park. I mean, you talk about him *all* the time, do you know that? To be honest, I don't care on Shelby's behalf – she wasn't interested in him in the slightest and God knows, the poor man deserves some attention – but Bernard? It's just not on, Freya.'

'I'm sorry,' I say. 'I didn't mean to upset you.'

'Don't apologise to me. It's not *me* you're cheating on. Although it's upsetting you didn't feel you could tell me. How long have we been friends?'

'I know, but I could hardly say, "Hey Lottie, I'm about to shag your sister's husband", could I?'

'Why not? She was doing it with Max!'

I sigh. 'I'm so sorry, Lottie.'

She holds up her hand, the universal stop sign. 'You know what? It doesn't matter. I'm past caring.'

'I don't want to lose you,' I simper.

'You're not going to,' she says testily.

'I have feelings for him,' I tell her.

'No.' She shakes her head. 'I don't want to hear about this, Freya. Not today. Don't make today about you. Today is about my sister.'

'I'm sorry,' I say for the third time. 'Can we just do the dishes and not talk about it then?'

She shrugs. 'Help me get some more glasses down. We've run out and there are some spares in the top cupboard.'

I climb up the wooden stepladder obediently and pass Lottie one long-stemmed wine glass after another. Then she looks up at me and says, 'End it, Freya. For Bernard's sake. He is a good man.'

I nod, even though I know I can't and I won't.

She reaches for the glass I'm handing her. Our fingers meet on the crystal stem at the same time, but Lottie doesn't let go. There, on the rim, is a lipstick print. Fuchsia, made from unmistakably plump lips. Shelby's colour, Shelby's lips.

Lottie touches her own lips. 'Shelby,' she whispers on an inhale of breath.

The wine glass drops into the Butler sink, where it smashes into four, neat pieces.

'Lottie?' Piers comes running and Lottie falls into him and sobs. He nods to me to indicate I should leave and so I retreat to the fireplace and stand awkwardly between my husband and my lover.

I find Lottie outside half an hour later. The garden is fragrant with the start of spring. Sunlight floods across the fountain, like specks of glitter being twisted between the fingers of whatever god exists, sprinkled onto this idyllic, peaceful spot in the world. I hadn't realised how claustrophobic I felt inside until I am out here, in the fresh air.

Lottie hears me approach but doesn't turn around.

'It's beautiful in summer.' She stares straight ahead.

'It's beautiful *now*,' I say.

'Carole tells me you suspected something was going on between Shelby and Max,' she says, still without turning. 'How did you know?'

'I saw them at Esperance Motors on the night of cheese and wine at yours. They were together, I saw them kiss. I didn't tell you.'

'Wow, it seems like there's a lot you're not telling me.'
She turns to face me.

'I didn't mention it because you were anxious as all hell
that night, Lottie.'

'But you told Carole?'

'She asked me and I couldn't lie.'

'Carole's told me before that Max has no money,' says
Lottie. 'He's completely reliant on Carole financially. That
house belongs to her parents and Max and Carole never
bought them out, they just vacated for Carole and Max to
move in when they got married.'

'So?'

'Think about it,' says Lottie. 'He's worked for Graham
Parkes for twelve years and has never been promoted,
except for recently, but earns a ton of cash. More and
more cash every year. Isn't that weird? He has the cushiest
gig ever. And he got to have my sister on the side.'

Lottie's eyes fill with tears. 'I think he panicked when he
knew she had rumbled them. He thought he would lose it
all, and he was going to end up rich if it killed him. Or he
killed someone else.'

I watch a butterfly skitter past us and up towards the
fancy fretwork of the white exterior of the home. A moment
later, it comes back, its wings vibrant with orange, the colour of flame, and I wonder, is this Shelby stopping by, like
the lipstick on the glass.

'Carole did tell me at cheese and wine that she'd cut
him off if he did anything with Shelby, but that doesn't
exactly confirm Max is guilty,' I say.

Lottie turns towards the bi-fold doors. Inside the house, Max is deep in conversation with Bernard by the fireplace. He has his back towards the photo on the easel, as though he can't bear to look at Shelby, to be reminded of her striking beauty. I scan his body for signs of guilt. Would a grieving man put his hand in his pocket like that? Would a grieving man bow his head so low and stare at his shoes, or is that the behaviour of a guilty one? I just don't know. But what I do know is that I've known this man since school and I've never once seen him acting violently. But then again, money does strange things to people, doesn't it? It bends their morals, makes them malleable.

'Think about it,' Lottie says. 'Shelby would have threatened all sorts if he'd tried to break it off. You know what she was like. I mean, she walked into the ocean twenty years ago because she wanted to make him pay for flirting with Carole. She wouldn't have let him go. She would have killed him first.'

She takes a breath and continues. 'The fact is, someone did it, and it's likely to be someone she knew. I know where I'm putting my money. And I'll bet Carole has her suspicions, too. She knows more than anyone that the only thing Max really loves is money. Shelby at least had the hope he was in love with her, but Carole just has to put up with the fact that the man she loves only ever wanted her cash.'

Strangely, my heart hurts for Shelby. I wonder, for a second, if she was a victim in life, too.

'Do you think Max loved her?' I ask. 'Shelby, I mean.'

'Maybe.' Lottie shrugs. 'But he loves money more than he's ever loved any woman. I'm sure of that.'

She pulls out a packet of menthol cigarettes. 'I haven't smoked for years, but do you know what? Today I feel like it!' She lights a cigarette with a shaky hand and offers the pack to me.

'Would you believe, I found these stashed in my own kitchen? Behind the compost bin!'

I feign shock about Carole's fag stash and take one out of the packet she's offering me. It's not a white flag, but it's close enough. We stand in silence for a moment.

'Will you talk to the police about it?' I ask. 'About Max?'

'You bet I will,' says Lottie, a picture of calm. She turns to me. 'Max might be smart, but he's not indestructible. If he killed her . . .' Her eyes fill with tears. 'If he did it, he won't get away with it.'

I put my arm around my friend, and we turn to walk back to the house. I watch the scene in front of me through the glass of the oversized bi-fold doors. Tino nods earnestly as he chats to Bernard, which makes me feel decidedly on edge; Marella sweeps effortlessly around the room with a silver tray of vegan quiches on one arm, like she has become accustomed to life in Lottie's palatial abode, like she fits in. And then there is Max with his grey pallor and hooded eyes, staring at his shoes. Maybe it's because of the photo, but again it feels for a moment as if Shelby is present, watching us all, and waiting for the person who really did it to trip themselves up.

Chapter Twenty-Five
Shelby

Before

Dying has turned me into an even bigger celebrity. None of them can take their eyes off me at the end of school formal. I catch Kylie Baker staring at me as I walk in through the swing doors of the school hall in my second hand black cocktail dress.

'Wanna take a picture?' I look her dead in the eyes.

Kylie's face flushes red. 'Sorry Shelby,' she says and stares at her ugly clutch bag.

On the stage Mr Flynn taps the mic and makes a little speech to welcome everyone. He says, 'I'd also like to send our warmest regards to Shelby Brennan. We're glad you are feeling better, Shelby.'

Theo Alexandrou shouts out, 'Better? She was dead!'

'Dead hot,' sniggers Jimmy Riley.

I give him the finger.

The big girl from the beach with the dyed red hair and a nose ring gets riled up. 'Have some respect,' she hisses at Jimmy and his crew, as if I need someone to defend me.

'Chill out, Maz,' says Jimmy.

'Well, I've risen now, haven't I? So you can all get stuffed,' I snap. It still hurts my ribs to talk too loudly. My head buzzes from the noise of it all, the crowds and the voices. It's as if I'm trapped in a cage and people are staring in, waiting to see what I will do next.

Mr Flynn says, 'Okay, settle down everyone.'

I already feel like I need air, so edge myself backwards towards the doors. That's when the girl with the nose ring taps me on the shoulder. 'I've been thinking about you all weekend,' she says, which is so creepy. 'Have you been okay?'

'Fine,' I say, and the way I say it is like, 'Do I even know you?'

She knows that's what I'm thinking, because she says, 'I was there last weekend. I put the towels over you,' she says. 'You've been through a lot.'

'Yeah,' I say. 'Thanks.' I take a few steps further back. I don't like her in my space.

'If you ever want to talk, I'm a good listener,' she offers.

'I have enough mates, so no thanks,' I say, and her smile drops. She lollops away crestfallen as Eminem's 'My Name Is' starts to blare out of the hall speakers, and stands alone in the corner of the hall.

Lottie scurries up to me in her long, bottle-green velvet dress which has about as much sex appeal as a history text book.

'You okay?' she asks.

'Why does everyone keep asking me that?'

She shrugs. 'Just checking.' She nods at Nose Ring. 'What did Maz want?'

'Nothing much. She was there at the beach that night and now she wants to be my best friend or something.'

Latto appears. He wraps his arms around my waist from behind and kisses me. 'Maybe she fancies you.'

'She did have a good gawp at my tits on the beach.'

My breasts, exposed to everyone. Johnny Turretson finally getting to cop a feel.

Later, Nose Ring walks into the bathrooms while I'm there and I ignore her, although I notice in the mirror that when she walks into the stall, someone has stuck a Post It note on the back of her dress that says, 'Lesbo'. Part of me wants to tell her it's there, and I almost do, but I don't want her getting ideas about us being friends, so I don't bother.

What I do instead is I tell Kayla Sanders that Fat Maz is gay. I tell her that she gawped at me, on the beach. Like, properly stared. I don't know exactly why I do it – perhaps it's to take the attention off me and my near-death drama. To give them all something else to talk about. I try to forget about it after that and just drink and dance. I let Max kiss me for ages in front of everyone for the whole of 'I Want It That Way', because so what if everyone's watching?

At the end of the night when I'm waiting for Max with a cigarette on the front steps, Maz walks right up to me and gets in my face.

'Did you tell everyone I'm gay?' she asks.

I don't even look at her. 'Why would I bother to do that?' It's not a lie. I didn't tell everyone, just Kayla, and I can't help it if Kayla has a massive gob on her, can I?

'Kevin Besser said you told Kayla Sanders I like girls.'

She's got her hands on her hips now and she's talking really loudly. A small crowd begins to gather around us. It emboldens me.

'Well, you do though, don't you?' I shrug.

'I helped you last Saturday night, Shelby,' Maz says, and her face is all blotchy and red because she's angry. 'I prayed for you and you haven't even asked my name.'

'That's because I know it.'

'What is it?'

'Marion.'

'No, not Marion. It's *Maz*. Maz Wright,' she says. 'I'm into Pink, sci-fi novels and boys – not girls. Although if I was into girls, it would be absolutely nothing to do with you.'

'I don't really give a shit . . .' I begin, but she's warmed up now.

'I might not be as "cool" as you,' she uses her fingers to make quotation marks, 'or as pretty, but I sure as hell don't deserve to be abused by you for being kind. I helped save your *life*, Shelby, and you treat me like I'm a piece of crap?'

I don't really know what to say because I'm not used to people standing up to me, so I sort of stare her down nonchalantly with my eyebrows raised, until she shakes her head and mutters 'unbelievable' and turns her back on me.

'Whatever *Marion*,' I say and Leila O'Hara and Millie Yang from maths start to laugh. 'Get stuffed.'

And that's it. I have socially annihilated her, whatever her name is. Just like that.

I get the guilts when we're walking home and when Latto pokes me with his finger and says, 'Cheer up, babe,' I ignore him. I can't stop thinking about how she'd said, 'I might not be as pretty as you, but I don't deserve to be abused for being kind,' and the only word I can use to describe how I feel – and it's an unfamiliar sensation – is shame. I was a total bitch and the thing is, I couldn't help myself.

Instead of going straight home, we go to the dunes together, to our place. I don't tell Latto I'm nervous about being near the ocean again, but he senses it when I grip hold of his hand as we rise up to the peak of the sand hills and the ocean looms, fearsome, beyond.

'You okay?' he asks, and I nod.

'Really, how are you, after what happened?' We sit side by side. He doesn't try to sexy-kiss me, or get his hand up my dress like usual. Instead, he brushes my hair behind my ear and the intimacy of the gesture takes me by surprise.

I almost tell him, 'fine,' but with Latto it is different. He knows me, he can see right into my soul. He knows me even better than Lottie thinks she does. Still, telling him this is like taking off my clothes and walking down the freeway. It's the same sense of vulnerability I felt when Dad died.

'Not great,' I say. 'Too bad everyone's spent the night reminding me about it.'

Latto lights up a cigarette. 'I thought you were dead for sure.'

'Were you scared?'

'Course I was.'

'Good job lightning doesn't strike twice, hey?'

He sits up to exhale his smoke. It spurts out like the dirty fumes from an exhaust pipe before dissolving into the ocean breeze.

'Why'd you do it, Shelby?' he says. 'Why did you walk into the water?'

'I don't know,' I tell him.

'You can't swim.'

'I know.'

We sit in silence, save for the waves and the seagulls squawking as they chase one another across the surf.

'Did you want to off yourself?'

'No, that wasn't it.'

'Was it to do with me talking to Carole Parkes?'

I don't say anything, just twist a blade of marram grass between my fingers. Sea grass. It feels soft to the touch, even though it grows in the most arid of conditions. The toughest grass you'll ever see.

'Maybe,' I say. 'I was pissed off.'

'What the hell, Shelby?' He runs his hand through his hair, which is slowly growing back, offering the very slightest twist of the golden curls that lie beneath. 'I wouldn't go with her if you paid me. Couldn't afford it! I just get on with Seb, that's all. Plus, Cam asked me to ask her if she wanted to buy some more weed. He told me to sweeten her up, if she happened to come along. You know, to see if some of her mates wanted to get weed, too. He needs some more punters up this end of town. *That's* why I was talking to her.'

'Okay.' I shrug.

'It's late,' says Latto. 'We should go.' We get up and start walking to the clearing in silence.

'So you don't wanna screw her then?' I ask as we walk between the trees.

'No!' he says.

'Do you think she's hot?'

He stops by a stately fig and leans against it. 'She's not a dog, but like I said, she's too rich for my blood. Anyway, it doesn't matter what she looks like, because I love you,' he says casually, even though it's the first time.

'I love you too, Max,' I say. And I mean it. He's the only guy who gets me, the only guy I'll ever want. I might only be seventeen, but I know it.

He grins, a broad one that swallows his whole face.

'Max, and not Latto?'

'Max when I'm being serious.'

He kisses me long and deep. 'You and me Shelby, always, okay? I'm gonna get us out of Shivers Beach and one day we'll live here, in this town, and we'll be rolling in cash with a ton of kids. Just you watch.'

'In Esperance?' I laugh. 'Yeah, right!'

'Why not?' he says. He is serious. 'Give me one reason.'

'You'd need to win the Lotto first.'

'It's got to be easier than that,' he says, taking a penknife out of his pocket.

'Since when do you have a penknife?' I ask.

He laughs. 'I always carry one. You never know when you might need one – like now.'

He lifts his hand and carves our initials ML & SB into the trunk of the fig tree, slow and steady. Then he outlines the letters with a heart.

'That's so cringey,' I laugh, but my heart feels full.

We get our exam results six weeks later and that's when everything starts to go to shit. The letters come through the post. Lottie scoops hers out of our rusty letterbox and

tears open the envelope. I leave mine on the kitchen counter while I eat a bacon sandwich, which just about sums
up my give-a-shit factor. I get a TER score of 50, while
Lottie gets 74. Latto aces it, with 97, which is the highest
result any kid at Shivers Beach High School has ever got.
They put a photo of him in the paper and he almost dies
of embarrassment.

'You still stoked about your results?' I ask him as we
sit in a booth at KFC in Shivers about a week later. He's
quiet and sort of nervous, like he's forgotten how to talk
to me.

'Course,' he says. 'Your food okay?'

'It's KFC. Tastes the same as it always does,' I say.
'You're acting weird.'

He takes my hand. 'I need to talk to you,' he says, 'about
Carole Parkes.'

My heart stops. 'What about her?'

'Her dad's offered me a job.'

I look up. 'He's what?'

'He's offered me a job.'

'Doing what? Like, gardening or something?'

He laughs. 'No, you dope.'

'What job then?'

'Just listen, would you?' He's swapped 'ya' for 'you', like
he's trying to be posh. 'Her dad runs a venture capital business in the City and he heard about my results, and that,
you know, I'm good at maths.' He has grown six inches
taller. 'He's been looking for an intern at his company, so
he called this morning and asked if I was keen. I told him
dead set I was! Graham Parkes, he's called. He wants *me*

in his company, as soon as I can start. I'm gonna get paid a shitload *and* get travel expenses. I have to smarten up though, y'know, borrow a suit and get my hair tidied up and stuff.'

The room spins around me and everything is a blur.

'How did he know about your results . . . ?'

Latto sighs. 'How would I know? I guess he read the paper. Aren't you pleased?'

'Sure.' I shrug. 'It just seems too good to be true. What about uni?'

'Nah, this is a much better opportunity. I'm not gonna earn cash at uni, am I? My old man agrees. This is the fast track to getting rich. Have you seen their house?'

'You know I've seen it.'

'Then you can see it's a no-brainer!'

'Yeah, but surely it's not just about the money?'

'Isn't that why people *go* to university? So they have good earning potential? This puts me on the fast track.'

'As an *intern*! You're hardly a member of the board yet, are you?'

'Thanks for being pleased for me.'

But how can I be pleased? I don't want him getting close to her. *Closer.*

'I *am* pleased, Latto,' I lie. 'I just—'

'Better start calling me Max now,' he interrupts. 'I'm going up in the world, babe. I told you it would come together and it has. Don't you trust me?'

'Yeah, of course . . .' I twist the end of my ponytail around my forefinger. Everything is changing and I don't like it.

'Shelby, listen to me: this is our ticket out of here. Me and you. Out of this hellhole and somewhere with prospects.'

I'm pretty sure he means Esperance, and, even though he's included me in his grand plan, there is something about the way he is acting that unsettles me. I could compete with another girl because of the way I look, but I don't know if I can compete with the lifestyle, with the pot of gold he's searching for.

'Chillax,' he says. 'Nothing will change. It's not like I'm going to up and move to Esperance! Not yet.'

Not yet.

But it does change. Max (the boyfriend formerly known as Latto) calls me at lunchtime on the Friday of his first week at his new job.

'I can't see you tonight,' he tells me while he chews on something indeterminate on the other end of the line. 'Graham wants to take us out for a slap-up dinner as a first week pat on the back.'

'Who's "us"?' I ask.

'Dunno, a couple of the boys from the team, I guess. I'll come round first thing in the morning tomorrow.'

'Sure,' I say.

He doesn't show until five the following afternoon. 'Sorry babe,' he says. 'But I got trashed last night. Graham took us to this *unreal* place by the harbour. The bill was six hundred bucks and he got out his black Amex, and paid it, just like that!'

I pull on a jumper over my T-shirt and we walk to the bus stop to the City, a route we've done a thousand times, but somehow, my hand doesn't fit into his as easily as it usually does. He seems taller and I have shrunk.

'Where are we going?' I ask.

'You'll see!'

I don't ask anything else, because I don't care where we are going, as long as I'm with him.

Darling Harbour is packed when we arrive, hundreds of people dressed in going-out clothes, headed towards the PLAYD cinema. 'Are we going there?'

'Yep, surprise!' Max grins. 'Tickets to the premier of *Cast Away*!'

I look around at the throng of people headed towards a thick red carpet lining the route to the doors of the cinema. 'It's amazing,' I say. 'But I thought we were going to sit and smoke somewhere. I would have dressed up in something decent . . .'

'You look great, don't worry.'

'How did you even get tickets?'

'Graham's on the board at PLAYD.' He shrugs.

'Wow,' I say. I'm feeling a bit out of place but I decide to roll with it. I take Max's hand and he leans down and kisses me. When we move apart, I look up and she is in front of us. Carole. She is in a bottle-green sequinned mini dress, her yellow hair loose, legs tanned.

'Max!' she squeals. 'Two nights in a row. Daddy said you were coming!' She kisses him on both cheeks, the rich way.

Two nights in a row?

'Oh, hi,' she says and looks down at me in my thongs. 'Shelley, isn't it?'

'Shelby,' I say. 'I think you know that.'

She smiles patronisingly. 'Yes, Shelby, that's it. Sorry!'

Max looks uncomfortable.

'I felt *so* bad about what happened to you in the water after exams,' Carole says it in a baby voice, feigns concern. 'We were all so worried about you. Are you okay?'

'I'm good,' I say, stony-faced. I don't like the way she is talking about it.

'It couldn't have been easy having so many people see you like that.'

'I don't really give a shit,' I say. 'Should I?'

Max tightens his grip on my hand. It's a warning not to kick off.

'Of course not,' Carole says. 'I'm just glad you're all right now. The water can be so scary if you can't swim.'

She turns away from me to Max. 'It was so good to hang out last night! Such fun.'

Max bristles. 'It certainly was,' he says, like he's had elocution lessons. 'Please thank your father for me.'

'I will.' She smiles and turns. 'Ciao!'

Max clears his throat and pulls me along.

'You didn't tell me she was out with you last night,' I say, and I hate myself as soon as it's out because it makes me sound needy.

'You didn't ask,' he shrugs. 'Anyway, why does it matter?'

'It matters because she wants you to fuck her, and something tells me daddy's little girl always gets what she wants.'

'Are you saying she made Graham employ me because she fancies me?'

'I bet she was the one who suggested it.'

'You're damn right she did, because she heard about my exam results. I *earned* this job, Shelby. This wasn't a favour because some chick has the hots for me!'

'So you're admitting she's after you?'

'Yes. No. I don't know!'

I turn to leave.

'Oh, come on, Shelby. Don't have a strop. Come watch the film.'

'Get stuffed,' I say and turn on my heel towards the bus stop.

It's only later, as I climb into bed to the gentle sound of Lottie's snoring, that I realise Carole must only have known that I can't swim because Max told her.

Max doesn't call the next day and it eats at me. He calls on the second day and says, 'I thought you needed some time to calm down', which winds me up massively because I'm not the one in the wrong.

'Don't call me again,' I snap and hang up.

By the end of the week, I don't care who's in the right and who's in the wrong because I just want to touch him. It's been five days – the longest we've gone without seeing one another – and so I swallow my pride and message him.

We meet at the beach. 'Look at the moon,' I say as we walk along the sand. 'It's huge, lights up the whole beach.'

'Uh-huh.'

He stares ahead and walks as if he's in a trance, arms hanging loosely by his sides. Occasionally, he kicks the sand. When we reach the rocks, he says it.

'I think we should break up.'

I feel the blood drain from me. My head feels light.

'What?' It comes out as a whisper.

'Break up,' he says.

'It was only a stupid fight! You wanna break up over that?'

'No, I don't mean *really* break up,' he says. 'I mean, we should fake it.'

I stare at him. I don't understand.

'Hear me out.' He sits me down on the black, volcanic crop that's blanketed with oyster shells, holds me by the shoulders and looks deep into my eyes. 'It'd be a temporary break-up, and it wouldn't be real. Look, I reckon I can get a leg up at the company, earn more money,' he says, 'if I go on a couple of dates with Carole.'

My gut twists. 'Are you serious?'

'Listen to me. We'll "break up" for a while in public, and I'll go out with Carole for a bit. I'll get in with Graham, you know, go out on the yacht, go to a few dinners, that kind of thing. Then when it fades with Carole, which it will, we'll get back together, you and me.'

'No, this is insane. Why bother?'

'Didn't you hear me, Shelbs? Money. For *us*. Why else? If we want to end up in Esperance, do well for ourselves, then we have to make sacrifices!'

'Like screwing Carole Parkes?'

He doesn't look at me. 'I wouldn't screw her,' he says. 'I'm talking short term. She'd get bored of me, it'd die a natural death, and then you and me will get back together.'

I look out to sea, try to take it in. Think of us, on this beach, just weeks ago, Max at the edge of the bonfire with

Carole, laughing, her tucking her hair behind her ear. Him flipping the lid off a bottle of cider and handing it to her. What is he saying? Does he want us both? Is he letting me down gently? The thoughts dart about my head like dust motes in the sun, but then I think of the things he says to me when we make love and I know he is mine. How could he not be?

'She'll think you left me for her.'

'Nah, we'll say it was mutual.'

'She'll know.'

'Who cares? It doesn't matter what she thinks, 'cos *we'll* know the truth. Think of the potential of all of this. The *money.*'

I want to tell him that I don't care about the money. That I would live in Shivers Beach until the day I died if it meant he was with me, always, but I don't. Instead, I say what Shelby Brennan is expected to say: 'Whatever. Sounds like fun.' I straighten my back and swallow the lump that's lodged in my throat.

Max smiles. 'That's my girl! Think of where we're headed, Shelbs!' He kisses me lightly on the lips and it feels okay because he is proud of me. 'No one's ever coming between us in the long run. Look, I'll prove it. Give me your wrist.'

He takes out the penknife he carries everywhere, with its little scalpel-like blade and picks up my wrist. In the soft flesh below the curve of my palm, he carves the letter M like he did in the tree. It stings like hell. The wound oozes blood and he picks up my hand and sucks on the flesh. He looks me in the eye as he does it.

'Till death us do part,' he says.

It's like marriage, but it is not. The same, but different. Then he turns over his own wrist and presses the knife to his flesh. He carves an S shape, taking care to make the top half the perfect curve. When he has finished, he shows me his wrist. The bottom of the S barely bleeds, it is little more than a cat scratch, but the top half oozes blood, and I can't help thinking as I look at it, that the top-heavy bleeding makes it look more like the letter C.

At Kayla Sanders' birthday party at Shivers Beach Surf Club the following week, I pretend I'm good with breaking up with Latto.

'Aren't you gutted?' Janice Lee asks as she slathers on copper-coloured lipstick. 'Thought it was serious.'

'Ran its course,' I say. 'He's a bit of a dickhead really.'

'Shame.' She studies my face. 'I heard he's with that blonde snob from Arlingford Ladies, now.'

'Really Janice?' I snap. 'And why are you so interested in Max Latimer, exactly?'

Janice stutters. 'Um.' Her eyes dart towards Kayla. Kayla shrugs and does an 'eek' face.

'I didn't mean anything by it, Shelby. Honest,' she says and takes a gulp of her vodka tonic.

I see Freya and Lottie at a table on the other side of the room and make my way towards them.

'Hi Shelby,' Freya says.

'Hi,' I tell her.

'Thought I'd come back and see the old crew,' she says, like she thinks I care.

'What was Janice Lee on about?' Lottie asks. 'Looks like you spooked her.'

'She was just sticking her nose in, as usual.'

'Asking about your break-up with Max?' Lottie suggests.

'If you must know, she was asking about him and Carole Parkes.'

'Well,' Lottie says, 'Max has always liked money.'

'Oh shut up, Lottie, it was a mutual decision, okay?' I snap. The insecurity eats at my guts like acid, but then I touch my wrist, the place where Max carved our initials, and the knots go away. 'I'm going to the bar.'

I try to remember how to put one foot in front of the other, but for some reason I can't seem to remember how to do that basic thing I've been doing since I was ten months old. At the bar, Candice Aitken and Sylvie Wills step aside to give me space – it's just something people do around me. I don't thank them, just lean forward to order a red wine and add to Kayla's dad's bar tab. Its warmth temporarily numbs the aching sensation at the back of my throat. I miss Max. I miss him so much.

Just as I'm turning back towards the party, Fat Maz walks past. She is wearing a black 1950s-style prom dress with white polka dots. Her hair is bright red and she's paired the dress with maroon Doc Martens over red tights. As she passes, she knocks my elbow and red wine leaps from the glass and slides down my wrist into the crevice of Max's initial. The wound hasn't healed yet and it stings like acid. I jump back and our eyes meet: mine cold, hers apologetic. She holds her hand up, asking for a stalemate.

'Watch it, *Marion*,' I snap, seeing the hope drain from her eyes, and presumably all hope for humanity too, if the girl she saved from drowning can't even be nice to her. The guilt wells up but if I'm nice to her, or she's nice to me, I'll cry. 'Get the hell out of my way.'

She eyeballs me, her wide, welcoming pupils narrowed to pins. She is not scared of me like everyone else. She takes a step forward so her face is an inch from mine. She smells of CK One, of hair spray and cheese and onion crisps.

'Like I've told you before, my name's not Marion, it's Maz. Got that?' She taps her temple with her finger. 'Maz, as in Marella. Not Marion or "Fat Maz" as your dick of a boyfriend calls me . . .'

I flinch.

'Who the hell do you think you are to treat me like dirt? Do you even *know* me?' She moves in even closer. I'm aware in my peripheral vision that Janice and Kayla are watching the exchange, but I stay rigid, on the spot. I get the weirdest nervous compulsion to laugh, it happens to me sometimes, and I do it, just at that moment. I laugh in her face.

'You know what, Shelby? You are vile,' she cries. 'If I'd have known just *how* vile when I was trying to save your life, then I would have left you there to rot. You know everyone is giving me shit at school because of you? Because you told everyone I was staring at your tits when I was actually trying to stop you from dying!'

She's crying but I'm still smiling. I can't make myself stop. No one has ever confronted me like this and my face does not know how to react. It's a smile that's one step away from a sob.

'I hate you, Shelby Brennan!' she sobs. 'You're a heartless bitch!'

Then she turns on her ugly Doc Martens and runs off, and Shane Gibson shouts out 'dyke' after her.

I don't know how I get back to Lottie without collapsing, because my whole body is wracked with the shakes, but somehow I do. Lottie can tell I'm messed up – I can see by the way her left eyebrow twitches – but she ignores me and carries on talking to Freya.

It's a boy called Saxon who eventually comes to the rescue, probably because he's always wanted to get it on with me.

'Hey Shelby, you okay? Let's go outside for a smoke,' Saxon says, and he pulls me out of the stifling room and through the double doors into the air, where I can finally breathe. I imagine it's Max hauling me out, and I let myself be led. Later I give Saxon a hand job behind the lifeguard station, just because I know it will get back to Max and I want to hurt him as much as this whole shitshow is hurting me.

SUNDAY

Chapter Twenty-Six
Lottie

The late afternoon sun beats down on the last of the spring hydrangeas, and I find myself filled with something that feels like hope as I cradle my coffee in the back garden. My anxiety has all but gone. It is odd, but it is almost as if, now the worst has happened, my brain has let go of the niggling fear that it might. Initial grief trumps every human emotion – the happiness, the anger, the worry – and anaesthetises it. And while I still grieve, for my last immediate family member, for the sibling with whom I shared a womb, there remains hope. I have realised my grit. I am still here, and where there is life there is hope – and there *is* life!

Marella knocks on the patio doors and waves. She's been inside the house all morning helping to clean up, to empty the dishwasher and shift furniture back into place, to clean fingerprints off the French windows and spray disinfectant on the kitchen bench. Now she is done, she will return to her little apartment on the border of Esperance and Mooney Waters.

I jump up and go inside.

Marella hands me my Sass & Bide maternity dress, folded and washed in my own machine. She obviously didn't realise it was meant to be dry-cleaned. 'Thank you so much for the loan of the outfit,' she says.

'No, Marella, thank *you*. You have been wonderful,' I say. There's no need to mention the dress – not after everything she has done to help. 'It's been lovely having you here.'

She suddenly slaps her forehead with her palm and points to the occasional table in the far left corner of the living room. 'Oh no, look! I've missed some glasses. I'll just give them a quick wash and dry and then get out of your hair.'

'It's okay, really. I'll do it later. Thank you for everything, Marella.'

I'm keen for her to leave now – the house has been filled with visitors since Shelby died and I just want to get back to normal. I want to be alone with Piers so that we can dissect everything that has happened, so we can flop back on the sofa and rest our feet. I am utterly exhausted.

'Where is Piers?' she asks.

'Upstairs, getting changed, I think.'

Marella looks at her feet, awkward. 'Um . . .' She shuffles her weight onto the other side. 'I just wanted to mention something before I go.'

It occurs to me she has been looking at me oddly since she arrived, keen to divulge something.

'It's probably nothing . . .' she says.

'Go on.' I feel the slight itch of impatience.

'It's just that before Shelby died . . .' She stops. The impatience turns to dread for some reason.

'What is it?' I feel my heart rate quicken.

'It's just before she . . .' Marella begins. 'Before she um . . .'

'Oh for God's sake, just spit it out, Marella!' I snap.

Marella flinches and my hand flies to my mouth. 'Oh goodness,' I say. 'I am so sorry. I didn't mean to snap. I'm just so emotional . . .'

Marella smiles and takes my hand. 'It's really okay,' she says. 'You're under so much pressure, I get it. And I wasn't exactly being succinct. Let me start again.'

She takes a slow inhale.

'You see before she died, I spoke to her . . .'

Piers appears in the kitchen and both our eyes snap up. Marella jumps and takes a step back.

'Would you like me to give you a lift anywhere, Marella?' he asks, oblivious.

'It's fine,' Marella responds with a tight smile. 'I can walk home.'

'What were you going to tell me about Shelby?' I glance at Piers, who is studying his phone with a frown. 'You said you'd spoken to her right before she *passed*?'

Piers looks up from his screen. 'You chatted to Shelby?'

'Oh, it's nothing important,' Marella says, but she does not look Piers in the eye. 'It was just in passing, that's all. She seemed happy, that's all. I just wanted to tell you.'

I wonder if I should be concerned, if there is something more to this, but then I dismiss it. Why would Marella have spoken to Shelby about anything other than the time of day? And why wouldn't she tell Piers if it even *was* something more? But I don't ask. I don't want to push her. She would tell me if it was something important.

'Thanks for letting me know,' I tell her. 'It really is a comfort. And of course thank you for everything you have done over the last couple of days. You are a true friend.

Please do take some flowers with you – there are so many and I can't keep them all myself.'

Marella smiles at me. 'I will,' she says. 'For the shop.' She gathers up the contents of two vases, wraps the stems in a plastic shopping bag she drags from her handbag, and heads towards the front door. Piers opens it for her.

'Thanks,' she mumbles and I feel a sigh of relief as he shuts it behind her.

We are finally alone, and Piers opens his arms. I obediently fall in.

'Thank God that's over,' he says. 'I have been so proud of you these last couple of days, my darling. You've held it together beautifully. You are so strong. The great pretender.'

I free myself from Piers' arms and look up at him, pleased. Even as the mourning sister, I have pleased my husband. And he is right – I *have* done well. I have said goodbye to my sister in style. I have given her the send-off she would have wanted, and, when her body is finally released to us, we will do the last formality, the burial, privately, as a family.

'But now it is over, we need to talk about the money,' Piers says and I feel the familiar sense of dread. The money problems haven't died with Shelby. Our code-breaker is dead. How will we access the money without her? The fact is, Shelby's death means we will have to find a new way to recoup our losses.

'Yes,' I sigh. 'We do.' There is so much to talk about, so much to do. Like going through Shelby's personal items, her clothes. Tino has agreed I should be the one to do it, to give what I want to charity and sell anything that is valuable.

The doorbell makes us jump ten feet apart.

'What's Marella forgotten?' sighs Piers and marches to the door.

But it is not Marella. Instead, an unfamiliar man and woman stand either side of the welcome mat.

'Dr and Mrs Denton, hello,' says the man. He is short and dressed in an ill-fitting suit, with dark brown hair that looks like it belongs on a Lego character. The woman is tall, a redhead with a splattering of freckles and age spots. She offers a warm smile.

'I'm Detective Sergeant Angela Murphy and this is Detective Senior Constable Jason Wu from the homicide squad,' she says. 'I'm sorry to intrude on a Sunday.' She looks around us and inside the house, down the hall, as if we're hiding something inside.

'No problem,' says Piers. 'We've just finished cleaning up after my sister-in-law's wake yesterday. Please do come in.' He steps to the side and gestures with his hand for the two detectives to pass him. 'Please head on through to the living room – it's at the end of the hall.'

The detectives step over the threshold and walk down the hall and we follow them. Piers looks at me and raises an eyebrow.

'You okay?' he mouths and I nod.

Senior Constable Wu looks around the room. 'Nice house,' he says. His eyes settle on the large photo of Shelby on the easel. 'I must say, that is a very striking picture of Mrs Massini.'

'She was very beautiful,' I say.

'Twins, weren't you?' Murphy asks as if she can't quite believe it. Just the smallest difference in DNA to make the older sister entirely more striking than the younger.

I nod. 'Shelby was a few minutes older,' I say, like those combined seconds made all the difference.

'Once again, we are so sorry for your loss,' she says.

Wu steps forward. 'We won't keep you, Mrs and Dr Denton,' he says.

'We wanted to let you know that Mrs Massini's body has been released for burial. The autopsy report has come in – and it's a little surprising actually. Would you like to sit down?'

I glance at Piers.

'What do you mean?' I ask.

DS Murphy regards me suspiciously. 'This information is not for public consumption at the moment, and we are only telling you this because you are the victim's family, but the post-mortem concluded a couple of things. The first was that your sister had sexual intercourse shortly before her death.'

Piers and I look at one another. *Max.*

'With Max Latimer?' I ask.

'We cannot divulge that information, Mrs Denton. I do apologise,' says Murphy. 'Not at this stage in the investigation.'

I nod. I don't need the answer because I know it already. 'What's the second thing? You said there were a couple of things.' I brace myself for more.

'Yes,' says Wu. 'We can tell you with certainty that your sister wasn't killed by asphyxiation, as we originally thought.'

My world caves in all over again.

I look at Piers as if he has the answers I'm so desperately grappling for.

'You mean Shelby wasn't strangled?' Piers asks.

'She was, but that wasn't the cause of her death,' says Murphy.

I can't believe what I'm hearing. I put my hand to my chest to comfort my racing heart.

Piers' eyebrows furrow. 'I don't understand,' he says. 'Not strangled?'

My body begins to shake violently, and Piers takes my hand and squeezes it tight.

'It appears likely the strangulation merely rendered her unconscious,' says Murphy, matter-of-factly. 'The pathologist concluded that the moment of death came later.'

Wu looks directly at me. 'The marks on your sister's head are consistent with her skull smashing against rock,' he says, and everything goes black.

MONDAY

Chapter Twenty-Seven
Carole

Max walks downstairs, carrying his washbag. It gives me a start to see him. He's been respectful of my wishes not to linger inside the family home since he moved outside to the granny flat. He shouldn't need to – the granny flat is a self-contained, two-bedroom cottage, with a fully-equipped kitchen and bathroom, with a little vegetable patch on its very own front lawn. Room enough for a small family. Max had it built soon after we moved in so we could separate from my parents when they visited. He never said as much, but I know that was the reason behind his keenness to add to our portfolio of bedrooms.

'You made me jump,' I say.

'Sorry,' he says, his face painted with an expression that's bordering on pathetic. 'I forgot to take my razor. I didn't realise you were home.'

'It's a Monday morning,' I state, because he knows I'm home on Monday mornings. 'My routine hasn't changed just because we're separated.'

Today I will go to the shops; tomorrow Ryan and the cleaners will come; Wednesday I do Meals on Wheels in Nash Lake – none of that is any different now I have evicted my cheating husband from the family home.

'I don't like that word,' says Max.

'Which one?' I ask, but I know, and it hurts my heart to act this cold.

'Separated,' he says.

I turn away to hide the tears that threaten to form and wait until I hear Max sigh and the screen door that leads to the vast garden click shut.

I am in that peculiar wasteland between anger and sadness. I grieve for the man I have adored since I was a teenager, but I will not take him back after what he did to me with her. I will continue to be civil for my children, because Max is a good father to them. He's always been the cut disinfector, the nit comber, the bike-rider, the joke-maker, the cushion-fort builder. He still is all those things, just without me. And I will learn to live with it, because the truth is, my hatred for Shelby was just as strong as my love for Max – and she's not going to win this particular battle, even from the grave.

I watch him walk down the garden, his head bent low, and part of me wants to run after him and beg him to come back, to just say, 'Let's forget it and move on,' but I am stubborn and I am proud, and I always have been. But more than anything, what example would I be setting Olivia if I took him back? If I showed her that a cheating man deserved to be forgiven? Or to Otto, that it's okay to do the dirty on your spouse?

They come for him in the afternoon, like I always knew they would. They stand at the door with grey, hangdog faces, and solemnly introduce themselves. The same detectives from the scene of Shelby's murder, only with duller eyes this time. No sparkle of a dead body to excite them.

Detective Sergeant Murphy steps forward. She would be quite attractive with a facial peel and a wax strip to the top lip. 'Hello again, Mrs Latimer.'

'Detectives.'

'May we please come in?' she asks.

'Of course.' I smile and lead them into the kitchen. I gesture towards the sofa and return to the kitchen to fill the kettle. My EpiPen has dropped from the small rattan basket it sits in beside the teabags and so I pop it back in its rightful place, just in case. You never know when you might come across a rogue peanut. These two certainly look as though they may put a bag or two away in the squad car.

I switch the kettle on.

'Thanks, but no need,' says Murphy.

'Nonsense!' I reach up to pick out to bone china mugs from the cupboard and a teapot. I can't abide tea that's made in the mug.

'No thank you,' says Murphy, firmly this time. 'We'd just like a quick word with your husband.' This is not a social call.

'Max is in the granny flat at the bottom of the garden,' I tell them.

'Oh?' DS Murphy's right eyebrow shoots up.

'Yes,' I tell them. 'He's. . . painting it.'

'On a work day?'

'He's working from home today.'

Why should I tell them our business? Why do they need to know that I've thrown him out for the affair? Even if it is only as far as the end of the garden where the jasmine trails a scented path to the beach.

The detectives share a look. 'Could you let him know we're here?'

I sigh and get out my phone to ring Max's mobile. I am not the kind of woman who catcalls down the house, and besides, Otto and Olivia are upstairs doing their homework, and I do not want them alerted to the fact there are two rather scruffy-looking detectives in our living room sniffing around their father.

Max answers on the first ring. 'Carole?' he asks hopefully.

'The police are here,' I tell him, matter-of-factly. 'You need to come up to the house.'

I pour the tea from the pot into mugs, and flinch as a drop hits the tender flesh of my wrist. Hannah is usually the afternoon tea-maker, but she's clocked off already today. It's probably for the best, not that she's not discreet.

Max arrives with wet hair.

'Good afternoon,' he says, studying Murphy and Wu as they stand in front of the sofa. 'Won't you sit?'

The detectives ignore him.

'Hello again Mr Latimer,' says Detective Senior Constable Wu. 'You might remember us from the crime scene. The *murder* crime scene?' he clarifies, as if there has been more than one.

Max nods. 'Of course,' he says.

'Been swimming, Mr Latimer?' asks Murphy.

'Showering, actually.'

'You don't shower in the main house?' asks Wu.

'Not on this occasion, mate.' I notice his accent slip in to Shivers Beach speak, as if he's trying to identify with the man and woman who have snubbed our elegant Coco Republic sofa and who were most definitely not born and raised in Esperance. He's trying to be one of them, to tell them, 'I'm just a regular guy, like you!' It's chameleon-like, the way Max slips between the two accents, the two worlds. He's lived in each for almost exactly half of his life.

'As you know,' begins Wu, 'we're investigating the death of Mrs Shelby Massini and we were hoping you would come to the station, voluntarily at this stage, to help us with our inquiries.'

'Surely you don't suspect . . .' I look at Max and back at the detectives. 'Max would never hurt anyone!'

'At this stage, Mrs Latimer, we just have a few questions, and we were hoping your husband would come with us – or follow us in his car. Either works for us.'

'But why? Why Max?' Even I know it's a stupid question. They have to talk to him, just like they have to talk to everyone.

'Mrs Latimer—' begins Wu.

'Are you charging him?' My hands are on my hips.

'Not at this stage,' says Murphy.

'So you're saying you might?'

'It is possible,' says Murphy. 'If we find more evidence that implicates him in the murder of Mrs Massini. But at this stage, as I just said, we are inviting Mr Latimer to talk to us of his own free will, under caution.'

'Caution?' says Max, and I can tell he's rattled by the way his left eyebrow quivers.

'Yes, Mr Latimer. It is procedure,' says Murphy.

'Caution?' I parrot. 'What does that even mean?'

But I know, because I've heard it a hundred times on TV. *You do not have to say anything. But it may harm your defence if you do not mention when questioned something which you later rely on in court.*

'As I said, Mrs Latimer, it's procedure.'

'Don't you need evidence?' I ask. 'And what if you don't find it?'

'Then Mr Latimer would be free to go.' I don't like the way she says 'would'.

'You mean he *will* be free to go.'

'Carole . . .' Max begins.

'If he's an innocent man,' says Murphy, with a faint glint of amusement in her eyes, 'then yes, your husband *will* be free to go.'

I close my eyes, feel the nausea swell in the very pit of my stomach.

'I'll come,' says Max. He looks around him in what I can see is panic. 'I'll just get my wallet and keys.'

He rummages around in the basket on the kitchen bench and then slowly turns.

'I didn't kill her,' he says. 'I may have . . . I may have had *sex* with her that night, but I didn't kill her.'

The pain hurts like a knife in the heart. Wu glances at me.

'My wife knows everything . . .' Max explains.

Murphy and Wu regard Max with impassive expressions. They are not remotely shocked by this revelation, and I realise it's because they already know. Of course they do. Max's DNA would have been all over her. Max knows it too.

'I would never have hurt her,' he says

Murphy holds a hand up. 'I'm sure you didn't, Mr Latimer,' she says. 'Although in our experience, most killers actually deny they are killers, so you'll understand us wanting to proceed with this chat in more a formal location.' Her voice is dripping with sarcasm. 'Just, you know, to clear everything up. Like we said, it's your choice, of course. You will be coming with us voluntarily.'

I've seen the movies. Max is a suspect, just one who's not under arrest. Yet.

'Do I need a lawyer?' he asks.

'It's up to you, Mr Latimer. You can have a lawyer or a support person,' says Wu.

I stand up.

'Not Mrs Latimer though. We don't usually allow . . .'

I turn to Max. 'Shall I call Bernard?' I ask.

Max shakes his head. 'Not yet, darling,' he says and I flinch at the term of endearment. 'I'll let you know if I need him.'

Otto comes down the stairs in his school uniform – grey pants, white shirt and a green and red striped tie.

'Dad?' He looks at Max and then at the officers. 'Who are you?'

'Hi mate.' Wu bends down. 'We're the police and your dad is helping us answer some questions about a crime.'

Max ruffles Otto's hair on the way to the door. 'Maybe next time you can come in the squad car with the lights, kiddo? Right, Detective Sergeant?'

Murphy shoots him a weary 'don't push it' look.

'Okay,' says Otto, unsure. 'I'll see you later, Daddy. To watch *Lego Wars*?'

Max's voice is reed thin. 'Yep. I'll see you later, buddy.'

He walks alongside Wu to the car, while Murphy hangs back. She puts her hand in her pocket and pulls out a white business card. 'Take this, Mrs Latimer,' she says. 'In case you need to talk to me about anything.' The insinuation is slight, but it is there – that I am withholding something that could implicate Max.

'Such as?' I snap, and vow to put it in the bin when she has left.

As soon as the door is closed, I feel a crushing sense of emptiness and I hold out my arms for my son to fall into.

'Why's Daddy going with them?' Otto asks.

'Because he's so important that they need his help to solve a crime.' I hope he can't hear the burning in my throat or see the tears forming.

'Is it to do with Lottie's sister?'

'Yes.'

I try to keep my face neutral, but kids are so perceptive. I watch the car drive away and the tears pool hot against my eyeballs. I'm watching a marriage with love and trust and two babies, but not without its share of complications, disappear down the driveway. Even in death Shelby has stolen him from me. Does that mean she has *won*?

Otto tugs at my hand. 'Mum?' he asks. I barely register him. 'Mum?'

I kneel down to his level and look into his eyes, sniffing back my own emotions and salty tears and forcing them down another route, down the back of my throat like acrid liquor. I can't let my baby boy see the anguish I'm in on account of his father.

'Yes, darling?'

Otto looks at me, his brow creased.

'Dad didn't *do it*, did he? He didn't hurt her?'

I sit back and grip Otto's shoulders, look square into his eyes.

'No,' I tell him, firmly. 'No he did not. And you must not ask me that again, do you understand?'

I will not entertain another option. I have to believe Max is innocent, and even if there is a single per cent of me that has pondered his guilt, I cannot let him go down for Shelby's murder. How would my children ever survive it? How would they ever make it in the world with their father inside a jail cell? They wouldn't! They couldn't! What would people *think*?

'I didn't really think he did,' says Otto, alarmed. 'You believe me, Mum, don't you?'

I pull him in to me and breathe in the scent of his hair, the biscuity smell of his scalp. God I love this boy! And how I love his father, still. Love him and hate him. Want him gone, want him close. See the bad in him but see the good too. Max may have cheated on me with her, he may have lied to me, broken my heart, but I know him. I know he is a good man. I have to believe that. I have to believe it for my children.

Max is not a murderer. Max is not a murderer.

If I say it enough times, maybe I'll start to believe it.

Chapter Twenty-Eight
Shelby

Before

'How's your girlfriend?'

Max and I lie naked in the sand. It is one in the morning, six months after we 'broke up', and the sand is still warm from the intense heat of the day.

'I'm meant to be giving this stuff up,' he says. 'It's not a good look in finance. Plus I've got to stay sharp, you know, for work. Can't have this stuff fuddling my brain.'

He passes the joint to me.

'Nah,' I say. 'I've gone off it.'

Max nods. 'I get it,' he says. 'How's your mum?'

'She still has lung cancer,' I say. The irony is she never smoked. Just spent years breathing in the air from Dad's Marlboro Reds.

'Want me to stub it out?'

'Nah.'

He inhales deeply.

'You didn't answer my question,' I say. 'How's your girlfriend? How's Carole?'

'Don't call her that.'

'What is she then?'

He smiles. 'A means to an end.'

'Oh come on,' I say. 'You must like her a bit.'

He exhales smoke rings, one little puff after another, doesn't answer.

'You done it with her yet?' I ask, my heart fluttering.

'We said we wouldn't talk about it.'

'But I want to know.'

'Just drop it, Shelby, okay? If you must know, we haven't,' he says. I wait for the word 'yet', but it doesn't come.

'Anyway, she's saving herself,' he says.

'What for?'

'For marriage!'

I laugh. 'Bull.'

We stare at the stars in silence. We have met up here every Friday night for the last six months, had sex, told one another how much we love each other. It is three months since Max got promoted from intern to shadow trader on the stock floor, the boss's special mangénue.

'When you think about it, marriage would be the ultimate way to seal the deal.' Max exhales. 'I mean, theoretically if I married her, and then her old man popped his clogs . . . or even if we just *divorced* . . . you and me, we'd be quids in.'

I laugh, because I think he is making a joke.

He turns to me like the idea is just dawning on him. 'It's not a bad plan, Shelbs. I'd be set in the company if I married her. Old mate would promote me to trader for sure. Once I'm at a certain level and I've made a name for myself, I could get out of the marriage and the company and get a slice in the divorce settlement.'

I stare at him, open-mouthed.

'People do it all over the joint. Marry for money, I mean. If I married Carole, I mean not now, but *eventually*, then we'd be set for life.'

My mind flits forward a year, how it would feel walking through Esperance on Max's arm, and Carole seeing us, knowing that he was always mine.

'We could *both* do it,' Max says.

I stare upwards. I can make out Jupiter glowing over-head and see the formation of Orion's Belt. Think of a world outside of Shivers Beach, in a mansion with French shutters and billowing cotton curtains.

'Get married to other people?' I ask, just checking I heard it all correctly. Not just him, but me too. Married to someone who isn't Max. I know then; I understand. Because he wouldn't allow that unless he was sure his plan would work. That it would work out to our advantage, eventually.

Max nods. 'Why does it matter who's married to who?' he says. 'We'll always be together.' He fingers the letter on his wrist. 'We're playing the long game, remember?'

'Sounds messed up to me,' I say.

Max laughs. 'It's all hypothetical, babe. It's not like it's really ever going to happen.'

Lottie and I bury our mother at Shivers Beach Cemetery five months later, and a few weeks after that, Max and Carole announce their engagement.

Lottie creeps into my bedroom on a Saturday morning (we've been upgraded to a bedroom each now we're the only people in the house) and presents the newspaper to me.

'You need to see this,' she says, her face annoyingly grave. Like the undertaker at our mother's funeral.

'Waking me up? This had better be good,' I warn her. I take the paper from her hand, study the page. It takes a few moments to register, to find what my sister wants me to see. And then I see their faces, in black and white. A photo, not bigger than a passport photo really, two heads in close, smiling. Carole looks smug as hell, the cat with the cream. Underneath the photo, their two surnames are hyphenated: PARKES-LATIMER.

The blurb reads: *Graham and Rosemary Parkes of Esperance are thrilled to announce the engagement of their only daughter, Carole Georgina, to Shane 'Max' Latimer, of Mooney Waters . . .*

Of Mooney Waters? It almost makes me laugh. They've even polished his upbringing!

The couple will marry at Esperance Catholic Church on 14 May.

'They look so happy,' says Lottie, then covers her mouth dramatically. 'I didn't mean . . .'

'Whatever,' I tell her. 'I couldn't care less.'

'Are you okay?' She touches my shoulder hesitantly.

I shrug off her hand and turn away. 'Fine. Can you get off my bed?'

'Sure,' she says and gets up and leaves the room.

The first tear trickles down my cheek, hot and angry, forging a path for the others behind it.

In the afternoon, Max calls me.

'I need to see you,' he says.

'Why? What do you need me for when you have her?'

'We talked about this,' he says. 'It didn't come out of the blue.'

I meet him at Mooney Waters this time, at the far end of the beach. The surf is massive; white horses pummel the sand aggressively. Every crash sends a volt of rage up my legs from my toes.

Max pulls me towards him and I resist, but what always happens, happens. I fight until I don't want to any more – and the reason I don't want to is because somehow the idea of losing Max to Carole in the eyes of the law is making me relive my grief about losing my mother. I let myself be held, because I need the comfort.

Max kisses me long and deep, then nestles his head in my hair.

'I miss you,' he says.

I pull away. 'Nice photo in the paper, *Shane*.'

He doesn't look at me.

'Will she be Parkes-Latimer, or just Latimer when you get married?' I ask.

Max sighs, does his hand-through-the-hair thing.

'I don't know,' he says, staring at the sand. 'You know I don't love her. She'll never understand me like you do. We'll never have what you and I have.'

'Then why are you doing it?'

'For us.' He grabs my shoulders. 'The long game.'

'Stop saying that!' I snap.

'But it is, Shelby! Don't you see? We wait it out. We play the game and we get the money and we have a *future*.'

I look to the sea. It has the power to consume me, to drown me, and so does Max. I can't fight either of them, but they both have the potential to end me.

'I don't want to lose you,' Max says. 'Tell me what to do and I'll do it. I don't know any more. I just know I want to make a life for us.'

'By fair means or foul?'

'I guess.'

'Do you love me?' I ask. 'Do you?'

His eyes are red, his face drawn.

'You know I love you, Shelby.'

He means it. He is telling me the truth. He really is doing it for us. I swallow the lump in my throat as if it's phlegm. Why shouldn't we take from her? From Carole? Why the hell not? Even if it's just to see her face when he leaves her for me. I take his hands in mine and I look deep into his eyes. I can do it. I *can*.

'End game,' I say and Max nods.

Max hears the resolve in my voice, my confidence. But it is all an act, because underneath my fragile ribcage, cracked and broken on the beach two years ago, my even more fragile heart no longer feels like it has been merely sliced in two but that it has been finely julienned and scattered in a pan of bubbling oil.

On the eve of the Parkes-Latimer wedding, Max drives to my house in the new silver Mercedes-Benz Graham and Rosemary Parkes have bought him as a wedding gift, a welcome to the family, if you like. He beeps the car shut with a key fob.

'Fancy,' I say, running a finger over the bonnet.

'Don't touch,' he jokes.

I press my finger down harder on the metal. Max smiles.

'Isn't she a beauty? I'll take you for a spin after our holiday.'

He means his honeymoon in Cyprus. But the word sounds too trite to say. I don't like his use of the word 'our' either – as if they are a united front.

'I can't stay long.' Max pushes my hair back, out of my eyes. 'I have the pre-wedding dinner to go to. Also,' he laughs, 'I don't want some bogan to key my car.'

'How long have you got?' Because that's what our relationship is dictated by now – by Carole's schedule. Her plans, her wedding, her rules – the ones that she has imposed on her fiancé, that have increasingly kept him away from me. And it's only going to get harder from tomorrow.

'Half an hour?' Max shuts the front door behind him.

Half an hour with Max before he leaves me to marry Carole. We walk to my bedroom and Max pushes me against the door and kisses me.

'How's it going with him?' he whispers in my ear.

I pull away. 'Fine.'

'What's his name again?'

'You know what his name is,' I say.

'Tino Massini, what a stupid name.'

'It's Italian,' I say. 'He's an Italian stallion.'

'Stallion my arse.'

'Jealous?'

'You bet I am. Sounds like a dickhead.'

'How's your fiancée?'

Max smiles. 'Needy,' he says. 'Stressed out, emotional.'

All the things a bride should be.

'When are you seeing him next?' Max asks.

'Tomorrow,' I say. 'While you're getting married.'

Max sighs, puts his hand up my T-shirt. 'Bet he's all over you like a rash,' he says.

'Mostly.'

'I hate him.' Max puts his hand beneath the waistband of my shorts and my body responds to him. His fingers move like scissors in the moisture that's there.

'Bet he doesn't make you feel like this,' he whispers in my ear. His breath is warm, urgent.

Max is one hundred per cent right; Tino doesn't make me feel like this. No one ever will.

I have been dating Tino for two months now. Tino is from old Italian money in Esperance. His parents came over from Puglia back in the 1950s and worked their way to wealth. He doesn't give a shit that I'm from the rough end of the peninsula – I think he gets off on it, sees me as his diamond in the rough. Loves the look on his school chums' faces when he walks into a bar with me on his arm, loves to see their faces when they ask me, 'So where did you go to school?' and I say, 'Shivers High.'

I never hid it from him, not even the first time we met. Because I guess that first night, I didn't care who he was, or what he thought of me. I wasn't looking for him, even though I knew I needed to meet someone, like Max had. Lottie and I were at the Starlight Bar in Mooney Waters when he sidled up to me at the bar, trying to find an in. He opted for the most obvious.

'Can I buy you a drink?' he asked. Disappointingly unoriginal, but pleasingly attractive.

He was tall – taller than Max, but with similar golden hair, and it tumbled into his eyes when he turned to look at me. His jaw was squarer than Max's, and he was clean-shaven, but there was a strange sort of semi-resemblance there. He felt familiar, somehow. Like Max, but not. Like eating, say, generic chocolate instead of Cadbury's. Or using a rip-off perfume from the markets in Boorie Point, instead of the one from the perfume counter in Hennicks & Douglas.

'No thanks,' I said, knowing he'd ask again.

'Are you sure?'

'Yes.'

'Listen,' he said, and leaned in. 'I'm not doing this for me.'

He placed one hand on his heart and gestured with the other towards a man with brown hair at the bar who was gawping in Lottie and Freya's direction. 'That's my mate Piers,' he said. 'He thinks your friend is gorgeous and wants to talk to her. Can you help? You might be doing her a favour if you let me buy you a drink.'

'Which friend?'

'The light-haired one,' he said, and I realised he meant Lottie.

I looked at him again. He had a rugby shirt on with jeans, and a gold signet ring on his pinky finger, expensively straight teeth: a private-school boy through and through.

'If it helps his cause, I should let you know Piers has great credentials,' he told me. 'He's training to be an obstetrician.'

'And you?'

'Boring technical stuff, for mobile phones.' He smiled. 'We both live in Esperance.'

'Figures,' I said. He looked confused but smiled nonetheless.

'Do you know Esperance?'

Oh yes, I thought as I studied his face, *I have been with Max on every inch of that sand. I know it like I know the lines on my palm, the freckles on my own body.*

'You could say that.'

'What about you?' he asked.

'Shivers Beach.'

I studied his face. It didn't fall. He didn't turn away from me. His top lip did not turn up. He just nodded. 'So why this bar?'

'Why not?'

'Fair enough. So, can I buy you a drink now we're a little better acquainted?'

'No thanks,' I told him again.

'Why not?'

'Because I don't want to be picked up by some entitled private-school boy,' I lied. 'You're coming across as a bit desperate.'

He smiled, bit his lip. 'And you're coming across as rude,' he said. Then he walked away and didn't look at me again, however many times I glanced up and willed him to stare.

That was when I knew I wanted him.

Max lays me down on my single bed in the room I once shared with Lottie.

'I meant it,' he says. 'I love you so much.'

Our moans are more urgent than they have ever been before. When we're done and roll apart, I notice that Max's eyes are wet.

'What am I doing?' he asks. His voice catches. I have never seen him like this before, not even when I died on the beach in Esperance.

He turns to me, holds my face in his hands, wipes my tearful eyes with his thumbs.

'The end game,' I hear myself say again. 'The money, remember?' And it's like we've done a total flip and now I'm the one persuading him.

'I'm not choosing her,' he says. 'You realise that.'

He is not choosing her. He is choosing the money. Money for us, for our future together.

'I know,' I say, even though really, I don't know anything any more.

We dress in silence, the room thick with emotion, with sadness. Max stands on the threshold of my bedroom and we stare at one another for a long time. He goes to leave, but then turns back. He takes my chin in his palm and pulls my face towards him. There is so much tenderness in the touching of our lips that it is almost too much to bear – every emotion of the past and the present combining, a vortex of longing and tenderness and regret. It is a good-bye of sorts, but not. Because it is written in the stars for us both: together until the end, till death do us part.

Max turns and walks down the corridor, and I hold my breath as I listen to his feet on the floorboards and then, finally, hear the front door close. The gentle, expensive hum of his car engine isn't enough to put a damper on the spirits of the black and white fairywrens on the branches of the eucalyptus tree outside my window. They chirp happily as they go about their day, because *their* lives are not tangled in knots. They do not stand on the edge of a sixty-foot cliff with their tiny bodies on the precipice, waiting to fall.

TUESDAY

Chapter Twenty-Nine
Freya

I sit on my front veranda with my morning coffee and watch the lorikeets landing on our state-of-the-art bird house. Bernard knows the distinct difference between his crested tits and his spotted peckers. It is just another stride he's taken into old age – one that's pushed me further away from him and into the arms of Tino.

But it was always going to happen. If I'm honest, I knew I wanted Tino the moment I saw Shelby talking to him at the Starlight Bar in Mooney on the day we met him. Tino was the most striking guy there: strong arms, tanned skin, the delicious curl that fell into his face. He was like an Italian version of Max! Taller, more angular in his features, but similar, nonetheless. Like a Roman god. I remember thinking to myself, *Well, if she doesn't want him, I might have a chance.* But then she decided she *did* want Tino and what Shelby Brennan wanted, Shelby Brennan got.

My phone pings. **Come and see me later tonight?** Tino writes, and I smile.

Love to, I reply.

Things are moving on between us, fast. Constant messages, declarations of desire. He features in my dreams, no longer as Luca, but as himself.

I think back to the night of Shelby's murder, how intense it had been between us. I hadn't wanted romance, or a four-poster bed. I'd simply wanted to be touched by

Shelby Brennan's husband, by the man who had picked me over her. I hadn't realised then how quickly it would turn from desire to affection, but maybe the affection was always there. Maybe we needed one another: two lost souls, destined to be together. Two people in miserable, defunct relationships, drawn together by attraction but also the human desire to be held, supported, wanted. And now I want him in a different way to the way I wanted him before she died. Perhaps it was written in the stars that she would die in the clearing. Perhaps she had to die in order for that to happen, to pave the way for me and Tino.

The postman hurls a rolled-up newspaper over the fence and it snaps me out of my Tino-induced trance. I get up and retrieve the bundle and start to unfurl it, though I don't have to look at the whole face of the woman on the front to know immediately who it is. Shelby smiling in full technicolour, and beside her a large photo of Max. The words on the front page read:

CRIME OF PASSION? Dead woman's tryst with married man on night of murder

Murdered Esperance woman Shelby Massini enjoyed an illicit tryst with her married former lover on the night of her death, it has been alleged. The *Esperance Morning News* has been informed that Mrs Massini, 42, enjoyed a private meeting with Max Latimer, also 42, shortly before she was strangled in the clearing beside Esperance running track.

Shit, I think to myself. *Poor Lottie and poor Carole.*

My mobile rings on the table beside me. Lottie.

'Oh Lottie' I gush into the receiver. 'I've just seen the paper. Are you okay?'

'Yes, yes,' she pants. 'But never mind that. They've arrested him. Max. They've taken him in.'

I feel my heart speed up. This is significant.

'Arrested him?'

'Yes! Carole says he was cautioned at the station yesterday and they went back later on for the clothes he was wearing on the night Shelby was killed and they've just formally arrested him. The fact he had sex with Shelby right before she died is incriminating enough, but I told them all about Carole threatening to cut him off and the fact he lives for money.'

Lottie is elated, breathless.

'Have they charged him?' I ask.

'Not yet, but they will. That's what they do next.'

'Wow,' I say. 'This is huge. Poor Carole.'

I look out of the window. Lottie is convinced of Max's guilt, but I can't quite believe it. He's not an angry man. Or is he? Shelby must have driven him crazy, just like she drove every man crazy. It wouldn't be unheard of if he just flipped. I mean, everyone flips sometimes, don't they?

The truth is, I don't know what to think. We all wished Shelby dead at one point or another, didn't we? Every one of us has a motive: Max, Tino, Carole – even me!

But Lottie doesn't have an eye on anyone else. She has found her man.

'He planned it, Freya,' she says down the line, her voice bouncy and excited. 'Just like we said.'

We?

'He met with Shelby knowing Carole was going to cut him off if he didn't end it somehow and he strangled her and then pushed her backwards and the impact cracked her skull. That's what killed her, a cracked skull!'

This isn't like Lottie, all this excitable talk of broken skulls.

'How's Carole?' I ask.

'Carole?' Lottie asks, like it's the wrong question. 'How is *Carole*?'

I change tack. 'How do *you* feel?'

Lottie takes a deep breath and lets it out.

'Relieved,' she says. 'Relieved.'

Chapter Thirty
Shelby

Before

Graham Parkes is an old mate of Tino's father Luigi, so Carole is invited to our wedding, which take place a little over a year after hers, and only six months after Lottie weds Piers. She comes with her brother Sebastian, mum Rosemary – and, of course, Max. Rosemary looks like she's got some giant bird on her head, and Carole just looks plain as anything, her little pot belly suggesting she's let herself go now she's married.

I don't have much of a say about the guest list because, as I came to realise in the preamble to Lottie's wedding, rich people like big weddings because it is a chance for them to show off to everyone they know just how wealthy and entitled they really are. The parties they throw to celebrate their children's nuptials are essentially a chance to celebrate themselves. Since I've been living in the Massini's beachfront pied-à-terre for the last year, I've let Tino's mother Cathy arrange most of the wedding. All I have to do is rock up wearing something amazing (Cathy insisted on custom Stella McCartney), pick a few canapés and turn up with a smile on my dial. I can't complain. I've got a priceless antique sapphire ring belonging to Tino's Italian nonna on my finger and a two-week holiday to Amalfi included in the package. After all, didn't Max say we should marry for money?

Lottie has been beside herself about the wedding, dreamily thrusting magazine cuttings of veils, bouquets and bridesmaid dresses in my face. She wants a peach dress; I want her in black. I picked a YSL A-line number because why not now it's on the Massinis' tab?

'But black?' she said when I showed her what she'd be wearing. 'Really?'

'It's slimming – and a lot sexier than the sacks you usually wear.'

'Okay,' Lottie agreed, but she looked anxious as hell about wearing something that exposed some flesh. Then she said, 'You know I won't be able to wear a dress like this for long. I mean, not now I'm pregnant.'

'You're what?'

'Pregnant,' Lottie grinned. 'We're having a baby.'

At least she had the decency not to announce it at the wedding.

'Congrats,' I told her. She grinned and stepped in to give me a hug. She clung on tightly and stroked my back and it felt like my torso was being trapped in a vice.

'Thanks,' she said. 'I'm only seven weeks, you know, so it's early days. But my boobs might be a little much for the dress you like . . .'

'My wedding, my rules,' I said. 'I had to wear baby pink for you.'

'You took it off after an hour.'

'And you haven't let me forget it.'

'Freya would love to wear the black if you'll ask her as well.' She put her hand on her belly.

'Freya? To be my bridesmaid?'

'I could be your maid of honour and she could be a bridesmaid. Two is better than one.'

'Are you serious? Why on earth would I ask *Freya*?'

'Don't be mean.'

'Are we talking about the same Freya who spent the whole time pining after Max while I was with him and now can't keep her eyes off Tino? Wanting to shag my ex *and* my fiancé hardly makes for bridal party material, does it?'

'She's your friend, Shelby.'

'She needs to get laid.'

'She is! By Bernard Harrington. He's a barrister, actually. Very well off. Piers knows him from rugby. He's a bit older, has a couple of kids. But she doesn't seem to care. And he's crazy about Freya by the sounds of things.'

'Okay good, she can stop being obsessed with my love life then.'

'I still think you should ask her. She's been your friend for years.'

'A friend of yours,' I say. 'Not mine. It's not happening. I can't think of anything more disingenuous than asking Freya Morton to be my bridesmaid. She can go fish.'

The night before the wedding, two boxes are delivered to my hotel suite in the six-star Harbourside Hotel. The first is a pair of diamond earrings, dainty, understated. The card reads, *The long game*. The second is from Tiffany &

Co., in a large, turquoise box and it arrives with an envelope. I open the box within the box and the diamonds sparkle shamelessly. A bracelet made from brilliant cut diamonds. I pull the card out of the envelope. 'Something almost as beautiful as you are! Tino xx' it reads. I put on the earrings from Max and fall asleep.

Twelve hours later, I walk up the aisle towards Tino, with my fiancé's diamonds on my wrist and my lover's in my ears. Lottie fluffs out my train and then adjusts my veil, which doesn't cover my face, and steps out ahead of me. I am halfway up when I see them, Max and Carole. Carole looks at me like she's the most jealous woman alive, but there's also a bit of a smirk, like she knows something I don't. Max, on the other hand, looks anguished. Until he glimpses the earrings, because I reach my hand up and touch one with my finger, give him a little sign, and he smiles. But then I look away towards my husband-to-be. Tall, handsome, self-assured, capable. Able to cope with me. Perhaps he *can* be more to me than Max. He smiles at me from the altar, lopsided, sexy, and I smile back. I leave Max in this moment, and I walk towards the man I am going to marry. As I arrive next to Tino, he takes my hand in his confidently. Like he is in charge of me, just like I need, because otherwise I will walk all over him.

'You look stunning,' he says. 'Hello, Mrs Massini.'

After the ceremony, we eat a three course meal and we dance and everyone tells me how beautiful I look. And when Tino does his speech and talks about how we met and how he will never meet a woman like me again, Max gets up and leaves to go to the bathroom. I clock him coming back – he has the glazed expression he gets when he has smoked a spliff. Carole looks at him distastefully and asks him something. He shrugs and shakes his head. Then she hisses something at him, which with my limited experience of lip reading, looks like 'Tell her, now!'

A team of ten wait staff wander about topping up champagne glasses. I lose track of the amount of times my glass gets refilled. I'm just turning back to the table when I hear a female voice that is vaguely familiar.

'Champagne?' she says, and I turn. And there she is, the girl from school . . . Maz. The one who tried to save me at the beach. The one who launched at me that time in the RSL at Kayla Sanders' party. I don't know what to say to her. It's awkward that she's serving me at my own wedding in black pants and a white dress shirt, while I'm dripping in diamonds and Stella McCartney.

'Hi again,' she says and looks me in the eyes. It is definitely her. Last time I saw her, she had red hair and now it is a kind of coconut brown, but the nose ring is still there. 'It's me – Maz from school? You look incredible,' she says.

'Thanks,' I say and offer her nothing. Part of me wants to talk about that night on the beach, to acknowledge it, but for some reason the words don't form. So instead I say the first thing that comes to mind, which is, 'Please can you top up my glass?'

She looks at me with pursed lips and says, 'Of course. Enjoy your day!'

Veronica, the wedding planner, comes running up to me holding her iPad.

'It's four o'clock,' she says. 'Time for the first dance! We can't get behind schedule.'

Tino appears and pulls me in close, kisses my temple.

She nods to Piers, who's our MC. He taps the mic. 'Ladies and gentlemen,' he says. 'Please line the dance-floor for the first dance!'

Tino pulls me to the centre of the floor, and I feel the cringe-hit of this Hallmark moment prickling my skin. I glance across the room and see Max, and expect him to be smiling at my awkwardness, but instead he stares at me like a miserable drunk.

I can barely remember which song Cathy picked, but then the music begins. It's 'Can't Take My Eyes Off Of You' by Frankie Valli.

'I really *can't* take my eyes off of you,' Tino whispers in my ear. I lean against him, the way I do with Max, and for a moment, as we sway, I imagine that Tino's chest is Max's. They're not dissimilar. The same, but different. At the end of the song, the drummer crashes the cymbals dramatic-ally, and Piers shouts into the microphone: 'Ladies and gentlemen, Mr and Mrs Massini!' Ahead of me is a giant wall of flowers spelling out our names: SHELBY & TINO. The words sit a little wonkily, like they don't quite work together.

The dancefloor vibrates with the thud of feet, but after an hour or so, the tempo slows. Luigi takes my hand for 'My Baby Just Cares for Me', and twirls me around mer-rily. Sweat has collected on his belly and underarms and I try to avoid it touching my dress.

Max appears out of nowhere.

'Can I have this dance?' he asks. He leans in and takes my hand from Luigi.

'Oh, yes of course,' says Luigi. 'That's probably a good idea seeing as I'm a little out of puff!'

Max laughs. 'Shelby and I are old school friends,' he says, even though Luigi hasn't asked.

'Lovely,' says the old man, clearly relieved to sit down before he has some kind of cardiac episode. 'Enjoy your dance.'

As Max pulls me in close, my smile stays pasted. I can't give anything away. I glance around the room, but no one has noticed us yet. Not even Carole. She is chatting to Lottie in a corner and they are both smiling. They chink their water glasses together and laugh. Lottie pats her belly protectively. She's twelve weeks now and she's had the big scan, so she's telling anyone who'll listen. She motions towards her breasts as if to apologise for their voluptuousness in her tight-fitting dress.

Max whispers in my ear. 'You look edible.'

He is drunk. I can smell it on him.

'Not now,' I say through ventriloquist's teeth.

'I want you.'

'No.'

'Come upstairs with me.'

'Max!'

'I love you, Shelby.'

'Not *now*,' I hiss.

'She's pregnant . . .' he slurs. 'Carole.'

And in a moment of perfect serendipity, the music stops. I step away from Max and look up at him.

'No,' I say.

'She wanted me to tell you.' The band kicks in again.

'Here?' I hiss. 'At my *wedding*?'

'She's not stupid, Shelby. She knows how I still feel about you.'

I glance across the room, and there is Carole with my sister, each with their hands on their own bellies, protective. She is smiling at me. She is telling me that she is the one who holds the trump card now. She is saying, 'It's time to give up now, I've won.'

It's too much. Carole is carrying Max's child.

I turn to Max. 'This stops *now*,' I tell him and push him roughly away. 'It's over.'

He ignores me. 'I don't want a baby with her. I want you.'

'I mean it,' I say. 'I won't do this any more. A baby is a game-changer, don't you think?'

'No.' Max grabs my wrist. He squeezes tight. 'I need you. I can't live without you.'

'Darling?' says Tino, appearing out of nowhere. He looks at Max's face and then at mine.

'Just having a dance,' says Max, dropping my wrist.

Tino looks confused, like he's trying to work out the connection between us. He puts his arm around me, pulls me in close and I am grateful for it. I am relieved someone has my back, even though I always thought it would be Max.

'Ahh, yes,' he says. 'You're from Shivers Beach too, aren't you mate?'

Max doesn't respond, because he knows Tino is having a dig.

Tino smiles at Max, but it isn't genuine, his eyes don't crinkle this time. 'Then you'll know how amazing my wife is.' *My wife, not yours.* Then he takes my hand and leads me away from my past.

In the hotel lounge, Freya sits with her older boyfriend Bernard and Lottie sits on Piers' lap, stroking his creepily large gynae hands as they rest on her belly. Tino and I sit down.

'How do you know that bloke again?' he asks Freya.

'That's Max Latimer, the Shivers High School stud,' Lottie purrs. She looks at me and adds with a glint in her eye, 'Sorry! But that *is* what we used to call him.' She turns to Tino, with a conspiratorial smile. 'Tino, you must have heard about Max?'

Tino's eyebrows knit together. 'I know he's married to Carole, but I didn't know he was an old school friend of yours.'

'More than that,' Lottie giggles. 'He was Shelby's first love – although it was more like obsession.'

I kick her in the shins with my Jimmy Choos, but the tulle softens the blow.

'Hey, stop kicking me, Shelby.' She pouts. 'Tino is a big boy and more than secure enough to know it's all in the past. You're not the jealous type, are you, Tino?'

'Not at all,' Tino smiles. If only he knew the extent of my love for Max, how it filled every inch of my body like blood, from the age of seventeen, and how it still fills me now. He might be jealous then! He picks up his whisky tumbler and shakes around the ice.

'High school was a long time ago,' I snap. 'Shall we drop it?'

It's awkward for a moment, until Freya's middle-aged boyfriend gets up. 'Anyone for a drink?' he says. 'I'll go to the bar.'

'No mate,' says Tino. 'You enjoy yourself, I'll go.'

I watch his broad back as he strides to the bar and muscles in next to Max. I watch him lean in and order champagne, and then I watch as he jabs his elbow sharply forward, slamming it into Max's rib cage. I watch as Max recoils in pain, his hand flying to his side. Watch his lips say, 'What the hell?' as he turns to square up to the man next to him, only realising it would be a futile contest, since Tino is a good few inches taller and quite a bit broader. I want to rush to Max, but I won't. Not now he is going to be a father. I am married and perhaps it is finally time for this stupid youthful folly to end.

Tino turns away from the bar, a smile flickering on his lips as returns to the table with a round of drinks. He puts the tray down and passes me mine, then chinks his against it and says, 'To us.' Freya and Bernard throw their glasses in too, and Lottie holds up her water.

Later, when the tunes have stopped and Veronica has retired her iPad, Tino carries me over the threshold of our suite. He lays me down on the bed and kisses me long and hard and deep, and this time I don't think of Max. I tell myself not to. I tell myself that if this is marriage, how hard can it be? Perhaps I'll learn to love it, learn to love *him*. After we have had sex – because it is not making love quite yet – I go to the bathroom to take my make-up off, and slip into the silk negligée my husband had shipped from

Rigby & Peller in London. Tino comes up behind me, and puts his hands round my neck.

'I love this neck,' he says and squeezes gently, then bends down to kiss the spots where his thumbs have been.

'You're mine now,' he whispers against my earlobe.

Later, as Tino snores gently beside me, I receive a message from Max.

I need to see you, he says.

No, I reply immediately. **It's over,** I write, buoyed by the strength of being a wife and the feeling that maybe, just maybe, I can love someone else. That someone else gets me like Max. **Do not contact me again.**

I delete his number from my phone, even if his phone number is so irreversibly etched on my heart that I could recite it fluently backwards.

I hold out six whole weeks before I go back to him.

Chapter Thirty-One
Lottie

St Paul's is the only thing that keeps me sane on the morning of Shelby's funeral. Somehow working through bundles of clothes gives me a strange sense of comfort, especially the ones from deceased estates. The expensive, designer items that come in are usually from people who have died, because most family members don't want to be bequeathed a pair of Kate Spade heels or a handbag – these items are too personal because they used to sit on a body that is now cold. Instead they come to us, where members of the public, people who weren't close to the dead, rummage through, unaware of their provenance.

I have donated eight black binbags full of clothes, accessories, trinkets. My sister's life reduced to straining garbage sacks. Part of my life, too.

I'd gone through my wardrobe after I'd done hers, found things that reminded me of her, clothes I couldn't bear to wear. Before long I was in a frenzy, pulling items off hangers – things of mine, of Piers', of Isobel's, overwhelmed by an insatiable need to start afresh, all of us. It was cathartic, it was freeing – it was a closure of sorts. Or at least an initial sealing. The scar left by Shelby's death will never fade, but the wound can slowly heal. When Max Latimer's head is on the spit, it will scab over good and proper.

Marella pulls me into a hug. 'You're so kind to bring Shelby's things – on the morning of her burial of all days,' she says. 'It isn't an easy day for you – especially not with that horrid newspaper article, too. Do you know who tipped off the press?'

'I've no idea,' I shrug. I want to tell Marella I don't really care about the article, because it only makes Max's arrest look more expected, more *just*. That it exposes him for who he really is. I don't tell her that the article isn't actually a bad thing because it can't hurt Shelby any more but it can sure as hell make Max look bad! I could explain all of this, but I don't, because my hating Max doesn't need to concern her. I'm so tired of it all.

Marella touches my arm. 'Don't think about it,' she says. 'Come on, let's take everything inside.'

She hauls the bags out of the car one by one and we carry them to the shop. I hug each black bag as if I can't bear to let it go, while Marella holds a bag in each hand by the tenuous handles. Lastly, she lifts out a box that's full of handbags. As she pulls it out of the back of the car, the scent of Shelby fills the air momentarily, before catching on the breeze and travelling off elsewhere.

It had been strange, at Tino's place. At the wake, he'd been jovial, almost hyper – but ten days later, it was as if he'd suddenly realised what had happened and that Shelby was gone. The house was shrouded in darkness, only lit by the odd strip of filtered sunlight through the blinds. He answered the door in joggers and a white T-shirt, his stubble overgrown. He looked sad, innocent, humble, like the man I'd always known. Not the one who'd slept with Freya, who'd cheated on Shelby. But even though I wanted to be angry with him, I couldn't.

'Lottie,' he'd said, pulling me into a hug. 'Come on in. You know where everything is.'

He led me through the house and up the stairs anyway.

'I made a start,' he gestured at the piles of clothes chucked roughly on the unmade bed. 'There's nothing I want to keep.'

He paused in the doorway. 'You know I still loved her,' he told me. 'Even at the end.'

'Did you?' I ask. 'What about Freya?'

'Freya?' He ran a hand through his hair. 'Oh Lottie. It's been a huge mistake. It started as a ploy to try and make Shelby feel something for me. I loved her so much. *Too* much. And I could never make her feel the same.'

'I get it,' I say. 'Just be careful with Freya, okay? She's vulnerable.'

'Nah,' he said. 'She wanted to get back at Shelby as much as I did. All the times Shelby treated her like shit, treated both of us like shit . . .'

He'd left me alone after that, in the room they'd shared as husband and wife. To sort, to classify, to reject. I picked up her favourite handbag – the quilted Chanel, took out her purse, looked at the receipts. On the day she died, she'd gone to Only Organic and bought a slice of carrot cake and a chai latte; for some reason she'd kept the paper receipt. There were business cards: hers from Esperance Motors, credit cards bending at the side, $67.25 in cash. A note written in a scrawl: *The End Game xo*. In the pocket of the bag was a packet of gum, a pair of tweezers and yet another wand of her favourite lipstick, Go Fuchsia Your-self. I wound up the stick and dragged it over the back of my hand. 'Oh Shelby,' I whispered as I breathed in the familiar waxy lipstick smell.

I went through every handbag like this, emptying methodically and putting it in the cardboard box. Each so beautiful, but too close to my sister to keep. Too used by her. I only kept the YSL Loulou for Isobel – she'd always loved that bag. Maybe she wouldn't want it, or maybe she would, but I couldn't bear to part with it.

The clothes were simpler. I didn't want much, only a couple of key items. I couldn't do it. I emptied the pockets – a receipt here, a hairband there – and bundled them up: the kaftans, the shorts, the tops, the dresses, the shoes, saving a couple of things for Isobel. I folded them neatly and placed them inside thick black bin liners.

'The box is big ticket items,' I tell Marella, as though I'm organising raffle prizes at a village fete. 'Mostly handbags. The black binbags are clothes.'

'Are these Tino's?' she asks, opening up a bag of men's clothes.

'Nope, they belong to Piers,' I say. 'There's some of Isobel's stuff in there for the teenage section, too. A couple of dresses she's grown out of.'

'Wow,' says Marella, unzipping a heavy suit bag. 'This one looks expensive!'

'It's a little too tight these days.' I shrug. 'What can I say? Piers likes his cheese.'

I hand over a pile of pinstripe shirts that have seen better days. My husband's work 'uniform' of fifteen-odd years.

'Out with the old,' I say.

'Catharsis.'

'Something like that'

'There's a crack in everything; that's how the light gets in,' says Marella reflectively.

'Leonard Cohen.' I smile. 'Shelby loved Leonard Cohen. Figures, really.'

Marella picks up the cardboard box and takes it into her office. 'I'll need to Google some of this,' she says. 'Find out how much it goes for second hand.'

'A lot. We should put on the Facebook page that we've had some designer items come in,' I suggest. 'Maybe have a special sale. I know lots of women who'd love some of this stuff, and the men's items too.'

'Great idea,' says Marella. 'We could hold a sale next week, during the day.'

'Sure, whatever you think.' I force a smile. 'I don't know if you're really into designer stuff or not but if you want anything of Shelby's, you know, please, just take it.'

'Oh, Lottie, I couldn't . . .'

'I mean it. I'd rather you have it than some of the vultures in this town.'

'Thank you, Lottie,' Marella tells me and pats my hand.

'Will Isobel go to the funeral this afternoon?' Marella asks.

'Yes,' I tell her. 'I think it will be healthy for her to say goodbye.'

'They were close, weren't they? Isobel and Shelby?'

I look up at her and nod. 'Yes, they were.'

'So alike in looks too. Isobel almost looks more like . . .'

She was going to say Isobel looks more like Shelby than me. I know. I've heard it before. But I don't want to hear it today, so I gather up my jacket, phone and car keys.

'Okay, I'll be off,' I tell her. I don't want to be there for the ceremonial hanging up of my dead sister's clothes. Or my living husband and daughter's for that matter. I have a burial to attend.

'Are you sure I can't make you a quick cup of tea . . .'

'No!' I snap.

Marella blinks and a small crease forms in her brow.

'I mean, no thanks,' I add. I can't seem to fight the irritability right now. Marella is bearing the brunt of it.

She smiles and touches my arm. 'I just want to help,' she says.

'I know,' I smile. 'I'm so grateful for everything you've done, but I'm fine. I'll be in touch. Okay?'

The truth is, I want her to stop wanting to save me.

'I need to get home to Piers,' I tell her as I turn towards the door.

'And how *is* Piers?' she asks, and I slowly turn around. There is something in the way she delivers the line, how she asks the question. Something sinister. Something strange.

'Fine,' I say. 'He's at work. Why?'

'Oh, nothing. It's just . . . it must be so hard on him. Trying to look after you and Isobel. I mean, it's draining, isn't it? I mean, it's such a gamble, dealing with grief – you don't know what you're going to get, day-to-day. I'd bet my last dollar on the fact he is feeling this epic loss as much as you. I mean, you invest so much in a relationship.'

I look at her face as she talks.

Gamble. Loss. My last dollar. Invest.

She stares into my eyes and I stare back. Gone are the warm, fine lines around her eyes and the open, dilated pupils. Now they are pin-pricks. Dots that stare across at me. What does Marella know about us? About me and Piers? About the *money*?

'I'm not sure I follow?'

Marella's face changes again, brightens.

'I'm not saying anything, just how hard this must be for you.' She smiles and turns away.

But I can't shake the feeling that she is trying to tell me she knows something.

I reach the front door and come face to face with Carole. Out of the frying pan and into the fire. Mascara rivers down her cheeks and her skin burns red.

'You!' she says, pointing at me. 'What did you tell them?'

'Me?' It comes out like a squeak, like the old Lottie.

'You know Max has been formally charged,' she spits. 'Not just cautioned, but *arrested*! What the hell did you say to the police?'

She steps towards me, gets right into my face. I look to Marella for help.

'Carole, I . . .'

'What did you tell them?'

'I told them the truth, Carole,' I cry, and I hear my voice take on a tone I haven't much heard before. 'I told them about Max's past with Shelby and that you'd threatened to cut him off if he cheated!'

'No!' she screams. 'You are my best *friend*! You *know* Max would never do this and you're trying to frame him! He is the father of your *godchildren*, Lottie! He might have been thinking with his dick,' she shouts, 'but Max would *never* hurt anyone, including Shelby!'

She jabs her finger at my décolletage, lifts her hand up as though she might pull my hair. Marella's reaction is quick, strong and her face is contorted in a grimace, like she's lifting weights. She steps in and lifts Carole away from me.

Carole steps back and grips her wrist in pain.

She looks Marella up and down, her face painted with disgust. Like she's been touched by a leper. 'Get *off* me, you freak. Who even *are* you?' she says.

Marella looks stung and it's a look I recognise. A look on a face from years ago. And then it dawns on me. Marella was there at the beach the night Shelby almost drowned. The girl who hated Shelby. Marella is Fat Maz. I *do* remember her from Shivers High, and she *did* hate Shelby.

'Marella,' I say, evenly. 'Please get off Carole.'

'Don't worry, I'm leaving!' screams Carole. 'Lottie, you're dead to me. Do you hear me? *Dead!*'

Shelby is dead to me and now Carole is, too. My legs feel like they will fail me, and I have to hold the side of the table with the kids' toys on it to steady myself.

'Carole,' Marella snaps. 'Lottie is burying Shelby this afternoon. Go easy on her.'

Carole looks at Marella. 'He is the father of my *children*!' she cries, and she slumps to the floor, her legs out beside her like Bambi, black tears dripping onto her white linen pants. After a few seconds, she pulls herself together and stands up again, the old Carole back. 'I'm getting out of this hellhole,' she says and marches to the front door, but not before doing a double-take at an Armani military-style jacket perched on the shoulders of Nell the mannequin in the window.

We bury Shelby straight after lunch. We stand in a semicircle of three – me, Piers and Isobel – around the rectangular pit in Shivers Beach Cemetery next to the plot where our parents were both buried. The headstone, made from shiny black granite, looks out of place amid the crumbling, mossy stones: ovals, squares, angel statues, crosses. The only flowers are on our parents' grave: a bunch of lilies a week, or maybe two weeks old. The sticker on the cellophane says White Bloom Flowers – the florist in Esperance. I hadn't realised Shelby ever came here.

The heat bears down on us – there's no shade from the imposing, dilapidated church, and the earth around the grave is cracked and thirsty. The stifling breeze brings with it the acrid liquor smell of the bin in the corner of the graveyard, which overflows with bottles and cigarette packets and all sorts of rubbish.

Tino doesn't come. He tells us he already said his good-byes at the morgue and at the wake. Poor Tino, always so sweet and gentle. Tino who has the guilt of Freya to deal with, a mistake he made. An error of judgement. It must be killing him, and I understand why he has chosen not to be there. Shelby treated him so badly at the end – the separate beds, the snide comments, the belittling. It makes me so sad to think that she didn't give him a chance, espe-cially after everything he did for her.

Isobel stands at the foot of the grave. She cries softly, rocks back and forth, stares at the mahogany coffin six feet down. We play 'Everybody Hurts' by REM, the anthem of our teenage years, as we throw our handfuls of earth on the wood. I imagine my sister, listening from down below, her head on a satin pillow. Her head bashed in at the side. At least now Max Latimer will rot in hell.

The song ends, and that's when my tears come. They come and they stay and for the first time, my daughter falls into me and holds me like a daughter should hold her mother. And then, only twenty minutes after we have arrived, we step out of the dry, arid heat of Shivers Beach and into the cool air of the limo to go home.

'Why did you give all of Auntie Shelby's stuff away?' Isobel asks me.

I tell her it's because it's too raw to handle. That I need to have closure.

'What about me?' she asks. 'I wanted some stuff to remember her.'

'I saved you the Loulou bag,' I say. 'But I don't want the rest of it in the house.'

'Why?'

'Because she's dead, Isobel.'

'You just don't want any of her stuff because you're jealous,' Isobel says.

'How so?' My voice is weary. I am so very tired.

'Because she was always so funny and cool and nice. Everything you're not. You were awful to her. *Awful.*'

'Awful? Because I cared about her?'

'The way you spoke about her to Dad.'

'What?'

'Always slating her. You hated her and you were jealous of her.'

'Why would I be jealous of Shelby?' I snap.

'Because I've always wished she was my mum and not you.'

That's it. I can't hold it in. 'You're so like her,' I cry. 'Self-absorbed, selfish. Two peas in a pod! That's why you're so obsessed with her! I wish she'd been your mother too, then I wouldn't have to deal with you!'

'Dad?' whimpers Isobel and begins to sob.

Piers doesn't react, just stares ahead. I turn and look out of the window, ignore my daughter's tears. She needed to be told.

As we pull up outside the house, Freya calls. When she has finished expressing the obligatory sympathy and asking how the burial went, she tells me Carole is holding a small, impromptu gathering later on and Freya thinks I should come.

'I know you guys had a falling out this morning, but I think you need to be there to show her your support, and at least hear her out. I think she'd like to talk about Max.'

'I can't,' I tell her. I am exhausted emotionally, and every one of my limbs ache. I want to get inside, change out of the uncomfortable black lace dress I wore to my sister's graveside. 'Besides Carole won't want me there.'

'She doesn't, if I'm honest, but I think you need to make a strategic decision to be there – I mean, strategic in terms of your friendship.'

I sigh. 'I don't know, Freya.'

'Look,' she interrupts. 'Carole deserves to be heard. It can't hurt. She really believes Max is innocent – she has to because of the kids. Just hear her out.'

I can't believe what I'm hearing. I don't say anything. I can't.

'Oh come on, Lottie. When you break it down, do you *really* think Max would do that to Shelby? Murder her in the park?'

I don't have an answer. 'Money talks,' I say.

She sighs. 'Look, he might be money-motivated, but Carole is right, he is not a killer. Even if she did cut him off, I can't see him murdering anyone.'

I sigh. I cannot believe what I am hearing. Is Carole paying her or something? There is no way in hell it wasn't Max. The man who shot at possums with an air rifle? Don't they say the lust for blood starts in the teenage years?

'Look,' says Freya. 'I know you want to find out who did it, of course you do. But do you think you might *want* it to be Max, so you can have an outlet for your anger? Carole would put her life on Max being innocent and wants to prove it, for Otto and Olivia's sakes as well as hers. She loves him, despite what he may have been doing with Shelby. Anyway, she says she knows who did it, and she can prove it.'

'Who does she think did it? Who else is there?'

'I don't know. The park flasher? Carole has a theory or two. But theories aside, when you break it down, you and Carole really need one another right now. You are both going through hell. You've both lost someone close to you.

It's a different type of grief, but what she's going through is still grief nonetheless.'

That much is true.

'Just think about it.' Freya says. 'That's all I'm asking.'

'I'll think about it,' I say and hang up.

Chapter Thirty-Two
Freya

Carole opens the front door at Summerfield and nods at the pesto dip I'm carrying. 'Over there on the table,' she says. I carry the bowl covered in cling wrap obediently into the living room and set it on her antique oak coffee table to join the bowls of carrot sticks and celery, along with a large vat of tzatziki. I don't know how many people she's hoping for, but as far as I know she's only invited me and Lottie, so her julienning skills (or Hannah's, as I suspect) may have been slightly wasted.

She follows me in. 'You're the first to arrive.'

First in, and I'll be the first one out – I have a date with Tino to keep.

Inside the open plan kitchen-meets-living-room, candles burn in between family photos that Max hasn't yet been erased from, like a shrine to the dead. In the corner of the room is a large whiteboard on wheels, and at the top, Carole has written 'Suspects' and underlined it. But there's nothing, not a single name, underneath.

'Where are Olivia and Otto?' I ask her.

'Skating rink,' she says. 'With Hannah and her kids.'

She pours a glass of prosecco and hands it to me as if this is a lovely spring soirée, and not a meeting to discuss the innocence of her husband, incarcerated for murder most foul.

'Please,' says Carole, beckoning me to the couch, 'have a drink and some nibbles.' She is holding a red whiteboard pen, and she wheels the whiteboard over to the middle of the living room. I sit to attention like a schoolgirl as she taps her watch.

'Not that I care, but is Lottie coming or not?' She examines her fingernails.

'Yes,' I tell her.

The door opens.

'Speak of the devil,' says Carole.

Lottie walks in, back straight, head high. She is a different woman these days. It's like Shelby's death chased that frightened little mouse right under the table. She is wearing a pair of leather pants with a mohair jumper and heels. It's so unlike her. It's almost as if she's realised life's too short to dress like an extra from *Joseph and the Amazing Technicolour Dreamcoat*. The only sign of the old Lottie is the homemade hummus she's proffering in a ceramic bowl.

Marella scurries in behind her. 'Hi,' she says, and holds forth a bowl of beetroot dip like a sacrificial chalice. 'I hope you don't mind me joining you.'

'She's with me,' pouts Lottie. 'Moral support.'

'I made a dip,' says Marella awkwardly. 'Beetroot.'

Carole ignores her.

'Looks lovely,' I offer without conviction.

'Well, well, well.' Carole glares at Lottie. 'Are you here to accuse the father of my children of murder again?'

Lottie holds up her hands. 'I didn't implicate Max, Carole. I simply told the detectives the truth about Max and Shelby's *history*. If Max is innocent, it will be proven.'

Lottie clearly doesn't think for one second Max is innocent, but she is doing it for the sake of her friendship. Carole's left eyelid twitches at the word 'if'.

'Believe what you want,' she says. 'I *know* Max is innocent – and so do the police, which is why he's been arrested
but not charged. They can't prove he did anything, and
that's why they're going to have to let him go. I'm not
going over old ground here. The point of this gathering
is to work out who did kill her, despite whether you, with
your infinite knowledge of police pathology, believe it was
Max. You *are* open-minded, aren't you, Charlotte? Surely
you of all people want to work out who killed your sister?'

Lottie bites her lip like a small child, and so she might:
Carole has just called her Charlotte. I can see in Lottie's
face that she thinks the right man has been linked to the
crime and that marking out motives on a whiteboard is
futile, but shrugs to suggest she will go along with it. Anything to placate Carole. I feel so sorry for her. She doesn't
want to lose her friendship with Carole, even if it means
swallowing the truth about Max.

'Well,' stutters Lottie, as she sits down on a rattan foot-
stool, 'you may find out there is more to the murder than
you thought, although I'm not permitted to say.'

Carole looks annoyed and is about to say something
when she clocks Marella positioning herself right on the
edge of her Coco Republic sofa.

'Marella, please can you just sit in the middle, you'll
damage the upholstery,' she snaps. 'It's a sofa, not a milk-
ing stool.'

'Sorry Carole,' mumbles Marella.

Carole pulls a lid off a whiteboard marker with a flourish.

'Eat the dips please, people,' she snaps. 'Hannah didn't make fresh tzatziki for nothing. I mean, I would have made it myself, but what with everything going on . . .'

Marella's hand shoots forward towards the carrot batons.

'So, given Max didn't murder Shelby, we're going to work out who *did*,' says Carole.

Marella glances at Lottie. 'Lottie, are you going to be okay with this?' she asks.

Carole glares at her.

Lottie nods. 'It's fine,' she says. 'I've been through it all with the police. Of course it's hard, but I can handle it. Like I said, I want justice for Shelby.' She sits up straight and crosses one leather-clad leg over the other.

'Nice pants,' Carole says, and then remembers she's pissed off. 'The police have been absolutely useless . . .'

'They have to cover all bases,' I say, playing devil's advocate.

'Max is languishing in a holding cell,' barks Carole. 'So I hardly think they've "covered all bases".'

'Okaaay,' I say and nibble on a cucumber stick.

'Right, let's start with the suspects. There's Piers, of course . . .' Carole begins.

Lottie's eyes widen. 'Now Carole, that is hardly fair . . .' she starts.

'I mean he didn't exactly *like* Shelby, did he?' Carole says.

'Actually, he was at the hospital delivering a baby,' says Marella.

'Not that he needs an alibi,' sniffs Lottie. 'Piers wouldn't hurt a fly.'

'He could have done it on his way home.'

'Actually, he couldn't, because I saw Shelby at the park just before eight thirty,' I say. 'She was in her fluoro shorts running in that sort of model-like way she has, I mean *had*. I arrived at Lottie's less than ten minutes later and Piers walked in pretty much straight after me, so he couldn't have done it.'

'*And* you were there when Shelby's text came through,' simpers Lottie. 'Please stop, Carole, I've been through enough.'

'See?' says Carole. 'It isn't nice when your husband is accused of murder and you know he didn't do it, is it? Regardless of your rather feeble protestations, there's no denying Piers has the *motive*.'

Lottie looks seriously annoyed, because it's dawning on her that they asked her here just so she could accuse Piers.

'What's his motive?' I ask. I genuinely don't know.

'Because Shelby always belittled him,' says Carole. 'Or maybe she was having sex with him too.'

Lottie's skin burns red.

'Now hold on,' says Marella.

'Who are you? The bodyguard?' asks Carole. She turns to Lottie. 'It isn't beyond the realms of possibility, is it?'

Lottie stands up. 'No! Piers would never . . .' She sniffs back the beginning of a sob.

'Oh, wind your neck in,' snaps Carole. 'I'm not serious about Piers. We all know he's way too pathetic to strangle someone. Anyway, it seems he was too busy with his hand up another woman's vagina that night. Oh sorry, I mean *delivering a child*.'

Lottie's nostrils flare. 'It was a caesarean!' she snaps.

'Whatever,' says Carole. 'Anyway, I'm not even talking about Piers. I'm talking about the other person with motive – Tino.'

I sit up straight. 'No way! You don't think . . . ?'

Lottie glares at me.

'Yes way!' Carole says. 'His motive is clear, isn't it? His wife whoring it around town.'

I don't like the way this conversation is going. Tino would never touch Shelby, never. He was too apathetic about her to hurt her. He just didn't care about her enough.

Marella gets up. 'I'm just going to the loo . . .'

'Sit down, Marella,' barks Carole.

'Sorry,' says Marella, and sits herself back down.

'She was not *whoring* it,' Lottie hisses.

'Hmm,' says Carole. 'But she wasn't *faithful*, was she?'

'Nor was Max,' Lottie blurts out.

Carole sighs. 'No, Lottie, he wasn't. And coming to terms with that has been *devastating* for me.'

Marella gets up again. 'I really do need to go to the bathroom,' she says apologetically and heads off down the hall.

'So anyway, as I was saying, Tino was one person with a motive.'

I shift in my seat. Tino had been with me all night and then he'd gone straight home, hadn't he? I'd watched the rise and fall of his buttocks as he crossed the sand. He'd messaged me when he got home. He wouldn't have done that, would he, if he was busy murdering Shelby? But unfortunately for Tino's defence in the Court of Carole, Lottie is the only one who knows this – and I'd like it to stay that way.

'But there's no actual evidence against Tino,' I say. 'You know, just to be fair to the poor man. He is way too nice to do anything so brutal.'

'Apparently Ted Bundy was "a nice man" too,' says Carole, using her fingers as quote marks. 'Charming, in fact.'

'Oh come on,' I say. 'Tino's hardly a mass murderer, is he?'

Carole shrugs. 'That leaves one other person then . . .' She lowers her voice to a whisper and glances up the hall. '*Marella.*'

'Marella?' Lottie whispers. 'That's ridiculous.'

'Is it?' hisses Carole. 'Then who do *you* think it is, Miss Marple?'

I can see the cogs in Lottie's brain wheeling round, slowly. She looks towards the bathroom like she's trying to move chess pieces on a board.

'The park flasher?'

'Police ruled him out,' Carole says impatiently, but she doesn't elaborate, presumably because by ruling out an opportunist, she's making Max more credible as the killer.

'I know it's not Marella,' Lottie says. 'I mean, what would be her motive for killing Shelby?'

'High school?' I shrug. I hate to agree with Carole, but there is a historical motive there, and even if it's unlikely, I'll take anything that shifts the focus off Tino.

'What about high school?' whispers Lottie, following Carole's gaze up the hallway in the direction of Carole's downstairs bathroom.

'I heard Shelby *ruined* Marella in high school,' says Carole.

'Oh, please,' Lottie hisses. 'Are you seriously trying to tell me Marella would kill Shelby because of a high school vendetta? Hardly enough of a motive, otherwise we'd all go round killing the people who bullied us. You'd be dead fifty times over by now, Carole.'

Carole rolls her eyes.

'Carole has a point,' I say. 'It was worse than bullying. Shelby wrecked her. Made it into a bad thing that she liked girls, which ended up not even being true. She demeaned her, made sure everyone called her Fat Maz. Then Shelby was awful to her at her wedding, when Marella turned up serving drinks. I saw Shelby click her fingers at her!'

'Yes, but you don't kill someone because of that.'

'Ahh, but you *do*,' I say, embracing the new suspect. 'It's in every murder novel! Look at how she swanned around at Shelby's wake, handing us all duck pancakes . . . keep-your-friends-close-and-your-enemies-closer behaviour to me.'

'Entirely possible,' says Carole. 'Where even *was* she on the night Shelby was killed?'

'She was at the vet's,' whispers Lottie. 'Rocky got a piece of glass in his paw and she had to take him to the after-hours vet in Mooney.'

'Maybe she bumped off Shelby on the way there?' I offer.

Lottie shakes her head. 'There's no way it's Marella. She can't even organise a pile of second-hand clothes, let alone plan a murder. *Trust* me.'

We hear a flush and fall silent. Marella walks back in and sits on the edge of the sofa. Her dress is tucked into the back of her tights.

'What did I miss?' she smiles.

'Nothing,' we all say in unison.

Carole sighs. 'Well I'm buggered if I know who did it. But I know it wasn't Max.' She turns to me. 'I've already contacted Bernard about defending him if he ends up being charged.' She quickly adds, 'Not that he will be.'

Lottie fixes me with an accusatory stare. 'Freya? Is this true?'

'Um, he hasn't mentioned it,' I tell her. 'But, I mean, he does like to help where he can.'

'But he *can't*,' pleads Lottie. 'Tell him it's a conflict of interests. He'll get Max off for sure. Even *if* he did it.'

'That's the whole point,' says Carole, adding a 'duh' for good measure. 'Bernard's a good man. He'll help us if Max is wrongly charged. I mean, he'd have to! The kids wouldn't recover if their father went down for a murder he didn't commit, even if we're not together any more.' Carole's eyes fill up and her chin wobbles, and let me tell you, she is definitely not what I'd classify as a pretty crier.

'Um,' begins Marella, 'I'm going to play devil's advocate here, and *please* don't shoot the messenger, but there's the small fact that Shelby and Max, err . . .'

'Had sex right before she died?' I offer.

'Yes, that,' says Marella. She doesn't say 'allegedly' like they did in the newspaper, and Carole doesn't dispute it, either.

'Yes, he did. You are right,' Carole snaps. 'And I hate him for it. But do I think he's a murderer? Absolutely not. Max is a good man and if you think I'm going to let him languish in jail after fifteen years of marriage, then none of you know the meaning of loyalty.'

I don't like to point out that Max obviously doesn't either.

'Max messed up,' Carole says, her voice catching. 'He let her reel him in. But don't you all see? That's what Shelby did to everyone: to Max, to Tino, even to you, Lottie. Wound them in, made them obey. Max may have cheated, but he's not a killer . . .'

Lottie opens her mouth to speak, but I shush her gently with a squeeze of my hand. She brushes it off and stands up with wobbly legs.

'I'm leaving,' she says. 'I can't listen to this any more. My sister is dead, and I'm very sorry Carole about what that means for your children, I really am, but everything points to Max. You can scribble on your whiteboard all you want, but it doesn't dispute the facts. He was the last person to see her alive.'

Carole shrugs. 'The truth will out. And anyway, Lottie, what were *you* doing on the night of the murder?'

Lottie's skin flares red and I'm about to tell them both to calm down when Carole starts to make this weird gurgling sound in her throat, as if she's about to cough up a furball, and her hand flies up to her jaw. She begins itching her skin wildly and her lips begin to swell and turn an eerie grey-blue.

'Can't breathe!' she says on the inhale. 'Peaaaa-nut . . .'

'Peanut?' repeats Lottie, her eyes wide. 'But you can't eat peanuts . . .'

Carole claws at her throat and spins around the room, looking for help, for air.

'Does she have an EpiPen?' Marella grabs Lottie by the shoulders. 'Lottie? An EpiPen! Where does she keep it?'

Lottie just stares at Carole, panic-stricken.

'Where the hell is it?' I run into the hallway, and grab Carole's handbag, but all I can find is a half-eaten protein bar, a pair of Chloe sunglasses, a tampon and some hand sanitiser. I tip the bag upside down and shake it, but nothing else comes out.

Marella is in the kitchen, pulling back the kitchen drawers in a frenzy, throwing things out and up onto the counter: bottle openers, spoons, measuring cups. She empties out the teabag canister and the little rattan basket beside it, but the search is fruitless.

'Not here,' she says and charges into the pantry, tossing out medical boxes onto the kitchen bench and then emptying them out: pain relief, cough syrup, bandages, rehydration tablets all tumble onto the marble benchtop. But no EpiPen.

I grab my mobile with shaking hands and dial 000. It seems to ring forever, unlike when you dial someone by accident and they pick up straight away.

'Ambulance,' I yell at the operator. 'My friend can't breathe! She ate a peanut. She's allergic. We need help, now!'

Marella hurls herself up the stairs. 'I'll look in the upstairs bathrooms,' she calls. 'Lottie, look in the downstairs bathroom.'

Lottie stays still, her face frozen with panic. I race to the downstairs loo, the phone tight to my ear, but a search of the cupboard above the sink yields nothing apart from some various teeth cleaning implements, a hairbrush and a copy of the *Financial Times*.

Carole is now lying on the floor, clawing at her neck. Marella, who has realised her search for the EpiPen upstairs is futile, and now has nowhere to look, falls to the floor beside Carole, and strokes her hand. 'It's okay, Carole, stay calm,' she says, cool as a cucumber. 'We are getting emergency help. Don't panic, you're going to be okay.'

I give the address, hang up on the operator.

'First available,' I say like I'm waiting for an Uber. I sit down and survey the room. 'An ambulance is on the way.'

Carole's eyes are closed, her chest barely moving.

I get up and pace the hallway. The room reeks of fear and adrenaline, and in the middle of it is the frozen outline of Lottie, watching us as we spring to action and bark and shout.

Her face is ashen, but her expression is eerily calm.

Chapter Thirty-Three
Shelby

Before

Max calls me on Tuesday afternoon. 'Carole's at Lottie's for the cheese and wine thing later. Meet me at the garage?'

'Why the garage?'

'I want to show you the car.'

'I've seen the car,' I laugh. 'I work there.'

'I know, but *I* want to show it to you.'

When I get there, he is leaning against the sign that says, 'Esperance Prestige Motors, Serving You Since 1995!' I unlock the showroom and we go inside. In the distance, I can see Freya in her fluoro running club top, pounding the pavement on her way home from the reserve. We move to the side of the showroom and I put my arms around Max's neck. I turn to look out of the window and see Freya standing still now, squinting to see us. I smile at her and shrug, telling her exactly what she's dying to know and I plant a kiss on Max's lips. Freya looks flustered and jogs on. Frankly, I don't care who knows about us any more. It won't be long before they all know anyway.

Max hands me a bag with the logo of a London lingerie brand on it. 'Happy birthday,' he says. He kisses me deeply, thrusts his hand under my top and rests it on the small of my back.

'I've missed you,' he says.

'Me too. You know what you can do about it,' I say.

Leave her. Just do it. Leave her.

'Six months,' he says. 'Six months until we've been together fifteen years – that's what the prenup says. That's what will ensure we're set for life. And even then, we can't just jump into a relationship – it'll be too obvious, and she could contest the money.'

'The money, the money, the money!' I snap. 'It's always about the *money*, isn't it? I mean, you don't ever mention your kids.'

'Oh no.' He shakes his head. 'I love my children. I would never hurt them. That's one of the reasons why I can't leave yet.'

'But you will in six months?'

He turns from me.

'Or will you? Tell me, Max, because I don't understand.'

'You're not being fair. It's easy for you – you've managed to back out of your marriage, you've made that step, I haven't. Carole isn't a bad person . . .'

'She isn't a good one.'

'Actually, she is. You don't know her like I do.'

'You are kidding me. Are you really doing this?'

'Shelby.' He takes my hands. 'I want to be with you. I want to wake up with you every day, forever. I want us to be happy. But I have to do it in the right way.'

'You mean wait for Carole's money to come in before you dump her?'

'Are you serious? I've done all this for us.'

'For us?' I snap. 'You've dressed in designer suits, bought yourself God knows how many cars, swanned around like a big bollocks for *us*? When is there going to be an "us"? We made this pact years ago and you're still there, driving your cars and curating Carole's diamond collection. You're still waiting for the right time after two kids!'

'The long game,' he says quietly.

'But how long? When we're in our fifties? Sixties? Seventies? When we're *dead*?'

I shake my head. The realisation has dawned on me that Max will never leave Carole because he's too comfortable. And perhaps part of him loves her too.

'Six months, Shelby. Six months until we can get out of here and we'll be sorted for life.'

'Six months, and then how long? You're a coward.'

Max shakes my hand away roughly.

'Come on, Shelby, admit it. You love all of this creeping around.' He is worked up now. 'You'd be bored shitless if you lived with me in a house with shutters. You know you would. Why do you think I agreed to any of it? To keep you! I wouldn't have been able to otherwise.'

I let the words sink in. I never told him how much I loved him, did I? I only pushed him away. How could I have got this so wrong?

'No,' I tell him. 'You went after the money.'

He shakes his head. 'We both did, Shelby. We both did.'

'I've waited for you,' I tell him.

'No,' he says. 'You didn't wait. You got married too! Do you know how hard it was on your wedding day?'

'My wedding day when you announced your wife's pregnancy? You're selfish, Max. You know it and I know it. You'd kill your own mother for the money.'

'Don't you dare . . .' he starts but he doesn't finish.

'No! You made me a promise!' I roll up my sleeve, show him his initial, now faded, on my wrist. 'If you don't walk away, I'll tell Carole everything, I swear to God.'

Max's face flares to match mine and he turns. 'You wouldn't.'

'I will tell her. About how it never stopped between us, about the pact we made: the long game. I will tell her and then I'll walk away and you'll never see me again.'

'You know you wouldn't,' he repeats.

'Try me.' I push his shoulder hard, he stumbles, and for the first time in almost two decades, I see a wicked flash of anger in his eyes, directed at me.

Chapter Thirty-Four
Lottie

The ambulance arrives in less than five minutes, even though time stands still and it seems like an hour. Freya sighs with relief and says 'thank God' as the sirens whoop-whoop their way along Esperance Parade. The ambulance stops outside Carole's front door and the red and blue of the lights flash through the front window.

Carole is blue and lying in the centre of the floor, a photo of Max smiling down at her from the mantelpiece. His skin is pink and he is full of life, but Carole's is grey. A half-eaten carrot stick lies beside her. She looks as though she is almost dead.

'Who put peanuts in the dip?' Marella says, hysterical.

'Oh God, was it you, Lottie?' Freya shrieks.

Everyone is panicked but my body is paralysed with fear. I can't move. All I do is watch them all as they flap and fluster and try to help Carole. It's as though I am an outsider, peeking in. I try to speak, but I can't.

'Lottie?'

I blink twice.

'Lottie?'

I open my mouth, shake my head slowly.

'Well, someone did!' Freya is holding Carole's hand. 'Stay with us, honey. You'll be okay.'

She gets up and flies back into the kitchen, starts opening random cupboards – and even the fridge – in a last-
ditch attempt to find Carole's EpiPen.

I stay frozen to the spot. I cannot take my eyes off Carole. I am watching a woman die – just like my sister died.
I am terrified. I cannot move a muscle. I cannot help her,
just like I couldn't help Shelby.

Does this make me responsible? Does this make me a
killer?

Chapter Thirty-Five
Freya

The paramedics arrive a minute later. They don't mess about. They jab Carole with adrenaline and cover her face with an oxygen mask and wheel her into the back of the van. They tell us one person can go with her in the ambulance to Mooney General Hospital, and I volunteer since I'm the calmest at this point, although Lottie – who's paler than a carton of skimmed milk – manages to persuade them to let her come too by saying she feels a bit faint. I think she is just terrified to be alone.

Marella says she'll stay behind at Carole's place so that there's someone there when Carole's kids get home from the skating rink with Hannah.

One of the paramedics radios ahead. 'Severe anaphylaxis,' he booms. 'ETA at General in ten minutes. It's touch and go. Have resus ready.'

The ambulance tears down along the road to Mooney, weaving in and out of cars with sirens blaring. It seems like the ten-minute journey takes an hour. Carole is under a foil blanket and a paramedic is hovering over her with electric pads, as if she's expecting her to go into cardiac arrest any second. When we get to the hospital, they race her off and I wonder if it is the last time I'll see her.

But it isn't, because Carole pulls through. Just two hours after she is admitted, the swelling has almost entirely gone, save for her lips, which only look like they've been nicely enhanced. It's a bit too early for 'maybe you should think about getting fillers, they suit you' comments, so we just fuss around her in her hospital room, smoothing her sheets and mopping her brow with a wet flannel, until she says, 'Oh for God's sake, please get that filthy thing off me.' Lottie, who's got her colour back by this point, rings Piers and says she's going to stay over at Carole's house because Carole doesn't have anyone else now Max is languishing in a cell. She points out someone needs to keep an eye on Otto and Olivia and relieve Marella who needs to go home and let Rocky out.

Carole spends the next couple of hours dozing, only waking up periodically to say things like, 'How many times have I told you all not to bring peanuts? It's not rocket science!' or to look at herself in her compact mirror and say, 'Christ alive, I look like I've been exhumed.'

Just before ten o'clock, Lottie and I head back to Carole's. I need to pick up my handbag which I left there in the race to get to the hospital.

After Marella has gone, I pour us two shots of whisky.

'Crikey, that was close,' I say in perhaps the biggest understatement of the twenty-first century. 'I mean, how did it even happen? We all know about the peanut thing.'

Lottie shrugs. 'I've never been more scared,' she says. 'I thought we were going to end up burying Carole, too.' Her eyes fill with tears. 'I just couldn't move, I just *froze*.'

'It's okay,' I tell her. 'It was a shock. But the good thing is Carole's going to be fine.'

'Thank God Marella was here,' she says. 'She's rather handy in a crisis.'

'We should probably work out where the peanuts came from, so it doesn't happen again,' I suggest.

We scour for the dip bowls to do some sample tasting, to try and work out how a humble (and deadly) little nut managed to rub its venomous juices on something that Carole ate. But Marella has not only washed the little ceramic bowls in the dishwasher, she's done it on an extra hot cycle so that any hard evidence has been irretrievably obliterated.

And then I see it, in the rattan basket beside the tea-bags. Carole's bright yellow EpiPen, glaringly obvious, yet somehow invisible just hours before.

Chapter Thirty-Six
Carole

I feel like I've been hit by a freight train. My lungs are sore and my windpipe aches from trying to pull in air. My ribs are painful and my neck hurts from where my nails drew blood.

The inability to breathe is terrifying, but the panic makes it worse. Like a fish out of water, you flip and flap and fluster, praying you'll get some air.

To say I'm relieved is an understatement, because how will I prove Max's innocence if I am dead? And to put up with Shelby in the afterlife would have quite literally been the nail in the coffin. So here I am, in a vile white hospital gown that does nothing for my figure, with a canula dug into my hand. I look normal again. My lips have finally deflated and I no longer resemble a newspaper advert for bad surgery.

I'm so tired.

Olivia has finally stopped calling from Marella's phone, now I've reassured her I am fine. But it could have been much worse. *Death* worse. I wish Max were here. I miss him so much.

I don't have to miss him for long, because at some point during the night, he is there at my bedside. He is in the same clothes he was in yesterday, with stubble on his face. It is mostly grey now – how did I never notice this before?

'They didn't charge me, Carole,' he says. 'There were fibres under her nails from the killer's clothes – they weren't mine. They let me go.'

I close my eyes and hope I'm not dreaming. When I open them again, he is still beside me.

'How did a peanut get into the house?' I ask him. 'Every-one knows peanuts can kill me! Do you think someone did it on purpose?'

'Shhh,' Max tells me. 'You need to rest.'

I close my eyes again. *Think, Carole! Think!*

I can't even remember what I ate. It only takes a trace. An indelicate smear of peanut on a spoon used to mix, or the gentlest touch of the deadly nut on the rim of a serving bowl. Each enough to constrict my windpipe, to send me to an early grave.

I can't think it was deliberate. But it doesn't evade my thoughts that all of the people close to me tonight know about my allergy: Max, Freya, Lottie, Hannah, even Marella.

Every single one.

Chapter Thirty-Seven
Freya

I leave Carole's at around eleven o'clock. Bernard is not yet home because he's so tied up with the Framlingham case. The house feels old somehow, empty, *chilling*, with the crime novels everywhere and the fountain pens and the paperweights and the barrister wigs. There is nothing young in this house. No passion, no air. I think of Carole who almost died in her own home and I feel a sharp pang of panic. I do not want to die here, in this airless place. I need to get out. It's as if *my* throat is swelling and *my* airways are closing. I cannot breathe.

Bernard is a good man, Carole said. He *is* a good man, too good to stay with. The fact is, I can't do it any more. Not when I'm in love with someone else. And while I know Tino and I can't be together so soon after Shelby, because it just wouldn't *look* right, it's just a matter of time until we can make it look seamless. People have always expected Bernard and me to split up on account of the age gap, so there will hardly be shockwaves rolling through the community. Once they have said their 'I told you so's, they will understand.

I bite the end of the fountain pen I bought for Bernard for our seven-year anniversary, a Mont Blanc. It's so hard to find the right tone when you're telling your husband you intend to leave him, but I am hyped up on adrenaline now. I remove the pen from my mouth, and I begin to write.

My darling Bernard,

When you read this letter, I will be gone. I know you will have noticed a change in me, of late, and I want to explain why. When we married, I was so happy, swept off my feet, but recently I have realised I cannot do it any more. Darling, the gap between us suddenly feels like fifty years and not twenty-seven. I can't live the life of an old woman at forty-one. I can't stay home and wait to die. I feel like my life is slipping away like grains of sand through my fingers. I love you deeply, but I'm sorry to say that this love has turned platonic. I will always cherish our time together, but I need some space to reconnect with the person I've forgotten I am. I have taken a rental apartment nearby and will be back for the rest of my things in the coming week.

Here are my keys – I will arrange with the cleaner to let me in when you are at work.

I'm so sorry. Freya x

I place the letter in an envelope on the kitchen bench and look up at the clock. It is eleven thirty and Bernard will be home soon. I load up an overnight bag, put it in the back of the Mercedes my husband bought me for my fortieth birthday, and pull back the gear stick with the hand that usually wears the diamond he bought me at Tiffany's on Fifth Avenue, the hand which is now devoid of jewels.

I will spend tonight at Tino's, for company. It's not a relationship yet, but who says it can't be? Who says that what started out as revenge – a means to get back at the woman who always got the guy first – can't be something more? The thought excites me. The idea of Tino excites me. The way he wants me, the way he *needs* me.

I pull into his driveway with a smile on my face. Tino answers the door in his dressing gown, and the surprise on his face suggests he's shocked to see me. 'I was just . . .' he starts. 'Never mind! Come in.'

I stand in his living room with photos of Shelby staring out from every surface. I'd never noticed before, but the whole house is decorated entirely in *her* style: modern, angular shapes, a crisp, marble tabletop, black blinds, black and white photography books arranged neatly in stacks, a sleek black candle dead in the centre. There is nothing that shows Tino's character here – no soft edges. The room seems cold, like a show home. The lighting is dim and a takeaway bag sits on the floor beside the La-Z-Boy chair. Tino's phone is in his hand. I look at the screen, the image, a video on pause, is of the back of two people's heads at a wedding.

'What's this?' I ask.

Tino turns it over. 'Just scrolling,' he says.

'I wondered if I could stay tonight? We did say we would see one another, and I had a crazy evening. Carole had an anaphylactic shock and then . . . well, I've left Bernard.'

'Wow,' Tino says, scratching his head. He places his phone screen-down on the mirrored drinks trolley beside him. It's achingly Shelby. 'Yeah, sure,' he says. He doesn't ask about Carole.

'I've just got a couple of bags, if you could help me with them. I don't want to leave them in the car outside.'

'You want me to get them now?'

'If you wouldn't mind.'

It feels awkwardly polite.

'Sure,' he says, tightening his dressing gown cord. 'Make yourself a drink. I'll be back in a minute.'

I walk to the drinks trolley and take the heavy, crystal lid off the whisky decanter, pick up a tumbler and pour myself a dram. My second of the night. One for Carole, one for Bernard. Tino's phone is in front of me, and I don't know why I do it – a sixth sense maybe – but I turn it over, and click the little sideways triangle on the video to make it play.

The footage shows the back of two heads, looking forward. They turn and they kiss; it is Shelby and Tino.

'Happy wedding day, wife,' he tells her. 'I will love you forever.'

'Till death do us part,' says Shelby.

I click off and I scroll some more. Tino has a file on his phone called 'Shelby' and I open it. And there she is. Her eyes, her lips, her smile. Thousands upon thousands of photos of Shelby. Intimate ones, loving ones, striking ones.

I look around the room. She is on every surface, every wall. The sofa cushions, the glass in my hand. Her dressing gown is on the seat Tino has been sitting on, as if he has been smelling it. I finger the rim of the glass.

He didn't just love Shelby. He was obsessed with her. He still is.

'What are you doing?' Tino is in the doorway with a bag in either hand.

I look down at his phone in my hand. 'I was just . . .'

'That's personal,' he says and lurches forward, dropping the bag and snatching the phone.

'You still love her, don't you?' I ask.

'Always,' he replies quietly. He clicks on the video on the screen and stares at it as if I'm not in the room. Then he emits a terrifying sob. He wipes his ruddy face, and, all of a sudden, it is crystal clear.

'You did it to hurt her, didn't you? Us, I mean. You wanted to get back at her for treating you so badly.'

He doesn't answer for a moment, and then he looks at me and says, 'Yes, but isn't that why we both did it, Freya? To get back at her?'

He is right, but that doesn't mean it doesn't feel like rejection. Because even though it started that way, hadn't it become something more? The way he had touched me on the day of Shelby's wake, that wasn't revenge, wasn't it? How could it have been, when she was already dead?

'But what happened at the wake . . .' I begin.

'I'm sorry Freya,' he says. 'I was confused.'

I nod. I get it, I do. I make my way over to my bags, open the door and walk through it, close it gently behind me, in a gesture of respect for the grieving widower. Even with the door closed, I can hear him. He is sobbing now, his silhouette at the window clutching a phone which flashes with colourful memories of his dead wife.

Suddenly I don't feel so bold. I want to go back to my house. I haul my bags back to the car and drive the short distance home. I see Bernard though the clear panes of glass that border the front door, like the emerald-cut diamond of my engagement ring. As if in slow motion, he picks up the letter, looks at the envelope and puts it down to pour himself a drink. I watch him for a moment, an old man bumbling about his kitchen. What will happen if he reads it? My heart aches for the hope I have lost, for the promise of Tino and a new life.

This is my chance at freedom. This is the chance I have to walk away from mundanity and start afresh. But then, where will I go? Who will look after me? How will I afford to live? I'd have to get a job, get an income. I could do that, couldn't I? Could I?

'No,' I say to myself. *He cannot read that letter!*

'Bernard!' I bang on the door, call his name. He doesn't register, because, like many of his faculties, his hearing is on the turn. *Oh God, no!* I need him to let me in. 'Bernard!'

I watch, panicked, as he tears open the envelope with the fat forefinger of his right hand. Runs it along the paper like a sausage. He pulls out the letter from the envelope.

No. He cannot do this.

I bang harder and he looks up, as if he can hear something pesky, but he can't quite work out what.

I ring the bell. I'd forgotten we even had one.

'Bernard!' I cry. 'Please!'

He looks up at the door, sees me and waves heartily, like he's excited to see me. He ambles, the letter hanging from his fingers, down the hallway to the front door, the paper catches the air and flutters.

'Darling,' he says. 'I've been waiting up for you. You left your keys on the side.'

'Did I?'

He kisses me on the forehead. 'You did. And your rings are upstairs by the bed. You mustn't leave them there. They could get lost.'

'Sorry,' I mumble. 'I was cleaning earlier and took them off. I didn't want anyone to see it flashing in the park, you know, not while there's a killer on the loose.'

'Clever girl.' He smiles. 'And what's this? Have you written me a love letter?'

My hand darts up instinctively for the paper and he pulls it out of my reach. 'It isn't a Dear John, is it?' He looks at me, deadly serious, and then laughs. 'I'm joking, my darling.'

He hands it to me.

'It isn't meant for you,' I say quickly. 'It's a letter for Lottie. I wrote to her tonight. You know, she's had such a tough time, and there's nothing as meaningful as a hand-written letter!'

'Oh dear! I'm so sorry, darling. I assumed it was for me and opened it. I assure you I didn't read a word, but you'll need to pop it in a new envelope now.'

'That's fine.' I smile and let out a sigh. I walk into the kitchen, legs wobbling. 'So, is the Framlingham case all tied up?' I ask, trying to keep my voice steady and my face free of emotion.

'Just about,' Bernard says. 'I'm exhausted now, though. Time to hit the hay. I'll go and lock the front door.'

I watch him lock us inside and blink back the tears. It is a prison of my own making.

The next morning, I leave the house early to head to St Paul's. Lottie is writing price tags and attaching them to a pile of clothes when I get there. She has in her hands a sequinned mini skirt. 'Sass and Bide,' she says. 'Shelby's.'

'Oh.' I stand back. I don't like the idea that Lottie is pricing up something that's been worn by her dead sister.

'Please don't be weird about it,' Lottie says. 'I'd rather her stuff was here than in landfill. At least it's benefitting someone less fortunate.'

'Listen,' I tell her. 'I just wanted to let you know, in case you haven't already heard, that Max has been released without charge. Carole texted me late last night.'

Lottie doesn't look up from the dress as she fixes it on a wooden hanger. 'He'll be back when they get enough evidence,' she says. 'They have to release suspects until they get enough evidence to charge them.'

'Yes, but they've proved it wasn't him, Lottie. Max didn't do it. Carole told me they tested his clothes and ruled him completely out.'

Lottie's face reddens.

'You can price that one at twenty bucks,' she says.

'Lottie . . .'

'Hang it up, then!' she snaps and I take it from her and hang it on a rail.

I shift on my feet.

'Are you okay?' I ask.

'Fine,' says Lottie, shaking out a leopard print sundress and taking it to the window, where Nell, the mannequin, stands naked. She slips the dress over Nell's head. 'You? I take it you didn't come here just to tell me about Max. Spit it out.'

'I just wanted you to know I broke it off with Tino.' It's a slight twist on the truth.

'Good,' says Lottie. 'It was the right thing to do.'

My eyes fill with tears because I've messed everything up. 'He's still madly in love with Shelby,' I tell her.

'I could have told you that,' Lottie sighs, looking up at me wearily.

'I can't stay with Bernard,' I say. 'I just can't do it any more.'

'What are you doing, Freya? Asking for my permission to leave him? It's nothing to do with me. You got yourself into this mess, you sort it out!'

'But Lottie, I just . . .'

'No!' Lottie snaps, which I hope is just the grief talking. 'Pull yourself together. I don't have time for this. I've just lost my sister and found out the man who killed her is apparently getting away with it! I don't have time to help you sort out whatever pathetic little crisis you're having with your husband.'

I stand and look at her, wide-eyed. I never knew how much like Shelby she could be.

I turn to leave. 'I'm sorry,' I say.

Lottie doesn't reply.

Outside, I stand and watch her labelling and hanging clothes. She holds an old suit of Piers' in her arms and embraces it as if it is bringing her comfort. Poor Lottie. So full of grief, loss and pain. I have been so hard on her. I feel such remorse that I stand for a moment, wondering if I should go back inside the shop and apologise, tell my friend I'm sorry for making it all about me.

Chapter Thirty-Eight
Shelby

Before

I have an important errand to run on Thursday on Esperance Parade, but, as usual, you can't fart in this place without someone knowing. And today that someone is Carole Latimer. She is in the flower shop buying some gawdy arrangement, so I slip past as quickly as possible and head towards St Paul's, but I know she sees me, because she hovers behind a tree for ages looking in my direction. It's creepy, really.

I need to talk to Marella, under the guise of an apology for what went down at school.

She's in the window when I walk through the door of the shop.

'Marella?' I call out as I browse a rack of clothing. It's nice in here, homely. The old lady in the corner says hello and offers me an Arnott's Mint Slice.

'Yes?' Marella steps down and faces me. There is no recognition on her face as far as I can see. Maybe this is a wasted journey.

'I wondered if I could have a few moments of your time?'

'Fine.' She smiles thinly. She dusts off her hands, leads me in to her office and gestures at a plastic seat on the opposite side of the desk.

'You might not even know who I am, or remember me, but . . .'

'Of course I remember you, Shelby,' she says matter-of-factly, unemotional.

'Look Marella,' I say. 'I was completely out of order at school, calling you fat and stuff, but that was a long time ago.'

Marella looks up at me and shrugs.

'It's fine,' she says, because she knows that's as near to an apology as she's going to get. 'I agree, you were awful to me, but it didn't ruin my life in the slightest, you may or may not care to know. I went on and got a doctorate and now I'm working here in Esperance and I have Rocky, so I'm just fine.'

'So we're good?'

'Yep, we're good . . . So why are you really here?' she asks. 'It's not to apologise.'

I sigh. 'Actually, there is something else,' I tell her. 'I'm here because I need you to keep a secret for me. And it's big.'

She walks over to the open window and shuts it firmly.

The next night we meet at the dunes, on my request.

On my way to you, beautiful, xo he tells me in a message before he finds me at the usual time, in our usual spot. We meet and make love on the sand like we always do, and I know it is the last time. But Max doesn't.

'I'm sorry about the other night,' he says. 'I didn't mean to get so riled up. But the making up is the best part, isn't it?'

I wriggle back into my running tights and turn to him.

'You know everyone suspects we're doing this, don't you Max? *Everyone.* I can see Freya knows – she's always watching us. I knew she was there at the garage the other night – that's why I made a show of kissing you. I don't want to keep it secret any more. I'm sick of it!'

'What?' he says. 'Why would you do that?'

'Because I want you to leave her, Max, and you're not fucking doing it!' I tell him, standing up. 'This is it, your ultimatum. Do it now or lose me. I'm sick of this. I don't want it any more. Choose.' *Me or the money.* He doesn't know I've got over eight million untapped dollars sitting in a Bitcoin account – and the password in the palm of my hands.

He looks at me and I know. 'I can't leave her,' he says simply. 'I can't leave my kids.'

Here is my answer. Twenty years too late. 'You're never going to leave her, are you?'

He looks down, shakes his head and whispers it. 'I can't.'

I think in my heart I've always known.

My throat burns, my heart aches. 'Say goodbye Max,' I tell him. 'To me and your precious money, because I'm going to tell her, like I said. I'm going to make good on that promise.'

If he'd only chosen me, he could have had both! But I'm not going to tell him that, because I needed to know what meant the most to him – me or the money. And he chose the dollars.

'Shelby . . .'

He goes to grab my wrist but I shake him off, turn and run, weaving in and out of the sandy pathways that lead to the clearing. I briefly glance back to see the look on his face, but he has disappeared. After a few yards, the squeaky cool sand turns to rock and then to mulch, and

I slip my flip flops back on. I stop by the fig tree with our initials on its trunk: ML & SB. I trace the letters one by one, feel the ragged dips and troughs of the wood. Then I hear a noise behind me, the crack of a twig underfoot, the squelch of wet leaves. See a man's tall silhouette. He says my name on the intake of breath.

'Shelby!'

'Leave me alone.'

'Don't be like that.'

He steps forward and holds out his arms to me, and I step back. He opens his mouth like he wants to say something, make amends of some kind. His hands are now on my shoulders. He looks in my eyes with genuine emotion before they seem to glaze over and turn to steel.

He moves his fingers inwards, towards the base of my neck. At first it almost seems like a gesture of intimacy, his fingers tickling my skin, before they stiffen.

I try to pull away. But he squeezes tighter. I try to gulp, but I cannot.

I try to move my torso, but I can't do that either. Not with his hands on me. I grab the tree, finger the initials of Max's name, try to grasp hold on something, anything. Feel the sting of my fingernail as it rips clean off. I try to scream for help but my voice has gone, it comes out as just a whisper.

'Help!' I try again but he squeezes harder.

I cannot breathe, only stare and blink, blink and stare.

My arms flail and, as my fingers bend like claws, pull at the twigs. Clutch at straws.

He cannot look at me as he throttles me, so I say her name to him. The name we both know so well. The name that might shock him into stopping what he's doing to me.

'Lottie,' I choke out.

His eyes narrow but his hands don't move.

'Oh you stupid, stupid girl,' Piers says as my thoughts start to blur and everything goes black. 'Whose idea do you think this *was*?'

THURSDAY

THURSDAY

Chapter Thirty-Nine
Carole

The doorbell rings, a stately ding-dong, and I ignore it because I'm too busy scouring the *Esperance Observer*'s Facebook page for updates on the park flasher. Everyone's talking about the shock arrest. It makes a refreshing change from them talking about Max.

He is back in the granny flat again. A free man. A cheating scumbag maybe, but not a murderer *or* a flasher. Last week, the same paper's headline read: *Is Latto the Flasho?* And it had almost broken me. I'd picked up the kids immediately from their respective schools in case someone in Olivia's year had spied the offending headline on social media. But as it happened, the park flasher has been identified as someone else entirely, thank God. Someone altogether rather surprising.

'I'll get it,' calls Hannah from the kitchen, where she is slicing her homemade banana bread for Olivia and Otto's lunchboxes, which, of course, if the children ask, I will pass off as my own.

Freya comes scurrying up the hall into the kitchen.

'I need to talk to you,' she says.

'I've just read about it,' I tell her. 'I have to say, I didn't expect it to be the old duffer from the charity shop. Although Lottie did tell me Ron liked to take his clothes off. But, exposing himself at the park?'

'*Ron* is the park flasher?' Freya seems shocked. 'Ron from St Paul's?'

'Yes. That *is* what you're here for, isn't it?' I ask, re-arranging the sunflowers on the benchtop.

'No, Carole!' she snaps. 'As if I'd come over here to chat to you about some old man flopping his cock out at the park!'

'Touchy!' I chirp, organising the stems.

Freya sighs. 'Listen, I just need to run something past you.' She pulls shut the French doors that separate the room from the hallway. 'It might be nothing but it's just been bugging me . . .'

'Go on,' I humour her.

'The suit Piers was wearing the night Shelby died . . .'

'What about it?'

'Piers had on this bespoke tweed suit. It was kind of hipster-like. I remember thinking it would look great on a Hemsworth or someone, but just not on Piers, because he's so preppy. Anyway, he came in with blood all over his shirt and I said to him, "You've got something on your shirt"– and I remember this really clearly – Lottie said the suit meant a lot to them as they'd got it in London on their honeymoon.'

'And?' I sigh.

'Well I can't be sure, but I think I saw Lottie with the same suit in St Paul's, pricing it up. I mean it could have been a similar one, but I can't get it out of my mind – it looked like the same one. It didn't dawn on me until later.'

'I don't get the significance of any of this,' I tell Freya, because frankly, I have more to think about at the moment than Piers' dubious fashion choices.

'Carole, you are not *listening*,' pleads Freya and there's something in her manner that makes me suddenly want to focus.

'Piers gives away a ten-thousand-dollar bespoke suit to charity? The one he wore on the night of Shelby's *murder*? Why would he do that?'

'You think it was Shelby's blood?' I ask.

'Yes! Lottie *always* dry-cleans his work clothes. She would never give away a suit like that unless she *had* to get rid of it. Or he *made* her.'

'But Shelby was strangled; there wasn't any blood when I found her.'

'I don't have an answer for that,' says Freya. 'But don't you think it's strange? She said she'd never get rid of that suit.'

'You're saying Piers killed Shelby and made poor Lottie dispose of his clothes?'

Freya sighs. 'I don't know, but stranger things have happened.'

I can't quite get my head around it. But the fact is, murderers are often family members, everyone knows that.

'But what about the fact you saw Shelby on the track *and* Lottie spoke to her after Piers got home?' I ask, playing devil's advocate.

'Lottie *said* she got a text,' shrugs Freya. 'But I didn't see it.'

'Yes but you saw Shelby.'

'I saw what I *thought* was Shelby, but it was dark and I could have been mistaken.'

'Who else would it have been?'

'I've been stuck on this point myself, but I thought about it and I think it might have been Lottie.'

'Don't be silly. Lottie's white as a sheet and she runs like Bambi.'

'Maybe she faked it. I can't explain it. I haven't worked it out yet.'

I mull it over. Suspecting Piers is one thing, but Lottie? Lottie wouldn't hurt a fly – she'd be too terrified. She gets anxious watching *CSI*, so I can't imagine her having any involvement in crime of any sort.

'I can't explain it,' says Freya. 'I don't want to doubt her, because well, she's Lottie. But I never for one moment thought Max could have done it. He's not that kind of man.'

'Thank you, Freya,' I say. I haven't always seen eye to eye with Freya, but I do trust her.

'So what do we do?' Freya asks.

I chew on my cheek, weigh up what needs to be done. There is, on the one hand, Lottie, my best friend. And then there is Max, the man I have always adored. One of them loyal to a fault for over twenty years, the other only pretending to be. But the choice I have to make is not easy, is not black and white. It is a choice between my best friend and my cheating husband. It is the possibility of getting justice for a dead woman I hated to the detriment of her sister whom I adore. I look at Freya and shrug.

'There's only one thing we can do,' I tell her as I walk to the mantel and pick up the plain white business card that's underneath my statement vase of lilies. 'We call the police.'

FRIDAY

FRIDAY

Chapter Forty
Lottie

I lie by the pool with an Aperol spritz, enjoying the afternoon sun and reflecting on my coffee with Marella this morning. I took her to Only Organic to tell her I was leaving St Paul's, and she'd been quite upset.

'But why?' she'd asked, gulping down her full-fat latte as I sipped on my black coffee.

'Because it has too many memories,' I told her with a sniff. 'I don't know if it's just Shelby's clothes or something, but I find it hard to be in the shop since she died, so I'm afraid I won't be coming back again.'

Marella sighed. 'You and Ron, both gone in the space of a week,' she said. 'What a shame.'

'It is,' I said. 'I wish I didn't have to leave.'

It was a lie, of course. I didn't want to stay, not one bit. Too much water under the bridge at that shop, too much second-hand baggage.

'What can I say? I'll miss you,' Marella said.

'Me too,' I lied.

The sun beats down on my legs, giving a layer of colour on the skin I've been hiding away under floral prints. I close my eyes, watch the world turn orange under my eyelids, open them again and survey my domain: an azure pool, sandstone tiles, a slender green palm tree casting a shadow from on high over my left big toe. A black house spider pulls a cicada into its web and wraps it tight in the corner of the sun-lounger. Over and over she works to trap her victim in an impenetrable cocoon. She looks innocent and graceful as she does it, she cowers and makes herself small when she feels threatened, but inside she is filled with deadly venom, an inbuilt urge to kill.

I hear the doorbell ring, ignore it, and take a long sip of my cocktail. It tastes sweet and bitter. Bitter-sweet. That's what it's like to be sisterless: a little bit bitter, a little bit sweet.

I wonder if I did love Shelby once, but I can't think of a time I did. She was never tender, always cruel. Everything I see in her, I see in Isobel, and that's why I can't feel for my daughter what most women feel for theirs. The reason I wish she had been Shelby's child and not mine. I've tried to love her, I really have! But she is too like my sister. And I blame Shelby for it.

Isobel and Shelby, two peas in a pod.

The bell rings again, interrupting my reverie. I sigh and put my drink on the arm of the lounger, gather my floral kimono and slip it on. I walk barefoot along the hallway, see the figures through the frosted glass of my front door, hunched in deadbeat grey jackets. Most out of place in this colourful, flora-rich spot of the world. I don't want to let their drabness into my world, but I have to.

Detectives Sergeant Murphy and Senior Constable Wu from the homicide squad stand on the other side of the threshold.

'Hello,' I say, gathering the fabric of my gown. 'Won't you come in?'

'Thank you, Mrs Denton,' says Murphy and steps inside. Her smile is not as vibrant as it was last week, instead she is studying me, looking for signs of weakness, of guilt. I notice there is a uniformed police officer waiting by a squad car outside in our driveway. He stands with his hands behind his back, his gun in his holster.

'Is . . . is everything all right?' I ask, giving my best anxious face.

'Mrs Denton, where is your husband?'

'Piers? Why do you need to see him? Is it something I can help you with?'

'This may seem like a strange question, but does your husband possess a tweed suit?'

A bespoke suit made in London years ago. A suit made from the finest Scottish tweed by the most esteemed tailors in Savile Row.

'Yes,' I tell them. 'He does. At least he did until yesterday.'

Wu glances at Murphy.

'Piers asked me to take it to the shop – I mean, to St Paul's, the charity shop where I work. It had become a little snug, you know, around the waist. When I took my sister's clothes and things, I bagged up a few items of his, too. Mainly things he's grown out of.' I pat my stomach to make my point about Piers' expanding waistline.

'Thank you, Mrs Denton,' says Wu. 'In the spirit of full disclosure, we should let you know we have the suit and are examining it in the lab. Just as a precaution.'

'Oh?' My voice is feeble. 'I'm afraid I dry-clean all of Piers' suits, including that one. I did it before I took it to the shop. You can't send dirty things to the charity shop, you see. I mean, people do, but . . .' I falter. 'Gosh, have I done something wrong?'

DS Murphy's eyes crinkle into a smile, but her lips do not. She studies me as if she thinks she knows something about me.

'It's no matter,' she says. 'That won't make a difference.'

'I'm sorry?'

'We found some fibres underneath your sister's fingernails and on her tongue and neck. Microscopic fibres we cannot trace because they are so unique. Tweed, of some kind.'

Shelby's fingernails stuffed with fibres from a bespoke suit? I feel my blood drain. Oh Shelby, how you must have fought to hold on to life as it slipped out of your grasp!

'And . . .' I simper. 'You think these fibres are from Piers' suit?'

'Oh, we just want to rule it out. But in the meantime, we're keen to get hold of your husband . . .'

I feel the panic set in.

'Where is Mr Denton today?' DS Murphy asks again, as casual as if she's asking about the weather.

'He's at work, of course.' I look at my phone on the coffee table, and she follows my gaze.

'No need to tell him we're on our way.' She smiles. 'We don't want to concern him!'

I nod. 'Of course,' I say.

The feeling is overwhelming: shock, fear and anger, all rolled into one.

But mostly I am disappointed.

Disappointed in Piers.

He had one job.

How the hell did he screw it up?

'So,' says Murphy for the third time. 'Can you confirm your husband is at the hospital?'

If I have to throw him under the bus, then so be it!

'Yes,' I tell them, my hand over my open mouth, the shocked little wife. Poor, put-upon little Lottie, always ready to help.

'Maternity ward. Delivery suite seven,' I say. 'He'll be there until four.'

Chapter Forty-One
Carole

On Friday afternoon, shortly after Freya calls to tell me Piers has been arrested, Max and I go to visit an apartment in Mooney. Somewhere he can stay for a few weeks while we work out what is going on with our marriage. The apartment is horrible – riddled with damp and 1960s carpets – and the idea of Max and the children staying there pains me. I wonder if that was Max's intent when he picked it from the apartments on offer online, if it was a way to stall for time as he tries to win me over. And my God, is he trying!

'Thanks for coming with me,' Max says as we walk back to the car. He goes for the driver's seat, but I make it clear I'll be driving. I don't want him assuming his role in our relationship is the same as it has always been.

'It's fine,' I tell him. 'I need to check it out if the kids are going to be staying there.'

'I miss you and the kids so much,' he says. 'Just being at home with you all.'

I do not reply.

As we drive along the bitumen road with the heat snaking upwards, I feel nothing but an incredible lightness in my shoulders. The air smells of diesel oil and hope.

'I'm so sorry, Carole,' he says as I negotiate the one-way system to get us back on the main road. He looks older, sadder, *greyer*. 'I mean, for everything.'

I stare at the road ahead, see the sunshine, the green of the trees, the possibilities. The rain has stopped now and everything is swathed in sunshine again.

'You were going to leave me for her, weren't you?' I ask him as I indicate right. Max is not surprised by the question.

'I thought about it,' he says, staring ahead. 'But I couldn't do it. It wouldn't have lasted. I was just carried away with it all, with her. Infatuated, I suppose.'

I snort. 'For over twenty years?'

Max bites his lip. 'Maybe. With Shelby it was a bit of history, a bit of obsession,' he says. I see the dark circles under his eyes, the baggage of a man who is grieving. 'I can't explain it. It was like she had a hold on me. But it could never have worked between us. It would have been toxic.'

'You couldn't live with or without each other, isn't that what the U2 song says?'

'Something like that.'

It dawns on me that I am talking about my nemesis without hate. And it isn't a new thing. I've realised that Shelby and I had something in common – we loved a man who let us down. For her, he represented home. He represented security. But he couldn't give her everything. The man she loved consistently chose me, for whatever reasons. Oh yeah, I came with money, sure – but it was real. The birth of our children? That was real. The cuddles with Otto and Olivia in the middle of the night? The nights we talked for hours about TV shows, argued about politics; when I helped him clear out his mother's home after she died and held him as he cried? Those things were real and Shelby knew it. Just like I knew he loved her with a passion he could not replicate with me. In the end, we were both victims of loving Max. He ruined us both.

'What shall we do?' Max asks me, as I turn onto the highway. 'Do you want me, still?'

I stare ahead. Yes, I want him, he is all I have ever wanted. But I don't want to be second best. I cannot live with that.

'Can you stop the car?' Max asks. I pull over on the side of the road near Mooney Park. There are a few runners there, ants in a line, making their way around the circuit, past a clearing like the one where Shelby met her death. Past high trees that perhaps hold all of their secrets in their boughs, like in Esperance. The secrets of the running club: desires, hatred, jealousy, camaraderie, love.

'Carole.' Max turns to me, puts his hands on mine. 'I messed up. I'm not going to lie to you – I wanted her and I couldn't let her go. But I wanted you and the kids, too. That's why I didn't leave. I want to come home, now. To you and to the kids. I want to be with you. I don't want to live in some shithole miles away from you all.'

I look into his eyes.

'Do you love me more than you loved her?'

'Of course I do . . .'

'No, Max.' I look him dead in the eyes. 'No bullshit. Do you love me more than you loved her?'

He breaks eye contact with me and stares ahead. 'Yes,' he says, but his smile does not reach his eyes.

It is all the information I need.

'I want you gone by tomorrow,' I tell him. 'Stay with Tino until you find somewhere, I don't care. But you need to leave.'

'You're serious?'

'Deadly.'

'But Carole . . . ?' He turns to me, his hands clasped together. Maybe he thought the apartment viewing was just theatre, histrionics. A chance for me to punish him before welcoming him back home. 'Please.'

I have a good side, I am not devoid of emotion, or love, or empathy. But I know when I deserve better. My children deserve better. Olivia needs to know that you don't ever need to be second best in your own marriage. Otto needs to know how to treat a wife. I am glad their father is free, and I will fight for him in many ways, but I am not going to be there as his consolation prize. I do not like second-hand things. I never have.

'No,' I say, softer this time and restart the engine. 'I'm sorry Max, but it's over. I deserve more, can't you see?'

He stares ahead.

'But where will I go?' he eventually asks.

'It's not my concern any more,' I say and pull out onto the intersection. 'I'm sorry.'

I stop at the crossroads and indicate. The large bottle-green road sign in front of us has two arrows. The left points to Shivers Beach and the right, to Esperance. I take the sharp right, while Max stares sorrowfully to the left.

SATURDAY

Chapter Forty-Two
Lottie

They let me have ten minutes with Piers after they charge him with Shelby's murder.

'Get Bernard on the phone, darling.' Piers squeezes my hands. He looks so tired, so old. 'I need to lawyer up.'

I don't think there is much a lawyer can do for my husband now. Fibres under the fingernails? I'd say it's pretty conclusive. Guilty as charged.

Piers begins to cry, softly. I withdraw my hands. I hate it when he is pathetic. I hate it when *I* am pathetic, but it is a role I have had to play. I have had a starring role as the fretful, put-upon wife, and let me tell you, it gets you so much further in life than bulldozing your way through. It gets you a big house, a doting husband, a group of friends you can slyly manipulate. It allows you to get away with murder. Oh, I'm sure I've been anxious in the past, but never about Shelby. Those dreams were never premonitions. They were manifestations. Scenes I would create in the middle of the night as I lay awake that I would embellish. I would try to make them so vivid that maybe, just maybe they'd come true. Maybe, if I dreamed she would walk into the water and drown, she would! And would you believe it? She did! All I had to do was tell her I'd dreamt it, put the idea in her head . . .

I look at Piers, sniffling like a child. 'Pull yourself together,' I snap. 'For God's sake.'

'We can kill her, and we can frame Max,' I told Piers the week before, after Shelby told us she would not give us the Bitcoin password. Greedy old Max Latimer, who dangled a carrot in front of my sister's nose for two decades, who had his cake and gorged on it, too. 'She meets him every Friday for sex and that's when we should do it. The storm will wash everything away!'

I planned my birthday dinner for the Friday night because it was the night Shelby always met Max. Then when we heard the forecast, the flooding and the winds, so perfect for destroying evidence – well, it was the perfect storm.

'Are you being serious?' Piers had asked.

'Deadly. You know she's going to ruin you. Ruin *us*.'

'But if she's dead, how will we get the password?'

'We'll find it. I'll go through all of her stuff, her bags, her drawers. I grew up with her Piers! I know the places she hides things!'

'But' – he'd turned away from me, scratched his head – 'we won't get away with it.'

'We will,' I said. And I knew right then he would do it, for me. You see, it's easy to create an illusion that you're the downtrodden wife, but believe me, it's rarely the wife who's the downtrodden one. Piers hasn't made a decision that I haven't put in his head for almost twenty years! Sometimes I've even convinced myself that Piers is mean and controlling, but it couldn't be further from the truth.

'I don't . . . I don't know.' Piers shook his head but I knew he was chewing it over. There were so many reasons. Eight million of them!

'She'll never give us the password while she's alive,' I said. 'She's better off dead.'

And I was right. Shelby wouldn't give it to us because she had something on Piers. She knew about money Piers had stolen, over the course of the years, from the women's shelter floating account – it was the account he was trusted with as esteemed chairman of the board. Shelby had seen the accounts. She'd threatened Piers. 'I'll expose you if you come after the Bitcoin money,' she'd said. 'A gynaecologist ripping off a women's charity? It doesn't look good, does it, Piers?'

With Shelby gone, I knew I could get the password back, go through every possession she ever owned, you know, posthumously. Rifle through her phone, her laptop, her diaries. I'd just have to wait for the police to give her phone back. And I did it. When Tino gave me her mobile I tapped in the password (her birthdate – how original) under the guise of sending myself photos from her camera roll. I scrolled her notes, her emails. I dug about in her bags and in her purses and her pockets until my fingers bled. I traced the outline of the cornices of her ceilings. I peeled back the velvet of her jewellery box, took a screwdriver to the mini safe under her bed. Pulled off the heels of her shoes. Ripped the pockets off her designer jackets. I was frenzied, mad!

But in the end I couldn't find that damn password. But all is not lost. I have found a man in America who says he can unlock the password in fourteen days for a thirty per cent share. We can take that gamble for $8.3 million! I mean, six million is better than nothing, isn't it? It will pay off our debts and set us up for life.

Later, when I'd taken Shelby's possessions to St Paul's,
I also took the clothes Piers had worn to strangle my sister – the ones he had put in the washing machine drum
in front of Freya, just to be safe, along with the suit and
tie. 'A suit from Savile Row in London,' Marella had said.
'How amazingly generous!'

The truth is, I'd dreamed about killing Shelby a million
times, but in the end, it had been surprisingly easy. We had
an unwitting alibi in Freya. She didn't know it, of course,
but we played her like a pawn. Poor, loyal Freya, who, as it
happens, wasn't that loyal to Bernard.

I'd collected Isobel from dance on the night of the murder, got dressed in my high-necked floral maxi dress, with
the kaftan on top, poor little sun-deprived Lottie, always
covered up! But underneath, I was wearing a pair of tiny
running shorts and a pink fluoro crop top, just like Shelby
always did. I'd lightened my hair earlier in the week, of
course, on Carole's advice, and given my body the once-
over with a tanning mitt and a daily dose of pool-time,
so that anyone running on the opposite side of the park
would see my beautifully dark-skinned sister, alive and
well, plodding along the track at eight twenty. I knew
Freya would be out running because she mentioned she'd
be coming to me straight from the track. I only needed
her to get a quick glance of Shelby. I drove to the reserve,
and parked outside Isobel's dance studio, pulling off my
kaftan as I did. I waited until Freya was on the far side of
the track and stepped out in my fluoro so she'd see me,
or rather Shelby, but not up close. It was easy to mimic
the way Shelby ran, chin up, arms in an arrogant march. I

ran for less than a minute and then I got back in the car, slipped my kaftan over my running gear and waited for Isobel, who was late to emerge as usual. I remember the little princess got in and said, 'Ugh, why do you always dress like you live in a commune?' and I thought, *Little do you know!* When Piers and I arrived home, Shelby was visibly safe and well, because Freya had just seen her! Then just to cement the idea she was still alive, Shelby sent me a text message! The little beep to my handset courtesy of Piers in the other room.

That was all we really needed – alibis at the time of the murder. That and a money-hungry lover in Max, who was about to get cut off from his equally materialistic wife because he'd been rumbled cheating on her. It was as if the stars aligned when Freya glimpsed Shelby and Max at the garage and mentioned it to Carole.

In fact, fate intervened rather neatly, firstly in the form of Ron, the park flasher, who provided an alternative suspect if we couldn't frame Max. There was also the foreboding weather (I'd been sure to point it out, 'Something awful always happens when there's a storm'), which would give us a better chance of hiding evidence at the crime scene, or so we thought. What better time to commit murder? I planted the hype about my dreams being vivid. I told everyone how anguished I was about my sister, how fearful I was that she would be taken from me. How I'd seen a man standing over her, a man who was tall and broad and not unlike Max. Calling the newspaper and telling them about Max and Shelby and their secret tryst on the evening of the murder just served to gild his guilt!

The truth was, Piers had gone straight from little Anne-Marie Cairns's birth to the clearing. It was dark by then. He'd found her there, fresh from fornicating with Max. And he put his hands around her neck and squeezed until she was dead. Or until he thought she was – thank God she fell on a rock, another twist of fate!

Don't get me wrong, it wasn't as if I breezed through murdering Shelby. It's been harder than I thought. You see, I did love her in some ways. Not in many, but in some. Perhaps purely by virtue of sharing a womb, of feeling part of a pair somehow. And she was my captor, sure enough. I couldn't blossom with Shelby there, I couldn't breathe. She stifled me, embarrassed me, belittled me, gave me nothing aside from distance. She was a bad egg on the outside with a core that was partly decayed, but also inherently good. Two flawed eggs fertilised – but only one of us tried to disguise it.

Dad knew. He knew my tendency to choose to be bad rather than good. At first it was just fits of rage, but then the anger settled, and I'd quietly vent. He watched me as I scratched the faces off my dolls with the end of a compass, pull their heads off systematically. Then it got worse. The desire to hurt animals (he'd seen me holding the neighbours' cat under the water, pulled me off it before it drowned), the time I held a knife at Shelby's throat. And that's when he threatened me with hospitalisation, asked Mum to investigate a psychologist. 'She isn't right,' I heard him whisper one night when I should have been in bed. 'She needs help.'

And all I could see in my future was a white straitjacket and a cell – and a future watching Dad and his darling Shelby become ever closer without me. Everything they did was together – it was like there was some kind of umbilical cord uniting them, some piece of DNA that made them love one another above anyone else. And I couldn't stand it! And so when they were singing in the car and laughing and sharing a moment of intense joy together, I pulled the handbrake on the freeway and the car pirouetted across the road and killed our father. I didn't even care in that split second that I could get hurt too – the adrenaline and the fury were running hot in my veins, my pulse pounding in my temple – and so I did it, and it all happened in a split second, and I didn't even close my eyes as we hit the ute. Shelby hadn't seen me pull the handbrake because her head was hanging out of the window, her hair flowing behind her and her mouth open in song.

But I always wondered if she suspected. 'Dad would *never* do that,' she said defiantly, when the police concluded that our father had decided to kill us all, on impulse.

Even so, after that I thought it best to wear a different personality as a disguise. Lovely kind Lottie, so sweet and *anxious* – and, in time, I came to believe I was that Lottie, too. And then I met Piers, and everything was suddenly okay. I didn't have the violent urges or the need to suppress my hatred for Shelby any more, because I had finally overtaken her in money and stature – and I had a baby, too! Even if that baby grew every day in the likeness of her aunt.

Am I sorry that Shelby paid with her life? No I am not. Because my sister's death was my rebirth. Oh, I felt sorry for Carole – she'd been a loyal friend, after all. I hadn't meant for her to become collateral damage. I'd just needed her to stop campaigning to free Max, to stop finding loopholes in his almost-proven guilt. If he got off, then they'd look elsewhere for the murderer, wouldn't they? All I had to do was hand Marella a knife that just happened to have been used for Isobel's peanut butter sandwich when we prepared the dips in my kitchen. Just a trace in the beetroot dip, but enough to kill a person with a severe allergy. I felt bad after that, honestly, I really did – Carole and I have been friends for years, and were indelibly linked by our unspoken hatred for Shelby. But she had to go. And even though she didn't die, despite me plucking the EpiPen from its usual home in the basket beside Carole's English Breakfast teabags and slipping it into deepest corner of my raincoat (believe me, it was trickier to return later that night with Freya sniffing around) the episode was enough of a shock for her to realise there were greater forces at play and that she needed to back the hell off.

Piers leans in across the table. In the corner of the room, DS Murphy stands tapping the screen of her phone. She looks up momentarily and says, 'You've got two more minutes,' before she drops her head down again. As far as she's concerned – as far as *everyone's* concerned – Piers' guilt is a done deal.

'Lottie.' Piers leans in close. 'Maybe we have a case here. I mean, I may have tried to kill Shelby, but I didn't succeed.

It was the fall that killed her, the rock – the detectives said so themselves. Technically I didn't murder anyone.'

'What?'

'Don't you see, Lottie?' he whispers. 'I didn't actually kill Shelby – her death was accidental. As far as I'm concerned, I just threatened her, got rough with her with my hands on her neck. I never pushed her, she just fell. How can they prove I pushed anyone? Get me Bernard – maybe he can help.'

I look at Piers, shackled and ready for the slammer, and I feel an overwhelming desire to laugh at the preposterousness of what he's saying, the stupidity. Instead, I let out a sob and jump back in mock horror. 'What the hell are you talking about?' I whimper, loud enough for Murphy to hear in the corner of the room. 'Are you telling me, Piers, that you're confessing to strangling Shelby?'

Piers looks confused. He looks from me to the window and back to me again.

'You know I am Lottie,' he says, through gritted teeth. 'You know I am because you asked me to do it.'

'What are you saying? How could you?' I gasp, as Murphy's gaze flies from me to Piers and back again, as if she's watching the final of the Australian Open.

Piers nods and begins to clap his hands together as much as he can wearing a pair of steel handcuffs. It's like watching a seal clap.

'I always knew you had the capacity to be a scheming bitch, but I didn't know quite how much,' he says. 'You're going to find yourself all alone in this world, Lottie, do you realise that?'

I stare back at him. What he doesn't realise is I can re-invent myself. If I've done it once, I can do it again.

'Oh Piers,' I whine. 'Why are you saying these things?'

Murphy inches forwards.

'You're forgetting one thing, my darling,' says Piers. 'You helped me! Who took my suit to the dry-cleaners? Who slathered on the fake tan and dressed up as her sister for a night-time run?'

'Proof?' I ask and tap my fingernails on the table.

'Won't your watch have recorded the spike in your heart rate?'

'Tenuous,' I tell him. 'I seem to recall running across the carpark to collect Isobel from dance.'

'Then who faked the text message from Shelby saying she was going to be late? It's surprising Starsky and Hutch here haven't worked that out already.' He looks at Murphy. 'No offence,' he says.

'None taken.' She smiles. 'Anyway, lovebirds, you're going to have to hurry it along,' she says. 'There's a nice, luxurious cell waiting for Mr Denton out the back.'

Piers tries to reach my phone, but I pick it up and put it in my pocket.

'Being coerced into writing a text message and unwittingly taking a dirty work suit belonging to my murderous husband to be cleaned don't make me guilty of murder now, Piers, do they?' I smile.

'No,' he spits back, with the most bitter of smiles on his face. 'But they make you an accessory.'

Part Three: Rebirth
Six Weeks Later

Chapter Forty-Three
Freya

I stare out of the car window, watch the uniformed pack of Arlingford girls lug their bags inside the gate and turn around for a last glance at their parents. Isobel looks back, sees me, and waves. I wave too before I turn the car in the direction of home.

Isobel is doing surprisingly well, given where both her parents are. A life sentence for Piers, eighteen months for Lottie. Lottie was told that if she pinned it all on Piers, she would get less time, so that's exactly what she did.

'I knew my husband wanted to kill my poor sister,' she sobbed during cross-examination. 'But I only found out after he did it. I didn't know what to do. I felt duty bound to protect him! I made a vow in front of God to be loyal to him.'

He called her a lying bitch as he left the courtroom. 'It was her idea,' he cried. 'She wanted Shelby dead! I didn't even kill her – don't you see? She hit her head on a *rock*!'

Lottie had clutched at her chest, pulled at her understated Dior pussy-bow blouse, looked about, desperately. 'Please don't shout, Piers,' she whimpered. 'You're *scaring* me!'

In the end the jury found Lottie not guilty of murder, but guilty of aiding a murderer, of providing him an alibi and hiding the evidence in the form of his suit. She sobbed as she was led away, calling to Carole and me in the viewing gallery, promising us she didn't know a thing about Piers' evil plan. 'And I thought I had issues,' Carole said.

Bernard left me that same afternoon.

'Sit down, Freya,' he said, leading me through the hallway of our home to the sun room where the dust motes swirled in the midday sun. He gestured at the velvet armchair with the gold studs in the arm. He'd been acting strangely for a while: hushed phone calls, late night walks, weight loss, that kind of thing. He even had a strange smell about him.

He sat down beside me, took both of my hands in his. 'I have something to tell you,' he said. His eyes watered, his cheeks were hollow and so I knew what he was going to tell me before he said the words: he was dying, cancer was eating away at him, and he would soon be dead. I would be a widow. I'd braced myself for the words.

But instead he said, 'Freya, I have met someone else.'

My head whipped up.

'You've what?' I put my hand to my temple, shook my head. 'I'm sorry, what?'

'I've met someone else.'

'*Met* someone? So you're not . . . dying?'

'Not that I know of.'

'You can't have met someone,' I'd said, incredulous. 'You don't go out.'

'I do go out sometimes, Freya. I really am so sorry.' He ran his hands through his hair. 'I feel utterly wretched about this, but I needed to be brutally honest with you. I believe the relationship I have formed with this lady is going to be very significant.'

I was speechless. *I* was the one who had had the affair. *I* was the one stuck with a soon-to-be septuagenarian. *I* was the one who had desperately wanted out.

'Darling Freya,' Bernard continued. 'I feel as though I am decaying in this relationship of ours. I love you dearly, but I am aware I've turned into rather an old fart lately. I don't want to pop off this mortal coil without living a little bit more. I think we age one another.'

Hold on, wasn't this exactly what I'd written in my letter to *him*?

I looked at him then, and it all made sense. The weight loss was down to the slimming effect of excitement and adrenaline, not sickness!

Bernard looked flustered. 'I've drawn up a very generous settlement. You'll be well looked after, Freya. You'll have the Mooney house, of course, and I'll help you every step of the way. It will be a fresh start for you.'

I looked out of the window and thought back to the letter I'd written him just weeks previously, caught up in the whirlwind of my affair with Tino. A letter to end a marriage. It was despicable. The way I had treated him, taken advantage of him, disregarded him, dismissed him as old and pitiful, when really it was he who pitied me.

I took his face in my hands and looked deep in to his eyes. 'Thank you, Bernard,' I said. 'For everything. I hope you and this lady, whoever she is, will be happy together.'

It is quiet when I open the door. Billie, my rescue cat, nuzzles my legs as I walk through to the open plan kitchen with its white walls and its wooden chairs and crab-pot lights. This is Mayfin Cottage, my gift from Bernard, a weatherboard two-storey home on the beachfront, a little way from the women's shelter. From the master bedroom window I will soon be able to see whales migrate, doing their annual journey between June and October, throwing up their spray into the winter sun. From the back window, I can see the diggers on site at the shelter – expanding it to add twelve more rooms for homeless women and children, thanks to an anonymous donor. If I open both windows, there's the most incredible salty breeze that whirls through the house. Sometimes I just stand and breathe it in. I have always loved this house, and Bernard knew it. That's why he gave it to me. He is a good man, and by all accounts, a happy one. When I found out who he was seeing, I was baffled, I really was. Because I do know her, you see. I've known her a very long time. But after I'd digested it, chewed it over, I realised it made perfect sense. *They* made perfect sense. She will be good for him. Better than I was, or could have been.

Isobel's room is sea-facing too, and covered in posters of pop singers I've never heard of. Oh yes, that was another by-product of Lottie being jailed – guardianship of my goddaughter. Izzi (as she prefers to be called) is so like Shelby, and sometimes it takes the breath clean out of me. Just to see her striking that hip-jutty pose that Shelby always did or pouting with those full lips. I love having her, I can't tell you how much. The house feels young and fun. At the weekends, we go shopping at Mooney Mall together, or just go for a walk along the beach with a coffee. She talks to me about how everything went down. 'I'm going to be screwed up forever,' she says, and I link my arm through hers and tell her, 'No you won't, I've got your back.'

Not that I'm not just as scarred by everything as she is, but somehow, leaving Esperance has done me good. Helped me realise what's important in life. It's done the same for Izzi, I'm sure of it. She surfs, she helps out at the shelter on weekends, maybe to make up for what her father did, I don't know. She and Olivia Latimer do it together, head over there in their jeans and T-shirts and get busy helping the women who need it.

Izzi is still at Arlingford. She was set to lose her place after her parents went down, but a mystery benefactor stepped forward to pay the remaining five years of her fees outright, and so she's staying put. Every morning when I drop her at the gates at eight o'clock, I see them in the distance at the reserve, the running club, jogging together in a group, with Carole at their helm and their newest member, Marella, lagging a little behind.

Carole will sometimes see my car and lift her arm in acknowledgement, give me a smile. She looks out for Izzi too, takes her to dance if I'm running late. It's a big gesture of kindness in my book, to care for a child whose parents all but ruined your life. But in all honesty, we underestimated Carole – her kindness, her strength, her sense of self. Oh, she can still be as abrasive and vain as hell, but she is softer somehow, more human.

Carole was the one who suggested the new wooden bench at Esperance Reserve that sits at the opening of the clearance, dappled by sunshine on a warm, bright day. She gets that Shelby did the wrong thing, but she believes she was just as much a victim in the whole sorry saga. She and Shelby loved the same man, and he played them both for years. Carole sees this, but she also sees that Shelby was cheated by her sister, too. Let down by everyone who loved her, and ultimately alone in the world.

'Do you wish to contribute to the bench?' Carole called to ask, and I told her yes, I did. She was the one who found the words for the plaque online. It reads, 'Shelby Brennan Massini, 1981–2023. In death, we find peace.'

Sometimes when I pass the reserve, I see Carole sitting on the bench with a book or on her phone. She messaged me just last week. **Things aren't the same without you, Freya** she wrote, **Will you come back to the running club?**

I thought about it, but ultimately I declined. Too many memories, too much heartache, too much pretence. Maybe one day I'll revisit for old times' sake, but as an outsider. As a spectator, looking in.

Chapter Forty-Four
Carole

Olivia puts her arms around my waist and nestles herself into my shoulder. She is dressed in denim cut-offs and a white vest top, and her skin has a glow, thanks to the sun. Summer has arrived, resplendent, bringing with it breathtaking orange sunrises and light, hopeful evenings.

'I love you, Mum,' she says.

'You too,' I tell her. She's just turned fourteen, but she is taller than me now, and commands everyone's attention when we go anywhere. Tall, willowy, with deep-set dimples and bright green eyes. So like her father in looks, but so much like me in temperament.

'Please stop growing, Olivia Latimer,' I whisper into her hair.

She steps back. 'Do you still miss Dad?' she asks.

'Sometimes,' I tell her. 'But some things can't be fixed. It's not like I'll never see him anyway, is it? He's your father and I won't stop him being in your lives.'

Olivia nods and kisses my cheek. 'You're amazing, Mum,' she says. 'What you did for Izzi, with the school fees . . . it was incredible.'

I pat her back, my girl.

'That stays secret,' I tell her, my finger on my lips. 'Now go upstairs and get your stuff. Dad will be here soon.'

She smiles and runs up the stairs to pack her overnight bag.

I march to the bottom of the stairs. 'Don't think about packing my Louis Vuitton holdall,' I warn her. There's no way she's taking *that* to Shivers Beach! 'Use the Adidas!'

'Noted!' she calls in reply.

Olivia was devastated when she found out Isobel would have to leave Arlingford after Lottie and Piers went to jail. I lay awake the night Olivia told me the news, and at about 2 a.m., I realised I couldn't let it happen, which is why I contacted the school the very next day and paid the fees outright. I mean, why should Isobel suffer? That much money really is a drop in the ocean to me. It is not public knowledge, because not only do I not want people mistaking me for having a soft side (I have very swiftly learned that that's when they take advantage), but I don't want Lottie and Piers to rest easy in their flea-ridden single bunks under their scratchy blankets knowing I bailed them out after they tried to frame my children's father. Besides, it's rather fun to watch everyone try to guess who Isobel's mystery benefactor is – although Freya picked it in one. She phoned and said, 'If only more people knew that under that horribly prickly exterior, you're incredibly kind-hearted, Carole,' to which I'd told her to stop making such a fuss and pointed out she wasn't going to shift her perimenopausal weight gain if she didn't start running again sometime soon.

Max arrives at about seven o'clock.

'Olivia? Otto, come on,' I call up the hall. 'Your father is here.'

He stands in his tracksuit and leans against the door frame. He runs his hands through his hair, looks at his watch, taps his foot on the welcome mat. He looks older somehow.

He gazes out across the lawn, takes it all in.

'The grass looks great,' he muses.

'It does,' I say. 'Ryan's here today.'

Max smiles at me. I nod back, cordially.

'You look great,' he says.

'Yes,' I say. 'I do!' There's nothing like a new haircut to make you feel brand new.

He is about to say something else but I beat him to it.

'So, you'll have them back tomorrow at three?' I ask. 'My father wants to take them to a garden party in Esperance North.'

'Four more like,' says Max. His vowels sound a little loose. 'We're going ten pin bowling.'

Christ alive! *Ten pin bowling? How horrendous!*

'How delightful,' I say. 'Four should be fine.'

Max smiles. It looks like he's gained a few pounds and his temples are greying. He wears a grey tracksuit and muddy trainers – the kind of attire I always frowned upon. It doesn't particularly smack of self-care, an outfit like that.

Max nods his head towards the house. 'So, are they coming out or not?'

I turn around. 'Olivia! Otto!' I call up the stairs. 'Your father is here! Come *on*!'

The children fly down the hall and dodge between our bodies.

'Move, dipshit,' says Olivia as she nudges Otto towards Max's car.

Max grins as we watch them pass. Then he turns to me.

'How are you, Carole?' he asks. 'I mean, really?'

'Fine,' I tell him. 'How are you? How are you settling into your new apartment?'

Max looks embarrassed. 'It's pretty small.'

'And what's it like being back in Shivers Beach?'

Max looks at his feet. 'Look Carole, it doesn't have to be like this. We should be a family – you, me and the kids. It's not right, me being so far away from all of you.'

I look into his eyes. 'Max,' I say, and I reach out for his hand. I take it and wrap it in both of mine and he looks at me, hopefully. 'You lost that privilege when you decided it was a good idea to have Shelby Massini on the side.'

I pat his hand and drop it. He scratches his chin, walks away from me, raising his arm in a wave to Ryan, who is clipping the hedgerow. I see Max vastly differently these days – more with pity than desire. Ryan, on the other hand? Let me tell you, there's absolutely no pity there! Freya says I always had an eye for a bit of rough!

I call out goodbye to the kids as they climb inside Max's gunmetal grey Audi. Oh, he still got to keep one of the cars. I couldn't have him driving my children around in an old rust bucket, could I?

Max's wheels crunch on the gravel as the car heads up the drive. He makes a left onto the road that lies flush with the sand dunes, and, as he passes the driveway that snakes towards the old Massini home with its lights on again and its new residents inside, I can just make out his head turning right, as if he's looking for her, wondering if she's home.

I turn around and walk through the house, via the kitchen, and out of the sliding doors towards the garden patio where Ryan now sits, enjoying a well-earned beer after flogging himself with the lawn. A single bead of sweat trickles from underneath the arm of his T-shirt and down his right bicep, which shines deliciously in the afternoon sun. So delightfully rough.

'Another?' I ask, holding a brown bottle in the air.

'Why not?' says Ryan, and reaches out his right hand.

Our fingers brush as he takes the bottle and our eyes lock.

Why not, indeed.

Chapter Forty-Five
Lottie

I don't have much to do in here. They're afraid of me. They do what I tell them.

I didn't want to have a middle class name, it doesn't do. Not in here. So I've told them my name is Shelby. I strut around with my head high, my hair pulled taut in the meanest of ponytails, slicked back with gel. I tell them I'm born and bred Shivers Beach, drop my 't's and dilute my consonants. I glare at them from under dark, kohl eyes, unless they find and confiscate my eyeliner, and then I have to wait until I can somehow obtain another. One eyeliner cost me one hundred dollars, can you believe it? The orange jumpsuit wouldn't have suited the old Lottie, but somehow it suits me, the person I am in here. Shelby Brennan. My sister, reborn.

'Shelby?' Cathy's in for theft. 'Can I get you anything?'

I'm an accessory to murder, you see, so they're scared of me.

'Breakfast tea,' I tell her. 'You know how I like it.'

They don't know Lottie, the anxious little weakling everyone else sees. But I know her, and I want to be her again, with the nice house and the pretty dresses. I'm already preparing to go home to Esperance, to find that Bitcoin password and live my life again. No one else knows about the money, you see, not now Shelby's dead and Piers is locked away. They don't have to know.

I pick up a pen and begin to write. I write for hours on paper that's stamped *Shivers Beach & Peninsula Women's Jail and Psychiatric Hospital.*

> *Dear Carole*
>
> *It's been six weeks without any contact with anyone from Esperance. No one will write to me, not Freya and not even Isobel. Why is that? I swear to you, Carole, I knew nothing of Piers' evil plan until much later. He duped me, too. I have lost my sister, my husband and my daughter because of him. The fact is, I'll be out of here in eighteen months and I like to think you'll welcome me back into the fold. Will you, Carole? Will you come and visit me, perhaps? For old times' sake? Could you do that? So I can explain everything to you?*
>
> *If you see Isobel, please tell her Mummy loves her.*
>
> *With all my love, Lottie xx*

I send a variation of the same letter to Freya and Marella. A week later, Carole's comes back unopened with the words 'RETURN TO SENDER' written in her haphazard scrawl and underlined three times.

It's okay, I think to myself, two out of three isn't bad.

I have all the time in the world.

Chapter Forty-Six
Marella

The sun beats down on the pavement, making it look like a slick of oil. It's almost too hot to run today, but I have to. I am determined to get fit, to make this second chance I've been given work to my advantage. I stand in the shade of my porch and look up at the front of my house where the jasmine creeps up the diamond-shaped trellis and settles on the windowsill of the master bedroom upstairs. I look at my reflection in the glass of the French windows. I am slimmer, much slimmer these days, on account of everything that has happened. My stomach is almost flat, held in place by the tight elastic of my vest top, which bears my name underneath the words, *The Running Club*. Carole has redesigned the logo, just to freshen things up after everything that happened.

'Marella!' Carole jogs towards me and stops. 'Morning! I'm so glad to see the top fits. You really do look wonderful. You'll be in the next size down soon. What an amazing effort. You must have lost at least ten kilos.'

'Thirteen,' I tell her. Unlucky for some, but not for me.

I smile at Carole with my new, whitened teeth. They were a little crooked before, until I invested in Invisalign. I paid a visit to Lottie's colourist too, for some highlights. In fact I took Lottie's next appointment – after all, she won't be having her hair done where she is. Not for a long time.

It hadn't been my plan to live in the heart of Esperance. I'd always been happy in my little apartment on the out-skirts. But as I got to know Lottie, and I saw what life was like for her, how easy, how effortless, I began to dream about it.

And then I came into money. A lot of it.

It was the day of Shelby's funeral when Lottie walked into St Paul's with Shelby's things. 'There's a lot of stuff in here that's valuable,' she said. 'A lot of it is personal stuff. Handbags, wallets and things.' She looked sad as she played the part of bereft sister.

'Can you deal with it?' she asked. 'Take anything you like, of course. It's all a little too close to her for me to keep.'

It was a little patronising, of course, but then again, it was meant to be.

After she'd gone, I made myself a coffee and set about emptying the box of handbags she'd given me. A Kate Spade purple tote; a Dior rucksack; a battered Prada clutch. I priced them up for sale, delighted that they'd make so much money for St Paul's. And there, right at the bottom, was Shelby's trademark Chanel bag. The inter-twined Cs had come loose and hung off a little – nothing a touch of Superglue wouldn't make perfect again. I picked it up and smelled it. It smelled like Shelby: fresh, slightly leathery, expensive.

I remembered her sitting in the office with me the day before she died, clutching that bag, offering a lame apology for being so vile at school, as if one half-arsed 'sorry' would make up for the torment I endured as a teenager. Then she told me why she was really there: 'I'm here because I need you to keep a secret for me,' she said. 'And it's big.'

I nodded and away she went, spilling the beans about Piers, about how he'd stolen over a million dollars from Mooney Women's Shelter over a period of five years. How he'd started with fifty thousand dollars here and sixty thousand dollars there, and then it had multiplied. She had the proof and she'd photocopied it. He was mad at her because she knew about it, she said. And because she'd forgotten some password he was looking for – something to do with a Crypto Wallet. It wasn't anything significant, she said, but he was mad at her nonetheless because he liked to be in control.

'Anyway, can I leave the papers with you, about the shelter?' she asked, producing a wad of bank statements and documents, decorated with orange highlighter. 'Where they can't be found? Piers is mad at me for finding out. I need them hidden. Can you do that?'

And I had done it, like good little compliant Maz. I'd locked away the papers in the filing cabinet that only I could access, and I'd promised I wouldn't tell a soul. Not even Lottie, because I'd assumed she didn't know what her scumbag husband was up to. And I *didn't* tell anyone, not until Max was framed and Carole went into anaphylaxis, and then I made the decision to hand them over to detectives Murphy and Wu – after all, that was Piers' motive right there, wasn't it?

Although, here's the real kicker. Piers was telling the truth when he said he hadn't killed Shelby, that he hadn't finished her off.

And I know this because I was the one who did it.

It wasn't intentional. It wasn't planned. But when the opportunity presented itself, I took it.

Let me explain.

I've always had a keen interest in Shelby. At first, I wanted to get to know her because she was the cool girl at school, but after the night she drowned and shamed me for trying to help her, I was so angry. She ruined my reputation, made me a subject of ridicule. As the years went on, I couldn't forget her – couldn't forget how vile she'd been, how my parents had spent hundreds of dollars in therapy as 'Fat Maz' got to grips with the effects of her cruelty, the names, the accusations. I kept setting up meetings with her, hoping she would make amends so I could move on with my life (it's what my psychologist suggested) and believe me I tried: at Kayla Sanders' birthday party, at Shelby's wedding when I answered Cathy Massini's advert for wedding caterers; when I got a job at a charity shop in the town she lived in. I waited for the apology but it didn't come. Then it did, of sorts, when she came into the shop, and all I could think was, *You still want something in return!*

On the night Shelby died, I was walking round the running track with Rocky, who'd just been patched up by the vet because of glass in his paw. He was walking quite normally, and so I decided to take him out for a quick loop of the park, which the vet had okayed, of course. I felt it was too late to go to Lottie's by that point, and I didn't want to leave Rocky alone. Rocky made his way through the bushes into the clearing, and that's when I saw her there, lying there in the dirt. She was woozy, regaining consciousness, and her neck was badly bruised. She saw me there in the twilight.

'Marella?' she slurred, confused. The confusion turned to relief. It was as if she felt safe, as if she thought I would hoist her up and take her away from the clearing and from danger.

'Shelby?' I whispered. 'What's happened to you?' She held up her hands to her neck. 'Piers,' she said. 'He tried . . .'

She couldn't get her voice. She bent down to try and pick up her bag, swaying. She was delirious. That's when I saw the rock on the ground behind her. I don't know why, but I picked it up. It wasn't too heavy, maybe as heavy as a brick.

Shelby looked me up and down, her eyelids drooping. Then she seemed to come to. She looked at me the same way she looked at me at Kayla Sanders' party, the same way she looked at me at her wedding – with amusement. Like I was nothing.

Then she said, 'What you gonna do with that rock, Fat Maz? Kill me?' And she laughed.

So I brought the rock down and I smashed it into the back of her skull, and I watched as she fell back to the ground. I stayed to check her chest was no longer moving, thinking how glad I was that she was finally dead after so long wishing she was. Those years of torment just melted away as if they'd never happened! Then I ran home with poor, limping Rocky, whose vet visit gave me the perfect alibi.

I slept like a baby that night.

I went into St Paul's the day after Piers was arrested and I sat there and looked at the Chanel bag that had been gathering dust on top of my paperwork. The bag belonging to the woman I had killed.

I stroked the soft leather and undid the zip. There was nothing inside – Lottie had cleared out every receipt, every rogue cent – save for the black, silky lining, which had come away at the seams. Easy to stitch. I put my finger in the hole and wiggled it, and something sharp found the soft skin behind my fingernail. I pushed my forefinger in some more and connected with a rectangular piece of card. A card that had been put inside the lining and sewed up afterwards; it was too big to have fitted in the hole otherwise. I saw how the stitching came apart easily as I tugged it out.

The front of the card read:

SHELBY MASSINI
ESPERANCE PRESTIGE MOTORS
ACCOUNTANT
21 INNERMAN ROAD 2188. CALL 0417 7663219

On the back was a scrawled line of numbers and letters: *0cfwd-ffw37h-777jgzms.*

Then the words: *PiersNeverPickPasswordsWhenYou're-Drunk @ twin81*

I flipped over the card again, and studied it. It was covered in pen dots, and tiny circles, and that's when I noticed it. The pattern, I mean. I was a maths whizz at school, I was always on the lookout for a code. The pinprick dots were heavier underneath certain letters.

SHELBY MASSINI
ESPERANCE PRESTIGE MOTORS
ACCOUNTANT
21 INNERMAN ROAD 2188. CALL 0417 7663219

The highlighted letters spelled B I T C O I N.

I remembered what Shelby had said about Piers and the CryptoWallet, so I logged on and entered the details, just to see what it was all about. I entered *PiersNeverPickPasswordsWhenYou'reDrunk @ twin81* and I waited as the circle on the screen spooled and swirled and then, there it was in front of me: the number eight followed by six other digits: $8,357,214.

I felt my heart thumping in my chest, but I knew what to do.

It only took a few seconds to send the funds into my own account. I had no qualms – that's the beauty of Bitcoins. They can't be traced. Your money is only yours if you can remember your password.

First of all I made a large, cash donation to Mooney Women's Shelter. Two million, to be precise. Double what Piers owed them. A week later, I bought Tino and Shelby's home, a stone's throw from Esperance beach (how she would have hated that!) and, because Tino couldn't wait to leave the neighbourhood after the truth about Lottie and Piers came out, he sold it for half of what he should have. I splashed out on some new home furnishings, as well as a brand new wardrobe, a gym membership, a new car. I sent the Chanel tote to the handbag doctor for repairs because old habits die hard! And then, when poor Rocky lost his battle with cancer (oh, it was devastating), I bought an adorable Pekinese. It was Carole's suggestion.

'Such well-bred dogs,' she said. 'Nothing against dear old Rocky, but they're so much *neater* than mongrels.' I called my darling Peke Lady Luck.

Of course I also donated a large sum to St Paul's, to give the shop the refurb it desperately needs. I have grand plans to make it into a go-to destination for designer recyclables – to make it achingly fashion-forward, to raise as much money for people who aren't as lucky as me. And Carole's going to help me do it. I wonder what Shelby would think, of Carole and I working together! Oh, she would hate it, I'm sure!

I don't need anything else, you see. I don't need limitless millions – I just wanted a home! On my first afternoon in Casa Marella, I poured myself a glass of Moët and sat in the swinging chair with Lady Luck on my lap, and I said out loud, 'Here's to you, Shelby!' And that's when the blue butterfly had landed on the balustrade in front of me. I watched as it danced about before landing inside my empty water glass.

'Didn't I do well?' I asked the creature as it flitted and whirled, irritated by its temporary imprisonment.

Like I said, I hadn't anticipated living in Esperance – it wasn't my style. But here's the thing: it sucks you in, this place, the beauty, the almost robotic perfection. I had to have it: the lifestyle most people only ever dream of.

I'm just pleased I got away with it.

'Marella?' Carole taps her Apple Watch to denote this is no time for daydreaming.

'Good to go!' I clap my hands together.

'Ugh, Marella is so *formal*,' Carole says. 'Can I call you Ella for short? It's such a lovely abbreviation – so feminine!'

I nod. 'Of course,' I tell her. Ella. I like it.

Carole smiles. 'Right then, let's go.'

We reach the reserve less than a minute later. Hannah, Carole's housekeeper, waits by the water fountain in a fluoro running top emblazoned with the club logo. Across the grass, Max jogs past the clearing. He has gained weight since Shelby died.

'Don't mind Max,' says Carole. 'He still runs along here before he picks up the kids some nights,' she says. 'He misses Esperance, I think.'

I watch Max forge forwards, his body against the wind, going nowhere.

'How is it going with Bernard?' Carole asks.

'Oh, it's only been a few dinner dates.' I smile. Only a few, but each so enjoyable. He deserves so much better than the philandering wife he had. Oh yes, he knew all about Freya. He may be greying at a rate of knots, but he's definitely not stupid.

'Hannah!' Carole calls. 'We have a new runner! You two know one another, right?'

'Of course we do,' chirps Hannah. 'We met on the um, *peanut* night . . .'

'Nice to see you, Hannah,' I say.

She looks me up and down. 'You too,' she says. 'You look great.'

'Thanks.' I smile.

She is right. I do look great. I'm a new woman! I am a butterfly emerged from a cocoon, a chick fleeing the confines of the nest, a phoenix from the ashes!

Marion. Fat Maz. Marella. Ella.

My foot taps the pavement, my new wrinkle-free forehead glistens in the summer sun. I close my eyes, let the orange flood my eyelids.

Ella.

And just like that, I am reborn.

Acknowledgements

The idea for *The Running Club* came to me on a loop of my local park with my son as we watched a group of runners repeat the same circuit in the rain. I began to write as Covid took hold, escaping the real world in Esperance. As the first lockdown eased in Sydney, we travelled as a family to the NSW south coast and it was a little tree-lined clearing that led down to the sand dunes near Manyana that became the setting for the murder.

Luckily, my wonderful editor Kimberley Atkins liked the synopsis for *The Running Club* – despite me describing it absolutely terribly to her on Zoom – and so I fell head-first into the world of Shelby and co. Thank you Kim for gently persuading me to choose characterisation over an overload of red herrings. As ever, I am endlessly grateful to you, Amy Batley, Katy Blott and all at Hodder & Stoughton for your expertise and enthusiasm for this book, and *The Trivia Night* before it. Meg Kennedy, Melissa Wilson, Nicky Luckie and the Hachette ANZ team: the way you have embraced my books has been such a thrill and I'm so thankful to be part of the Hachette ANZ gang.

Marina de Pass, you are amazing. Thank you for loving this book from the first read and for juggling it along with all-things *The Trivia Night*. I can't imagine finding a better agent or agency. Infinite thanks also to Araminta Whitley, Helen Mumby and of course to the most wonderful and entertaining lunch partner, Mark Lucas.

The writing community is a beautifully supportive one. Sally Hepworth, the blurb quote you provided for *The Trivia Night* arrived as I began the editing process for this book. It occurred to me around this time that maybe I *can* actually write. It can't be a coincidence and I'm truly grateful for your kindness. Thanks also to Helen Cooper, Harriet Walker, Anna Downes, Nicola Moriarty, Ber Carroll, Patronella McGovern, Veronica Henry, Sarah Pearse, Rachael Johns, Anthea Hodgson, Jacqueline Bublitz and Michael Robotham for your support of *The Trivia Night*.

Vanessa McCausland and Cath Adelbert, thank you for reading this book when it was in its roughest form and cheering it on at such an early stage. Jill Walters, your expert police advice saved me from a few scary plot holes. Natalie Young, thanks for being such a thorough copy editor.

Thanks also to Louise Roberts, Sarah Swain, Julie Cross, Bev Hudec, Emma Levett, Lucy Elliot, and The Faber 'Twinklings', as well as the fabulous community of writers on Instagram who are always on hand to offer positivity and support.

Jayne Murphy, Debbie Wise and Leonie Lincoln: you're always on hand to shoot the breeze over a lychee martini when writing days are tough – I love you! Fiona Pogson, Janaya Laws, Alice Ierace and Nina Dorn – you girls make me laugh (a lot) and I'm sure half of the rubbish we discuss makes its way into my novels. George Blaskey (miss you, mate), Jamie Halcro-Johnston, Pip Prentice, Jenna Macdonald, Tanya Andrews, Gerry Davies, Bob Fox, Glenda and Phil Planten . . . just thanks.

Mum, I grew up watching you write lists, diaries, cards, letters – thanks for passing on the genes, and for your and Dad's continual encouragement.

To Raff, Sav and Bug – guess how much I love you? I promise I will dedicate a book to you when I write one with less 'adult hugging', murder, flashers and rude words. Rob, you can't have this one either (you got the last one, let's not be greedy), but know I love you and am so grateful for all you do for me. Not least for reading this book when you'd rather be cracking on with an Iain Banks novel instead.

The Running Club is for my sister Joanna, who has always encouraged me without an ounce of competition, unlike Shelby and Lottie. I love you, Joey.

And finally, to all the amazing booksellers, readers and bloggers who have encouraged me along the way and who picked up the book before this one and enjoyed it, and possibly even reviewed it, my heartfelt thanks. Your confidence in me means everything.